I0699653

Shroud
of
Darkness

Also By Shane Miller

<u>Darkness Series</u>

Prelude of Darkness

SHROUD
OF
DARKNESS

SHANE MILLER

BOOK TWO

Copyright © by Shane Miller 2025

All rights reserved. No part of this publication may be reproduced, stored, or transmitted in any form or by any means, electronic, mechanical, photocopying, recording, scanning, or otherwise without written permission from the publisher. It is illegal to copy this book, post it to a website, or distribute it by any other means without permission.

This novel is entirely a work of fiction. The names, characters and incidents portrayed in it are the work of the author's imagination. Any resemblance to actual persons, living or dead, events or localities is entirely coincidental.

Shroud OF DARKNESS
Book 2 of the Darkness Series

Library of Congress Control Number: 2025909102

ISBN: 979-8-9855631-3-9 (Hardback)
ISBN: 979-8-2820532-2-7 (Paperback)
ISBN: 979-8-9855631-4-6 (ebook)

First edition: May 2025

10 9 8 7 6 5 4 3 2 1

Book Cover Design by ebooklaunch.com

For
Gordon & Marian

... and the many weekend trips to the ranch

Prologue

Scotland, 1898

Isaac hit the ground hard; his body convulsed in pain as he rolled to his back, trying to breathe. Overhead, on the grassy knoll, two figures—one in a black robe, the other in purple—towered over him. Their robes billowed in the wind as their metallic masks glinted in the moonlight. As he struggled to regain his breath, uncertainty of what would happen next made his blood run cold. His throat grew tight as their gaze bore into him.

The air around Isaac seemed to thicken as he gasped for air between fits of coughs as his lungs started to reboot. His body trembled with fear as dozens of cult members, clad in crimson robes, encircled him like a flock of vultures closing in on wounded prey. Their metallic masks concealed any trace of humanity, leaving no indication of what they would do with him. They waved their arms and hands over him in some form of ritualistic dance, each chanting something different. Their voices merged into a rising cacophony of rhythmic vibrations that paralleled Isaac's heartbeat.

"Enough!" came a shout from the leader adorned in gray robes trimmed with blood red. His voice resonated with power as it sliced through the air.

The crimson-clad cultists scurried away, putting Isaac between them and their leader. Isaac scrambled to sit up and clutched his chest with one hand as he took his first full breath. His heart pounded as he leaned on his other hand for support and stared back at the leader, unsure of his intentions.

Through the haze of pain and confusion, the obsidian cross in the distance drew him in. The child, callously thrown at the cross by the leader moments prior, was partially absorbed by it. Half of his tiny, bruised body was buried deep in the blackness of the cross. An ominous purple light pulsated from deep within, reflected off the child's anguished visage, forever frozen in a perpetual state of distress.

Standing guard next to the cross were two figures in purple robes that flanked the child's father. He was severely beaten with his arms bound behind his back while their hands gripped his arms and shoulders.

The leader pointed an accusatory finger directly at Isaac. "Seize him!"

Isaac's body tensed. He clambered up to stand, wanting to run, to evade the approaching crowd behind him. However, it would be in vain. They closed in, grabbed his arms, and hoisted him up. His trembling legs barely supported his weight as they forcefully bound his arms behind his back.

The purple-clad cultist from above jumped down from the overlook and slinked toward Isaac, wrapping his arm tightly around his shoulders. He pressed his cold metallic face against Isaac's ear and barked, "Quit your squirmin'," then grabbed a sizable chunk of hair and ripped it back, inflicting knife-like pain. He kicked the back of Isaac's knees in one swift motion, forcing him to kneel before the leader. Isaac cried out, his scalp throbbing where a chunk of hair had been torn away with his arms wrenched high above him. He looked up at the leader with tears in his eyes, pleading for mercy.

The leader took a few steps toward Isaac and lowered himself to one knee. "You shouldn't have come here," he said, shaking his head in pity. "Or should you? The answer to that question won't be resolved at this juncture. However, here you are, so perhaps this is how it all should be."

Isaac's gaze flickered from the leader to the ominous cross and back again, his mind racing for a means of escape. "Let me go, and ye'll never see or hear from me again."

"It's far too late for that," the leader scoffed. "Perhaps it would be best to have the Alluring Knight command you to walk out into the ocean until you reach the distant shores of the Americas?"

Isaac briefly thought it over. This guy was clearly mad, and taking his chances in the frigid ocean seemed like his best option to get away.

"Or..." the leader trailed off, relishing in Isaac's desperate hope.

"Aye!" Isaac interrupted with urgency. "The ocean."

The leader laughed as he poked Isaac in the chest. "This pitiful fool seems to think he holds sway over his own fate."

Behind Isaac, the other members groaned and chuckled at him, reveling in his helplessness. With his options swiftly dwindling, he silently cursed himself again for not seizing the opportunity to flee with his horse when he had the chance. A surge of apprehension prickled at the nape of his neck as he scanned his surroundings, searching for any possible means of escape.

"I can see it clearly now," the leader said, voice dripping with intrigue. "You believe you can plunge into the ocean's depths and evade our grasp."

Ripping off his mask, the leader revealed a wicked grin, his eyes gleaming with malice. Despite his youthful appearance—fair skin, slicked black hair, and a smooth face that placed him no older than his mid-twenties—an ancient unsettling aura clung to him.

"You should know that the Alluring Knight didn't earn his name for his good looks. He is a deadly adversary, and you, my dear, are no match for him."

Isaac stammered, "I-I don't—?"

The leader patted Isaac's head condescendingly. "Understand? Of course, you don't. You're just an underdeveloped, feeble-minded creature, merely a slave to your own primitive brain."

Isaac threw a desperate punch at the leader's face, hoping to catch him off guard and create an opportunity to escape. His fist flew past the leader as he swiftly leaned back, evading the feeble attack with ease.

"Pathetic," the leader retorted.

A deep, commanding voice pierced the night as it boomed over them. "Blood Knight!"

Isaac glanced upward, eyes widening at the sight of a newcomer adorned in a yellow robe standing upon a nearby mound.

The leader donned his mask, his irritation evident as he stood up. "What is it now? Can't you see I'm dealing with this cretin?"

"The Sovereign One seeks an audience with this stranger."

The leader's fist tightened as he shook his head in defiance. "This is none of his concern. I'm the leader now!"

"Are you?" the new figure countered.

"Of course not!" he shouted, kicking the ground in frustration. "My time has yet to come—but it *will* come. Oh, we've both seen it, haven't we?"

"Come," the yellow Knight beckoned to Isaac.

As before, a fog enveloped Isaac's mind; he felt his consciousness slip away as he found himself drawn toward the yellow figure. He felt the same feeling pushing him when he first arrived at the shoreline and saw the ethereal lights emanating from the cultists off in the distance. Something then had compelled him to investigate the lights, leading him into the hands of this cult, and now it was propelling him forward yet again. His body felt as light as air as he ascended the mound, joining the figure garbed in yellow. Casting a final glance at the leader, he watched as his rigid form retreated back toward the obsidian cross. Only a tiny portion of the unfortunate child's foot still protruded from its darkened base.

Isaac looked back toward the yellow Knight. Every fiber in his body pulsated with the will to bolt out of there. He thought maybe it was fear keeping his feet planted in front of this cultist, but a spark in the back of his mind told him something much more severe was afoot, holding him in place.

"What dae ye want with me?" Isaac's voice shook.

The figure in yellow bowed his head and silently walked on, his fingers intertwined as if in prayer. Isaac found himself obliged to follow, unable to resist the inexorable pull.

"The Sovereign Knight has foreseen your future and shall guide you upon your destined path," the yellow figure whispered.

"What path? Do you mean he'll let me leave?"

The yellow Knight answered his question with silence as he led Isaac further into the unknown. The distant cries of the child's father faded into oblivion, replaced by the crashing waves as the proceeded forward. He wrapped his arms around himself, seeking warmth amidst the growing chill as ice particles formed on his beard. With each step, his worries about returning home intensified. His heart sank, tears held at bay, as he realized that he would never again behold his wife and child. A wound so deep and irreparable that it seared his soul.

Up ahead, a horse-drawn carriage seemed to materialize through a fog that Isaac hadn't noticed before. Standing beside the carriage was a woman draped in a flowing white robe. Her smooth alabaster skin and dainty features revealed a beauty reminiscent of a Greek statue, carved by a master craftsman. She exuded a sense of timeless grace as she held the reins of Isaac's Shire horse in her delicate grasp.

"It can't be," Isaac whispered in disbelief.

The yellow Knight bowed to her, then took a few steps forward and opened the door to the carriage.

A plump, elderly man in celestial blue robes stepped out of the carriage. His neatly trimmed white beard, connected to the half ring of hair encircling his bald head, gave his round face an elongated look. Around his neck, he wore a shimmering metal pendant, embedded with a mesmerizing blue X that emitted a powerful glow in the pale moonlight.

Isaac's legs trembled as he fought to remain standing. A sense of immense, almost god-like power radiated from the man in blue.

A smile formed on the old man's lips as he looked at the woman and said, "It appears all is not lost—for the artist has arrived."

Chapter 1

United Citadel Field Unit Beta Team

Logan stood behind Leah and watched as she raised her pistol and fired at her target. It had been over six months since the New Orleans mission, where the Beta team rescued her and Maeve, but it came at the expense of their father and friend Detective Connor Kaplan's life. Logan glanced back at the two sun-bleached double-wide trailers where they were staying. He never planned on any of this, but since Detective Kaplan and his ex-wife were now gone, he figured it would be best to sell their homes and relocate to the west side of Las Vegas, far on the outskirts.

While the New Orleans mission had failed, for Logan, it felt good to reconnect with his sister after almost thirty years. However, he still felt incomplete, as if there was a large piece still missing from his soul, but he had a few ideas on why that would be. For one thing, his sister Leah was the same age, seventeen, as she was the last time he saw her, before her abduction by the Blood Knights when he was three years old.

In his timeline, Leah was never found, nor did he ever find out what happened to his twin brother, Lucas, a few days after Leah was taken. That memory of him frozen in the doorway of his bedroom as he watched a shadowy figure step out of the wall and turn his brother into black ash was always on his mind. Deep down he knew Lucas was dead, but his heart wouldn't accept it. It took many years before those vivid nightmares faded away—still, the feeling of being all alone in the world never left him. Which was exacerbated by being sent away with his mother to a safe house in Australia, where the two of them did their best to move forward by themselves.

After his mother died in his mid-teens, he left Australia to reconnect with his father, who was living in London and working as a member of United Citadel's Alpha team. He was doing the same thing now with Leah as his father had done with him, training another family member in special tactics to take down the Knights. The irony of it all wasn't lost on Logan.

Back in his timeline, the United Citadel, or UC, was a secret organization based in London, dedicated to ending the horrors of a growing cult known as the Knights, an organization the rest of the world refused to acknowledge. The most prominent sect, the Blood Knights, made their goal quite clear: obtain global control and put down anyone who resists.

The UC consisted of three branches—Assault, Defense, and Intelligence—where one member from each branch would be placed on a field team designated by a Greek letter: Logan from the Assault branch; team leader Eva from Defense; and her fiancé, CJ, from Intelligence made up the Beta Field Unit team. Through the use of the UC's Rift Generator technology, they had found their way to this new timeline just in time to see their old one fade away to darkness.

Leah took her finger off the trigger, lowered her gun, and tugged her ear protectors down. She flashed a smile back at Logan, proud of her near-perfect grouping on the human paper target twenty yards away. Indeed, Logan was amazed at how quickly Leah honed her skills. Given a few more years under her belt, he figured she'd be a better shot than him. But he knew shooting a paper target versus a live target were two different things.

"Not bad," he said.

Leah laughed. "Not bad? CJ says I'm a way better marksman than you are."

Logan rubbed his right temple. "First of all, CJ is an idiot. And second, this is a paper target."

"I know that—"

Logan held up his hand, cutting her off. "You're gonna miss your first time when it matters."

Leah's eyes narrowed. "I won't."

"Yes, you will," said Logan. "It has nothing to do with your skill level. It's all psychological."

Leah tilted her head to one side. "Uh-huh. So you're saying I don't have the guts to pull the trigger in the heat of the moment?"

"Nope. Not at all. You'll pull the trigger, but you'll miss. Everyone does the first time. That's why a shotgun makes the perfect home defense weapon. Even if you miss, you'll probably hit your target, even if it's just their arm."

Logan shifted his gaze toward the dirt road leading to their new homes. He shook his head as a small silver car made its way toward them with a dust trail that could be seen for miles—one of the reasons why he chose to live this far on the outskirts.

He turned back toward Leah and raised an eyebrow. "You expecting anyone?"

"No, of course not," she said, shaking her head. "No one knows I'm out here."

"Shit. All right, you go join Maeve in the other house and get ready to bug out. I'll join Eva and check this out."

Leah dug her heels into the ground. "I can help."

"Don't worry. Your time will come, and you are by helping Maeve. Now go!"

"Maybe it's CJ coming back?" Leah said, as she headed toward the house Maeve was recovering in after the New Orleans mission.

"Can't be." Logan opened the back door to Eva's house. "He's still out on his Recon assignment."

He scraped his feet against the dust mat and closed the door behind him. He could see Eva's curly blond hair as she stood at the front door, watching their visitor park their car through the peephole. The barren open floor plan, large front windows, and flimsy white walls didn't exactly give them much cover if they came under fire.

"Who is it?" he whispered as he moved behind her.

"It's some woman, but I can't say it's someone I recognize," said Eva.

"What's she doing?"

"From the looks of it, I'd say she's lost. She has a slip of paper in her hand, and it looks like she's lookin' around for an address."

Eva turned the door's deadbolt and twisted the doorknob. "Watch my back."

"On it," Logan said, unholstering his pistol.

Eva nodded to Logan and stepped outside. The woman looked up from her slip of paper and smiled. Her eyes, made larger by her glasses, darted back and forth between the two.

"Excuse me," said Eva. "Is there something I can help you with?"

"Maybe," she said. "Are you Eva?"

"Yes, I am," she said with caution.

"Oh, wonderful. I wasn't sure if I was in the right spot or not since I'm not from around here."

"I see," Eva said. "Which leads to why are you looking for me?"

"I was told you could help me by looking into my sister's situation."

"Hmm. And who told you this?"

"He said his name is Connor Kaplan. The way he talked, I assume he's a friend of yours."

Eva looked back at Logan, who had one eyebrow raised.

During the New Orleans mission, Logan was fairly certain the Detective Kaplan from this timeline had died, or was at least on his way out when Logan was forced to leave him. The other possibility was Alpha Team Leader Kaplan, his father from his own timeline, who had gone through the Rift Generator with the rest of the Alpha team months before the Betas used it. If Alpha team had made it here, it would definitely give them the leg up they could use.

"How long ago did you speak to Kaplan?" Logan asked.

"Oh, I'd say it's been about three days now when he gave me some airfare money to come find you," she said as she held up three fingers.

"Huh," said Eva. "And what would your name be?"

"Oh, I'm sorry. I forgot to introduce myself. My name is Iris Leroux," she said, as she held her hand out to shake Eva's.

Eva glanced at Logan again and whispered, "You recognize the name?"

Logan shook his head no.

Iris bit her lip. "Am I interrupting something? I can come back if this isn't a good time."

Eva took her hand and shook it. "Oh, no. I'm being terribly rude to you, and I apologize. You just caught us off guard."

"Sorry about that," said Iris. "I would have called, but your friend didn't have your number."

Logan holstered his weapon and stood aside as the two entered the living room. She seemed harmless enough, but he didn't want to take his eye off her. He closed the door and meandered behind the counter that divided the living room and kitchen while they sat down on opposing armchairs, giving him a clear view if she was up to something.

The counter creaked as Logan leaned on top of it. "How did you meet Kaplan?"

Iris took a piece of tissue from her white handbag and wiped her eyes. "He first showed up on the last day of my sister's trial two weeks ago."

"The end of August?" asked Eva.

"Yeah," she said.

"And what's your sister's name?"

"Rose Lombardi."

Eva picked up a notepad off the end table and jotted down some notes. "What was your sister on trial for?"

"First-degree murder for killing her family."

Eva looked up from her notepad and watched as Iris wiped away a couple more tears. "Oh, dear. I'm terribly sorry this has happened."

Iris let out a long sigh. "It's been the hardest thing I've ever been through."

"Am I correct to assume she was found guilty of this crime, but you believe she is innocent?"

"I know she didn't do it. She doesn't have a mean bone in her body at all."

"What was the evidence against her?"

"That's the major problem with this whole ordeal. Her fourteen-year-old son, the oldest of three, survived and told them she did it."

"And you think he's lying?"

"I don't know what to think anymore. I'm unsure how to put it, but I can tell you that he doesn't feel right."

"How so?"

"Well, now that's the problem. He looks and talks like Ted, but something is definitely off. It's like he's an imposter."

"Well, a traumatic event like that can change a person."

"Yeah, and I know that, but I'm telling you, something is definitely wrong with this whole situation."

Logan's ears perked up when he heard the back door squeak open. He saw Maeve, a former officer and Detective Kaplan's friend, frantically waving him over through the crack with Leah towering behind her.

It was still strange to him to see this younger version of Maeve, having known her rather well in the future when she was not only a member of the Alpha team, but his stepmom. Now, at thirty-six, she was only four years older.

"What? What is it?" he whispered when he joined them.

"I know who her sister is," said Leah.

"You do? How?"

"She was one of the doctors on the island where I was being held captive, before they relocated me to New Orleans."

"Right," said Maeve. "Your father and I found a medical file about a Dr. Lombardi when we went through the police station on that island looking for you."

"We have to help her," said Leah. "She was the only one there who fought to keep me from being experimented on. There's no way she could have done that to her family."

"Experiments?" asked Logan. "Are you talking about the Acolyte Serum?"

"I'm not sure," said Leah. "A lot of that is still hazy."

"All right," he said. "Wait here."

Logan moved back to his original position behind the counter and studied Iris. "Did your sister ever work on an island off the coast of northern California?"

Iris lowered her gaze and tapped her heel on the ground. "I'm not sure," she said slowly. "Her job often sent her to different locations."

"What kind of work did she do?" asked Eva.

"She was a medical researcher for Cognitive Endurance Incorporated."

"What kind of stuff was she researching?" asked Logan.

"I couldn't even begin to tell you. Rose never talked about that kind of stuff with me. But I know she loved her job and was with them for six years."

"You know where their main office is located?" asked Logan.

Iris shook her head. "I supposed it would be near her home in Kentucky, but I can't say for certain."

"How long ago did this crime happen?" asked Eva.

"March third."

"Of this year?" Eva asked.

"Yes."

She looked up at Iris. "And she's already been sentenced?"

Iris closed her eyes and nodded her head once.

"Maybe it's the British in me," said Eva, "but bloody hell, isn't that a little fast for a trial to take place in this country?"

"You're damn right it is," said Iris.

"Hmm," said Eva. "This has all been interesting, but I'm not sure how much help we can be after the fact."

Logan spoke up, "We'll look into it."

Eva looked up sharply at Logan. "We will?"

Logan motioned for Eva to join him in the kitchen for a quick impromptu sidebar.

Eva looked confused but held up one finger for Iris to see as she got up. "This'll take just a sec."

"Oh, okay." Iris looked back and forth between the two with her mouth slightly open.

Eva glanced at Maeve and Leah peering through the back door, then turned her attention to Logan. "I'm out of the loop on something here, aren't I?" she whispered.

Logan pointed his thumb over his shoulder toward the back door. "The tall one thinks Iris's sister was one of the doctors on that Shady Reef Island, and Maeve agrees."

"Ah," Eva whispered. "That's why you asked if she worked on an island."

"Yeah. If she was uncooperative and argumentative while working out there, I could see the Knights being none too pleased with her."

"Meaning she was set up to take the fall," Eva sighed. "I bet she made a good example of what can happen to you if you don't fall in line. Your life is ruined, and your loved ones are killed."

"Well, fear is a handy tool to have in your arsenal."

Eva smiled. "Yes, I do believe Machiavelli would agree with you."

Iris stood up, holding her handbag in front of her. "Is there anything else you need from me?"

"Actually, yes," said Eva. "About how old would you say our friend Kaplan is?"

Iris tilted her head. "Maybe in his mid- to late-sixties. Why?"

"Ah," said Eva. "That settles it then."

"It does?" asked Iris.

"Yeah, there's a junior and a senior, and I wasn't sure which one you were talking about." She smiled at the thought that their Kaplan from the Alpha team had made it here.

"Oh, I understand now," she said with a smile. "So, you think you can help me?"

"I'll do what I can," said Eva. "But I'll need a starting point, like a list of contact information of people I can talk to. Such as her son."

"Of course," Iris said, digging through her handbag.

She pulled out a business card and tapped it on the counter. "This is her lawyer, Thomas Ellis, business card. He should have access to everything you need."

Eva took the card and flipped it over to examine it. "Looks like he's also in Kentucky."

"Well, yes," said Iris. "Is that going to be a problem?"

"Oh no," said Logan. "I know a guy with a jet who thinks he's a pilot. Shouldn't be an issue for us."

Chapter 2

United Citadel Field Unit Beta Team

Eva stood at the front door with a smile and waved to Iris as she got back in her car and took off. Deep down, she knew there wasn't a lot she could do about her sister's situation, and that single thought wiped the smile off her face as soon as Iris was out of sight. However, if this was the Dr. Rose Lombardi who Leah knew from Shady Reef, perhaps that could shine a light on a new lead.

She had sent CJ to investigate Shady Reef several weeks ago after he healed from his gunshot wound in New Orleans. All he found was a burned down deserted island. Any information about what the Blood Knights were up to on that island was probably gone now. However, the late Detective Connor Kaplan did tell them about a sewer system, with some interesting things he discovered with Maeve while fleeing from the Blood Knights. It might still be undisturbed and worthy of a look-see, but now it was time to call him back. Then there was the matter of another older Connor Kaplan running around in this timeline.

Logan leaned up against a wall and crossed his arms. "How do you want to handle this one, Boss?"

Eva closed and locked the door behind her, then pulled out her mobile phone from her pocket. "First, I need to pull CJ back from the field."

Logan smiled, "I agree."

"Really?" said Eva.

"Yeah," Logan laughed. "He has his uses."

Eva joined Maeve and Leah in the kitchen, punched up CJ's number, and placed her mobile on the countertop dividing the kitchen and living room. She clicked the speaker on so they could all hear.

CJs voice came booming through the mobile in an instant. "Perfect timing. You're not going to believe who I've found."

Logan joined them in the kitchen. "My father?"

"No, Phillip Wallace. The odds of Alpha Kaplan showing up in this timeline must be astronomical."

Logan and the three women gave each other knowing looks. Maybe astronomical but someone who could fit the bill was meandering about.

Leah leaned toward the phone. "Who's Phillip Wallace?"

"He was a child who went missing in the early eighties," said Maeve. "An old friend of mine helped your father and me track down Jacob Wallace, Phillip's father. Both of you disappeared under similar circumstances, so we figured Jacob might be our best shot at finding you since he's been searching for Phillip for the past thirty-five years."

"Did he ever find him?" asked Leah.

"Sorta," said Maeve. "He made it to the island, and during the night, some Blood Knights entered his hotel room with Phillip and strongly encouraged him to leave or else."

"Whatever happened to them?" asked Leah.

"I can only speculate," said Maeve. "After Jacob rescued us from Shady Reef, he mentioned he had been keeping an eye on the Blood Knight's activity after his encounter with them on the island while maintaining his distance. Anything else he had to tell us was cut short when a Blood Knight's scout located us in Jacob's cabin, so he decided we should split up to increase our odds of escaping. I gather he went back underground, doing whatever he does to keep track of the Blood Knights. Anything about his son is a complete mystery, but it sounds like CJ might know."

"Well," said CJ. "I'm not sure what Phillip has been up to, but for now, he's staying in this small town called Plattesburg."

"Nebraska?" asked Leah.

CJ chuckled. "Yeah! How did you know?"

"That's where my dad grew up," she said. "This can't be a coincidence? Can it?"

"No," said Logan. "They're trying to lure us there."

"Still," said Eva. "He could have just as much information, if not more, about the Knights as Rose does. We can't pass up this opportunity."

"Who's Rose?" asked CJ.

"Another person of interest who might be able to help us," said Eva. "You wouldn't happen to have any information about a Rose Lombardi from Kentucky?"

"Hold on, I'll check."

Eva checked her watch, watching the seconds tick by as CJ searched the millions of databases he had stored on his wrist computer. It was one of the few things that annoyed and made her jealous about the Intelligence branch of the Citadel. They always had the time to double-check and cross-reference every minute detail of anything they were researching or investigating. In the medical field, she had to know precisely what she was doing or stand aside for someone more skilled. The last thing you wanted to do was get lost in the eighteenth hour of an emergency surgical procedure and lose a patient due to your lack of knowledge.

"Well," said CJ. "This is unexpected."

Eva looked up at Logan, her eyebrows raised. "What did you find?"

"Other than a small blurb about her arrest, I can't find any other information about a Rose Lombardi from Kentucky in this timeline. Usually, I can find some form of voter information and old addresses, but there's nothing like that here. Even the archive sites come up empty."

Eva smiled. "I noticed you said *this* timeline. What else did you find?"

"Loads of information from our timeline."

Maeve's face went pale as she looked upward when CJ said "timeline." Her mouth went ajar when she tilted her head to one side with vacant eyes that were all too uncanny. Eva had seen that same expression before on some locals during her first mission in South Africa.

Maeve's lips quavered as she whispered, "Convergence."

"What?" Eva asked.

Maeve stood there in silence, her expression unchanged.

Leah leaned away from her, eyes opened wide and fixated on Maeve. Her voice trembled as she said, "What's going on, Maeve?"

Logan clapped his hands in front of Maeve's face. She squeezed her eyes shut as she shook her head with strands of red hair getting stuck to her face from the sweat that coated her brow. She held up one hand to her forehead.

"I'll be all right," she said through labored breaths.

Eva reached out for Maeve's free hand and wrapped her fingers around her wrist to check her pulse. She looked up at Maeve and asked, "Are you sure?"

Maeve pulled her arm back and rubbed her wrist. "Yeah, I'm fine. Just had one of those quick little migraines. That's all."

"Uh-huh," said Logan.

"That's not what it looked like to me," Eva said.

Maeve glared back at Eva. "Well, that's what it was."

Eva stood her ground and stared at Maeve. "What did you mean by *convergence*?"

"I didn't say that!" Maeve yelled.

Silence filled the room. This was the first time Eva had seen Maeve snap at anyone like that, and it bothered her. She watched Maeve's eyes for any subtle hints that the Knights had compromised her. After all, they did have Maeve for quite some time, and it was the only clue Eva had in determining if Maeve was an Acolyte, one of the Knight's poor souls they can control. Thankfully, she never saw any proof to suggest she was, but that was assuming the Acolytes behaved the same way here as they did in her timeline. Still, she knew she had to investigate it further; she just had to ensure her timing was right, and her words were perfect. One wrong step and Maeve would likely shut down completely.

CJ piped up on the mobile, "Uh, guys. You still there?"

Maeve wiped a single tear from her eye. "Sorry about that. It's just with getting abducted and losing Kap. Then there's the possibility of an older Kap from another timeline here. I guess my emotions finally caught up to me."

"Happens to the best of us," said Eva.

Logan leaned forward, leering at the phone, resting his arms on the countertop, he asked, "What can you tell us about the Rose from our timeline?"

"Well," said CJ. "She won a bunch of awards and grants in her research in human psychology, mainly dealing with something called cognitive control."

Logan groaned. "You mean like mind control?"

"I'm not entirely sure," said CJ. "I'll have to get back to you on that one."

"Oh, no," said Eva. "It's nothing like that. It's more like a skill set that allows you to override your more basic impulses to make better decisions with the goal of changing how you operate and feel as a person."

Leah smiled. "Like a self-help program?"

"Yeah," said Eva. "Something like that. CJ, what else did you find?"

"Well, it says here she lived in Kentucky with her husband, and it looks like she has three dependents."

"Hold that thought," Eva said as she turned to collect the notes she had made while talking with Iris. "The oldest one is Ted, right?"

"Yeah, Ted or Theodor, followed by Hector and Marco."

Eva smiled. "And she works for Cognitive Endurance Incorporated?"

CJ chuckled. "Right again."

"What about a sister named Iris—"

"Leroux?"

"That's the one."

"My records show she's here too in our timeline, but not the one we're in now."

"How can that be?" Leah said, exasperated. "She was just here."

Eva jotted down another bit of information on her notepad. "There's always the possibility she wasn't who she says she was, or her information has been erased too."

"Well, yeah. I guess," Leah said under her breath. "But couldn't she have traveled here like y'all did?"

CJ spoke up. "Not likely. Our Rift Generator was a well-guarded secret. Very few people knew about it, let alone, had access to it."

"We're diving into pointless speculation now," said Eva. "None of that can be confirmed or denied at this time, so we need to keep moving forward with facts."

Leah responded, "But, what about—"

Logan stared at her, shaking his head no.

Eva sighed. "We'll come back to this topic when we have more information. Until then, I'm invoking Article III Section II. Logan, you'll join CJ in Nebraska and see what information you can extract from Phillip Wallace."

"Copy that," CJ said, while Logan nodded his head.

Eva continued, "You two will go by the subunit team call sign Bravo. And Maeve, you'll be joining me in Kentucky, while Leah, you'll remain here."

Leah raised her hand. "Hold on. Shouldn't I be going to Kentucky?"

All eyes were focused on her now.

"I mean," Leah hesitated. "I'm the one who knows what she looks like. I could help identify her or something like that."

"Yes, you could," said Eva. "But I've got something more important for you."

Leah rolled her eyes. "Please don't treat me like I'm five years old."

Logan shook his head again, his expression neutral.

Leah scoffed. "Shake your head all you want, but I'm a part of this as much as you are."

"Which is why you'll be filling my position as ops manager. I need someone here to remain in contact with both teams, and to organize all the information we'll collect."

Leah lowered her gaze, her cheeks flushed. "Oh," she said sheepishly.

"However," Eva said. "I don't want you here by yourself."

Leah opened her mouth but paused. "Yeah, you're right," she said. "Besides, I don't really want to be by myself right now."

"Nor would I," said Eva. "Now, who can we get to stay with you?"

"What about Forsyth?" Leah asked. "He's a friend of my dad, and probably the best lieutenant Metro PD has."

Maeve chimed in, "Probably not."

Leah scrunched her face up, confused. "Why not?"

"He's dealing with some issues stemming from when he helped out your father and me in locating Jacob Wallace."

"What'd he do this time?" asked Logan.

"Well, according to Chambers, he violated a bunch of policies when he tapped into a couple of criminal databases to run a check on Wallace. Which is how he found his mugshot and last known location."

Eva's spine shivered, and her cheeks and fingers tingled. "This is bad, isn't it?"

"I hope not," said Maeve.

CJ spoke up, "Who's this Chambers person?"

Leah pinched the bridge of her nose. "Oh, he's that short, crusty detective who worked with my father and is always negative about everything."

"Actually," said Maeve. "He'd be perfect to have hanging out around here."

Leah's eyes widened. "Oh, no. Not him."

"Yeah, him," said Maeve. "He already knows they're from the future, so that's one less headache to deal with."

"That settles it then," said Eva.

"But—" Leah interjected.

Eva picked up her phone. "CJ, Logan is on his way."

"Sounds goo—"

Eva ended the call, shoved her phone back in her pocket, and turned to Maeve. "Go talk to Chambers and see if he can do it and find out how quickly he can get over here."

"Oh, he'll do it. I'll just have to treat him to a free meal at the diner first. I'll be back in a couple of hours," Maeve said as she dug her car keys out of her jean's pocket.

Once Maeve was out of the house, Eva took a seat at the small round table, shoved into a corner by the kitchen, and motioned Logan to join her.

Logan said, "Hey, Leah, how about you fire off a couple more rounds, and I'll join you shortly."

Leah's eyes drifted back and forth between the two. "Fine, but you better be bringing your A-game this time. None of this 'I'm so good my second shot went perfectly through the first hole on the target' nonsense."

Logan smiled. "Practice makes perfect, so get to it."

Leah let out a huff and left through the back door.

Eva leaned back in her chair, her arms folded. "I want to keep an eye on Maeve. That's why she's coming with me."

Logan rubbed his chin. "Yeah, I figured it was something like that. You think she could have been turned into an Acolyte?"

"I'm not certain. I can't say either way at this point, but I intend to find out."

"All right, just make sure to watch your back."

Eva smiled. "To the end."

Chapter 3

United Citadel Field Unit
BRAVO SUBUNIT

Logan pulled off I-76 after he crossed the Colorado-Nebraska border. His eyes felt heavy as he slumped further down into his seat. A tingling sensation took hold of his leg as numbness set in, just as the car turned onto the only road into Plattesburg.

Well, at least that'll give me something new to focus on, he thought, trying to keep at least one eye open. He had left Vegas at 5:00 a.m., and after fourteen hours with only two quick stops for gas, he was ready for bed. With a heavy hand, he punched the button to roll down the window, hoping the cool, fresh air would give him the extra kick he needed to stay awake until he made it into town. Memories from long ago flooded his mind as the smell of the Platte River filled his car. For Logan, it felt like he was here a lifetime ago, and until now, he had forgotten he had been here at all. Memory was still hazy, but he could remember coming here with his dad to see his grandmother for a lovely Christmas visit. It would have been just a few months later when that Shadow Man turned his brother into ash.

Logan's body shook as a chill ran down his spine. It was all he could do to wipe that memory from his brain, though a quick follow-up with a bottle of Irish whiskey would lock that memory away for a decent amount of time. Still, that event happened a little over six months ago in this timeline, and that grandmother should still be here. He had never really met her in his timeline, and he knew the one here wasn't really his grandmother, but she would be a close enough approximation. That is, if he were to believe CJ's theory on time travel and unlocking different dimensions.

The way CJ explained it was when you are in timeline A, and go back in time, you are now in timeline B since you were never in the past in timeline A. So, in reality, they used the Rift Generator to punch a hole that allowed them to cross into timeline B. In turn, the people here may look like the ones they know from timeline A, but in truth, they are different people with different life experiences.

His brief trip down memory lane ended when he turned onto the main street in Plattesburg. Most of the structures on this stretch of road were old two-story red brick buildings, with large display windows highlighting all the pricy antiques they had to offer. Scattered in between were your mandatory hardware store and one-screen movie theater surrounded by local eateries and what looked like a dive bar. Large neon signs lit up the early night, giving it that retro 1950s vibe for the two blocks that made up their "downtown" area.

Logan pulled up to P. Berg's Tavern, wedged between the theater and another antique store, and slammed the gear shift into park. He groaned when he saw CJ through the window wearing his usual blue Hawaiian shirt and white ball cap with tufts of brown hair poking out behind his ears. He was perched at the bar, using it as a backrest with his elbows propped up on it, running his mouth about whatever nonsense he thought sounded cool. Although it did bring a smile to Logan's face when the couple CJ was annoying decided to get up and leave.

Logan got out of the car and meandered into the tavern. He gave a subtle nod to the couple CJ chased off as he stepped inside. *Ah, dammit,* he thought, when CJ raised his hands high above his head to flag him down as if he was a giant jet airliner. Logan returned the gesture with a simple two-finger salute and slid onto the stool next to him.

"I thought you boys in Recon were masters at blending in and going unnoticed," Logan snapped.

CJ chuckled and held up two fingers for the bartender to see. "Oh, look around here. You're the one who stands out like a sore thumb with the 'don't approach me, or I'll kill you' crazy look in your eye, whereas I'm the life of the party."

Logan rolled his eyes. "Clearly. And by the way, was it just that one couple you ran out of here today, or is there always this ten-foot zone around you that others won't cross other than that poor sap who's bringing us our drinks?"

"Thanks, Gil," CJ said as he reached for his drink and took a sip. "And I don't know what you're talking about."

Logan smiled. "Somehow, that doesn't surprise me."

CJ waved to another couple in their mid-fifties at the far end of the room, then pointed up at the ceiling. The couple nodded, and proceeded to climb the stairs to the loft.

Logan took a swig of his drink. "More friends of yours?"

CJ shook his head. "Nuh-uh. New leads. They lived next door to the house Phillip rented, where they found the murdered bodies of his landlords. They should be able to help fill in some of our missing holes."

Logan gripped his right hand into a fist. "You're telling me the bloke we're after is a murderer?"

"Ah, I'd put him more on the probable suspect list."

Logan shook his head. "And this wasn't something you thought was important enough to talk about yesterday?"

"Well," CJ hesitated. "Y'all seemed so interested in Rose, I knew I wouldn't get a chance to bring it up until later, and by then, Eva had already hung up on me."

Logan sighed. "And when you texted me where you wanted to meet, you figured I still didn't need to know?"

CJ stood up with his drink and patted Logan on the head. "You see, us boys in Recon know exactly when information needs to be distributed among the other departments. It's a nifty little skill we all have."

Logan looked up at CJ, his eyes narrowed. "Well, we men in Assault know precisely how to extract information from idiots who think they're running the show."

A nervous grin stretched across CJ's face. Looking past Logan to the bartender behind him, he held up his glass and pointed at it. "We're gonna take these to the booths upstairs, Gil, if that's all right with you?"

The bartender shrugged. "Um, sure. That's fine as always."

CJ nodded. "Thanks, Gil. I owe you one."

"No, you really don't," Gil mumbled.

Before the exchange got any more awkward, Logan got to his feet and said, "Lead the way."

Upstairs, a few patrons were situated at tables in the middle, with four booths shoved in the front of the building that featured the large windows overlooking the street. With fewer patrons up here, it gave off a more intimate setting for those wishing to escape all the noise down below. The couple, who CJ flagged down earlier, looked toward him when they saw them trot up the stairs and motioned for him to join them at their booth.

The gentleman, wearing a dark button-up shirt and jeans, reached out and shook CJ's hand. "Thanks for meeting us here. We thought it would be best not to discuss this when our kids are home."

Logan shook the man's hand as he slid in next to CJ.

"I'm Owen, and this here is my wife, Nora." The man cocked his head to one side as he studied Logan's face. "You look kinda familiar. Do I know you from somewhere?"

Logan glanced at him as he took his hand back. "'Fraid not. I just got one of those types of faces. The name's Logan."

Nora, who wore a faded red T-shirt and jeans, smiled broadly. "Oh, are you British?"

Logan chuckled. "Oh, no. I'm American, but I grew up in Australia."

CJ smiled and took another sip of his drink. "Yeah, you're doing a bang-up job blending in," he whispered.

Logan mumbled back, "Still leagues ahead of you."

"Anyway," said CJ. "How about you tell us how you met Phillip."

"Sure," said Owen.

Nora leaned forward, placing her hand on her chest. "This will all be on the record now, right?"

"You betcha," said CJ.

Logan leaned over to whisper into CJ's ear. "Who do they think we are?"

CJ laughed and took another sip of his drink. "Oh, come on. It's all right. They know we're undercover reporters."

Logan raised an eyebrow. "Are we now?"

"Cool it," CJ whispered as he took another sip.

Nora looked around the room, her eyes wide with fear as she tapped Owen's arm.

Owen's smile went flat as he stared at Logan. "Who are you guys, really?"

Logan waved CJ aside before he had a chance to speak. "We're investigators."

Nora leaned in and whispered, "Like the police?"

Logan shook his head. "No. We're more like, er, what's the word I'm looking for …" Logan paused. "Freelance."

"Good one," CJ chuckled. "The word he's looking for is private investigators. Our client wishes to remain anonymous, and I apologize for the ruse."

"Oh, I see," Nora said, with a slight frown. "That's all right, but could you tell us why your client is interested in Phillip? It'll help us decide if we want to help or not."

"Sure," said Logan. "You see, both Phillip and our client's daughter disappeared in a similar way when they were kids. We want to get in touch with him to see if his case is related to hers. It might help us in locating her."

Even though we've already found Leah, Logan thought.

"Right," said Nora. "I think we can help then."

"Ace," said Logan. "Could you tell us how long you've known Phillip?"

Owen licked his lips. "Let's see, when was that, Mother? Four years ago?"

Nora nodded her head. "That's right. It was at the end of May 2015. Our neighbors, Carl and Jean Norman, were looking to rent out their basement."

Logan raised an eyebrow. "You guys get a lot of renters in this place?"

"Actually, yes," said Owen. "You'll catch a lot of kids out of school looking to spend their summers fishing while taking on some handyman type of work."

"Uh-huh," said Logan. "And that's when Phillip showed up."

"Right," said Nora. "Now you said he was like a runaway or something like that?"

"Not quite," said CJ. "Child abduction would be a better fit."

Nora's face turned white. "Oh, my word," she said as she held her hand over her mouth. "I would have never guessed that at all. Are you sure you have the right Phillip?"

"Yeah, CJ," said Logan. "Are you sure we're after the right person?"

"That I'm sure of. But I'll explain how I know in a bit."

Logan leaned back in the booth, picked up his glass, and swirled the liquid around. "'Bout how old would you say Phillip is?"

Nora bit her lip. "Well, I reckoned he'd be approaching fifty if I had to guess."

Logan placed his drink down and groaned as he wiped his hand down his face. "And that didn't seem strange to you? Some random bloke showing up in a town this small lookin' for work?"

"Well," Owen hesitated. "It did at first, but once we got to know him, he turned out to be a really nice guy."

"That's right," Nora jumped in. "He was always so polite and helpful. He would often help Owen out in the field, movin' pipe for free."

"Then what did he do for money?" Logan asked.

"Oh, that was never a problem for him," said Owen. "You see, he was always collecting cans and scrap metal to turn in and was a wiz at plumbing. Made quite a few bucks getting some of these older home's pipes up-to-date."

"So, when did it start to turn south?" Logan asked.

Owen shrugged. "Well, let's see. I believe it was right after Easter last year. Right, Mother?"

"Why heavens, yes. That was when his friend showed up."

"Hold on," said CJ. "You never mentioned this friend to me before."

Nora smiled. "You didn't ask the right questions, dearie, like Mr. Logan."

CJ chuckled. "All right, you got me on a technicality. So, who's his friend."

Nora stared at her right hand as she drew an imaginary circle on the table with her finger. "Never did catch the fella's name, but he had this cold aura around him."

"Aura?" Logan asked.

Nora huffed. "Okay, a vibe. You could just tell he was up to no good."

Owen took Nora's right hand and held it, giving it a couple of good squeezes. "You'll have to excuse Mother for that. She gets a little touchy when folks question her senses."

Nora turned to glare at Owen. "I know what I felt," she said quickly.

Logan's face turned red. "I'm sorry, I didn't mean anything by it. So, um, do you know what his friend wanted?"

"Well, no," said Nora. "Not exactly. I only saw him briefly once myself when he was fighting with Phillip."

"What kind of fight?" CJ asked.

"They were in his backyard late at night, screaming at each other," said Nora. "It was so loud, I'm surprised they didn't wake the whole neighborhood."

"What was it over?" asked Logan.

"Well," said Owen. "His friend wanted him to go back home with him wherever that was."

"Oh," said Logan.

"Yeah, he was beggin' and a pleadin' that he must go there to get checked out."

"Something medical?" asked Logan.

Owen shrugged. "Not sure, and I didn't feel right asking him about it. His business isn't my business."

"Yeah," said Nora. "But in hindsight, I wished we would've because it was after his friend left, that's when he started to act really strange."

"How so?" Logan asked.

"Well," said Nora. "For starters, it was right outside this bar that Gil saw him banging his head against the sidewalk. He was screaming about tryin' to get the worms out of his head."

"Worms?" asked Logan.

Nora pursed her lips together. "Yep. Worms."

"What happened after that?" Logan asked.

"Gil called the Normans, and they came and picked him up. Took him down to Denver to one of those specialty hospitals for all the good that did."

Logan sighed. "Nothing they could do for him?"

"Nope." Nora scoffed. "Gave him some pills, a pat on the head, then sent him off."

Owen shook his head. "Now, Mother, that's not exactly true. He did pretty well for over a year."

"Well, of course," Nora said, waving her hand aside. "Owen's right about that part, but I tell you, he was never quite the same after his friend visited him."

"Could you describe this new behavior?" CJ asked.

"Well, I could tell he was fighting something awful in his mind. He was having a battle of wits, and something was pulling him to things he didn't want to do."

Logan sneered. "How could you tell?"

"He would be in the backyard almost every morning doing that whisper-yelling as he fought with himself. And, of course, last month, my youngest—our biological youngest, that is—went over to their house to check on the Normans, since I hadn't seen them for a while and they weren't answering their phone. That's when he found Carl slumped over in his chair from a head wound, and Jean strangled to death in her bed."

"Must've scared the hell outta your boy," said Logan.

Nora nodded. "Oh, it did. But talking with the cops about it seemed to have put him at ease."

"Whatever happened to Phillip?" asked Logan.

Owen cleared his throat. "A deputy found him in the basement that night and hauled him off to Ogallala two days ago, but he escaped before he got there."

"And I can fill in this part," said CJ. "A farmer found the police cruiser abandoned in his alfalfa field. It didn't take long for a bunch of cops to come from all over and comb the area. Hell, some even came from as far as Omaha."

Owen leaned forward over the table. "That's right, but we never did hear if they found anything."

"Well, they still haven't found Phillip or the deputy," said CJ, "but they did find a faint set of bloody fingerprints."

"Let me guess," said Logan. "Phillip's."

CJ snapped his fingers. "Ten points to the fellow with the accent. Lucky for us, his prints were still in the system when they fingerprinted him at school."

"Huh," said Nora. "I didn't know they did that."

"Yeah," said CJ. "Must have been some school program they had in California during the '70s."

Logan leaned forward to glance out the window. "So, he could be anywhere right now."

"Yes, which is why I was hesitant to talk to you two here," said Nora. "I've been having this feeling he isn't too far away."

"Oh," said CJ. "Your kids are home alone."

Owen winked at them. "Our youngest, who's twenty-eight, is home watching our two adopted teenagers. The doors and windows are locked, and they've been out hunting and shooting since they were kids. Believe me, they can handle themselves."

Nora glanced out the window, following Logan's gaze. "Who is that?"

Logan knew exactly what he was staring at. It was a shadow of a man with glowing blue eyes wearing a hat and a long coat against the building across the street. That image had kept him awake at night for many years and still haunted him to the very core of his body. That Shadow Man had stepped out of the wall, grabbed his twin brother by the shoulder when they were three, and turned him to ash.

"Not again," Logan snapped.

With a grunt, he shoved the table forward, got to his feet, and dashed down the stairs taking them two at a time. His grip on the rickety handrail barely saved him from toppling as his momentum outpaced his body. *Bang!* He burst through the front door to the street, his heart pounding. His eye's darted up and down the street as he searched for the shadowy figure.

He took a few more steps forward and looked back up at the windows above the bar and saw CJ, Owen, and Nora had their faces pressed against the glass, watching him.

Logan threw his hands up in the air and shouted, "Where is he?"

CJ shook his head and shrugged.

"Shit," Logan whispered.

Chapter 4

United Citadel Field Unit
Beta Team

The flight from Vegas to Louisville went off without a hitch—mostly. Things got a little tense when the security agent kept rescanning my passport. Not sure what the issue was, but after a long pause and a cheerful smile, he handed it back and waved me through. I'd had this lingering worry that the fake IDs CJ whipped up might trigger something, but Maeve and I made it through both airports without much hassle. I would like to give all the credit to CJ, but in reality, I knew it was CJ's friend in Intelligence, Nieminen, who's program CJ was using to implant the required information into various databases so we wouldn't get flagged.

I eased myself into the passenger's side of the gray rental car, opting for Maeve to drive. I hoped this additional task would be a good enough distraction to lower Maeve's guard as I poked around in her mind. Since her last outburst, Maeve had behaved perfectly normal, but the way she appeared disconnected from the world as she spouted "convergence," with no recollection of saying it, still needed to be investigated.

I waited for Maeve to leave the confusion of highway interchanges taking people to and fro around the airport before delving into her psyche. "So, how come you decided to become a cop? I know Kap was pretty much born into it."

Just a little grease to get her talking, I thought.

"Truthfully?" Maeve asked.

I laughed. "Not exactly the response I was expecting, but yes."

"I wanted a job away from the family business that didn't shove me into a windowless closet for eight hours a day working on the books."

"Yeah, it takes a certain type of human to fill that role, but if you love it, you love it."

Maeve pressed down on the gas as she gripped the wheel and zipped the car two lanes over to the left, forgoing the need to signal and check her blind spots. I gripped the handle on the door, thinking maybe now wasn't the best time.

"I take it then you've dealt with a lawyer or two in your career. You think we'll be able to get any information out of Ellis?"

Maeve shrugged. "Hard to say. Some of them can get quite chatty, but you'll generally have some difficulty pulling information out of them, even if it's public record. Our best plan of attack is to use him to get to Rose. If she gives the go-ahead, he'll likely answer all our questions."

I smiled. "I like the sound of that. And speaking of Rose, what information were you able to dig up about the facility she's at?"

"Ah, the Jasinski Medical Institute. Home to some of Kentucky's most disturbed individuals."

"Sounds horrid. You think we'll still be able to get in if Ellis refuses to help?"

"Perhaps, but it'll be tough."

I frowned at the idea of the new variable introduced. I knew that the best of plans could never account for all of them, and new ones would inevitably show up along the way, but I didn't have to like them.

"What would be the complication? I thought this country allowed visitors to converse with inmates?"

"It can vary depending on who you are and why you're there, but generally, you can get in if the inmate wants to meet with you in a state-funded facility. However, this one is privately owned and operated."

I shook my head as she added another variable to our already complicated situation. I could feel my heart sink the more I thought about it, but then I remembered some advice CJ had shared. This was back when our relationship was new, and our "dates" were covert trips to the shooting range to avoid raising any red flags with Citadel higher-ups. Since every designated field team member must be proficient in the other two members' duties, I found myself stuck behind my .338 Lapua rifle, swearing up a storm as each shot failed to hit the target.

Having to constantly recalibrate my Schmidt and Bender scope, all while battling the damn unpredictable wind, was overwhelming. That's when CJ leaned in, close enough for me to feel his breath in my ear, and whispered, "Slow down. Focus on the destination, not the journey. And don't forget to breathe."

His advice seemed counter to what you would expect, but it did work in that situation.

I took a deep breath and stretched my legs out the best I could in the confined space to try to slow down. I'll deal with getting into that private facility later, if it comes to that.

Maeve left the freeway a few miles east of the downtown area and meandered through a maze of side streets before finally turning onto Ellis's block. On my side, I saw the usual small-town lineup—two-story red brick buildings crammed shoulder to shoulder, with little to no parking for customers.

Across the street, though, it was a different world. Grand old Victorian-style homes stood proudly on display, their ornate trim and steep gables evoking the American dream of proud homeownership. Every so often, though, one of those same red brick commercial buildings was wedged awkwardly between them, breaking up the charm and making the area feel less like a neighborhood in which you'd want to raise a family.

"This is quite a peculiar stretch of road," I said. "Everything is laid out so haphazardly I'm not sure if it's supposed to be a business or residential district."

"Looks like they've been converting some of the homes into commercial space," Maeve said as she parked the car.

I got out and eyed the converted Victorian home I assumed was Ellis's office. I'm sure it was a lovely little home in its heyday, but not so much now. The ground floor, where I expected to see an expansive wrap-around patio, was stripped away and replaced with a glass office storefront with black metal beams for support.

Maeve got out and joined me with a snicker as she tried to contain her laughter.

I smirked. "What's scurrying about your head?"

"Well …," she said, her voice trailing off into a giggle. "You ever have one of those friends that was well past the age of getting a facelift, but did so anyway?"

"Um … maybe?" I said, and tightened my lips as I tried not to smile. Taking light of someone else's medical procedure wouldn't be decent of me.

Maeve laughed. "It kinda looks like what they're doing to all of these old homes."

As hard as I tried, a thin smile crept across my face as I followed Maeve inside the building. "Can't say I disagree with that assessment."

A paralegal working for Ellis was waiting for us as we stepped inside. His gray button-up shirt had become untucked in the front, with dusty handprints smeared on his dark blue slacks just above his knees. He flashed us a big smile when he made eye contact and gave a giant over-the-head wave with his free hand. Clutched in his other hand was a laptop wedged between two books on the edge of taking a tumble to the ground.

Maeve reached her hand out to shake his. "Why, hello there. I'm Maeve, and this is Dr. Lewis. We have an appointment to meet with Thomas Ellis."

The paralegal looked down at Maeve's hand and grimaced. "Oh, I don't think I should shake your hand right now. I've been digging through Tom's archives, and I'm bettin' the last time someone was down there was two presidencies ago."

Maeve retracted her hand with a chuckle. "Fair enough."

"I'm Ian, and you two are here right on the dot," he said as he ran his hand through his black hair to push down a cowlick, leaving behind a light trail of dust. "Your boss mentioned you two would be punctual, but I found most people are either early or late."

I leaned over to whisper to Maeve. "So, Leah's our boss now?"

"Well, you did kinda give her that impression," Maeve said out of the corner of her mouth.

Ian's forehead wrinkled as he raised his eyebrows.

"Oh, never mind us," Maeve said as she waved her hand aside.

I cleared my throat. "Is Thomas ready to see us?"

Ian pushed his laptop back into a less precarious spot . "Um, he should be. Just a second."

Ian sauntered to one of the two doors on the right side of the waiting room, rapping his knuckles against it before peeking his head through and said, "They're here."

A muffled voice replied, "Oh, good. Send them in."

"Right away," he said, opening the door.

"Thanks," I said as she passed by Ian, who nodded in return.

The second I walked into Ellis's office, I knew I'd stepped back in time into an old vintage cigar den. Mahogany wainscoting, so dark it was nearly black, lined the bottom half of the walls, connecting to evenly spaced wooden beams that stretched their way up to a ceiling with that same somber hue. Between those beams, burgundy wallpaper with golden damask patterns so rich they may as well have been dipped in gold lined the walls.

Behind a masterfully crafted, Prohibition-era desk sat Ellis. He was shorter than average, dressed in a gray pinstripe suit that had seen better days. His tie, a shade of blueish-gray, hung undone, leaving me to wonder if he had been up all night. His wavy hair was mostly gray now, but the flecks of light brown that shone through offered a nostalgic nod to his younger years that complemented his deep brown eyes.

Ellis motioned for us to enter. "Come in. Sit down," he said in a high-pitched raspy voice.

I sat in the green leather chair in front of Ellis on the left, with Maeve taking the one on the right. I snapped my head back at the sound of Ian closing the door behind us. As I turned around, I saw Ellis had his hand out to shake mine as he leaned over his desk.

I reached out to shake his and said, "Thanks for meeting with us."

I glanced toward Maeve with a raised eyebrow as I rubbed my hand after Ellis released it. "I'm happy to help out in any way I can," he said as he sat back down. "Dr. Lewis, right?"

"Yep, and this is Maeve."

Ellis nodded. "Nice to meet you. However, I must say, in my experience, it's uncommon to meet with a third party after the fact. So, what kind of business do you have with Ms. Lombardi?"

I leaned forward in my chair. "Her sister asked us to look into the matter."

"Oh," Ellis said, waving his hand aside. "I can save you a lot of trouble right now."

I cocked my head to one side. "You can?"

"Yep. I know all about what Iris is up to, and she reeled you two in hook, line, and sinker," he said, shaking his head.

Maeve pursed her lips. "Care to explain?"

Ellis chuckled. "Iris doesn't give a damn about her sister at all. It's the house she's after."

I leaned back in the chair and rubbed the bridge of my nose. "What does a house have to do with all this?"

Ellis intertwined his fingers as he cracked his knuckles, then placed his hands behind his head. "Maybe house is too simple of a term to describe this place, so let's go with mansion."

Maeve piped up, "How big are we talking?"

Ellis raised his eyebrows. "Big. The house itself is one of those modern takes on a turn-of-the-century two-story brick home with fireplaces sticking out on both sides, completely secluded on over one hundred acres of land. It's worth well over five million, so you can see why she is interested in the home."

I let out a heavy sigh. "Sounds lovely, but I don't see why Iris thinks she would have any claim to Rose's property."

"Eh," Ellis said, shrugging. "She kinda does in a roundabout way."

Maeve slapped her leg and chuckled. "Oh, I bet this is gonna be good."

"Miss, you don't even know the half of it," he said as he shook his head. "Their father rebuilt that house on the family's property toward the end of his life. After he passed, they both became the new owners according to his will."

"I see," I said. "So, naturally, with Rose locked up, she wants to be the sole owner of it."

"Not only that," said Ellis. "But she wants to sell it underneath her and pocket all the cash."

I raised an eyebrow. "But there's a snag."

"Yep," Ellis said with a snap of his finger. "Since one of Rose's sons survived, and with Rose in a mental institute, he stands to inherit all her shares. A stipulation their father put in the will to keep the house in the family, since Iris never had any children."

"I don't get it," I said as I shook my head. "Why have us look into this at all?"

"Hmm," Ellis said as he cocked his head to one side and tapped his chin.

"I know why," Maeve blurted out. "If we can prove Rose is of stable mind, then Iris can go to work on getting her to sign the house over."

"That's a good possibility," said Ellis.

"Yeah, it is," said Maeve. "But I don't think it's correct."

"I agree," I said. "That's not even close to the impression I got of Iris."

Ellis shrugged. "Okay, if you say so. But, I've gotta tell you that I've met many people who are just as convincing as Iris, and they have all turned out to be nothing more than petty liars and thieves."

Maeve had started to speak when her phone rang. She fished it out of her pocket and studied it for half a second.

"Excuse me for a moment; I need to take this call," she said, as she got up and left Ellis's office.

I turned my attention back toward Ellis. He was leaning forward over his desk, his head propped up by his left arm as he tapped his fingers on his desk. "Anything else?"

"Can you get me in touch with Rose?"

"Sure, I can arrange that, but it won't do you any good. Rose isn't saying a whole bunch nowadays. More than likely, she'll just decline your request."

"I see," I said as I leaned forward again. "Just tell her some people from the UC would like to meet with her."

Ellis gave a half smile. "Right, and who is the UC?"

I smiled. "Just tell her."

Ellis rolled his eyes as he picked up a pen and jotted the request down on a memo pad.

"Tell Rose the UC wants to meet her," he said under his breath.

Looking up at me, he asked, "Anything else, Boss?"

"Actually, yes," I smiled again. "Are there any details about that night you can talk about? Maybe something Rose said?"

Ellis's eyes locked onto mine. "Nothing I can share with you, Doctor. It's one of those client confidentiality things I'm sure you're aware of."

"Of course," I said. "The problem is I can't find any information at all. Not even who the officer on the scene was."

Ellis squinted at Eva. "Did you try the internet?"

I scoffed. "Of course, I did. I had my best man on the job."

"Really," Ellis said in a monotone voice.

I shook my head and made a gesture toward Ellis's computer. "You're welcome to give it a shot."

"Fine," he said.

I watched Ellis's face as it went through various stages of annoyance, followed by confusion before landing on frustration. I fought to suppress a laugh, being careful to keep my expression neutral.

"This can't be correct," Ellis said as the clicks from his mouse became faster and louder.

I smiled. "And now you can see the problem we're having."

"This is impossible," Ellis said, pushing the keyboard away with a thud. "I can't find anything about her or her family. And it is all public knowledge."

"Like it's all been erased."

Ellis lowered his voice. "That's right."

"So," I continued. "You think you could fill me in on some of the details?"

Ellis looked back at me and blinked a couple of times before saying, "Look, I would if I could."

"You would?" I counted.

"Yeah, but my hands are tied," he said. "But Detective Neil Morgan's aren't."

"And he was the first detective on the scene?"

"Yeah, and he also ran the investigation. You'll get more out of him than you would by talking to Rose."

"That may be true," I paused. "But I'd still like to see her, along with the house and her son, if I can."

"Yeah," Ellis said as he shook his head. "I can get you to her, but the house and kid are entirely different. In fact, I'm fairly certain the house is still on lockdown."

"Well, I guess we'll just have to improvise now, won't we?"

Ellis cleared his throat. "Well, will you look at the time? I've got a client showing up in ten minutes, so we should wrap this up."

"Sure," I said. "But one more thing."

"What is it?"

"Do you think she did it?" I asked as I got to my feet.

Ellis's cheeks reddened. "Well, to be honest, and yes, I know how that sounds coming from a lawyer, but I honestly go back and forth on this one."

I reached across the desk to shake his hand again. "I see. Well, thank you for your time."

"The pleasure was all mine."

I smiled back at him. When I turned the doorknob, Ellis said, "And I'm sorry if I came across a little annoyed back there. It's just that this has been a rough one that I am looking to put behind me."

I turned my head to look at him. "Think nothing of it."

Back outside, I found Maeve waiting for me in the car. It seemed somewhat strange that Maeve didn't rejoin me in Ellis's office, but then I noticed that she was still on her mobile.

"Yeah, I'll be sure to give her all the updates," Maeve said as I slid into the passenger seat.

"Leah?" I asked.

"Yep," Maeve said, hanging up the phone.

"Oh, that's terrific. What did she have to say?"

"As it turns out, quite a lot," Maeve said as she turned the car on.

"Oh, I hope it's good news!"

Maeve chuckled. "That would depend on your definition of good."

"Oh, dammit," I said. "Let's hear it."

"Logan checked in, and it sounded like tracking down Phillip won't be that simple."

"Typical," I sighed. "What else did he have to say?"

"Well, there was a bunch of swearing and blaming of CJ's surveillance skills, but he thinks he can straighten out that mess."

"Yep, that sounds like Logan."

"Yeah, sounded like he was making a mountain out of a molehill, but that's not the bad news."

"Uh-oh," I said.

"The situation with Forsyth isn't looking good."

"Oh, bloody hell."

"Yep. Chambers is currently with internal affairs, trying to defend Forsyth's actions."

"All of this, simply for looking up a person in the database?"

"Yeah. Chambers will try to explain that Forsyth wouldn't have been forced to do that if his captain hadn't passed the case off to homicide."

I sighed. "You think it'll work?"

"Nope."

"Damn," I said. "You know, I find it hard to believe that his inquiry was randomly flagged this quickly. Someone had to have turned him in."

Maeve stayed focused on the road ahead of them as she pulled away, never showing any signs of emotion. "You bet someone did. It was that same snake in the grass, his captain, who turned the case over."

Eva's voice shook. "Surely not."

Maeve laughed. "Obviously, you don't know her as well as Kap and I do."

"Actually," I paused. "Wasn't she the one who screwed up Kaplin's father's case so bad that they never found him?"

"The one and only."

Chapter 5

United Citadel Field Unit
BRAVO SUBUNIT

Logan lingered beside CJ in the middle of an alfalfa field, staring at an empty spot where the abandoned police car transporting Phillip should have been. The sun burned unabated through the cloudless sky, making it harder for Logan to contain his irritation for the current situation. Clearly, a team of detectives had already been through the area, and all that remained were bits of yellow plastic from the police tape scattered among the trampled plants. He groaned as he crossed his arms behind his back and gripped his left wrist. What once hinted at a promising lead now resembled a fool's errand.

Then again, he was more frustrated with CJ's poor intel because he was now out here instead of back in Vegas, keeping an eye on Leah. Being in the presence of people she trusted would be the best thing for her until her confidence returned. Training her in firearms and defensive techniques did help, but he knew she wasn't ready despite her enthusiasm.

Logan wiped the sweat from his brow and flicked it on the ground. "What exactly do you expect to find out here?"

CJ crouched down and yanked a few pieces of alfalfa up to study. Pulling the blades apart, he found a dark substance, smeared it between his fingers, then took a whiff of it. Holding his finger up for Logan to see, he asked, "Why would there be specks of oil out here?"

Logan shrugged. "The car could have hit a rock and punctured the oil tank."

"Maybe," CJ said as he stood up. "But if that was the case, I think there would be more than just a couple of sprinkles here on the ground."

Logan crossed his arms. "Only if the pan got punctured recently or had a slow drip."

"Right," said CJ. "We know Phillip's friend had been around, and I'm betting he sabotaged the car to help him escape."

Logan's face tightened. "That sounds like an awful lot of speculation. By that logic, you could also assume that Phillip's friend killed his landlords, but there's no evidence of either situation. Besides, if the car did run out of oil, why would it be way out here instead of on the side of the road?"

CJ frowned and tossed the plant back onto the ground. "Yeah, you got a point. This oil could just as easily come from some farm equipment."

"Yep," Logan said as he scanned the horizon. "I don't think we'll find much out here that the police didn't collect."

His eyes stopped when he spotted two figures perched on a small barren hill a few miles away watching them. He held his hand above his eyes, shielding them from the sun as he strained to get a better look at them. It was hard to tell from this distance, but they appeared to be wearing suits, with the taller one pointing something at them.

A fire burned at the back of his throat as he tried to swallow. "We're being targeted."

CJ collapsed to the ground and unholstered his pistol.

Logan glanced down at him and rolled his eyes. "Get up," he muttered. "If they were going to kill us, they would have done it already."

"Are you sure?" CJ asked as his voice shook. "From that far away?"

"Yes," he said. Although he knew he was partially lying to CJ. Only a handful of blokes could have made that shot from that distance, and he doubted one of them was on that hill.

CJ stood up, his gun at low ready. "Who are they?"

Logan shook his head. "Don't rightfully know. That's your department, not mine."

CJ glanced back at the path they made from their car to here and bit his bottom lip. "What should we do?"

Logan tilted his head to one side. "I'm gonna go see what they want."

CJ's eyes shot wide open. "What? Oh, tell me that isn't your real plan."

Logan smiled. "No. My real plan is to shoot them before they shoot us. That's why you're coming."

"Great," CJ said sarcastically. "You think it could be Phillip and his friend?"

"That would be helpful but doubtful," said Logan. "We don't have that type of luck. I'm bettin' on them being detectives wondering what we're doing."

CJ holstered his gun, reached for his backpack and unzipped a side pocket. He pulled out his binoculars, which he held up and adjusted. His brow wrinkled as he studied the two men, followed by a smile that crept across his face. "What the hell is *he* doing here?"

Logan tapped him on the shoulder. "Let me see."

CJ passed the binoculars to Logan, who wiped the lenses down with his shirt to annoy CJ before looking through them. "Is that Nieminen with a thermal cam?"

"Hard to verify now that the lenses are scratched, but I think so. The other guy standing next to him I don't recognize."

"Well then, let's go suss it out.," Logan said, returning the binoculars. "But keep your gun at the ready."

CJ packed the lenses away and unholstered his gun. "Right behind you."

Logan blazed a trail through the denser parts of that alfalfa field that stretched up to chest height, stomping and kicking rocks along the way to ward off snakes hiding in the area. Sweat beaded up on his forehead and dripped down the back of his neck, adding to the unpleasantness he felt being out there. Logan detested warmer climates, along with the local wildlife that thrived in such conditions. Given the opportunity, he often volunteered for assignments that took him to cooler temperatures. But times have changed. He had always been more comfortable hiding in the cold and dark until he learned about the Shadow Knight's ability to blend seamlessly in the dark.

Then there was the matter of the Shadow Man, and it was hard to deny the similarity between them. The Intelligence Division that CJ is a member of had never confirmed if the two were related. No matter how hard he pushed CJ for the information, he never said more than what scant information Intel had made public with the United Citadel.

Logan's eyes remained fixed on the figures as he pushed forward up the hill. The rhythmic sound of CJ's labored breath behind him distracted him. A thought flashed through his mind that adding CJ to some of Leah's training would be a wise decision. He nodded to himself as he filed that idea away for later.

A surge of anticipation traveled from his core to his fingertips, bringing his focus back to a razor's edge. He felt his right hand, guided by instinct, drift toward the grip of his pistol as they neared the top. He knew he couldn't afford to let his guard down since there was no guarantee this was the same Nieminen who had worked with CJ from his timeline.

Up top, Nieminen turned to face them while his companion with light brown hair remained obscured behind him. They were both dressed in black suits and ties that contrasted with Nieminen's white hair and blue eyes. Logan's expression remained detached; his eyes locked on the thermal camera still pointed at them. Typically, members of the UC used thermal cams to detect the elusive Shadow Knights since they can conceal their movements in a shroud of darkness; only their subtle heat signatures would disclose their presence. However, in broad daylight, that was impossible. Either Nieminen was looking for something else, or this was a giant clue that their intel on the Shadow Knights desperately needed an overhaul. It made perfect sense, given the scarcity of UC encounters with this particular sect of Knights.

CJ, following a step behind Logan, hesitated, then took a tentative step forward, his pistol at the ready. Logan raised his hand abruptly behind him, signaling CJ to halt. The pressure was on, and they couldn't afford any false moves now.

Nieminen lowered the thermal cam with a hint of satisfaction on his face. "Good job," he commended. "I see your brief tenure with the Alpha team has taught you not to trust anyone, even a friendly face such as myself."

Logan's eyes bore into Nieminen's, searching for any clues that might hint at the man's true intentions. During his final mission on the Alpha team, Intel discovered that one of the Blood Knight's Acolytes had infiltrated the old Beta team, resulting in their demise and the mission being labeled a catastrophic failure. It was Nieminen who had been assigned to clean up the aftermath and discovered the body of the dead Acolyte.

CJ piped up. "How did you get here? I thought you and the rest of Delta were stationed in Helsinki."

Nieminen winked at Logan, knowing Logan was helping him out in Helsinki before rejoining the Betas during their South Africa mission a while back. "Aye, we were there. After I completed that mission, Divisional Director Forsyth sent us through the Rift Generator."

A flicker of worry crossed CJ's face. "Where's the rest of your team then?"

Nieminen lowered his head. "They didn't make it," he admitted, his voice heavy with sorrow.

"What happened?" CJ asked.

"Yes," Logan demanded as he eyed Nieminen. "What happened?"

Nieminen wiped a bead of sweat from his forehead. "I thought I was working with someone I trusted, and you can decipher what happened from there."

"Yes," said Logan. "I've learned firsthand that trust can blind you from the truth. So, the real question is, how do we sort out who's who?"

Nieminen smiled. "That's where your brother comes into play."

Logan's eyes narrowed. "My brother's dead," he retorted sharply.

Nieminen's companion, who stood silently behind him, stepped aside, a wry smile across his face. "Oh, come now, baby brother. You know you have more than one brother."

Logan's eyebrows arched. The stranger did have a familiar-looking face, but his older brother died in childbirth long before he was born.

"C5?" he whispered, then raised his voice. "I mean, Connor Kaplan the fifth?"

"There's more than one Connor?" CJ interjected, looking back and forth between the two.

The man nodded, his expression tinged with a sense of nostalgia. "It's a family name, and I am the last one in the line. But I go by Quint."

CJ tapped Logan on the shoulder. "So, would that make your father C4?"

Logan nodded slowly as a flicker of recollection crossed his mind. From what his father told him, all the firstborn sons in the Kaplan line were named Connor, going back several generations. About the time Logan's grandfather came around they gave him the nickname C3 to avoid confusion at family gatherings.

"Yeah." Logan's voice dragged. "I vaguely remember being told my grandfather would tease him about how his nickname, C4, fit him so well as a kid because of the temper tantrums he would throw."

Still with his gun at the ready, CJ asked, "So how do we determine who's who?"

A smile tugged at one side of Quint's mouth. "Oh, just by using a piece of information I liberated from a Knight in a different timeline."

"Right, and how did you manage that?" Logan asked.

"Unimportant," Quint scoffed. "You two ever heard of Blaschko's lines?"

Logan and CJ shook their heads.

Nieminen interjected. "Think of them like zebra stripes. Each set of lines is unique to the zebra, yet appears identical to the untrained eye."

"Like a fingerprint," CJ mused.

"Somewhat, but these are more unique than a fingerprint," said Quint. "Humans possess similar patterns on their skin, invisible under normal lighting conditions."

"Okay, and your point is…?" Logan asked.

Quint chuckled. "Seems like the only consistency across these dimensional timelines is you're an impatient smartass, and I'm a miscarriage."

Nieminen cut back in to steer the conversation back on track. "Let me think how to put this so you'll understand."

A brief pause hung in the air before Nieminen snapped his fingers. "Yes, I know. Think of a vibration."

Logan's frustration seeped through his clenched jaw. "Huh?"

Nieminen pressed on, undeterred by Logan's injection. "Every constituent of the cosmos resonates in harmony with this particular vibration," he expounded with glee. "Every organism, every flora, every mineral, and even the fundamental particles themselves, all resonate at a frequency unique to each dimensional timeline."

CJ nodded. "So, what you're saying is that by scanning us for this frequency, you can discern which timeline we originated from?"

Nieminen's eyes brightened with approval. "Precisely," he affirmed. "By discerning the minute variations in your Blaschko's lines, I can deduce the precise dimensional world you emanate from."

"So, how does this work?" CJ asked.

Before Nieminen could respond, Quint interjected, "Oh, just take your clothes and gear off and toss them over here."

Logan unholstered his gun, his body rigid in defiance. "No. I'm not disarming myself."

Nieminen raised his hand to help calm down the rising tension. "Gentlemen, there's no need for such drastic measures," he assured. "Quint's just yanking your chain. All I need to do is scan your back into my wrist computer. It will only take a second. Just turn around and lift your shirts."

Logan's gaze shifted toward CJ, and he nodded, letting CJ know that he should go first. CJ's eyes widened as he shook his head.

"Uh, no," he protested. "You said not to trust them."

Logan's expression hardened. "I've got you covered," he said. "Now, why don't you do some Recon work and find out if this will work."

CJ sighed as he holstered his gun. "Oh, all right."

Nieminen swiftly manipulated a few buttons on his thermal cam before aiming it at CJ's back. CJ stood there, his discomfort palpable as he dutifully held up his shirt. Satisfied with his capture, Nieminen released the thermal cam, allowing it to dangle from the cord wrapped around his wrist as he went to work on his computer.

"Fascinating," he said. "You, my friend, come from E-12. That is the twelfth different dimensional timeline of Earth charted by the Knights, the very same timeline as myself."

Logan sneered. "Well, well. What are the odds of that?"

"One point less than astronomical," CJ said, lowering his shirt.

Quint flashed a half smile. "Not necessarily," he mused. "We have no idea how these shadow corridors the Rift Generators bore into work that connect these different timelines. For all we know, you may have just merely taken a leisurely stroll next door."

Nieminen held up his thermal cam again, his attention focused on Logan. "Your turn."

Logan shook his head. "No. I'm the same as him."

Quint let out a muffled laugh. "Come now, baby brother. There's no way you can know that for sure."

"Not about to turn my back on unfriendlies." Logan cocked his head toward CJ, his gaze still fixed on Nieminen. "Besides, I've been with him the whole time."

CJ held up a finger. "Um, that's not exactly true. We've been separated multiple times."

Logan groaned as he kept his focus on Nieminen.

CJ continued, "The first time we were separated was at the Blood's Knights mansion in Louisiana, where we found your sister and lost Detective Kaplan."

Quint's eyes narrowed. "Detective Kaplan?"

"Yeah," said CJ. "Your father from this timeline happens to be a detective, so we've been using that moniker to avoid confusion with the older version we know from the Alpha team from our timeline, or E-12 as Nieminen put it. He sacrificed himself to save Logan."

Quint frowned. "This is really bad," he murmured, shaking his head.

Nieminen, half distracted by the conversation, leaned in closer. "Louisiana, you say?"

"Yeah," said CJ.

"Interesting because that's where Forsyth was headed after sending us through the rift. He was working on some sort of plan but didn't share any of the details with me."

Logan interjected. "Unrelated. I want to know why you two are here."

Quint raised an eyebrow, a sly grin formed on his lips as he countered Logan's question. "Sounds like you're more interested in getting out of the back scan to confirm your identity. Now, I wonder why that would be?" His words hung in the air.

Logan clenched his jaw, his eyes fixated on Quint. He had hoped he could stall for some more time to devise a way to get out of the scan since he still didn't trust the two. But as luck would have it, Quint could see right through him and called his bluff.

Unable to back down, Logan drew a half smile and winked at Quint. "You first."

Quint's lips parted, poised to speak, when Nieminen swiftly interjected. "This game of cat and mouse is becoming wearisome. We're all here pursuing identical objectives. Our purpose revolves around locating Jacob's offspring, given his current deceased status. Extracting pertinent information from Phillip's cognitive faculties is paramount to putting us back on track and enabling us to effectively infiltrate and dismantle the Knights."

Logan raised an eyebrow. "Jacob's dead?" Last he heard, Maeve speculated that he went back underground after he rescued her and Detective Kaplan from Shady Reef.

Nieminen glanced back at Quint, who gave a subtle nod. "It would appear that way," Nieminen replied, his words drawn out deliberately as he carefully weighed each syllable.

Logan narrowed his eyes. "Appear?" he said with an undertone of suspicion.

Nieminen lowered his head. "The situation surrounding Jacob's presumed demise is a complex matter."

"Care to elaborate?" Logan asked.

Quint waved his finger at Logan. "Nope," he retorted. "We've answered your question, and now it is our turn, so assume the position for the back scan."

Logan let out a frustrated huff, knowing he had little choice but to comply if he wanted to get anything else from them. "Fine. Let's get this over." He turned around and lifted his shirt.

Nieminen swiftly manipulated the buttons on his thermal cam once more, capturing the necessary data from Logan's back while keeping one eye on CJ, who had now raised his gun and pointed it at them.

"This can't be?" Nieminen's voice trembled. His eyes darted from his computer to Logan.

Quint, unable to contain his curiosity, leaned in closer. His eyes narrowed as he peered over Nieminen's shoulder, trying to make out the tiny readings that had shaken Nieminen. "What is it? What'd you find?" he asked, his voice barely above a whisper.

Logan's attempt to remain composed faltered slightly. "Yeah, what is it?" he asked as he turned back around, his face paled as his heart pounded in his chest.

Nieminen shook his head as he looked perplexed by the information he was seeing. "It says that you are from E-Prime, which happens to be what the leader of the Blood Knights designated as his original timeline."

"You're mistaken," Logan quipped, trying to maintain his composure.

CJ echoed the sentiment they both were feeling. "What does that mean?"

"It means," said Quint, "that somehow this is your original timeline."

CJ shook his head. "But that's impossible."

Nieminen met Logan's gaze. "Apparently not."

Chapter 6

United Citadel Field Unit
Beta Team

My mobile went off far too early for my liking, at a quarter to four in the morning. Maeve's voice crackled through the speaker, informing me that Detective Neil Morgan was ready to meet us at a twenty-four-hour diner. Our original plan was to meet with Detective Morgan after his shift was over, but of all the rotten luck, a double homicide case got tossed to him at the last second.

I lay in bed staring at the ceiling, watching the shadows dance about. I listened to the rain pelting the window from a storm that rolled in. I couldn't help but be reminiscent of the days when I would have to force myself to make the trek on those rainy mornings to the university for those high-level early morning lectures no sane person would attend at those hours.

Begrudgingly, I was able to quickly throw on a fresh set of clothes and make my hair somewhat decent for our meeting with the detective. Maeve was already there when I reached the hotel lobby, impeccably dressed. I admired her knack for quick transformations, something I'd never quite mastered.

I smiled at her. "Just getting home from a hot date?"

Maeve rolled her eyes and lightly laughed. "I wish. I had difficulty sleeping, so I've been up for a bit."

"Sounds like your counterpart," I quipped.

Maeve frowned. "Kap?"

I stumbled, trying to deflect the topic. "Oh, no. Not him. Forget I even mentioned it. Just a slip of the tongue."

But I could sense Maeve was far from letting it go as we headed to the parking garage.

As she settled into the driver's seat, she flashed me a sidelong glance and a wry smile. "You know me from your timeline, don't you?"

"No, that's not it," I protested. But I knew it was too late for that. Maeve had already pieced it together.

Undeterred, she continued, "Yes, it is, and that's why you call Conner 'Kap' like the rest of his friends and I do. You knew both of us in your timeline. It all makes sense now."

"You're mistaken again," I said, hoping she would drop it.

"Nuh-uh." Maeve smirked. "I'm not turning this car on until you tell me how you know us."

Resigned, my shoulders slumped as I fastened my seatbelt. I could feel the corners of my mouth pull downward as I thought about what she was asking me.

"You know," I sighed. "Some things are better left unspoken."

Maeve put her hand on my shoulder. "Okay, I understand."

She started the ignition, and the car hummed to life. The rain streaked across the windows as she got on the freeway heading toward the diner.

Biting her lip, she ventured, "This is about Arthur, isn't it?"

A shiver sprinted down my arms, leaving goose bumps in its wake. "Who spoke to you of Arthur?"

Maeve's response held a momentary pause, her gaze distant. "Um, no one. It just came to me."

Bewildered, I stared back at her. "It just came to you?"

"Yeah, I know," she admitted sheepishly. "I get these sporadic fragments that drift into my head every now and then. I'd say ask Kap about it if you don't believe me, but..." she trailed off, then said softly, "but that's not an option anymore."

I offered her a sympathetic nod. "Well," I said, my tone softer, "that seems to be something unique to you. And yes, I knew both you and Kap rather well."

I looked over at her, torn between keeping a painful memory to myself or telling her everything. Ultimately, I couldn't find a good reason not to share, since it was only a matter of time before the truth would surface. I might as well rip the Band-Aid off now.

"We were on a humanitarian effort, Arthur and I," I said.

Maeve's curiosity was piqued. "Who's Arthur?"

"My elder brother," I clarified.

"I see," Maeve nodded. "I take it you two were close."

"Indeed, we were. He was the first of us to attend medical school at King's College."

"Impressive."

I nodded. "So naturally," I said as I winked at her, "I had to one-up him by getting into Oxford."

Maeve chuckled. "Of course you did."

"Eventually, he volunteered for an organization that assigned him to a remote village in Northern India to work on a mysterious disease that had broken out."

"What was it?"

"Not sure, but if I had to guess, I believe it might've been a potential Acolyte prototype the Knights were working on. Far more sophisticated than what Martin was infected with when you saw him on Shady Reef and subsequently killed in New Orleans by CJ, but that is a major assumption on my part."

"Ah," Maeve remarked.

"However, at the time, none of us had ever seen an Acolyte, let alone heard of them, and as far as I know, this prototype never got past stage one."

"What makes these different?"

"Well, that's a challenge," I admitted. "Because the UC could never determine the cause of this mysterious illness, but my best guess is how it's spread from host to host." I sighed. "Whatever it was, this illness eventually struck Arthur and several other medical personnel stationed there."

"Damn."

"When he fell ill, I brought him home to Norwich," my voice broke, "and isolated him at the university hospital."

"What were his symptoms?"

"It began with the semblance of flu-like symptoms progressing to rapid weight loss accompanied by visual hallucinations, paranoia, and followed by weeks of being in a catatonic state."

Maeve bit her lip. "That's intense."

My face flushed as I wiped away a tear. "Yes, it was incredibly difficult for my parents and me. Our only solace was that he was finally at rest a month later."

"Did he ever wake up from the coma?"

I nodded slowly. "Briefly. Right before he passed. His heart rate skyrocketed, and he opened his eyes and whispered one word... 'blood.'"

Maeve bit her lip. "Damn. How heart-wrenching."

I sighed and looked out the window. The drizzly, overcast sky mirrored the mood I was feeling. "After the day's events, you, well, I mean your counterpart in my timeline, visited me, and spoke of the Knights, their potential role in Arthur's demise, and gave me a week to decide if I wanted to join up with the UC."

Maeve raised her eyebrow. "I only gave you a week to decide?"

"You did." I smirked. "Though, it hardly took but a moment for me to commit. Because of Arthur, I do what I do now, not just for myself but for others. If I can help people find closure from dealing with the horrors brought on by the Knights, I bloody hell will."

Maeve smiled. "We both will."

The glowing neon sign of Dick's Cafe flickered against the gloom, beckoning us closer. Once inside, the comforting mix of freshly brewed coffee and vanilla pastries blended with the rain-soaked scent of the outside world. Soft unidentifiable country music played from speakers mounted in the ceiling, where muted lights dangled above the worn-out empty booths—minus one, where a middle-aged man sat looking through a weathered manila folder. At the counter was a server with gray hair and a smile, helping an older gentleman with his order.

Using some deductive logic, I assumed the tired-looking man in the booth was our detective. Water droplets shimmered in his unkempt hair, and the rain's toll was evident on his light jacket. While Maeve headed toward the counter to order coffee, I approached the man seated at the booth.

"Detective Morgan?" I asked, extending a friendly hand.

Morgan attempted to smile as he shook my hand. "The one and only," he said through a yawn. "You must be Dr. Lewis."

"That I am," I said as I slid into the booth. "But you can call me Eva."

"Sorry about the other night," said Morgan. "The detective on the night shift called out, so I was the only one available to take this unfolding case."

"No need to apologize," I said with a smile. "I've been in similar situations myself."

His eyes flickered to the window. A soft sigh escaped his lips. "Some people just don't know how to behave," he whispered.

I leaned closer. "One of the downsides to only seeing people at their worst."

Morgan nodded. "Speaking of similar situations, your assistant, Leah, said you wanted to talk to me about the Rose Lombardi case."

"Right you are," I said. "Her sister, Iris, reached out and asked if I could take another pass at it."

"Sure," he said slowly. "But I don't see the point. Of all the cases I've worked on, this one was fairly straightforward, and the trial has already come and gone."

Maeve returned with her drink and settled in next to me. "What'd I miss?"

"Just the formalities," I said, then turned my attention back to Morgan. "This is my colleague Maeve. She'll be helping me out on this one."

Morgan nodded. "Hello, and as I was saying, it pretty much was an open-and-shut case."

"That very well may be," I said. "But if you've got some time, I'd love to hear how your investigation unfolded."

Morgan adjusted his wristwatch. "I'm still good for twenty minutes. I gotta get home in time to ensure my oldest gets up in time for school. Since he's turned sixteen, he's been pressing the snooze on his alarm clock all the way through his first class."

"Oh." I chuckled. "This shouldn't take too long. I'm just interested in hearing your side of the case."

Morgan nodded and pulled a photograph of a young boy around fourteen from his folder. "This is Ted."

I piped up. "Rose's oldest child."

"Right," he said. "And the sole survivor of the rampage his mother went on."

"Any ideas on how he managed to survive?" Maeve asked.

Morgan leaned back in the booth and made a loud exhale. "By sheer dumb luck if you ask me."

"Can you elaborate?" I asked.

"Certainly," he said. "You see, Ted wasn't supposed to be home. After school, he went to a friend's house and then came home a little earlier than expected."

Maeve nodded. "Makes sense."

"Right," he said. "And that's when he stumbled across the aftermath."

"Oh no," I said. "How bad was it?"

Morgan's eyes darted around the diner to make sure no one was nearby. "It was bad-bad. He ended up stumbling across parts of his younger brothers dismembered in the kitchen sink when he went looking for a snack."

I covered my hand over my mouth. "Dear Lord."

"That poor kid," said Maeve.

Morgan nodded. "And that's just the beginning."

I leaned in. "What happened next?"

"Well, Ted hears some commotion upstairs, so he pulls out his phone to call us as he makes his way back outside, but ends up hiding in the pantry when he hears someone coming into the kitchen, which is where I found him."

"Did he see who it was?" asked Maeve.

"Oh, he did. It was his father stumbling through the door with a knife jammed into the area just below the neck above the shoulder."

"No kidding," said Maeve. "What did he do?"

"Didn't have time to do anything but close the door as silently as possible. Someone was following his father, and looking under the crack at the bottom of the door, he could see Rose holding some sort of wavy-bladed knife and plunging it repeatedly into Mr. Lombardi's back."

I rubbed the bridge of my nose, feeling the pressure building up in my sinus. "There is something that I have to confirm, but I'm pretty sure I know the answer."

Morgan eyed me warily. "Go on."

"Children can process trauma in, shall we say, unique ways. You think there's a chance he misunderstood what he saw?"

Morgan groaned. "No." He paused. "But I'll admit I had the same suspicions initially."

"Oh," said Maeve. "What changed your mind?"

Morgan sighed as he looked down at the picture of Ted. "Well, for starters, the medical examiner did confirm that Mr. Lombardi was stabbed below the neck just as Ted described. But we already knew that because the knife was still there when we found the body. However, there were also an additional thirty-nine stab wounds found in his back that may have come from the knife Ted described that Rose was using."

Maeve raised an eyebrow. "You never found that knife."

Morgan's shoulders drooped downward. "Unfortunately, you are correct."

I leaned my head to one side. "I'm missing something here."

Morgan's gaze narrowed. "What?"

"How can you be sure Ted isn't the murderer?"

"Let me tell you somethin'; this kid isn't faking it."

I raised an eyebrow, interested in where he was going with this. "How do you know?"

Morgan leaned in, his eyes now more intense than they had been throughout the conversation. "I've been doing this for far too long now. I've seen many people try to act or feign emotions and just outright lie. But Ted…" He paused as he looked back down at the photo. "The terror in his eyes, the way he trembled when he tried to speak—even the best of us can't fake that behavior."

"Perhaps," I said. "But since you never found the knife Ted described, how can you be so sure she wasn't set up by someone else? Also, I think it would be kind of hard to identify someone by looking through the crack under a door."

Morgan leaned back and rubbed the left side of his forehead. "You're not wrong. Looking through the crack under the door would be difficult. But there was some more evidence that led us to Rose and confirmed what Ted told us."

Maeve nodded. "Defensive wounds."

"You betcha, and a lot of them. We found biological material with her DNA under her other kid's fingernails that lined up with scratches found on her body. Then there was the partial blood pattern from Mr. Lombardi's neck wound on the wall in the upstairs bedroom, with a section missing that matched the blood pattern on her clothes, and that blood came back positive for Mr. Lombardi."

"Oh, I see," I said. "But for that to work, she would have to be taller than her husband or standing on something?"

"Right," Morgan continued, "she's just a smidge over 5'10", and he's five inches shorter. As I said, it was pretty much an open-and-shut case."

"What was the motive?" I asked. "Her lawyer mentioned that the theory was him figuring out that she was cheating on him, but if that was the case, why would she kill her own children?"

"The only person who can answer that is Rose," said Morgan. "It was speculated that if her husband did leave her, he would find a way to take sole custody of their children, which wouldn't be hard since Rose's job kept her away from home for months at a time."

"Right," said Maeve. "It's an old tale that I've unfortunately witnessed myself. If she can't have them, no one can."

"Bingo," he said. "And as for the affair, we were able to find the man she was cheating on her husband with." Morgan opened his folder and leafed through some pages. "Let's see here … ah, here it is," he said, pointing to a name on a loose-leaf paper clipped to the report. "His name is Mathias Kopache."

Maeve shot me a look, then turned her attention back toward the detective. "Did you say Kopache?"

"Yeah," Morgan said slowly.

"This Kopache guy," said Maeve. "Did he have gray eyes with blond hair and pale skin?"

Morgan's eyes narrowed. "You know him?"

"Yeah, if it's the same guy, I've met him once back in California," said Maeve.

Morgan clinched his fists. "Okay, what's going on here? Who are you two, really?"

I put my hand up in hopes of calming him down, but I feared it was probably too late for that. "We are exactly who we say we are."

"Nuh-uh," he said. "You're connected to this somehow. I just don't know how yet."

Maeve sighed and swirled what was left of her drink. "You're probably right, but what that connection is, I don't know yet. But I will find out."

"I don't like this," said Morgan. "If that's true, there's clearly more to this case than what we were able to uncover."

I cocked my head to one side. "Why did it go to trial so fast?"

"Oh, that bullshit," Morgan grumbled. "The DA figured they had more than enough evidence to bring it to trial despite the fact we were still interviewing other people who knew the family. The dumbass probably wanted to get it done and over with before his vacation."

"Still," I said. "I'm surprised they could set up a court date that quickly."

"Right, I know," Morgan said as he checked his watch. "But, if you would excuse me, I need to get moving."

I stood up and shook Morgan's hand one more time. "Thank you again," I said. "This has been very illuminating."

Morgan said, "Sure," as he turned to leave. We followed him out of the diner back into the rain. It was still dark outside, but the sun would soon be poking up over the horizon. Standing under the awning, Morgan took out a pack of cigarettes, lit one up, and blew the smoke out into the cold air.

"You know," he said, "the police stopped watching Rose's house months ago after our investigations concluded."

Maeve turned and whispered to me, "We can see the crime scene."

Morgan nodded, clearly hearing what Maeve had said. "Yes, but I advise you to proceed with caution," he said, taking another drag.

"That place has been vacant for a while, and I've heard reports of noises and lights in the windows. Wouldn't be surprised if some squatters have taken up residence."

"Absolutely," I replied.

Morgan flicked his cigarette into a puddle, where it fizzled out. "Let me know if you find anything."

He jogged across the street in the pouring rain, got into a car, and took off.

I turned to Maeve and asked, "How do you know this Kopache bloke?"

"Hmm," Maeve said. "You probably don't remember, or Kap never mentioned it, but he was the man that ferried us to Shady Reef and then abandoned us there."

"Sounds like we're on the right path, then," I said.

"Definitely," said Maeve.

Chapter 7

United Citadel Field Unit
BRAVO SUBUNIT

Logan's gaze remained fixed on the distant road that had brought them as he stood on top of the hill overlooking the alfalfa field. The familiar world he once knew was crumbling around him faster than a sandcastle caught in the tide. The original belief that he came from another timeline felt insignificant compared to the stark realization that this dimension was his true home. More so, Leah and Detective Kaplan from E-Prime weren't mere facsimiles, but his genuine family. Grief took hold of him as he recalled Detective Kaplan, his real father, sacrificed his life in New Orleans to save him.

He sniffed as he buried those emotions deep down so he could focus on the job at hand. There was still the matter of how, when, and why he traveled from E-Prime to E-12? For now, the only person who could probably answer that question was the one man he once believed to be his real father on the Alpha team. If Iris was right about bumping into him during her sister's trial, he knew it was only a matter of time before their paths crossed. Then again…

Quint's voice boomed deep into his subconscious, clearing his mind as he returned to his current reality. "Who are you?"

Logan stared back at him, his gaze hard as steel. "I'm exactly who I said I was."

Quint shook his head. "Cut the crap!"

Logan flashed a half smile, knowing any answer he gave Quint other than he was working for the Knights would result in the same reaction. But right now, that didn't matter, since CJ was the only one he needed on his side.

"Yeah, right. And how'm I supposed to know your little test actually works or does what you say it does?" Logan asked as he glanced at CJ.

CJ shifted right, re-aiming his gun at Quint, his knuckles white. "He makes a valid point."

Nieminen glanced toward Quint, his face motionless. "Indeed. He is correct in his assessment. This is a nascent technology."

Quint's jaw flexed as he ground his teeth, his face turned a deep crimson red. "The technology works. It's him that's out of place."

CJ opened his mouth, then paused. His eyes flickered between Quint and Logan as he considered his next move. "Look, Quint, all of us are out of place right now. Nothing we can say or do will change that. However, what you two can do is tell us what happened to Jacob."

Quint kicked the ground, sending a trail of dust and debris that settled a foot in front of him. "Fine! Whatever," he snapped, throwing his hands up and retreating to the hill's backside, where he gazed off into the distance.

CJ lowered his gun as Nieminen walked over to join them. "Is he always like this?"

Nieminen rubbed the back of his neck and raised an eyebrow with a lopsided grin. "Well, from what he's told me, his experiences have been notably tumultuous."

"How so?" asked Logan.

"Well, to start with, he's been traveling through many different timelines for which he estimates to be approximately four years, although the reliability of that measure is debatable, given how time functions across these sequences."

"What do you mean?" CJ asked as he scratched his head.

Nieminen explained, "He found an unusual dimension where the diurnal cycles seemed to extend to forty-eight hours, even though logically Earth in that dimension should still function as the others do. But his biological clock still treated it as two days."

Logan shook his head. "You've lost me."

"Hmm," said Nieminen. "I'll try to elucidate. So, for him, every year he spent in that timeline felt like two years. Quint also noted his mind felt like molasses while he was there. Such a sensation could be attributed to the effects of the prolonged diurnal cycle, resulting in a lack of proper rest."

As Logan listened to Nieminen's vain attempt at an explanation, he noticed a change in CJ's demeanor out of the corner of his eye. He seemed lost in thought momentarily as he holstered his gun and started tapping away on his wrist computer, ignoring Nieminen.

"Or better yet," Nieminen continued, "reading a single page in a book that felt like an entire chapter."

"Nieminen," CJ interjected. "Can I get a copy of that scanner program from you? It could come in handy, and I can take a look at how it works."

Nieminen nodded and held up his arm so both wrist computers were close to each other. "Make sure you isolate the program to your tertiary system chip."

"Of course," CJ said with a nod. "Don't want some rogue Knight program spying on us."

Logan kept his eyes on Quint as the other two ran the data transfer on their computers. In moments like these, distractions could be dangerous, and the last thing he would allow was for something to go wrong. Quint remained still, his back to them. Perhaps he was on the up and up, but trust was a luxury Logan couldn't afford; the UC had taught him that much.

Finally, Quint sighed and began stretching, his back producing a series of audible cracks. Both CJ and Nieminen paused their work and shifted their attention to him.

"A Shadow Knight would be easier to locate than Jacob," Quint remarked as he turned back around, rubbing his neck. "Jacob would vanish into the night as soon as he sensed you'd picked up his trail."

"Agreed," said Nieminen. "One could only ascertain his location if he allowed it."

CJ raised an eyebrow. "So, how'd you find him?"

"As strange as this may sound," Quint said, "it started by receiving an anonymous tip a little over six months ago."

Logan scoffed. "Bullshit. Who else would know you're here, let alone looking for Jacob?"

Nieminen locked eyes with Logan. "You are partly correct, but unfortunately, we've never discovered the identity of this mystery person. Their way of communicating with us varied each time. Sometimes, it would be in the form of a package delivery, a note slipped under the wiper blades of our car, or conveyed through unaffiliated intermediaries. But never electronically."

"Damn," said CJ. "This mystery man knew exactly who you are and what you're up to."

Nieminen cocked his head toward CJ. "Unfortunately, I would have to agree, given the circumstance. Yet the information has always led us to something we needed."

"Hmm," said CJ. "You think it could be someone from the UC?"

Nieminen glanced upward. "That would be plausible and a strong possibility, seeing as we've made it here to E-Prime."

CJ looked around, uneasy. "I wonder who else is here and if they're watching us right now?"

Quint shrugged his shoulders. "Maybe."

Nieminen continued, "Our last communique was delivered by a courier and directed us to a bar in Eureka."

Logan's eyes narrowed. "Isn't that where Jacob got arrested?"

"Well, well." Quint sneered as he shook his head. "Looks like someone knows more than they're letting on."

"Not exactly," Logan snapped back. "We only heard a snippet from Detective Kaplan, that's all."

Nieminen snapped his fingers. "I knew it."

"O-kay," CJ said after a short pause, stretching out the O. "Knew what?"

"I'll get there," said Nieminen. "So, the bar was close to closing when we arrived, and we took a seat at a booth near the back so we could see everyone that came in."

"Uh-huh," said CJ.

"A waitress came to take our order," Nieminen continued, his face tensing, "her expression went blank, and her pupils were enormous like she was void of all life."

Logan whispered to CJ, "Acolyte?"

CJ shook his head. "Don't think so."

"Well, whatever she is," said Nieminen. "She had every hair on the back of my neck standing up."

"Did she say anything?" asked Logan.

"Not a word. She pulled a marker from her pocket and scribbled down a set of coordinates on a napkin without ever looking down at it. The words 'go there now' followed," said Nieminen as he shivered.

CJ grimaced. "That's creepy."

Quint chuckled. "Oh, you think *that's* creepy? When she turned to walk away, it looked like the back of her head was covered in blood."

CJ shook his head. "Check and mate."

Nieminen nodded. "So, we proceeded to the specified coordinates, a remote maritime location a few miles north of Eureka. A rather suitable location for an illicit meeting."

"Or an ambush," Quint added with a cynical smile.

"That was a possibility, but it turned out to be neither," Nieminen continued. "We saw Jacob and two other people exiting a boat as we arrived."

"Any idea who the other two were?" asked CJ.

Nieminen nodded. "I wasn't sure at first, but the man looked like a younger version of Kaplan. It must have been your detective from here, making the other person Maeve. Then the three of them took off in an SUV."

CJ nodded. "That lines up with what we've been told."

"So, naturally, we found ourselves tailing Jacob's SUV through the winding roads of the forest late at night," Nieminen said.

"I'll tell you," Quint interjected, "those Redwoods are like another world at night. The tall trees seemed to touch the sky, blocking all light from the moon and stars."

"True," Nieminen agreed. "Which made it much easier to see the lights from Jacob's car, allowing us to keep our distance."

"Or so we thought," Quint added with a frown.

CJ grinned. "He caught on to you, didn't he?"

"It is a reasonable conclusion." Nieminen nodded. "I surmised he killed his lights before turning off the main road and onto a dirt path leading to his cabin. So, we took a tactical approach, circling around to come up from behind, hoping not to tip him off to our location."

Logan shook his head. "Well, I can tell you that your plan failed. Detective Kaplan mentioned Jacob saw two guys dressed in suits on his security cameras."

"I was afraid of that," said Quint. "We stumbled across a Shadow Knight with the same idea, forcing us to not be as stealthy as we should have been.

CJ's eyes widened. "What happened?"

"Well," Quint said, leaning forward, "Nieminen would call out the Shadow Knight's position as soon as he materialized on the thermal cam. Their ability to teleport between shadows can be lethal, but there's a split-second delay before they fully emerge, just enough time for me to get into place."

"Quint dodged and countered based on those call-outs," Nieminen added. "It was a coordinated effort until we smashed it in the face enough times for it to disappear for good."

"Why didn't you just shoot him?" asked Logan.

"Think about it," said Quint. "We couldn't risk making noise that would attract more of them to our location, and we still didn't have any clue what Jacob was up to."

"He is correct," said Nieminen. "And that was when Jacob flew by us on his ATV, but I believe he didn't see us."

"Where was he going?" asked CJ.

"To his grave," Quint said casually.

Nieminen's eyes narrowed as he shot Quint a look. "That has yet to be substantiated."

Quint smiled. "It seemed pretty definite to me."

Logan shook his head. "All right, what happened?"

Nieminen sighed. "We followed him as quickly as possible."

"Yeah," said Quint. "Luckily for us, he didn't go too far."

"When we caught up," said Nieminen, "we found him talking to this older woman standing in the middle of a meadow. Someone must have just dropped her off because she was standing there hunched over her walker in this peach-colored nightgown surrounded by fireflies."

"That doesn't sound too ominous," said CJ, intrigued. "But suspicious."

"You think?" said Quint, rolling his eyes. "Now, here's the best part. She holds up this black crystal that seems to burn hot red on the inside. The next thing we saw were thin black lines racing across Jacob's body.

"No," whispered Logan. "It can't be."

CJ gave Logan a look of concern, then turned his attention back to Nieminen. "What happened to him?"

"Well." Nieminen's voice trembled, barely above a whisper. "Flames snaked through the lines below his skin, and each flicker carried away wisps of ash from him, scattering into the wind."

Logan closed his eyes while CJ looked like he was processing a problematic equation. "So, the woman...?"

"Turned her attention to us," Nieminen continued. "She held the black crystal in one hand and pulled out a pendant around her neck with her other hand. It had a glowing white boxy letter 'C' that was pinched inward on the top and bottom."

CJ raised an eyebrow. "That's not just any 'C.' That's the runic letter Peorð."

"I had reached a similar conclusion," said Nieminen. "However, I don't know what it means in this context, but that woman is definitely a Knight and probably one we've never heard of."

Quint picked up the story. "The moment got even weirder when the pendant and the crystal both burst into flames. Took her out just like that," he said as he snapped his fingers. "She was gone, reduced to nothing."

"What happened to the crystal and pendant?" asked Logan.

Nieminen frowned. "We thought we could investigate the area where she vanished and snag them, but before we could get to it, about fifty Blood Knights swarmed the area and picked up her pendant."

"And the crystal?" CJ pressed.

Quint shook his head. "Not sure whatever happened to it, but we did see Phillip there with his arms tied behind his back."

CJ took a step back. "Sounds like Phillip is on the outs with the Knights."

Nieminen nodded. "That's how it appeared.

Silence fell between them before CJ's wrist computer buzzed. He looked at it, and, after a couple of taps, he said, "According to Nora, Phillip has been spotted back down by the river.

"Shit," said Logan. "We need to get to him before the cops do."

"Right you are, baby brother," said Quint.

Chapter 8

United Citadel Field Unit
BRAVO SUBUNIT

Logan and CJ raced back to the river in hopes of finding Phillip. Time was pressing down on them, and Logan wanted to locate him first since he still didn't completely trust Nieminen and Quint. Lucky for him, they had parked quite a distance away in some other field behind them, which gave CJ and him a good head start. As an added bonus, there wasn't anyone else on the highway to slow them down.

"Nora just sent another message," said CJ. "Sounds like the cops have been alerted to Phillip's presence."

Logan smacked the steering wheel. "Damnit! It must have been Quint or Nieminen. They knew they couldn't beat us to the location."

CJ furrowed his brow. "Or a local spotted him down there. I mean, he is the most wanted man in the area."

Logan sighed. "Yeah, that could be it too."

Coming close to town, he could easily make out a patrol car approaching them on the highway, likely scanning the area for Phillip. In the distance by the river, he spotted a cluster of police vehicles and dogs still scouring the area.

"Well," said Logan, "if Nora was right about Phillip being spotted by the river, he's givin' us all the slip."

CJ shrugged his shoulders. "Or they've already hauled him off and are lookin' for the body of that police officer. Either way, I don't think there is much we can do right now but wait and see what they come up with."

Logan groaned. "Eh, I hate sitting on my hands like this."

"Oh, I know that all too well," said CJ sarcastically. "So, what do you want to do now?"

"Give me a moment," Logan said, tapping his fingers on the steering wheel. "What do we really know about Phillip?"

CJ shot him a sly smile. "He's probably a nut and a homicidal maniac."

Logan groaned as he wiped his hand down his face. "Enough with the jackassery; tell me what someone from Recon would say."

CJ chuckled. "Better to be a jackass than an asshole, and they would say the exact same thing. However, I would point out that he did live here for a few years. It's very likely he's made some friends in the area who wouldn't have any problems keeping him hidden if they think he's innocent. Although that's assuming he hasn't taken them as hostages first."

"We'll see," said Logan. "Think it's time we pay your friend Nora another visit."

CJ's gaze fell to the floor. "You don't think he's with her or Owen, do you?"

Logan eyed the exit sign, indicating the turnoff to Plattsburg was coming up. "Don't know, but I intend to find out."

As he made his way toward the town, the engine noise grew softer as he slowed the car down to avoid drawing attention from the police. Passing through the main drag, it was obvious that word had gotten out that Phillip had been spotted, given how desolate the area was, with numerous closed signs in the windows. A few minutes later, Logan had parked the car outside Nora's place, a faded purple Victorian house that stood out like a sore thumb among her neighbor's more modest homes.

As they exited their car, he couldn't help but notice several police cars parked outside her murdered neighbor's house. They must have thought Phillip would be that stupid enough to return to the scene of the crime. Although, he himself had used that tactic in the past with some success, and CJ did have a point. After what the Knights did to him, chances are he's a nut.

Two teenage boys occupied Nora's porch, their posture tense as Logan approached. The elder, taller of the two, seemed to be the lookout and leaned in subtly to whisper to his younger counterpart. His eyes met CJ's and Logan's gazes as they climbed the steps. The younger one looked slightly on edge as he looked away, perhaps unsure what to expect.

CJ gave them a wave and a smile. "Hey guys, remember me?"

The taller boy leaned over again, whispering to his companion just audibly enough for them to hear. "That's the guy I was telling you about. The one that never stops talking."

Logan smiled at the candid observation. Before he could raise his hand to knock, the door swung open as if on cue. Nora stood on the threshold; her presence sent a chill down his spine that he wasn't expecting. He reasoned it was because she caught him off guard, but it still didn't feel right. The last time he felt that was when he was in the presence of a Shadow Knight at the Mayan Museum during a previous assignment.

"Why, hello there, young gentlemen. I just knew you'd be coming," she said.

Logan tilted his head toward the Normans' home. "Cops still searchin' for Phillip?"

Nora shook her head. "If those fellers think Phillip is just gonna wander on over there with all of 'em parked out front, then they are the biggest bunch of damned fools I've ever seen."

"Perhaps," said Logan.

Nora stood aside, pointing to a small room off the left that appeared to be the parlor. "If you come this way, there's much to discuss."

"Really?" said CJ as he entered. "There couldn't have been that much that has happened since last night."

Nora giggled as she closed the front door behind them. "Oh, well, deary, I've been quite busy."

Inside, the parlor was plastered in faded floral wallpaper with outdated furnishings. What caught Logan's eye was a tall, glass-fronted cabinet filled with an array of crystals and gemstones. That, plus a quick glance at a couple of books about psychics and tarot card readings, told him enough about her interests.

Nora ran her fingers down the top of a leather sofa as she walked around it and settled into an armchair perched in the corner next to a stone fireplace. She gestured toward the couch and said, "Please, take a seat."

Logan sat down and said, "All right, let's hear it."

Nora closed her eyes as she shook her head. "This business with Phillip has really opened my eyes to all sorts of possibilities," she said with a distant gaze toward the front window. "Phillip, you see, is but a pawn in a much larger game."

"Right," Logan scoffed. "And how did you come by this information?"

"That's the thing," she said with a slight tremble. "It isn't just one thing, but a bunch of little bits of information piled together."

Logan crossed his arms as he settled into the sofa. A lingering thought kept telling him that she would be making a bunch of wild leaps of logic with trace bits of information. Still, he knew there wasn't much else he could do now other than let her spin her tale.

CJ leaned forward, clasping his hands together. "Something has happened, hasn't it?"

Nora nodded. "I've been feeling a bit off after meeting you two last night.

"How so?" asked CJ.

"Well, dearie, I'm not sure how to describe it. But it started last night on the way home. We were talking about that shadow figure we all saw last night up against Marv's antique store, and that's when it hit me that I've heard about those things before."

Logan's ears perked up. "Where?"

"Oh, from the radio."

Logan tilted his head. "Really?"

"Yep," she said with a grin. "It was one of those late-night call-in talk shows from thirty years ago…," her voice trailed off. "Can't remember the name," she said, tapping her chin. "But I believe the fella broadcasted from the desert in the middle of nowhere."

Logan made a 'can you hurry this along' gesture with his hand. "What did he have to say about them?"

"Well, it's been a while, but a guest was saying those shadow people were some sort of interdimensional alien being observing us, and he was fighting with the other guest, some doctor out of Washington, the kind with a PhD, who thought they were echoes of past loved ones."

"Echoes?" asked CJ.

"Yeah, that's the term he used, but the way I interpreted it was like a latent image burned into an old monitor. Something you don't really notice except under certain conditions."

Logan groaned. "Well, I doubt the four of us would all have the exact same image of that shadowy bloke from last night burned into our brains."

"I'm well aware, Mr. Logan," Nora replied, irritated.

CJ waved Logan aside. "Never mind him. What happened afterward?"

"Well, when we got home, Owen had to head on back outside into the alfalfa field with my eldest son to fix a water pipe. The darn thing broke again, and you could see the water gushing high into the air from a mile away."

Nora leaned forward, looked around the room like a child getting ready to cross the street, and then held her hand up to her mouth to whisper, "That's when I saw him."

CJ raised an eyebrow. "Phillip?"

Her eyes went wide as she mouthed the word, "Yes!"

Logan jerked forward. "Why didn't you call us?"

"Because I had other things on my mind," Nora said dismissively. "Namely being, Phillip was leaving the Normans' house and heading back into the field where Owen and my son were."

"What'd you do?" asked CJ.

"Well, first, I tried to call them on their cell phones, but of course, they were in the house charging."

"Sounds about right," said CJ.

She paused, her eyes wandering momentarily before refocusing. "So, I followed him quietly from a distance with Beckett at my side. He's the taller one you passed on the porch while the other one, Milo, went out to warn Owen. Phillip made his way into our alfalfa field, lugging something he nicked from their home and disappearing amongst the tall alfalfa. We tried to keep track of him, but he had vanished." Her voice wavered. "Knowing he was so close, possibly watching us, was terrifying. My heart was racing the entire time, so we joined up with Owen, went back home, and locked all the doors and windows.

Logan raised an eyebrow. "So, did you call anyone?"

"Yes, I talked to Sheriff Wiese, and he drove around for a couple of hours lookin' for him."

Logan thought for a moment. "We need to find him before he gets further away or, worse, puts someone else in danger."

"Oh, honey, you're preaching to the choir," Nora quipped.

CJ held a finger up. "You know of any places you think he could hide?"

"As a matter of fact, I was just discussing that idea with Margaret from across the street."

Logan sighed. "That'll be Margaret Kaplan, I take it?"

Nora smiled and pointed her finger at him. "I had a feeling you two would know each other."

Logan shook his head. "Not exactly. I just know of her through an unrelated matter."

Nora waved her finger at him. "Oh darling, you're fibbing, and you know it."

"Oh," said Logan, "it's the truth."

Nora laughed. "Why, Mr. Logan, I've already talked to her about you, and she is well aware of your presence and how you are out of place."

Logan glanced at CJ, who shrugged his shoulders. "What do you mean by 'out of place'?"

"Like a strand of thread in a larger tapestry. Each one is weaved into the fabric with the utmost precision. However, up close, that one strand would appear to be out of place until you pull back and see the bigger picture."

CJ raised his gaze toward the ceiling and nodded. "That seems to fit."

"I don't know about that," said Logan.

Nora raised a finger, silencing him. "Be wary of the paths you tread, Mr. Logan. Not all is as it seems, but you've still got cards to play, and Margaret's your next one."

Logan cast Nora a weary look. "Sounds like you know more than you're letting on."

Nora smiled. "Just a strong feeling I've got."

She stood up and started shooing them out the door. "Now you get on over there and talk to her. She's been a dear friend to me and is a wealth of information."

Logan and CJ exchanged glances, nodded, and swiftly exited the parlor. Outside, the two teenagers were still leaning up against the porch railing, watching the police packing up their surveillance gear. Logan approached them. "Keep an eye out. If you see any guns drawn, get indoors."

The taller boy, Beckett, nodded. "We will."

Logan nodded in return and went across the street to Margaret's, his grandmother's home, with CJ in tow. From what he could remember, it was a modest, one-level, two-bedroom home, painted in a bright sunny yellow with white trim, which still appeared to be true in this timeline. Not sure what to expect, he took a deep breath and knocked.

Margaret greeted them almost instantly. Sweat glistened on her brow. Logan's heart skipped a beat when their eyes locked together. She looked just as he remembered her all those years ago. Her silver hair, highlighted with black streaks, was gracefully piled atop her head, with a few strands framing her face. Her tan dress, reminiscent of simpler times, hung loose against her slender frame. For the most part, she was technically a stranger to him since so much time had passed since he'd seen her last, but he could feel a definite connection to her.

She stuck her head out the door and glanced around the neighborhood with such vigor Logan thought they were about to be ambushed by some unknown assailant.

"Come in, quickly," she said softly, urging them inside with a swift hand gesture.

Once inside the living room, Margaret closed and locked the door behind them. Muted golden light shined on the lightly stained wood floors, creating a delicate harmony with the beige walls. The room was sparsely furnished, with only a green couch placed up against the back wall facing the front window. In stark contrast to the minimalist furniture, the walls were adorned with numerous photographs capturing happier times. Logan couldn't help but think of his grandfather, who had vanished sometime in the late nineties, leaving an undeniable mark on her life.

She tousled his blond hair and said, "I'd always wonder what you would look like when you grew up."

Logan smiled as his cheeks reddened.

"Here, have a seat." She gestured to the couch as she made her way to the kitchen. They hesitated momentarily, noting the old couch's fragile appearance, before settling in. Muffled sounds of shuffling chairs came from the adjacent room. Not long after, Margaret reappeared, pulling a wooden chair behind her.

Logan got to his feet when he saw her struggling with the chair. "Here, let me give you a hand with that."

Margaret stopped him with a wave of her hand, positioning the chair to face them. "Nonsense," she remarked, taking a quick peek at the curtains and tugging on the bottom to ensure they were closed tight. "I won't be treated like a guest in my own house."

"Oh, no," Logan said as he sat back down. "I didn't mean it that way."

Margaret followed suit and took a seat, smoothing out her dress in the process. Her gaze, stern and devoid of warmth, landed on them like an anvil. "I told Nora to send you two on your way out of town, but here you are, anyway."

CJ exchanged a confused glance with Logan before replying, "Nora implied that you would be expecting us. In fact, she indicated that you could help us find Phillip."

Margaret folded her arms, her body rigid like an old schoolteacher staring down a misbehaving student. "That sounds like Nora. Always going with her gut feelings while ignoring everything else."

Logan sat there in silence, mulling over some of his observations. There was something wrong about this whole situation, and he felt ashamed to admit it took him this long to put it all together.

"You're being watched," he whispered, just loud enough for Margaret to hear.

Her face softened with a subtle frown as she nodded in response.

Logan pinched the bridge of his nose as he reevaluated this situation. It all made sense in his mind. Quint had already visited their father's old stomping grounds. Hell, he could have easily used his family connection to get on Margaret's good graces and pump her for any information she had, which would explain why she knows about him being somewhat out of place. And when that didn't pan out, Quint hung around keeping tabs on her, knowing it was only a matter of time before someone interesting came stumbling by.

For all he knew, Quint could have been Phillip's friend Nora talked about. It seems reasonable to assume that he'd somehow come into contact with Nieminen after he took off from that late-night fight he had with Phillip that Nora told them about back at the bar.

Logan shot Margaret a smug grin oozing self-confidence. "So, where is me old best mate Quint?"

Margaret's brows furrowed in confusion. "Who's Quint?"

Logan grumbled. "My older brother. Who else?"

Margaret's demeanor never changed as she met Logan's gaze. "Your brother's dead," she said. "Died well before you were born. That's why there's such a big gap between you and your sister."

Logan sank back down in the sofa as all the cards he still had fell to the floor. His instincts kept telling him something else was going on with Quint, but now he wasn't too sure.

Logan's eyes narrowed, searching her face for recognition. "If that's the case, then how do you know who I am?"

Margaret started to speak before CJ cut her off. "Wait," he said as his right knee bounced from a nervous twitch. "First, tell us who's watching you?"

"I don't know his name per se, but he's very pale, always dressed in a suit, and his hands are cold as ice," Margaret said as she rubbed her hands together."

Logan turned to CJ. "Anyone you know?"

CJ shrugged. "Don't think so."

"How long has this person been watching you?" asked Logan.

Margaret stood and rechecked the front curtains while keeping her back toward them. Nothing but silence hung in the air as she lowered her head. A visible shiver shot down her body as she started to pace back and forth in front of them. Keeping her hands clasped behind her, she said, "He first showed up around the first of June in 1999."

"That would have been a couple of weeks after Grandad disappeared," said Logan.

Margaret stopped to look at him. "I believe so," she said before continuing to pace. "I was out in the garden tending to my tomato plants when this man showed up. So, naturally, I asked him if he needed help with anything."

There was a long pause as Logan and CJ watched her take a seat again before she continued. "He asked me if I knew where Kay was. He said he had some business with him and needed him to sign some paperwork for a project they were working on."

CJ turned to Logan. "Who's Kay?"

"That's the name his grandfather went by," Margaret said, pointing at Logan, then continued "Which was ridiculous for that creep to ask, since we'd already been divorced for fifteen years by then."

"Oh," said CJ.

Margaret went on, "None of the Connor men ever went by their first names besides Logan's father." After a chuckle, she said, "Guess he didn't like the little nickname, C4, he rightfully earned."

Logan smiled.

CJ leaned forward. "You ever find out what he wanted with him?"

Margaret nodded. "About a year later, this ancient-lookin' man showed up on my stoop. Said his name was Isaac, and he needed to have a word with me about Kay." Margaret glanced back toward the window as a car drove by. More than likely, Logan figured it was the cops leaving the Normans' house.

"Well," she continued, "he had a letter from Kay explaining he'd been caught up in some giant investigation into this cult out in California, which didn't make much sense to me since he was a detective in Las Vegas, but the letter was in Kay's handwriting."

CJ looked at Logan. "Your father and grandfather were both detectives in Vegas?"

Logan nodded. "Yeah, the old man joined up after my granddad vanished."

CJ refocused his attention on Margaret. "What else did the letter say?"

Margaret shrugged. "Not much more than that. It was that Isaac fellow who warned me about what these people were up to, and because of my association with Kay, he told me they would be watching me."

Logan shook his head. "What does this cult want with you?"

Margaret grimaced. "It's not me they're after, hon. You're the one they want. They seem to think you're the key to stopping it all."

"Yeah," said Logan. "I had to find out that one the hard way."

A sly smile crept across Margaret's face. "But they're wrong."

Logan and CJ exchanged a look of surprise. "How so?" asked CJ.

"On Isaac's second and last visit a few months later, he told me about how he knew an older you and a companion may be stopping by one day, and seeing how this was many years before you would be born, I wrote him off as a demented old fool, but then you were born. He talked about how there were more keys out there than just the one, and said I would know what to do when you two showed up."

"Really," said CJ. "What else did he say about us?"

Margaret scratched her head. "Now you see, that's the problem. I can't really remember since it was so long ago."

"Did you ever see that first guy again?" asked CJ.

Margaret let out a sigh. "All the time."

Logan's eyes narrowed. "Really?"

Margaret nodded. "Yeah, but he would never speak to me again. However, I would always see him watching me from across the street or through a window at the grocery store. Stuff like that."

"Man, that's creepy," said CJ. "Did you ever report it to anyone?"

"Yeah, I talked to the sheriff about it, but he could never find nor see him. In fact, no one in town ever saw him, so I just let it go before they all decided to get me committed. But that's how it was with him. I never saw him when I was lookin' for him, only when I was unexpecting."

Logan followed her gaze toward the front door. "Yeah, no wonder you're on edge. When was the last time you laid eyes on him?"

Margaret stood up and lightly stepped toward the door. "'Bout two weeks ago," she said, peering through the peephole.

Logan got up and unholstered his gun. He had to admit, the old lady had a damn good pair of ears on her since she heard the coming footsteps well before he did.

Margaret turned to look at him and waved him off. "Put that thing away," she said. "It's just Nora's boys."

Logan stood firm, with his gun at the ready, knowing full well this could be a trap set by the man with the cold hands. CJ followed suit and took up position in the kitchen, watching the back door.

Margaret shook her head at them as she opened the door on the first knock.

"Why, hello there, Beckett and Milo. What can I do for you two?" she asked.

Logan holstered his gun as he moved into view. It occurred to him that things could go south real fast if they thought he was holding the grandma across the street at gunpoint.

Beckett nodded at Logan when he came into view. "My little brother has something he needs to tell you."

Milo looked back at his brother, his big eyes pleading with him to let him go.

Beckett shoved him forward. "Tell him."

"All right, all right," Milo relinquished. "I saw Phillip jumping on the freight train that passed through here about an hour ago."

"Like a hobo?" CJ asked from the kitchen.

Margaret's eyes widened. "Milo! Why didn't you tell anyone?"

Milo's face reddened. "Because he's my friend."

"Well," said Margaret. "Friends in need can't be helped if no one knows the facts."

Milo twisted the toe of his shoe into the ground. "Yeah, I know. That's what Mom says."

"And she's right," said Margaret. "Now," she said, turning back to Logan. "I think you know when your path now lies."

Logan nodded. "Let's move out, CJ."

Chapter 9

United Citadel Field Unit
Beta Team

The early morning low sun pierced the dissipating rain clouds as Maeve drove us away from Dick's Café to search Rose's house. The more I thought about it, the more I worried if this was the right thing to do. From what Detective Morgan said, the place was pretty isolated. However, if caught, I wasn't in the mood to explain to the local police as to why I was trespassing on Rose's property.

Maeve's grip tightened on the steering wheel, her eyes never drifting from her lane as other morning commuters crowded in on the soaked highway. My mind kept circling back to that mysterious Kopache bloke. Seeing as he was the one who abandoned Maeve and Detective Kaplan on Shady Reef, and now had this connection to Rose, he was definitely a prominent figure in the Knight's organization. In fact, he could be another head Knight of a different sect, and the more I thought about it, the more I was sure of it. Logan reported his encounter with Malcolm, the leader of the Blood Knights, at the Knight's estate in Louisiana. During that mission to rescue Leah, CJ did shoot Malcolm, but another fellow rescued him. I'd bet everything that other fellow was Kopache. If I was right, that meant he is probably the head of the Shadow Knights.

My mobile broke the silence inside the car. Recognizing Thomas Ellis's number, I answered, my voice slightly hoarse from lack of sleep and the morning chitchat with Detective Morgan, "Eva speaking."

Ellis wasted no time.

"Eva," he began, his voice carrying a hint of drowsiness, "Rose has accepted your request to meet. Can you come to the Jasinski Medical Institute just outside Louisville right now?"

I exchanged a glance with Maeve, who nodded yes as she signaled to merge into a faster lane.

"Are they okay with us meeting her this early?"

Ellis chuckled. "Hell no. I'm just that damn good of a lawyer."

I smiled. "Well, we're on our way then."

"Great," he said. "I knew you would agree, so I'm just about there myself."

"You are?" I asked in disbelief.

"Yep," he confirmed. "I'll wait for you at the main front entrance. You know where you're going?"

I glanced back at Maeve, who raised an eyebrow as she tilted her head back and forth. "We have a rough idea," I said.

"All right," said Ellis. "It's fairly simple to find. Stay north on the 65 past the river, then look for exit 7-B. Take that one, then the first right, then just follow the road. It's pretty much a straight shot from there."

"Seems simple enough," I said.

"You'll know you're getting' close when you see the no hitchhiking signs."

"Lovely," I said.

About half an hour later, the looming silhouette of the Jasinski Medical Institute began to materialize amidst the dense foliage. Getting out of the car, the building, a behemoth of gothic architecture, seemed to tower ominously above us, its spires and turrets reminiscent of a church. Its ivory-colored stone walls stood out against the darker metal-trimmed roof.

I looked toward Maeve. "Did they just ask the architect to design a building that looks like an insane asylum out of an old horror movie?"

Maeve shook her head. "If they were going for a place that feels naturally unsettling, they nailed it."

As Maeve and I approached the entrance, a wave of anxiety flooded me. I knew the feeling was pure nonsense, but nevertheless, it was there like a vice pressing down on my heart. It didn't help that the only sounds were our footsteps echoing off the concrete pathway, amplified by the weight of the building's looming mass.

I spotted Ellis leaning against a nearby pillar, looking sharp in his crisp suit, a far cry from his appearance the last time we met. However, there seemed to be a slight trace of apprehension in his eyes.

"About time you two showed up," he teased. "I was just about to call it a day."

I did my best to convey a light-hearted chuckle that only fell flat. I took a deep breath to help gather my thoughts and said, "Let's not keep Rose waiting any longer."

Ellis tilted his head to one side, cracking his neck. "Agreed," he said, pulling open the giant heavy wooden door.

Cold air rushed against my face that felt like I was stepping into a morgue. I was expecting a dingy, old-looking hospital in disrepair, but thankfully, we were greeted with the exact opposite.

Polished white marble floors reflected the soft glow from elegant chandeliers overhead with pristine walls adorned with expensive artwork that made the place feel more like a museum than a mental facility. On the far-left corner sat a reception desk, where a middle-aged, uniformed nurse pored over some paperwork. She tapped the pen on the counter when she noticed us standing in the entryway.

As she glared at us, she pursed her lips together into a straight line. "You need to sign in here," she said, pushing a clipboard across the counter.

Maeve turned to whisper to me, "Geez, she really does fit the bill, doesn't she."

"That's probably why they hired her," I whispered back as I approached the reception desk.

The nurse focused intensely on Ellis as he leaned against the counter, watching us sign in. "Dr. Barnett will be furious with you for barging in like this," she said in a low voice.

Ellis smiled as he patted her hand. "Well, if he wants to stand between a client wishing to speak with her counselor, he's more than welcome to." A sly smile crossed his face. "But, as a lawyer, I would highly advise against that unless he wants to spend weeks standing in front of a judge while both local and federal inspectors are combing through this place lookin' for any reason to shut it down."

The nurse snatched the clipboard away just as I dotted the *i* in Lewis, leaving a line across the form. "Ms. Lombardi is ready to see you."

"Same room?" Ellis asked with a smile.

"Yes," she said with a straight face.

Ellis nodded and set off down one of the expansive hallways leading away from the lobby. The clicks of our shoes echoed out of sync until we rounded a corner, where six metal doors stood, five with red lights above them. The one on the right had a green light above it with Rose's name and picture displayed on a monitor embedded in the door. I gathered this must be a security feature to prevent you from bumbling into the wrong room.

Ellis held down a button next to the door until it made a clicking noise. He then pushed the door open and gestured for us to enter the dimly lit room, which didn't surprise me since I learned in school that muted lighting tended to have a calming effect on people.

Rose sat on the opposite side of the room, behind a thick acrylic panel with circular holes drilled into the center, each no bigger than a couple of fingers. She wore a yellow jumpsuit that appeared to be zipped up from the back. Soft, padded leather straps confined her arms and legs to what looked like a specialized wheelchair. Her head hung low as she stared at the floor.

"I'll leave you two to chat," Ellis said as he stepped back outside. Before he left, he pointed at a button next to the door, and said, "Hold this down when you are ready to leave, and the guard will unlock the door."

When Ellis closed the door, it loudly clicked as the tumblers inside slid into place, locking us in. Rose made a muffled moan as I turned back to look at her. She was now looking at us, but her eyes appeared to be unable to focus on us. Evidently, it was a side effect from whatever drug they had flowing through her veins. I just hoped she was lucid enough to talk to us, but I feared that wouldn't be the case.

Thinking back to how the front nurse acted toward us, I assumed Rose's current mental and physical state was intentional.

"Dr. Lombardi?" I asked, taking a seat in front of her.

Rose smiled when she heard her name, then shook her head in a way that looked like she was trying to shake loose the cobwebs.

"Yes," she murmured, her voice barely above a whisper.

Maeve stepped closer, her posture rigid. "Rose," she replied, her voice shaking ever so slightly. "Were you a doctor on Shady Reef?"

"Yes." She paused. Her voice was much stronger than before. "I was stationed out there working for Cognitive Endurance."

I leaned forward. "Did you know a young woman on the island by the name of Leah Kaplan?"

Rose nodded as her head bobbed back toward my direction. "She was a sweet patient of mine. Do you know if she is all right?"

I nodded. "Leah is back home safe and sound."

Rose smiled. "Oh, that's good to hear. I didn't think she would have made a good candidate for the research project."

Hmm, research project, I thought. Well, I guess that's one way to describe the process of abducting some poor soul to try turning them into an Acolyte. Still, at least Rose's brain was functioning well enough to answer our questions. "What exactly was the purpose of the research project, Rose?"

Rose's eyes narrowed. "I'm not allowed to speak of it," she said with a low voice again.

I found it strange that she would still protect the Knights after everything that had happened. With what they did to her family, then pinned their brutal deaths on her, what really could they do to her now other than to let her die?

Trying to use my best bedside manner and caring voice, I asked, "Rose, do you know why you are here?"

Rose flashed her eyes at me with a fiery gaze as she scrunched her lips together. "Because I'm a former Knight and those bastards set me up!"

"Which ones, Rose?" I asked.

Rose shook her head. "I can't say," she snapped.

Maeve approached the confined woman and got down on one knee, her voice now steady. "Rose, you and I have never met, but I've heard of you. I saw your name on a file back on Shady Reef in the police station, and I know you were helping Leah."

"Oh," she said slowly. "You're the one that got them all worked up that night, causing them to burn the whole place down."

"That does sound like that night I was there," said Maeve.

Rose jerked her hand up the best she could and pointed an accusatory finger at Maeve. "It's because of you I lost all my research!"

Maeve fired back. "And it's because of you and the stupid Blood Knights that Leah's father is dead!"

Rose turned her head away from Maeve as she stared at the corner of the room. "I don't know what you're talking about," she said under her breath.

I knew this was going nowhere fast, even from a casual observation. There had to be a way to open Rose up to get her to start talking. A trip to the pub might do the trick, but that was not an option here. Getting people to open up was one area in which CJ actually excelled, but it was far too late to call him in from Nebraska. I was going to have to tackle this one all on my own, and I was through playing mental games with Rose.

"Tell us what you know about Kopache and the Knights, or we'll walk on out of here along with any chance you have of being exonerated for the murder of your husband and two kids."

With a leisurely stretch of her neck, Rose chuckled. "Always straight to the point, huh? I admire that, but using the death of my family is no way to get me to talk."

I felt my face contort with anger. It was probably not the best emotion to display since Rose was smart enough to use it against me, but it was already too late. "You think we're playing games, Rose? Your family is dead, and you're in here, drugged and forgotten, while those responsible walk free! We can help you bring them down and get justice for you and your family, but we need information."

A smirk formed on Rose's face. "You really don't know how powerful they are."

"I have a good idea. The UC has been fighting them for more than thirty years," I said, as it just occurred to me that the UC didn't exist yet in this timeline.

Rose laughed. "The United Citadel is nothing more than a bunch of deflecting morons so paranoid they can't even be honest with each other."

I must say I was caught off guard by Rose's comment. Evidently, she knew more about what's going on than I had given her credit for, but she could also be making it up to see how we'd respond.

Rose leaned in slightly with a sinister grin. "But let's not talk about the UC right now. It's information about Kopache and the Knight you're after. I know the real truth about what happened to my family is incidental to you compared to that information."

I sighed. "Actually, you got it backward. We're specifically looking into the entire situation about what happened that night to your family at the behest of your sister, Iris. Information about Kopache and the Knights is just a bonus."

Rose's eyes widened, her confident facade slipping for a moment. "Iris sent you?" There was a genuine mix of surprise and apprehension in her voice.

"Yes," I said, softening my voice. "She believes you're innocent and wants justice for you and your family."

A small tear formed in the corner of her left eye. "She always was my biggest supporter." Rose sighed deeply, the weight of the world seemingly pressed down on her shoulders. "All right...but I can't say much in here." She lowered her voice down to a whisper. "They have people here on the inside."

I lowered my voice as well. "Are you sure?"

"Yes," she whispered back, then shifted her gaze toward Maeve. "Zeus is in the cell next to me."

I watched the blood drain from Maeve's face. "Zeus," I said, tapping my finger on my knee. "Wasn't he the guy on the island that ran the hotel you were staying at?"

Maeve nodded. "Yeah, that was him, but both Kaplan and I watched him get shot in the back of the head. There's no way he's here unless he's a corpse."

Rose smirked again. "His kind is not that easy to kill."

I felt a shock wave of energy shoot through my body. This was something entirely new the UC didn't know of. "What do you mean by 'his kind'?"

Rose continued with her smirk. "Get me out of here right now, and I'll tell you everything I know."

Maeve's hands clenched into fists, her knuckles turning white. "Do you really expect us to just waltz on out of here with you in tow?"

Rose groaned as we heard footsteps approaching the door. "Sounds like you've overstayed your welcome."

Before we could react, the door flung open, revealing a visibly agitated Dr. Barnett. A much younger Asian man in nurse's attire was standing to his right, looking uneasy.

The doctor's face was a shade of deep crimson as he barked, "What on earth do you think you're doing?"

Ellis appeared behind them and tapped the much taller doctor on the shoulder. "Why are you talking to my partners like that," he said with a wink toward us.

This only seemed to agitate the doctor more as the veins poked out of his neck as he turned to face Ellis. Shoving his finger into

Ellis's chest, he said, "You should know better than to interfere with a patient's treatment schedule. She's already a handful, and you throwing off her routine doesn't help!"

Ellis smiled back at him as he made a low-handed gesture for us to exit the room. "Dr. Barnett, a citizen's right to counsel is deeply enshrined in our legal framework, wouldn't you agree? Or perhaps there's a particular statute I'm unaware of that you'd like to enlighten me on?"

The rest of the room seemed to fade into the background as all the attention was now focused on the escalating volume. Subconsciously, I found myself backing away from the argument, taking a spot next to the nurse who had done the same.

Dr. Barnett's voice ripped through the building. "You lawyers are all the same. Always thinking you can barge in and disrupt the delicate balance we maintain here."

Barnett pressed his finger harder into Ellis's chest, forcing Ellis to step back. "You keep poking me," he said, "and I'll have you arrested for battery."

While Ellis and Dr. Barnett were battling wits to see who was the strongest, I thought it would be best to have a little chat with the nurse. Out of the three people I had met so far who worked here, he seemed far more timid and reserved. My best guess was that he didn't really belong here at all and was probably in an internship program.

According to his nametag, he was Aaron Sato. "Eva," I started, extending a hand that Aaron took gently, "and you are Aaron?"

"Yes, ma'am," he replied, still focused on Ellis and Dr. Barnett.

"Is the doctor usually all worked up like this?" I asked.

Aaron remained stoic in his response. "This is the first time I've seen him like this. Something is definitely wrong."

I lowered my voice, hoping to instill some trust in him. "Do you think it's because Rose was the patient we were talking to?"

Aaron looked at me for the first time. His face remained neutral, but his eyes revealed a deep, growing conflict inside him. "Has to be. I've had some interesting conversations with her during my rounds, and she's very different from everyone else that's been placed here."

"I appreciate your honesty, Aaron," I murmured. "We're just trying to help Rose, to uncover the truth. We never meant to cause any trouble here."

"You know," he began, his voice barely above a whisper. "Ever since Rose showed up, I'd catch glimpses of some unfamiliar faces around here when I'm making my rounds. They're not doctors or family, and certainly not patients. They always arrive late at night after most of the staff have gone home and leave right before dawn."

I shot a look at Maeve, who looked equally intrigued. I may have just found an ally in Aaron from the sound of it. "Do they interact with Rose?"

Aaron hesitated. "They go to her room and always have long sessions with Dr. Barnett afterward," he said with a slight tremble in his voice. I was starting to feel bad for him, knowing that if the Knights knew he was giving us this information, they'd more than likely kill him or try to turn him into an Acolyte.

"The next morning," he continued, "she would be calm and overly polite like she was fearful of something."

His sincerity was evident, and I couldn't help but appreciate his candidness amidst the looming threats around us. "Thank you, Aaron, and stay safe."

He nodded, and we both refocused on the ongoing confrontation between Ellis and Dr. Barnett that appeared to be winding down. Maeve nudged me. "Looks like we got what we needed for now. We'll come back for Rose when the time is right."

Ellis turned to look at us. "Let's get going. We've got other scheduled appointments to get to."

I nodded, taking one last glance at Aaron, who gave a slight nod of encouragement, reinforcing my belief that we had at least one ally in this facility. But then again, the Knights were a cunning lot, and it was always possible he was a plant from the beginning. There was no doubt in my mind that I would need to stay extra careful the next time I come back here.

Chapter 10

United Citadel Field Unit
Beta Team

Following our brief late lunch, we found ourselves on the outskirts of Rose's property, and I do mean the outskirts. The only indication we were in the right spot was a metal sign proudly bearing LOMBARDI RANCH, posted over a cobblestone road leading off yonder. This development certainly made the "Quiz the Neighbors" item on our checklist somewhat pointless unless they were watching Rose through a high-powered telescope that night.

Doing a quick survey of the area, I assumed the price tag on the land alone had to be more than what Ellis mentioned. He did say the sisters inherited the house from the father, and from what I was seeing, he had to have been a veritable tycoon. Naturally, this explained why Iris would be interested in gaining ownership of the house—selling it would set her up for life. Although, I suppose that one would have to assume that he also left a sizable nest egg for his two daughters. Granted, it wasn't unheard of for wealthy family members to give away all their fortune to charitable organizations under the belief that money not earned doesn't carry much value and can hamper one's ability to grow as a person. Then again, Iris may have already burned through her inheritance and was looking to replenish her coffers.

It took us a little over ten minutes to drive down that tree-lined road, even with Maeve's rather leaden foot on the gas pedal, before we pulled up to the house. As I gazed up at Rose's immense mansion, my stomach churned with a wave of uneasiness. The house seemed like a picturesque location to raise a family. I could almost hear the laughter of kids playing in the fields and the conversations they would have around a firepit on a crisp starry night, but now, that had all been replaced by the cries of horror and sadness.

Summoning my resolve, I took a deep breath, steadying myself for what we could be walking into. The scents of the nearby fresh flowers intermingled with the aroma of rain-soaked wood stacked neatly against the house. Unexpectedly, I could also detect a faint undertone of a metallic scent that reminded me of blood. A brief glance at Maeve told me she detected the same thing, likely seeping out the front door that was slightly ajar. My throat tightened as I thought about the possibilities behind the meaning of the open door. I had anticipated seeing the blood stains along with the aftermath of a police investigation, but now I was worried if someone else had already stopped by, and if they were still here or dead.

Maeve finally broke the silence in the air. Her voice echoed the concerns I was having. "I don't like the looks of this. The police would have secured the premises after they left." She gazed at the front door.

"No doubt," I reaffirmed as I unholstered my pistol. "We need to keep our wits about us and our sidearms at the ready."

Walking up the stone steps, I hesitated for a moment at the entrance, trying to better survey what was on the inside through the cracked door. The last thing we needed was to be assaulted by someone on the other side of the door the moment we stepped through. Maeve sliced her body to the right side of the door, her gun ready. She nodded at me, and I nudged the door open with my foot. Then she bolted through, her gun outstretched.

Once inside, we found ourselves in the foyer. To the left wall was a simple wooden bench for taking off and storing your shoes, with coat hooks mounted above bearing the names of each family member. Directly ahead, a hallway ran perpendicular to the length of the house with the living room straight across from us. To the right of us was a grand spiral staircase that must have been the one Ted heard his mother coming down that fateful night to put an end to his father's life. I quickly shook that feeling off, not wanting to dwell on that subject any longer than necessary.

We decided to commence our search on the ground floor, checking off each room for any oddities we might stumble across. Stepping into the hallway, I couldn't ignore the pervasive scent of blood emanating from the kitchen to the right of the living room.

"We might as well get this one out of the way," I remarked, gesturing toward the kitchen with the tip of my gun.

Maeve nodded in agreement and slinked toward the kitchen, taking care to check all the nooks and crannies for potential threats.

Two entrances led into the kitchen, and poking my head in through the first one, I could see the white marble countertops placed on top of dark wood cabinets, a large island in the center, and an unsettling pool of old dried blood between the two entryways marking the spot where Mr. Lombardi died. In the far-right corner, I could see the pantry door next to the fridge, where Ted must have been hiding from his mother. Taking a second pass at the room, I doubted that Ted could have seen anything from the pantry with that island in the middle.

"Hey, Maeve," I whispered, "how about you open the pantry door, and I'll cover you."

Maeve walked around the back side of the counter to avoid stepping on the dried blood. I positioned myself on the left side of the island and knelt with my gun pointed at the door. With extra caution, Maeve turned the doorknob without making a sound and pulled it open. Thankfully, the only thing stirring around was a cloud of dust.

As I stood up, my gaze was drawn to the sink. Stains of blood tainted the bottom, a silent reminder of where they'd found parts of Ted's younger brothers. I watched as Maeve stepped into the pantry to look for anything helpful that was left behind. It was apparent that she didn't seem to be as affected by the sights and smells of this dreaded place as I was, possibly due to her years as a cop. Despite having seen my share of corpses throughout my career, something about this scene unnerved me. Maybe it was because of the shared history with Rose, or perhaps witnessing the aftermath firsthand in person with the knowledge of what had transpired.

Maeve turned around in the pantry doorway, a look of concern creasing her forehead. "You holding up okay?"

Her voice pulled me back from my own introspection, making me realize how lost in thought I'd been. "Oh, I'm fine," I said through a nervous laugh.

"No, you're not," she asserted as she holstered her gun. "You're overthinking this and letting the stories of what happened here get to you."

I felt my eyebrows shoot up. "How'd you know?"

Maeve offered a reassuring smile. "I've seen that look before, and trust me, no one is immune from it unless you're some sort of psychopath."

"Well, that's good to know," I mused under my breath.

Maeve chuckled. "Kaplan gave me some advice when he noticed the same look on my face at our first crime scene."

"Oh?" I inquired.

"Yeah," she continued, "he said the key to clearing your mind is narrowing your focus and concentrating on the immediate task at hand. In this case, searching for clues in the pantry. Everything else will just fade away into the background."

"Just like that," I said with a snap of the finger.

"Yeah," Maeve affirmed. "I guess it would be kinda like when you're in one of those surgeries, and they have that surgical sheet draped over the patient, exposing only the operation site."

"Well," I said, checking the hallway to ensure no one was sneaking up on us. "That sheet serves multiple purposes, but I do see your point."

Maeve eyed the pantry door. "I've got an idea."

"I'm all ears if it gets us out of this room," I said.

"Nope," said Maeve, "but it'll redirect your attention."

I bit my lip. "What did you have in mind?"

Maeve's mouth stretched into a wide grin. "Let's test the idea that Ted could see his mother from looking under the door."

I eyed the area with Mr. Lombardi's dried blood, knowing I would probably be standing on it to make it an accurate test. After considering Maeve's idea for a moment, I gave in. "I was just thinking the same thing, and there's no better time like the present to corroborate Ted's story."

Maeve nodded in agreement, stepped inside the pantry, and closed the door behind her.

I moved around the island and positioned myself in the general area where Rose would have been. "Can you spot me?"

"Can't see a damn thing in here," Maeve said through a muffled voice. "Can you step closer?"

I tried to swallow a sour taste that formed at the back of my mouth to no avail. With a sigh, I moved toward the center of the blood stain. A cold breeze rushed against me that sent my teeth chattering. My mind raced back to the time when Logan felt the same thing at the Mayan Museum that preceded the appearance of a Shadow Knight.

"Maeve?" I asked, my voice barely above a whisper.

"Still can't see you," Maeve replied as she opened the door. "And I tried every possible position, including standing on my tippy-toes to peek over the door."

I watched the dimly lit area behind Maeve for any trace of movement. My heart raced with anticipation as I raised my gun. Maeve spun around, dropping to one knee with her pistol at the ready.

Seconds ticked by before Maeve stood up and holstered her gun. "Maybe we should take a step outside for some fresh air?"

I frowned and holstered my gun. "Apologies. Thought I saw something."

"Well," said Maeve as she approached the second entryway into the kitchen. "At least we can confirm that Ted didn't see Rose actually stabbing his father."

"That part is concerning." I felt my muscles tighten as I followed her. "Which means he's either lying or genuinely confused about what occurred that night. Either way, the cops and Ellis should have caught that."

"What the hell?" Maeve exclaimed, pointing at the bloodstained floor I was standing on.

I glanced down and noticed the stain had taken on a fresh, more juicy appearance. Lifting my foot, I saw blood pooling back into my shoe's indentations. "This can't be."

Maeve crouched down for a closer look. "It appears fresh. Maybe it's from a wild animal like a raccoon. The smell of blood could have attracted some unwanted attention from numerous woodland creatures, resulting in one nasty fight."

"Hmm," I said. "I've only seen those in a zoo. Are they that vicious?"

Maeve chuckled. "You keep raccoons in a zoo?"

I stepped away from the bloodstain and dragged my feet on the floor to try wiping the blood off the soles of my shoes. "Well, yeah, they're not native to England."

This isn't right, I thought. I was fairly certain all the blood in here was old and dry when we first entered, and I know I wouldn't have stepped in fresh blood. Yet, here I was, with fresh blood on my shoes. It was always possible it blended into the floor well enough, and I'd overlooked it. That would explain the smell, but still, I had warning sirens firing off. Something was amiss. Maeve tossed me a roll of paper towels of the counter to wipe the blood off my shoes.

"Let's check some more rooms," I suggested.

Maeve nodded in agreement, and we departed the kitchen to check out the living room. The space was grand, decorated with wealthy furnishings, but carried a feeling of warmth, thanks to the family portraits that adorned the walls.

"Well, well. Would you look at that," I said as I scanned the faces.

Mr. Lombardi was wearing a pendant with a red runic symbol on it that showed a straight vertical line with two more jutting off from the right-hand side. It was the same symbol CJ had identified as Feoh on the ring Logan had stolen from the Mayan Museum that granted us access to the Blood Knights temple.

"No way." Maeve moved in for a closer look. "Kaplan has a similar pendant he got from Jacob Wallace's neighbor."

"Lorelei?"

"Yeah. The one and only."

"Really?" I asked, intrigued by this new information Kaplan had conveniently forgotten to mention. "How's it different?"

"His has a blue 'X' on it instead of this red symbol." She tapped the picture. "Jacob mentioned it was a key that can unlock doors that can't be seen, but I'm not entirely sure what he meant by that."

"I think I might know," I offered up. "We used something similar to make a solid wall translucent enough for us to pass through at the entrance of a Blood Knight temple."

"Oh, that's probably it then."

New ideas swirled around in my head the more I thought about Rose and her family. I had always assumed Rose was the sole member of the family to join the Knights, but now I was considering the possibility her husband might have also been a member.

Next to the kitchen, we found the formal dining room with a shattered window. Maeve used some of her investigation skills to determine that a wild animal did indeed pass through here, indicated by the strands of hair and drops of blood stuck to the shards of glass on the floor. I haven't heard of small woodland creatures breaking windows to get into a house, but I guess it was possible. However, on second thought, it seemed more reasonable that someone else broke the window, and the critters came in later.

The tackiness of the blood indicated it was still fresh, which would explain why the blood in the kitchen was new. At the very least, we could close the book on the mystery of the blood, but it still didn't explain who broke the window and then left the front door open.

I followed Maeve into the library adjacent to the left of the foyer. The room itself wasn't overly spacious, but it stretched up through the second floor and was capped with a glass pyramid skylight. In the middle of the room sat an enormous desk facing the only window that surveyed the front of the house, which likely cost more than a luxury sedan. Bookcases lined the walls, only to be interrupted by a small spiral staircase that led to the second floor. From what I could see from the ground floor, the upper floor featured a circular walkway with bookcases embedded in the walls, along with various pieces of artwork hung up in between.

Maeve took a seat at the desk and propped her feet up on it. "What do you think the chances are that a crucial piece of information we need is scribbled in the pages of one of these books?"

I leaned against one of the bookcases, contemplating the horrid prospect Maeve proposed. "It would certainly complicate matters, but seeing how devious the Blood Knights are, it's plausible. We can start by searching for any obvious journals or diaries."

We spent the next hour searching the library, sifting through books and documents. Most of the items we found that stood out were standard family history records, old newspapers, and magazines. Dusk would be approaching soon, and it was about time we started to wrap things up.

I tilted my head back, rubbing a sore spot that had developed in my left shoulder. I spotted Maeve on the second floor, thumbing through a book. My heart skipped a beat when I noticed a painting hanging next to her. I bolted up the stairs, giving Maeve a good fright as she dropped the book she was holding and pulled out her gun.

"This can't be," I whispered, staring at the painting. It depicted a grassy meadow with a red dirt trail running alongside a pond accented with trees displaying their autumn colors. The sun hung low in the horizon, giving way to a star-field sky complete with a meteor shower on full display.

Maeve took a deep breath and holstered her gun. "What is it?"

My mind remained fixed on the painting, barely registering Maeve's question.

"I've been here," I finally uttered.

Maeve moved in closer to examine the painting. "You have? When?"

"After Ben sent us through the Rift Generator right before we ended up in this timeline, I found myself walking down this exact same trail," I said, pointing at the painting.

Maeve cleared her throat. "And you're certain it's not just a coincidence?"

I shook my head. "Quite sure, and how often do you come across a sky like that?"

Maeve's eyes widened as she took in the details of the painting. "I know that name," she said, pointing at the artist's name. "It's another one of Isaac's."

"Who's Isaac?"

Maeve tapped her chin. "I'm not entirely sure, but he painted this mural Kap and I found in the sewers after the Knights set that police station on fire back on the island."

"Hmm. Sounds like we have another Knight's name to add to the investigation list. But what's his connection to all of this?"

Maeve shrugged. "I have no idea, but it can't be a coincidence, *this* is just hanging here. We'll have to ask Rose about it."

I nodded. "Indeed, I will." I took the painting off the wall and tucked it under my arm.

Chapter 11

United Citadel Field Unit Beta Team

The sharp descent of the sun directed an eerie light on the mansion as Maeve and I hastily stowed the painting in the back seat of the car. The long shadows didn't help with the thought of a Shadow Knight being on the premises if the cold chill I felt in the kitchen was anything to go by. Then, there was nothing like stacking a robbery charge on top of a breaking and entering charge to boot. Maeve hesitated for a moment, glancing back at the house. "You sure you want to keep searching the house at this hour?"

I bit my lip. "Well, no, but I fear we might not get another chance."

Maeve sighed, "All right, but let's be quick. We're already pressing our luck as it is."

We made our way back inside, taking the grand spiral staircase up to the second floor. Off to the right of us was the main bedroom and laundry room. Outside the bedroom, I could see where the crime scene technicians removed a section of the wall. This would have to be where Rose stabbed her husband in the neck, leaving a blood spray pattern that Detective Morgan from the café mentioned. On the left were the three children's bedrooms.

We started with the children's rooms, saving the main bedroom for last. Maeve and I split up, each of us taking a room to help speed things along. The one I entered in the back corner was painted gray, with white trim. Model airplanes hung from the ceiling, along with various movie posters plastered on the walls, and a desk with some almost finished math homework resting on top next to a computer. Beside the walk-in closet, a door opened to a balcony with tables and chairs overlooking the pool.

I began my search methodically. Inside the nightstand, I found some comic books and a flashlight but nothing much else of interest. Continuing with my search, I found his desk drawer filled with some more school papers, colored pencils, and a bunch of candy wrappers. But crammed at the back of it, I found what appeared to be a green leather-bound graph paper notebook. Flipping through the book's first half, I saw examples of a board game he was designing, followed by some design layouts of his bedroom. However, occasionally, he would have some entries mixed in that were definitely not part of the previous designs. The cops must have overlooked this, since the room wasn't technically part of the crime scene, but I could see how they could be mistaken as part of the game. Leafing back a couple of pages, I found his first entry.

They came back again from the closet. Two of them dressed in purple to meet with Dad.

A few more pages later: *They met with Dad in the library. It was so cold and dark. Their friend in red came this time. He yelled about some research taking too long. Ted says he is going to follow them.*

His last entry says *Mom is in trouble, and Ted isn't Ted.*

Maeve stood in the doorway. "Find anything?"

I closed the notebook. "I might have," I called back, then brought her up to speed with what I had found.

Maeve leaned against the left side of the doorjamb. "Why would they use a secret passage to get in here?"

"They wouldn't," I said. "Unless one of them is a Shadow Knight. They can transport themselves through shadows, meaning all they need is a dark space to emerge from—something as simple as a closet."

"Right," said Maeve, "hence the name Shadow, but why not use the front door…" her voice trailed off. "Unless someone was watching them?"

"Maybe they didn't want the kids to see them," I offered up. "He mentioned Ted was going to follow them, and his last entry says Ted isn't Ted anymore."

Maeve winced. "That can't be good."

I shook my head. "No, it isn't, and Iris pretty much said the same thing."

Maeve gasped. "I must have missed that part. You think he's an Acolyte?"

"That is a concern of mine, and if true, Ted is probably the youngest person they've ever converted."

"Hmm," said Maeve. "Leah never mentioned Ted being out there on the island."

"True, but there's no dates in here," I said, holding up the book. "Without a proper timeline of events, who's to say when he was converted."

We continued searching the house, entering the laundry room next to the stairs. The room was dimly lit, but I could make out a bloody handprint and smears on the tile floor in front of the washer and dryer.

Maeve and I exchanged a worried glance, knowing this was probably where she cornered one of her kids. Next to the handprint, I noticed a ruler had been kicked to the side.

I knelt and picked up the ruler, examining it closely. Specks of white powder coated the top of it. Possibly detergent powder, but it had more of a chalky appearance. I scanned the rest of the floor and found a small divot next to the center tile. *So, the powder is from the grout, and someone was using the ruler to pry up one of the tiles, but why?*

My heart pounded as I crouched down to examine it more closely. "I think we need to pull up this tile."

Maeve nodded as she crouched down next to me. I wedged the ruler back in the slight indentation and gently applied some pressure. The tile wiggled ever so slightly before the ruler snapped in half.

"Oh, bloody hell," I whispered.

A sinister grin crossed Maeve's mouth as she unholstered her gun, raised the butt, and brought it down on the tile in one swift motion. I winced as the tile shattered with a loud crack, splitting it into three pieces. Clearing the fragments, I found a metal handle set into the wooden subfloor.

"Now, that shouldn't be there," I said as I pulled it up. The handle raised about an inch, then something below us clicked.

"There's something underneath us," Maeve whispered.

I smiled. "Definitely not a standard feature you'd expect to find in a laundry room."

"Mm-hmm," said Maeve.

We hurried down the grand spiral staircase, our footsteps echoing in the mansion's vastness. At the base, we veered off into the butler's pantry situated just beneath the laundry room. No doubt the latch mechanism triggered something in there.

Maeve began tracing her fingers along the intricacies of the back wall, searching for what I assumed to be some sort of switch or lever to open something in here. While she was doing that, I thumped on the right wall, hoping to hear an empty room behind it. Toward the back corner, I found the wall had shifted, revealing a hidden passage to the crawlspace under the stairs.

Crouching down, we entered. The air in here was much colder than I would imagine as it enveloped my body. I could feel my stomach twist into knots at the looming threat of a Shadow Knight being nearby.

Maeve panned her flashlight around, its beam gliding along the walls until it reflected off a gleaming object. Embedded in the wall was a knife, its curved blade similar to the one Ted had described.

"Looks like we found the second murder weapon," I said, my eyes still focused on the knife.

Maeve moved in for a closer look, taking care not to touch it. "This is exactly like the ones they were using on Shady Reef. Detective Morgan is gonna want to snag this baby for some fingerprinting."

Once outside, I pulled out my mobile and dialed Leah's number. Now was as good a time as any to give her an update. After the first ring, she answered. "About time you gave me a call. I've been waiting all day for an update."

Clearly, somebody didn't like to be left waiting in the wings, just like her brother. "Sorry about that," I said sheepishly.

"Well, don't keep me in suspense any longer. What did you find?"

I quickly summarized our findings with Leah, starting with the early morning meeting with Detective Morgan, dealing with Rose in the institute, and the interesting discoveries we'd made at Rose's house. I heard Leah gasp on the other end of the line when I mentioned the part about Rose's missing research.

"I might have an idea where she hid it."

"You do? Where?"

"I overheard my captors back in New Orleans discussing it right before my father rescued me. Sounds like Rose hid it before she fled home, which means it should be back on Shady Reef."

"If that's the case, then it probably got burned up in the fire."

"Maybe," she said, drawing out the word.

If she was anything like her brother, I had a pretty good idea of what she was thinking. "You're not going out there by yourself," I said shortly.

Leah laughed. "Oh, hell no. I never want to see that place again."

"Understandable."

There was a short pause before Leah spoke again. "What about that part about Ted not being Ted in the diary?"

"Something strike a chord with you?"

"Maybe." Leah hesitated. "Rose was always visibly distraught over something, but I never found out what it was. I'm just wondering if it had something to do with Ted?"

"Seems likely to me."

"Are you two going to talk to Ted?"

I glanced up at Maeve as she came down the front steps. "We've been considering it."

"It would be a dramatic turn of events if Ted turns up to be the real killer."

"True, but as it stands, it's hard to give a definitive answer. He could just as easily be an accomplice or completely innocent as he says."

"Huh, I wonder if Rose knew what would happen to her when she returned home from the island?"

I thought about it for a second. After all, Rose did know more than what she was letting on. "I wouldn't put it past her, but getting her to confirm anything is another issue, which reminds me, I need to let Detective Morgan know about the knife we found."

Leah sighed. "All right, I'll see if I can check in with Logan." Then she hung up.

I dialed Morgan's number, and after a few rings, his gruff voice answered. I could tell he was at a crime scene from the sound of it, probably the same one from last night.

"Morgan," he said.

"Hello, Detective, this is Eva. We met this morning at the café," I said, glancing back toward the car as Maeve leaned against it.

"Yeah," he said. "What do you need?"

"I've stumbled across an anonymous tip that you might want to check out the butler's pantry in Rose's house. Just thought you should know."

"Just stumbled across? Anonymous?" he remarked in a dry wit.

In the background, I could hear Maeve mumbling to herself. She seemed to be in some sort of trance as she danced around the car without a care in the world.

"Yep," I said into my mobile and hung up.

I turned my attention back toward Maeve, and it was evident something was severely wrong with her. Her eyes had that vacant, distant look as she mumbled and rambled incoherently. She continued to twirl around the car, her feet barely touching the ground.

"Life eternal never fading," she sang out. "Sky is not the same with a distant gaze."

I tried to approach her, but she continued to dance around away from me. This was something on a completely different level than what she had displayed before. My hands trembled as my mind raced to think of what I should try next.

Before I had a chance to call her name, Maeve bolted. Her pace was frenzied, and she made a beeline into the grove of trees next to the house. I sprinted after her, following the path she had taken. My breath caught in my throat as I weaved through the trees, hearing her feet pounding ahead of me.

I soon found myself at the entrance of an old, dilapidated barn that was no longer used. I stepped inside, the only sound being gravel crunching beneath my feet. Broken beams from the partial collapse of the barn's old hay loft dotted the ground with flecks of old hay scattered about. With the gentlest of breezes, I could hear the barn creek and moan—a sure sign it could topple down on us at any moment.

In the center, surrounded by shafts of moonlight that cut through the broken roof, stood Maeve. The fearful look in her eyes was unsettling, and moreover, was the gun she held tightly in her hand, its barrel aimed squarely at me.

"Maeve," I said slowly, attempting to calm my racing heart. "It's me, Eva."

Not a trace of recognition crossed Maeve's face. Her eyes were wide, and her hand trembled as she tightened her grip around the gun. She blinked a couple of times as if trying to push through the fog in her mind. "I can't trust my eyes," she said, voice shaking. "The shadows lie in a valley of no more."

Taking a deep breath, I stepped closer, holding my hands up non-threateningly. "Look at me, Maeve."

Tears welled in her eyes as she met my gaze. The gun was still pointed in my direction, but at least her arm was wavering.

"Maeve," I started, trying to mask the panic in my voice. "Give me the gun."

Maeve shook her head and pressed the barrel of the gun into her right temple. "It's not safe in here."

"Clearly," I stated.

Tears streamed down Maeve's face, the gun still pressed against her head, but like a flick of a switch, her eyes narrowed as she pointed the gun back at me. Every muscle in her body tensed as she licked her lips. "He knows the unknown, his heart as black as emptiness. Surviving by the transfer is the path to eternal life never fading."

I took another step forward, my heart on the verge of exploding. "Why don't you tell me who he is, and what he knows."

Maeve flipped back to her former state of mind, the barrel of the gun in her mouth, her eyes wide with fear, and for a moment, I thought she would pull the trigger. But then she dropped the gun and collapsed to her knees and pressed her hands against her head.

She raised her head, and her eyes met mine. "What's going on?"

"You tell me," I said as I picked up her gun, flipped the safety on, and placed it in my pocket.

Maeve looked around the barn, her eyes focusing on one spot like a bloodhound homing in on a scent.

"What is it?" I asked.

Maeve brushed my question aside as she crawled a few steps away from me toward the far end of the barn, brushing away bits of debris and turning over rocks. After a couple of minutes, she uncovered a peculiar-looking polished stone about the size of my fist. She held it up in the moonlight, giving it a dark, almost black appearance with deep red hues of color splashed on it.

"This is what the Knights are after," she said as she stood up and tossed it to me.

Catching it, I asked, "What is it?"

Maeve shook her head. "Don't know, but it's probably best if you keep a hold of it. Damn thing is making me feel uneasy."

I studied the stone in my hand, turning it over for any sort of marking that would scream 'Property of the Knights' but came up empty. "How do you know the Knights are looking for this?"

Maeve rubbed her hands. "Not sure if I do, if I'm being honest, but I've got this strong feeling that something led us here and wanted us to find this before they do."

"You know, this isn't the first time you've come under this sort of spell," I said, taking a picture of the stone with my mobile to send to CJ. "Kaplan mentioned something similar back on Shady Reef. Although it was nothing to the extent you displayed here, you did say the same phrase both times: 'life eternal, never fading.' Any ideas what it means?"

Maeve shrugged her shoulders and shook her head no. "I really wish I could tell you everything, but I swear, I have no recollection of saying that."

"Right," I said. My fear of Maeve being some sort of Acolyte or double agent intensified in the back of my mind, but on the plus side, at least I had her gun now. Then again, I've never known an Acolyte to behave this way. This had to be something different. Still, if she was indeed compromised, it must have happened long before she went to Shady Reef, or why else would she be repeating that phrase?

I glanced back down at my mobile as it buzzed with CJ's name on the caller ID tag. "Well, what is it?" I asked, keeping my eye on Maeve.

CJ laughed on the other end of the line. "And it's good to hear from you too, sweetheart, but what's with this picture of the rock you sent me?"

I smiled. "I was hoping you could tell me what it is. Maeve found it in this old barn by Rose's house and thinks the Knights are searching for it."

"Well now, that is interesting," he said.

"How so?"

"It's probably just coincidental, but this is a bloodstone."

"Of all the…" My voice trailed off. "Of course, it is. You think there could be any significance to it and the Blood Knights?"

"That sounds more like a Maeve question to me." CJ chuckled. "But I can tell you some history behind it."

My eyes narrowed. "What sort of history?"

"Well…," CJ paused. "Legends have it that it was created when a green Jasper gemstone was placed under Christ during his crucifixion. The red spots are said to have appeared on the stone when his blood dripped on it after some Roman guy shoved his spear into him, but naturally, the bloodstone has been around much longer than that."

"Really?"

"Yeah, almost every known culture out there claimed it would give them some special abilities. Usually granting them some sort of healing properties or making them invisible. Then there was a bunch of soothsayers that used to tote them around, claiming they granted them the ability of foresight or visions of the future."

"Like an oracle?"

"Yeah, pretty much."

I lowered my voice. "Maeve was acting all strange before she found it."

"How'd she know where to look?"

"I don't think she did know where to look. I think she was drawn to it."

CJ gulped on the other side of the line. "This sounds bad."

"Very," I said. "I'm going to go take her to the hospital tomorrow and see if we can't get some scans done on her."

"You know whatcha lookin' for?"

"I'm afraid not, but I hope it's something obvious for her sake. How's the hunt for Phillip going?"

"You're not going to believe this." CJ chuckled. "But Nieminen is here, and Phillip has snuck onto a train headed east."

This can't be, I thought, a tight knot forming in my stomach. "Our Nieminen? Your friend from Intelligence?"

"It would appear so," said CJ. "But Logan's still skeptical."

"Good for him. Where are you two now?"

"We're coming up on Chicago. Phillip switched to a bus in North Platte, and we'll see if he gets off there."

"All right, make it quick, and remember to keep me and Leah posted."

I could almost hear him roll his eyes as he said, "Of course."

"And one more thing," I said.

"Anything for you."

"Stay safe out there."

CJ laughed. "Don't I always?"

Chapter 12

United Citadel Field Unit
BRAVO SUBUNIT

Logan eyed Phillip's bus as it pulled into the depot near downtown Chicago. It let out a hiss as it sank low on its suspension, almost like it was dying right there on the side of the curb. He checked his watch—close to 11:00 p.m. The city's lights shimmered on the black river that cut through the area, separating him from the iconic Chicago skyline he'd seen in so many movies.

Phillip stepped off the bus, hands jammed in his pockets, shoulders hunched against the icy breeze blowing in off the waterfront. Ideally, Logan would've grabbed him the second he hit the pavement, but drawing attention now would just invite the kind of trouble that wore a badge.

The uncertainty of the situation unfolding didn't set well with him. He and CJ surveyed the scene as they sat in their rental car parked across the street. For one thing, they were far too close for comfort. Plus, there weren't a lot of people around at this hour they could blend in with. Fortunately for them, Phillip didn't seem to be all that aware of his surroundings.

"Well, look at that," CJ said as he nodded toward Phillip's direction. "Looks like someone made a friend."

Phillip had walked over to a sleek red car that had pulled up, and after talking to the driver, he opened the rear door and got in.

Logan shuddered as he looked down at his gas indicator on the dashboard. He had a little less than half a tank of gas, so if he had to stop to fill up, there was no easy way to keep track of them like the bus.

CJ glanced at the gauge, coming to the same conclusion. "We can't lose them."

Logan gave him half a smile as he pulled away from the curb. "I believe tracking them falls under your department."

CJ flicked his gaze toward Logan. "Seems like everything on this trip falls under my department," he said under his breath.

"When they start shooting, I'll take over," Logan replied as he watched Phillip's silhouette light up in the back seat from a passing streetlight.

As Logan followed the red car, they neared one of the bridges that arched over the river, the gateway to Chicago's downtown area. The bridge, illuminated by rows of lights, cast a golden glow over the water below, turning the river into a ribbon of shimmering lights.

Logan gripped the steering wheel, his eyes fixed on the cars ahead. The city's skyline loomed, a mix of historic and modern architecture, the buildings standing sharp against the night sky. CJ remained silent beside him, his attention sharply focused on his wrist computer tracking the red car through the city's traffic cams.

Once over the bridge, the red car weaved through the downtown streets before finally pulling into the entryway of a high-priced hotel overlooking the northern part of the Chicago River and Lake Michigan. Logan slowed the car and parked it on the opposite side of the street. Inside through the enormous glass windows, he could see Phillip with his new accomplice chatting with the front desk clerk.

CJ held up his phone and snapped a quick picture of the two. "I wonder if that's the friend Nora mentioned he was fighting with?"

Logan glanced at the photo on CJ's phone, scrutinizing the unknown man standing next to Phillip. "Send it off to her. She'd know."

Leaving the car, they made their way across the street and into the hotel, careful to keep a low profile. The lobby had its own spin on what Logan figured designers meant by modern, which basically meant big open spaces with lots of glass and white things.

CJ blazed a trail to the front desk, only stopping to give the doorman a brief nod. The vast expanse of glass and polished surfaces made Logan feel exposed, but there was nothing the Knights could throw at him now that would deter him. *To the end,* he thought.

Holding down the front desk was a younger clerk working on a computer terminal while her coworker was busy fielding a phone call. CJ stepped forward with a giant smile, his demeanor instantly warm and engaging.

"Good evening," he greeted, his voice friendly and confident. Looking down at her nametag, he said, "Beautiful night we're having, isn't it, Madison?"

"Wouldn't know since I'm working tonight," she said, tapping her foot, never looking up from her terminal.

CJ chuckled as he leaned slightly on the counter. "Ah, that's a shame then, but still, you are providing a valuable service. Why, without you here, I would be resigned to spending a chilly night on one of your city's finest benches."

She looked up at CJ, her expression softening as she tried to suppress a smile. "You sound like a man that's after somethin' he can't have."

CJ's smile widened, but he maintained a respectful distance. "You got me there on that one," he said with a chuckle. "My friend and I were hoping you could help us get a room. Preferably one with a view of the river. I betcha it would look magnificent from way up there."

Madison smiled back at him as she redirected her attention toward her terminal. Her fingers were a blur as she tapped away on the keyboard.

She smiled as she looked back up at CJ. "I might just have the room you're looking for."

"Oh, I like the sound of that," said CJ.

Madison nodded.

"Oh, but wait," he said with a snap of a finger. "We should probably have a room close to some friends of ours. They would have gotten here probably right before us; his name's Phillip Wallace."

"Oh, you just missed Mr. Wallace and company," she said. "The room next to his is still available if you're interested?"

Logan removed his credit card and slid it across the counter toward her. "We'll take it."

Madison picked up the card and did a double-take when she saw Logan's name on it. "Oh, Mr. Kaplan. Other members of your party have already checked in," she said as she took out an envelope from the desk drawer and handed it to Logan. "They left this message here for you."

CJ raised an eyebrow as he glanced at the letter. "Who's it from?"

"It's from Nieminen," he said, looking at the note inside. "Says they've already checked in."

CJ sighed. "A heads up would have been nice," he mumbled.

Madison handed over two room key cards to CJ. "Are you two part of that convention that's meeting here tonight?"

CJ smiled back at her as he handed Logan his room key. "Why, yes, we are. What tipped you off?"

Madison winked at him. "Oh, just a hunch. You guys have a certain aura about you. Plus, we've been expecting quite a few attendees. Your convention is quite the talk of the hotel. Definitely the most prestigious one we've ever had."

"Yep, you summed it up quite well, if I do say so myself," said CJ.

Madison brushed a strand of brown hair behind her ear. "Is there anything else I can assist you with?"

CJ tapped his fingers on the counter. "Nothing that comes to mind, but I'm sure there's something I'm missing."

"Well," she said, taking out a business card. "Here's my direct line and mailbox. I'll be here until 11:30, so just give me a little jingle when you remember it."

CJ tapped the card on the counter. "I'll be sure to do that, and thanks again for all your wonderful help."

As they walked away from the front desk, Logan couldn't help but feel a mixture of apprehension and contempt. While CJ was able to worm his way into getting exactly what they wanted, he worried that he may have tipped somebody off that they weren't exactly on the up and up. Only time would tell if CJ's actions added some complications to his job down the line.

Logan looked up when the doors to the elevator opened with a ding and followed CJ inside. It was a brief ride up to their floor, but it gave him some time to relax a little and reflect on his last update to Leah just before they reached Chicago. He wasn't entirely sure, but something in her voice told him she was up to something. He knew there was nothing he could say or do now to change her mind—if it was made up, it was already too late. And since she was a Kaplan, for better or worse, whatever she was planning was already in motion.

Once inside their room, CJ immediately got on his phone, and called Nieminen. "We're two floors up from you in room 1015," he said softly, peering out the window at the city lights below. "Intercepted a message, you say?" he whispered. After a few moments, he said, "I'll update you when we have more info."

Logan, meanwhile, pressed his ear against the wall, straining to pick up any sound from Phillip's adjacent room. All he could hear were indiscernible whispers. CJ smiled and shook his head as he pulled out his compact sound amplifier from his pack.

"Take a step back," he said, pointing the device at the wall. "There's an easier way to do that."

"Then hurry and get to it," Logan said as he took a seat on the bed.

He leaned back and watched as CJ panned the device up and down the wall. He couldn't help it when a sly smile formed on his face as CJ shook the device and redirected it at another section of the wall.

CJ lowered the device and shook his head. "All I can hear is the humming of their heater."

Logan gestured toward the opposite end of the room. "Why don't you go check them out, and I'll continue with Phillip."

CJ nodded and moved toward the other side of the room, his device in hand while Logan went back to pressing his ear against the wall. He held his breath so he could hear better. Listening, he heard footsteps followed by a door opening. Without a second thought, he sprang toward their door, pressing his eye up against the peephole, but to his dismay, he didn't see anyone out in the hallway, but that only meant they hadn't walked in front of his door. He turned back to look at CJ, who was still fidgeting with his device.

"Did you hear that?" Logan asked in a low voice.

CJ looked up and raised his eyebrows with a slight shake of his head.

Logan was already on the move as he opened the door. "Wait here," he said as the door closed behind him.

He quickened his pace in the rectangular hallway, making his way toward the elevators that ran down the central core of this section of the hotel. Rounding the corner, he saw Phillip standing there waiting for the elevator to open.

As he approached, the elevator dinged, and the doors slid open. Logan stepped in, positioning himself a few feet away from Phillip who punched the button for the ground floor.

He turned to look at Logan. "Which floor?"

Logan nodded and said, "The lobby works."

Silence fell between them as they rode the elevator down until Phillip turned to Logan, a trace of recognition crossed his face. "Have we met before?"

Logan shook his head and punched his accent up to 100 percent as he said, "Fraide not, mate, unless you've been on a walkabout round Sydney recently."

Phillip gave a small, polite smile. "My mistake," he said as he turned back toward the elevator doors.

As the elevator reached the lobby, Phillip stepped out first. Logan followed at a slight distance, digging out the clear circular patch they use to communicate out of his pants pocket and applied it behind his ear as he watched Phillip make his way outside to the front of the hotel. Logan picked up his pace, as he saw a cab pull up in front of Phillip.

Tapping the patch to make sure it was on, he said, "Phillip's getting into a cab. Start tracking cab number 58096."

CJ's voice came on the line loud and clear. "Roger that."

Logan watched as the cab pulled away, then turned and made his way back to their rental car and got in. At this time of night, he knew it wouldn't be too difficult to follow the cab, but that also meant he would be more visible.

"They just turned south on North Harbor Drive," said CJ.

"I'm on it," said Logan as he left the parking garage.

CJ's voice crackled as Logan rounded the corner onto North Harbor. "Also, I talked to Nieminen again. I told him the front desk clerk mentioned there is a convention happening here tonight, which, of course, he already knew about, and suspects the Knights are holding it. Which would explain why Phillip came here, and now his cab is strolling west on Randolf."

"Yeah, I see it," Logan confirmed. "But if the Knights are having some sort of town hall meeting here tonight, why would Phillip be leaving, unless…," his voice trailed off.

"Unless what?" CJ said with a sense of urgency.

"They know who we are, and they are trying to separate us."

"Understood," CJ said after a short pause.

Logan tightened his grip on the steering wheel as he continued to follow Phillip's cab, his mind working through the possibilities. If it was indeed a trap, he needed to be careful not to walk right into it. His eyes kept scanning his surroundings, looking for anything out of place that would indicate the presence of a Knight, or worse, that Shadow Man.

As the cab turned a corner, Logan's instincts kicked in. He slowed down, taking a moment to observe. The street was dimly lit, in this area, making a perfect place for an ambush. His stomach churned as he took it all in. Everything just felt too damn orchestrated. He knew CJ was smart enough to do the right thing back at the hotel, but he wasn't sure if he had it in him to do it. The risk-taking part of him had definitely subsided when he started dating Eva.

"CJ, I'm going to hang back. Something's not right here. Keep track of the cab's location for me," he said.

He waited for CJ to say something, but he was only met with silence.

Logan's eyes narrowed as the glint of headlights flickered to life in his rearview mirror and sliced through the darkness. He placed his hand against his chest, feeling his heart pounding inside. His guts told him this was no coincidence.

Without a second thought, Logan smashed his foot down on the accelerator. The engine roared, cutting through the quiet night as he sped past Phillip's taxi, the tires screeching in protest as he made a hard right turn, skidding into the wrong lane in the process. He glanced up at the rearview mirror. The car behind him kept pace as it trailed him through the empty streets.

"CJ, do you copy?" Logan tried to reach out again, but the line remained ominously silent. The tight squeeze of anxiety filled his stomach. What the hell had happened to CJ?

He pushed the rental to its limits as he weaved through the streets, trying his best to lose the car behind him with no success. It was only a matter of time before it rammed into the back of him, or, worse yet, he'd hit some poor drunk bastard trying to cross the street.

As he rounded another corner, Logan spotted a police car passing through an intersection. Without hesitating, he eased off the gas to use this new situation to his advantage and slid in behind the police cruiser. The car behind him seemed to hesitate as it slowed down before ultimately turning off. *Guess they figured their job is over,* he thought.

Ahead, he saw Phillip's taxi passing through another intersection, snapping him back to the task at hand. *About time something went our way.* Logan resumed his pursuit, keeping a safe distance while tracking the cab's movements. Unfortunately, he was too far away to see if Phillip was still in the car, but there was nothing he could do about that right now.

The taxi led him back to the hotel, completing a full circle that left Logan with a feeling that Phillip was no longer a part of the picture. He parked the car in a shadowed area nearby and, to his relief, watched Phillip get out of the taxi and head back into the hotel.

It was possible that Phillip assumed his plan had worked and he had lost Logan and came back to the hotel. Or the Knights wanted him to think that to lure him into a false sense of security so they could attack. His eyes scanned his surroundings again, but as before, nothing really stood out to him. Yet the feeling of being watched lingered, the sensation felt so thick he could taste it.

Finally, CJ's voice crackled through his communication patch, breaking his train of thought. "I'm here, I just made it to Nieminen's room."

Logan responded with a curt nod. "Copy that," he whispered.

Chapter 13

United Citadel Field Unit
BRAVO SUBUNIT

Seated in an uncomfortable hotel chair, CJ watched intently as the tiny blip representing Phillip's taxi moved down the street on his wrist computer.

"Understood," he confirmed with Logan, as his mind became a whirlwind of scenarios, none of them with a happy ending. One thing he did know for sure; he couldn't hang around in his room waiting for the Knights to come a-knockin'. He tossed his sound amplifier back into his pack, swung it around his shoulder, and gave thanks that Logan never bothered to unload his gear from the car.

Doing his best to move as stealthy as a seasoned operative, he peered through the fish-eye peephole and was grateful to see nothing threatening on the other side. With care, he twisted the door handle and eased it open wide enough for him to poke his head through. Sensing no danger, he set foot on the hallway carpet and took the first few quiet steps toward the elevator around the corner. He froze in place when he heard a ding followed by the familiar sounds of the elevator doors opening.

"Oh shit," he said under his breath, as he backtracked to take the long way around the rectangular hallway, hoping he wouldn't cross paths with whoever had just got off on his floor.

He passed his hotel room and slipped around the corner into the next hallway. Just out of sight, he pressed his back against the wall and crouched. His fingers danced around the side of his wrist computer and extended the small wire with a camera attached to the end. He angled it low, and around the corner so he could see anyone coming up the hallway, knowing full well he would look awfully suspicious in that particular position if they came up the other side.

Thankfully, right on queue, he saw two men dressed in hotel uniforms walking up the long hallway and going directly to his hotel room. The bigger of the two stood to one side as he covertly pulled out a gun while the other one fumbled around with the key card until the door clicked open.

CJ retracted the cable, his heart pounding. A jolt of urgency shot through him. With quick, silent steps, he made his way to the stairwell. He pushed the door in and entered the metal and concrete stairwell and was taken aback at how industrial the inner workings of the building were compared to the luxuries spent on just the parking structure alone.

With no time to gander at the cold surroundings, he dashed down the two flights of stairs but hit a roadblock when he found the door to Nieminen's floor wouldn't budge. His phone buzzed, indicating Logan was trying to get a hold of him, but for now, he would have to wait while he called Nieminen. He started to punch up Nieminen's number when a surge of adrenaline shot through him. He picked up the sound of two muffled voices talking at the bottom of the stairs.

Holding his breath, he leaned over the stairwell to see if he could see anyone making their way up—nothing. He slung his pack around, eased the zipper down inch by inch, and reached in. When his fingers found the grip of the sound amplifier, he pulled it out and threw on the headphones.

A man's voice came loud and clear through the headset. "Mystic one wants a floor-by-floor search of the complex before she arrives for the ceremony."

The other voice said, "And what if we can't find them?"

"Have no fear. Death will find 'em soon enough."

He closed his eyes as a lump formed in his throat. Seeing how it was his room being tossed, there was no mistake that they were talking about Logan and him. *Ah shit.* It sounded like more men were joining the search as their footsteps echoed off the metal stairs.

He looked back at the door to Quint and Nieminen's floor and found it curious they weren't after them as well, or were they? It only took half a second for him to realize that the only two possibilities were either they were already captured, or worse, working with the Knights.

The only thing he could do was to continue with his original plan, call Nieminen, and deal with the consequences later.

Nieminen picked up and asked, "Where are you?"

"I'm trapped in the stairwell just outside the exit door on your floor," he said in a hushed voice.

"What's happened?"

All the blood in his face drained as he heard someone open a door inside the stairwell above him. "They're after me; hurry and open the door to the stairwell," he whispered.

"I'm already here," Nieminen said, his voice flat, as the door cracked open.

CJ yanked the door out of Nieminen's hand and bolted through, nearly knocking him over in the process.

Nieminen tugged his shirt hem straight, then caught the door before it could bang shut and eased it closed without a sound. "Am I correct to presume you are being chased?"

CJ was slack-jawed as he looked back at him, his eyes wide with disbelief. "What the hell do you think I meant by 'they're after me'?"

Nieminen pulled out his key card. "I assumed this was one of the numerous times where you were being overdramatic."

CJ remained speechless as he stared at him.

Nieminen prompted, "We should continue our conversation in a more discrete location."

"After you," CJ said, gesturing down the hallway.

Nieminen pointed at the door across from the stairwell exit. "It's actually this one right here."

Slipping inside, CJ surveyed the room and noticed someone was missing. "Where's Quint?"

"In the bar downstairs, keeping an eye on who's coming and going."

He clenched his fists and took a deep breath to calm the mounting frustration building up inside him. The situation had escalated, and they were scattered all over the complex. He pulled out his comm patch and placed it behind his ear. "I'm here. I just made it to Nieminen's room."

"Copy that," came Logan's voice over the line.

CJ peered out the peephole and found comfort in the fact that it remained empty.

"You were right about them being on to us," CJ said under his breath, just loud enough for Logan to hear.

"What's happened?" asked Logan.

CJ spoke up so both Logan and Nieminen could hear. "Two armed men dressed like hotel staff entered our room."

"Ah, crap," said Logan. "Gettin' you outta the hotel's gonna be a real pain in the arse now."

"Your cover has been blown?" asked Nieminen.

"Yeah," CJ said, stepping back from the door and turning to face Nieminen. "Also, I overheard some chatter in the stairwell about a Mystic one ordering a sweep of the entire complex to find us."

"Us?" Nieminen asked as he gestured his finger back and forth between them. "Or you," he said with his finger pointed firmly at CJ.

CJ's eyes narrowed as he matched Nieminen's gaze. "Exactly," he said slowly. "How come they aren't after you too?"

Nieminen shrugged it off. "I can only speculate, but I'd suppose it would have to do with my penchant for being more careful than you two have been."

Logan's voice sounded off in CJ's ear. "Damn, I'm really hatin' that bloke right now."

CJ agreed with a soft hum, thankful Nieminen couldn't hear Logan.

CJ clenched his fists. "You're saying this is my fault? Hell, you're the one that left that damn note with our names on it at the front desk."

"Right," Nieminen rebutted. "Which tells me the gal at the front desk isn't working for the Knights, or else they would be after me as well."

CJ's face hardened as his mouth formed a straight line. "Perhaps you're the one working for the Knights."

Nieminen shook his head. "If that were true, you would have never made it up that hill in Nebraska."

"Nieminen's right," Logan whispered. "It was you who requested to have a room next to Phillip. That was bound to send up some red flags."

"Ah, shit," CJ mumbled.

"Hold on," said Logan. "It looks like Phillip is leaving the parking garage."

"On foot?" asked CJ.

"Negative. He's driving a car, and I don't see anyone else with him."

"Maybe he's making a getaway?"

Nieminen raised an eyebrow, having only heard CJ's side of the conversation. "Who?"

CJ waved him aside. "Don't wait for me. Start following him."

Logan's car revved to life as soon as CJ said 'don't.' "Already am."

"Phillip?" asked Nieminen.

"Yep," said CJ. "He's on the move again."

"What course of action are you going to pursue?"

CJ started to answer when Nieminen's phone rang. Checking the ID, he said, "It's Quint."

"Perfect timing," said CJ.

Nieminen continued, "Says he saw Phillip talking to a man dressed in a white suit with some other lookie-loo in a gray suit eavesdropping on them, and then Phillip left for the elevator."

CJ nodded. "Parking garage," he said, then paused for a moment. "I wonder who this gray-suit fellow is?"

Nieminen glanced at CJ. "Yes, he's here. It would appear the hotel staff are working with the Knights and are aware of the Beta team's position."

CJ responded with a stoic thumbs-up.

Nieminen looked back at CJ. "Quint's tailing the gray-suited man."

"Oh," said CJ.

Nieminen hung up and shoved the phone back into his pocket. "Have you been able to devise an extraction procedure for yourself, or are you evaluating an alternate course of action?"

CJ tossed his pack on the small desk that doubled as a table in the hotel room and took a seat. "I'm still working on that."

A sly smile emerged on Nieminen's face. "Perhaps you could shave your head to change your appearance? That should give you a few seconds of leeway in the event you come across one of those armed men again."

CJ tapped his fingers on the desk. "I'm thinking of something different."

Nieminen raised an eyebrow. "You want to do some recon work."

"No time better than the present," he said. "Besides, it might be my last opportunity."

"To test out the thinnest bulletproof weave ever created lining your undershirt?"

CJ chuckled as he pulled up his sleeve, showing Nieminen the scar from when he took a bullet in New Orleans. "Already tested and failed."

"Hmm," said Nieminen. "AD Sokolov will not be too pleased to hear his pet project has failed."

CJ pulled the sleeve back down and rubbed his old wound. "Yeah, I'm sure he'd be all heartbroken."

He closed his eyes and took another deep breath. His throat had tightened up on him making it hard to swallow. All the while, Nieminen appeared calm. *Man, that guy has one hell of a poker face.*

The thought of slipping away unseen gave him a flicker of hope—maybe he'd survive another night. But if he walked now, knowing he was this close to uncovering something new about the Knights? He'd never forgive himself.

CJ leaned back in the chair and laced his fingers behind his head. "You ever heard of a Mystic Knight?"

Nieminen sighed as he tapped his chin. "That's not a designation I am familiar with."

CJ raised an eyebrow. "Are you sure?"

Nieminen's composure changed to that of an astrologer pointing out the stars in the sky as he mumbled under his breath. His facial expressions fluctuated between uneasiness and doubt. It took him a few moments before he looked CJ in the eyes and shook his head. "It may be possible I've seen the term Mystic before, but I don't believe it was in connection with the Knights."

"All right, that settles it then."

Nieminen tilted his head slightly. "It does?"

"Yep, it does." CJ said as he rocked to his feet and stood up. "That gal at the front desk mentioned there was some sort of conference taking place here tonight that Phillip is, or now was, going to."

"Or she set you up to say more than you should have to get yourself flagged as an undesirable."

"Naw," said CJ. "I'm thinking she's just a regular employee making small talk with us."

"If you insist."

CJ chuckled. "I do, and like you said, if she was working for the Knights, they'd be bustin' down your door too."

"In theory, yes," Nieminen retorted.

"Right, and you and I both know there are more sects of Knights out there other than the Blood and Shadow Knights."

Nieminen scoffed. "Technically, that has never been proven."

CJ grinned as he shook his head. "You should run that nonsense by Ben the next time you…" his voice lowered as he remembered the sacrifice Ben made to keep the Rift Generator that brought them here running.

Nieminen raised an imaginary glass up. "To Ben."

CJ echoed his sentiments, his words barely audible. "To Ben."

Breaking the silence, Nieminen asked, "Am I to understand you want to attend this conference?"

CJ nodded as he regained his composure. "Damn right. If there is a new a sect of Knights here, I intend to find out everything I can about them."

Nieminen's head rocked side to side as he thought about what CJ had said. "All right, let's do this," he finally said. "What do you need from me?"

CJ smacked the side of his leg with glee. "First, I'm going to need you to run ops, and we'll have Quint take point."

"Leaving you with Recon."

CJ opened his pack, fumbling to pull out the equipment he'd been lugging around. "Wouldn't have it any other way."

"Naturally," Nieminen huffed. "I believe our first order of business should be for me to tap into their security cameras."

"Oh," said CJ as he looked at the time on his wrist computer. "How fast do you think you can get in?"

Nieminen opened the closet door and grabbed his laptop shoulder bag. He opened it up and pulled out a small box no bigger than a deck of cards that looked like it was being held together with layers of black electrical tape. On one end a small antenna wire dangled out that could easily be missed if you weren't looking for it, and on the other end was a cable several inches long that he plugged into the internet wall jack above the desk.

CJ picked it up by the little antenna and gave it a gentle shake. "My, my, this sure does look like a rushed job."

He scowled. "Which is more than I can say for the many devices you have never developed."

"Point taken," CJ rebutted. "What does this little guy do?"

"If we're lucky, it should be able to link us undetected to their security systems."

"And if we're not?"

A bitter smile crossed Nieminen's face. "I fear that outcome would necessitate the need for me to physically be present at their security station."

"Well, I'll make sure to cross my fingers then. 'Bout how long do you think it'll take?"

Nieminen typed up a few commands on his wrist screen. "I am unable to determine that. However, if it starts to take longer than an hour, we should investigate other options."

CJ shook his head. "Yeah, it's after eleven. I'm bettin' their little conference is getting close to starting."

Nieminen frowned. "I'm forced to agree with your assessment."

The knot that had been forming in CJ's stomach gave a firm squeeze, making it harder for him to think straight. If only he had more time, he was sure he could come up with a plan to get him up to that conference unnoticed. He glanced around the room, taking mental inventory of what could aid them. Other than the gear he had with them, though, he didn't see much else that would be of any use. Then there was the other problem of him not having the slightest clue when this conference would take place.

"All right." CJ sighed. "Get Quint back on the phone. We're gonna need another perspective on this little job."

Nieminen punched up Quint's number, and he must have answered it after the first ring since CJ could hear he was talking and rather fast too.

CJ leaned forward, trying to hear what Quint was saying. "What is it?" he whispered.

Nieminen nodded as he glanced at CJ. "He says there's a line of black cars pulling up filled with guests in white clothing, and they're filing into the lobby."

CJ glanced at the time. "Sounds like this conference is getting ready to start. Tell him to get some pictures of the guests, and does he know where they're holding this party?"

Nieminen shook his head. "He'll try, and no, but he has a plan to find out."

"Good to hear someone has one." CJ grimaced. "I've got a feeling I'm gonna be winging it tonight."

Chapter 14

United Citadel Field Unit
☆Operations Division☆

Leah smiled at the attendant as she exited the plane in California's Humboldt County, with her appointed babysitter, Chambers, lumbering behind. However, it didn't take long for the smile to fade as they approached Eureka in a rental car. Anger and rage had been her driving force for so long, but now something else was tugging at her. Her legs trembled as the memory of her captivity out here only those few months ago resurfaced, with echoes of the past she knew would never fully release her.

She subtly turned her face toward the window as Chambers glanced at her, hoping he couldn't see through the tough façade she was trying to put up. The lights on the dashboard reflected off him in the window, indicating he'd refocused his attention back on the road.

"Somethin' on your mind, miss?" his voice just above the hum of the car's engine.

Leah sniffed as she brushed a strand of brown hair back behind her ear. "Oh, what? I'm sorry. I didn't catch that."

Chambers shook his head. "Yeah, you did." He smiled. "You've got that dammed thousand-yard stare thing going on."

Leah blushed. "Oh, I do?"

Chambers nodded. "Mm-hmm."

"I'm just thinking of the best way to get out there," she said, knowing full well that it was a bluff. "There should be a restaurant just five miles or so down this stretch of road where we can park."

Chambers flashed her another glance. "Yeah," he said with a huff. "If you think we're gonna take a boat on out to the reef tonight, you're sorely mistaken."

Leah rubbed her forehead to subdue a growing headache. She knew Chambers would fight her on a few things, but not this. If the situation had been different, she would have left him behind without nary a word. However, the way things were, there was always a chance she might need some backup and who else but one of Las Vegas Metro's finest detectives, not counting Maeve and her father. At least, that's what she kept telling herself.

She smiled back at him. "Oh, I get that heading out there tonight isn't our best move."

"You're damn right," he muttered.

A sly smile crossed her face. "But I know you'll pretty much follow me wherever I go, or else you wouldn't be here."

Chambers gave her a sideways glance. "For now, but even I have my limits."

Leah's gaze refocused back outside as she watched the ripples play in the moonlight in Arcata Bay. She squinted as she stared into the distance, wondering if she could catch a glimpse of Shady Reef. A foolish notion, no doubt, since it would still be too far away on the best of days to see, but she had to try. She chuckled on the inside as she rationalized that the dangers the island once held were no more since CJ himself confirmed the Knights had deserted it. Unfortunately, it was short-lived, since she could vividly recall Logan going off on some of CJ's mistakes during one of their jabbing sessions.

It felt like only a few minutes had passed when Leah noticed they were pulling up to the Old Town Seaside Bar and Grill. She wasn't sure if this was the same place her father and Maeve had visited, but she could quickly call Maeve and ask. However, that was bound to bring up a line of questioning she wasn't thrilled about answering and, worse, put Eva on notice.

Chambers turned the car off and sighed as he stared at the restaurant. His eyes focused on the building while his demeanor remained stoic as he said, "This ain't right."

Leah did a double-take as she leaned forward to see what he was referring to. The only thing that stood out to her was the lack of patrons, but that didn't seem like something to really worry about on a weeknight. She scrunched her face as she looked back at Chambers. "What's not right?"

Chambers punched the button to start the engine. All the interior and exterior lights lit up as if a fighter jet had locked onto them. The engine whined and vibrated as it tried to turn over, then faded into dead silence. Shaking his head, he slumped forward, feeling around the bottom of the dashboard. He smiled when he pulled a lever that popped the car's hood. When he straightened back up, his smile faded as a waitress made her way toward them. "That young gal walking towards us," he said with a nod toward her direction.

"Yeah," Leah's voice wavered.

"She's been staring at us since the minute she could spot our car."

Leah gave him a hopeful smile. "Maybe she's bored?"

Chamber crossed his arms. "Nope," he snapped. "She was just ignoring that confused-lookin' fella right there in the doorway. Looks like he was tryin' to chat her up before we arrived."

The waitress pushed her face up close to the driver's side window. Her eyes were wide open with huge pupils as she looked around inside the car like a praying mantis searching for a snack. When her eyes zeroed in on Leah, her right hand shot up and politely tapped on the window.

Chambers looked at Leah as he gripped the handle on his pistol under his light blue flannel jacket. "Friend of yours?"

Leah pressed herself against the door, holding the handle with a white-knuckle grip, ready for a quick exit. "Never seen her before in my entire life," her voice trembled.

Chambers rolled down his window just enough to squeeze a finger through. "Can I help you with somethin' miss…" He glanced down at her nametag, "Cora?"

Her gaze remained fixed on Leah. "I knew you would come back tonight," she said in a soft, ethereal voice.

Cora's head turned as quick as a lightning strike as Chambers tapped on the window, her focus solely on him. Beads of sweat formed on his forehead as her vacant eyes bore into him.

Chambers cleared his throat. "I said, is there somethin' *I* can help you with?" he asked with emphasis on the "I" part.

Cora tilted her head, blinking twice. "You, I don't know," she said, then glanced back at Leah. "But she has been to the reef once before."

Leah loosened her grip on the door handle, leaning toward Cora. She didn't like the idea of this person she had never met knowing who she was, especially considering only the Blood Knights would have such knowledge about her in this town.

She gritted her teeth. "Back off, Blood Knight!" she growled.

Cora shook her head in defiance. "I'm no Knight!"

Chambers tapped the window again. "Then who the hell are you?"

"Just an observer," she said as she stood up and straightened her shirt.

Leah unbuckled her seatbelt and moved to open the door on her side. Chambers grabbed her arm, his grip tight as he jerked her back. "What are you doing?" he said through a forced whisper.

Leah's recent training kicked in as she grabbed a pressure point on his wrist and pulled his hand away, a move Logan had shown her.

Chambers jerked his hand back and massaged it, checking for broken bones. "Damn, that hurt."

Leah ignored him as she exited the car, slamming the door behind her. "Why are you observing me?"

Cora shifted her weight forward, resting her folded arms on the car's roof. Her thin silver bracelets clanked together, appearing brighter than they should be in the shadow she now cast over them.

"Master Dekker says you are only but a piece of the puzzle, but what part you play is still an unknown until more pieces fall into place."

Leah tapped her fingers on the car. "Master Dekker? So, is he like your boss or something?"

Cora smiled. "He's a conductor."

Leah glanced down at Chambers, who had unholstered his pistol and discreetly aimed it at Cora's midsection while she remained unaware of the potential danger.

Leah muttered, "That ain't helpful." Her words were meant for both of them, though she kept her gaze fixed on Cora. "What do you know about Shady Reef?"

Cora shook her head in quick jerks, almost robotic-like. "Bad place. You must tread carefully."

Leah shot up an eyebrow. "I thought the island was abandoned?"

Cora continued, "Master Dekker has left his boat for you. You'll find the Sovereign docked at the pier next to the warehouse behind us, but you must go now if you want to stay ahead of them."

"Ahead of who?" Leah asked.

Cora squeezed her eyes shut as she pinched the bridge of her nose. She swayed from side to side, appearing to be on the verge of losing her mind or simply passing out. Leah took a step forward around the car to catch or comfort her. She wasn't sure what she should do when she made it over there, but watching her fall backward and crack her head on the pavement would draw them some unwanted attention.

Cora shook her head again and held up a hand, letting Leah know to stop advancing on her. She blinked her eyes again. Her pupils returned to normal. "Whoa," she said, looking back and forth between them. "What's going on here?"

Chambers stared back at her with one eyebrow raised. "You approached us…," his voice trailed off.

Cora rubbed her temples and looked back at Leah. One tear streamed down her cheek, but Leah wasn't sure if it was out of fear or pain. "Are you okay?" she asked.

Cora nodded as she rubbed her hands together. "Sorry about that. I must've just had one of my little spells."

Leah took a step back. Clearly, there was something amiss with this woman, and she wasn't sure how to proceed with her. Her prevailing theory that she was a Knight still took precedence in her mind no matter what Cora had said. A knot twisted in her stomach as the realization of her vulnerability took hold. Her impulsive decision to leave the car's safety seemed rather foolish now, but she would never admit that to Chambers. The last thing she needed was word to get back to Logan, resulting in her being confined to the house until the end of time. Although that might happen anyway, once Eva knows she'd left Vegas.

She took a deep breath and straightened her posture. "Cut the crap," she barked out, mimicking her father's authoritative tone. "Your little act isn't fooling anyone."

A slight twitch appeared at one corner of Cora's lips as her face flushed. She tried to wipe away the tears streaming down her face, leaving behind dark mascara streaks.

Leah remained where she was, uncertain whether Cora's imminent breakdown was a ruse to lower her guard or truly genuine.

"Is there someone we can call for you?" Chambers asked.

Cora wiped away a few more tears, then looked back in the direction of the restaurant. She sniffed, then whispered, "I'll be fine."

"Are you sure?" Chambers asked.

The door to the restaurant flung open, and a man wearing a nametag holding a wet rag stood in the doorway. The lights behind him made it difficult to make out his face, but it was apparent he was angry.

"Cora, get your ass back in here!" he shouted, pointing at her. "You ain't off the clock yet!"

Chambers rolled down the window as Cora lowered her head, her arms folded as she scampered away.

Chambers stuck his hand out the window to wave at the man and said, "Sorry about that. She was answering some questions for us."

The man stood aside, letting Cora through the door. He looked at Chambers, shook his head, and went back inside.

Leah opened the car door and slid in next to Chambers. He eyed her as she fumbled with the seatbelt to straighten it out before she could fasten it.

"Where do you think we're going?" he asked. "The car's dead."

Leah let out a groan. "Great. What do we do now?"

Chambers unbuckled his seatbelt and flung it over his shoulder. "Well, I can tell you I'm not gonna wait around for some damn welcome party courtesy of these Knights to show up while I'm fast asleep."

"So, we're heading back to Vegas?" she asked.

"Hell no," he spat through gritted teeth. "I ain't walkin' back to the tarmac nor thumbing for a ride."

Leah already knew what he would say next, but she had serious doubts about heading out to the reef tonight. It was easy for her to take charge when it was five hundred miles away, but not so much now. Her stomach churned as she fought to keep her legs from shaking as she tried to suppress the memories of what happened to her out there. She clenched her hands into fists as she told herself it was now or never as she scanned the darkness behind the bar and grill.

"You're going to the reef?" she said.

"Damn right," he barked. "If the trippy waitress is any indication of the power they hold, they're gonna have one hell of a time finding me."

"How?"

Chambers smirked. "I intend to be unpredictable."

Leah's eyes lit up. "Oh, I see," she said. "So, you don't actually want to go there tonight, do you?"

Chambers snorted. "Hell no."

Leah smiled. "Well then, after you."

Chambers nodded and got out of the car as Leah followed suit. She hadn't noticed it before, but a nip in the air came off the bay, giving her goosebumps on her arms. As soon as they passed the restaurant, the world turned very dark on them, with only faint silhouettes of a factory and the sounds of water splashing against the shore to guide them. Leah pulled out her cell phone and turned the flashlight on. She waved it around to get a better look at her surroundings, but only Chambers faintly lit up. She frowned, turned it off, and shoved it back into her pocket.

"That little light ain't powerful enough," said Chambers, "but this one is."

A powerful beam of light shot out of Chambers's hand, lighting up the side of the factory. Rusty tin sheets lined the walls with faint lettering indicating it used to be a cannery. The few windows it had were all broken, more than likely by some unhappy soul chucking rocks at it.

He panned his flashlight to the right of the factory and zeroed in on a single boat tied up at the wooden docks. The main hull of the vessel was a deep blue with green accents that bobbed gently up and down. Running down the length of the side in big white letters was the word *Sovereign*.

"My hell, that thing is huge," exclaimed Chambers. "At worst, I was expecting a stupid little skiff or, at best, a derelict runabout. This is one of those damn crab boats they use way up north."

Leah started to speak but stopped as she pulled the neck of her shirt up over her nose and cupped her hand over it. She looked over at Chambers, her eyes wide. "What is that smell?"

Chambers grimaced as he sniffed the air. He groaned as he shined the light back on the factory. "Hell if I know, but it's coming from over there."

Leah took a couple of steps back away from the factory. "It smells like something is dead or worse."

Chambers chuckled. "What's worse than dead?"

"I don't know, whatever's in there. Why don't you go check it out?"

Chambers shook his head. "Uh-uh," he said. "I'm not about to go stumbling across a dead body, then spend the next few weeks trying to explain to a judge what the hell I was doing out here."

"Oh, that still may happen." Leah chuckled.

Chambers took off toward the boat. "Not if I can help it."

Leah set off in a short trot to catch up to him. A moment later, they were both standing on the dock. Chambers shone his light on a letter and key inside a plastic bag taped to the side of the boat.

"Our invitations?" he asked.

Leah shook her head. "I'm not sure," she said as she picked it up.

"Well, what's it say?"

"Give me a second," Leah said in a huff as she opened the bag. She unfolded the paper and held it under Chambers's light.

"Free to a good home?" he whispered as he read the note. "Signed Marcus Dekker? Who the hell is he?"

Leah shook her head. "Gotta be that guy Cora works for."

"Don't think so. Maeve's report said the guy's name running that joint was Malcolm," he said, pointing his thumb back toward the restaurant.

"No, I don't mean him…," her voice trailed off. "Wait a minute. You don't think that was Malcolm yelling at Cora, do you?"

Chambers shrugged. "Isn't he supposed to be the leader of the Blood Knights?"

"Yes!" Leah whispered through gritted teeth.

"Well." Chambers paused. "If it were him, I'd say we'd know by now."

Leah sighed. "Oh, I hope you're right about that one."

"So do I," he said as he slid the gangway ramp into position.

Once he crossed the ramp, he turned to give Leah a hand. "You remember what that guy's name was that ferried your pops and Maeve out here?"

"Kopache, I think," she said, then handed him the key for the boat.

"Hmm," he said. "That sounds like a last name. You didn't catch a first name by chance, did you?"

"'Fraid not," she said as she watched him climb the steps to the bridge.

"Why?" she asked as she followed him inside.

"Just a fleeting thought if this Marcus and Kopache guy are one and the same," Chambers said, firing up the engines.

"Don't think so," she said as Chambers dashed outside to cast off the lines holding them to the dock.

"But," she continued when he returned, "now that I think about it, Kopache's first name sounded something like Matias or Mathias."

Chambers glanced back at her over his shoulder. "You sure?"

Leah nodded as she lowered her gaze. "Yeah, I think I overheard the sheriff say his full name when they had me drugged up in that jail cell."

"Really," he said. "I never did hear that part of the story."

"Yeah," Leah whispered. "I can fill you in along the way."

Chambers punched in a couple of waypoints on the NAV system, then turned to face Leah. "Hold on."

Leah looked up at him. "What is it?"

"All three of their first names start with the letter 'M'?"

"Huh," she said. "That can't just be a coincidence."

"You're damn right," he said with a snap of a finger. "These three jackasses have to be connected."

Leah wrapped her arms around her stomach. Her insides felt like they were on the verge of releasing lava, as what she feared could happen was happening. "They're all Knights, and this is a trap."

A crooked smile crossed Chambers's face. "Well, we'll just need to stay one step ahead of them."

Leah wiped away a tear, hoping Chambers didn't see it. She could never forgive herself if someone else died because of her. First, there was her boyfriend, Mark, then her brother, Lucas, then her father.

Unexpectedly, a soft voice echoed across the back of her mind. She looked around the bridge, but only saw Chambers piloting the boat away from the dock. She closed her eyes as she tried to focus on it again. It sounded like a young child was trying to say something to her, but what it was she couldn't comprehend. She opened her eyes and nearly jumped out of her skin. Her heart pounded as she saw the shadow of a hooded figure with glowing blue eyes against the closed door they used to enter the boat's bridge.

Chambers' voice echoed through the bridge. "All right, let's see what this old gal can do."

Leah glanced at him and then refocused on the door, only to discover that the figure was gone.

Chapter 15

United Citadel Field Unit
☆Operations Division☆

Leah stood alone at the front of the bridge, a radio pressed to her ear. Chambers had left it with her when she insisted they check the rest of the vessel for any stowaways—something they both regretted not doing before setting off. Nearly five minutes had passed, and she had grown anxious for his check-in.

So far, the boat had been picked clean, save for some expired canned food that Chambers assured her would still be good eatin' in a pinch. But beyond that, there was nothing else of real value to them. Better yet, no Knight hid in the shadows, waiting to pounce.

She leaned forward, staring out the front window, catching sight of some sort of sea creature leaping out of the water near the ship's bow then slipping back down below the ocean's dark surface. It all happened too fast to get a good look, but she knew it was bigger than a run-of-the-mill dolphin, yet definitely smaller than a whale. She felt a pang of unease at the possibility of a shark tagging along the side of their boat. Accidentally falling overboard into the jaws of that nightmare ranked high on her list of worst ways to die. Perhaps that's why this Dekker guy left them his boat. The authorities would be hard-pressed to charge anyone if they died out at sea all by themselves, and it'd be easy for Dekker to say they stole the ship.

Chambers's voice crackled over the radio, "You say something?"

Leah looked down at the little unit and realized she had unconsciously hit the talk button. "It's nothing. How's the search going?"

Her eyes snapped to the bridge door when she heard someone knocking outside.

"The ship is all clear. Now unlock this damn door and let me in. It's freezing out here."

Leah spotted his face in the little window and rushed to the door to unlock it, letting him in. Chamber slammed the door behind him and rubbed his hands together as he blew warm air on them.

Leah raised an eyebrow as the cold, damp air blew past her. "Little nippy out there?"

Chambers took a seat along the back wall. His shoulders hunched as he wrapped his arms around himself. A faint clicking sound could be heard coming from his mouth. "You're damn right it is," he said. "But it shouldn't be."

Leah settled in next to the nav station across from him, her eyes tracking Chambers's every move as he rubbed his arms. She scrunched her nose and asked, "Isn't it usually cold out here?"

"Well," Chambers conceded, "my boat doesn't venture too far from San Diego nowadays, but I really don't remember this area being this cold. It's like there's a type of death chill in the air."

Leah cocked her head to one side. "Death chill?"

Chambers smiled. "Yeah, it's what you'd feel if the Grim Reaper was standing nearby getting ready to shake your hand."

"Oh," said Leah.

A chill ran down her spine, forcing her to jump out of her chair.

Chambers cocked his head to one side. "Somethin' scare ya?"

Leah pressed her hand to the lower part of her back and felt a cold spot. The ship's bridge felt warm to her, but now she wondered if there was some merit to what Chambers had said. After all, it's not like there wasn't some shadow figure in here earlier, and who knows? Perhaps that's the way a Grim Reaper would appear? *Well, shit,* she thought. *There's another frightening image crawling around my head.*

"Just a muscle cramp, that's all," she said with her best million-dollar smile.

"Yeah, that sounds like some grade-A bullshit to me."

Leah sat back down and rubbed her left leg, hoping it wasn't obvious that it was shaking. "Right, and to quote my father, you can be a real ass sometimes."

Chambers raised his eyebrows and pointed a finger at himself. "Me?" he said with a wink as a sly grin overtook him.

Leah leaned toward him, her cheeks flushed. "Yes, you," she barked.

Chambers waved her off. "Well, am I wrong?"

Leah lowered her gaze. "No," she whispered. "I think being out here again is starting to wear on me."

Chambers nodded. "As it should. No one I've met has ever gone through a situation like yours and came out unscathed." Chambers paused momentarily, the playfulness in his face replaced by a hardened fighter. "But I can tell you one thing, it won't be like last time."

Leah looked back up at him. Tears had formed in the corner of her eyes. "You don't know that," she whispered.

Chambers shrugged. "True, we're venturing into the unknown, but not unprepared. And unlike the last time, you won't be alone."

Leah looked out the front window and saw a wall of fog moving toward them fast as if all of it was being directed solely at them. Little rain pelts echoed through the bridge as they splattered against the glass windshield. The once-calm ocean swelled as wave after wave struck their boat.

"How much farther is it?" Chambers asked as he joined her.

Leah looked down at the nav's screen and frowned. "You tell me."

Chambers leaned over and studied the glowing screen. His eyes darted to the front window, but all that could be seen was the dense fog surrounding them, illuminated by the deck lights. Although they could feel the water was getting rough.

"This is bad, isn't it?" she said.

"Potentially," he said as he slid into the helm's station. "As long as these waves don't get bigger, and we don't run her aground, we should be all right." Leah raised an eyebrow. "Run her aground?"

"There's a lighthouse on that island, right?" he asked, bypassing her question.

Leah shrugged. "Seems like there was."

"You recall if it was operational?"

Leah shrugged and pulled out the life jacket wedged into a side panel under her station. She gave him a nervous smile as she tossed it on and tightened the straps.

Chambers nodded, donned his life vest, and refocused his attention back outside to the onslaught of waves crashing off the ship's bow. The wind howled as its speed intensified, which gave way to horizontal raindrops that turned to ice the instant they made contact with the vessel.

A loud bang exploded underneath them. Leah instinctively gripped the handrail mounted to her station. Her voice trembled as she asked, "Did we run aground?"

Chambers didn't answer her. Instead, he scanned the various buttons laid out in front of him while maintaining a firm grip on the handrail beside him.

"There you are," he said as he pressed one of them.

The monitors mounted above them lit up with live camera feeds of the inside and outside of the ship. Leah gave a sigh of relief when she saw no water flooding the lower decks, but a lingering concern remained in the air—they were still in danger.

She maintained her firm grip on the handrail as the ship tilted to the left. It lingered there far too long for comfort, but luckily for them, the ship could upright itself. A flash of painfully bright light lit up the bridge, accompanied by what sounded like an explosion that left her ears ringing. Every hair on her felt like it was sticking straight out of her body, overtaken by a static charge. The lights and monitors flickered, and the ship's power momentarily dipped before returning to normal. That was the closest she had ever been to a lightning strike. A nanosecond later, she noticed the lightning had cut through the fog, exposing a massive wave rushing toward them.

Chambers glanced at her. "This is gonna be a fun one," he sneered.

Leah opened her mouth but found it difficult to form any words. More adrenaline flowed through her body as the rising water pushed her back in her chair. Another lightning bolt ripped through the air, striking somewhere behind the rising wave. The ocean's inky appearance lit up to a translucent pale green, momentarily revealing the dark mass of a gigantic sea creature larger than their vessel hidden in the wave.

"What the hell is that?" she shouted.

"A problem if this damn thing goes under," he shouted back. Chambers pushed the engines to the max. The ship shook, and the engines roared as it accelerated to the top of the wave and crashed through it.

The memory of her being held captive here flashed through her mind as they flew down the backside of the wave. Even at the darkest point of her captivity, when fear had a firm grip on her, she was never afraid that she would die. She knew her father was looking for her and would find her before it was too late. He was Metro's best detective at locating a missing person. Her throat tightened as a single tear formed in her eye. While he was able to rescue her, her father had paid the ultimate price.

She glanced back at Chambers, whose grin only widened as he made micro-adjustments to the steering and throttle. Even with him by her side, she felt all alone. There was no one to come looking for her this time. Only Chambers and the cold chill of death knew where to find her.

The ship shuddered as it smashed through a smaller wave. The hull groaned as the bow angled itself to the right. Chambers fought with the steering to get the old gal to straighten out, but it barely made a difference.

Suddenly, he pounded his fist on his side console. "Damn it," he shouted.

"What is it?" Leah asked.

"I've lost the steering!"

Leah's eyes widened. "Can you fix it?"

Chambers let out a huff. "Not likely, and not before another giant ass wave capsizes us."

The deck beneath their feet vibrated as a deep, metallic howl echoed up from below, as if something were trying to tear the ship apart. The Sovereign took another hard turn to the right, then jerked downward as it surged forward.

Chambers ran his fingers over the controls, pressing buttons in quick succession. "This isn't right."

"What's happening?" she asked.

Chambers scratched his head. "I think we've snagged something that's towing us."

Leah took a deep breath, watching the ship's bow cut through the subsiding waves. Chunks of ice skidded across the deck, colliding and shattering into smaller pieces before slipping back into the ocean through the holes in the side of the deck walls.

"Should there be ice out here?" she asked.

"No," Chambers barked.

Curious, she noticed that whatever storm they were in had dissipated, giving way to a black, star-filled sky over a now calm, endless ocean. It was easy to feel that something was pulling them, but where it was taking them was anyone's guess.

"What do we do now?" Leah asked.

Chambers fiddled with the ship's controls for a moment, then sank back into his chair, defeated. "I don't think there's anything we can do unless you fancy going for a swim."

"After you." Leah smiled.

She unconsciously pulled out her phone to call Logan for help, but as expected, she didn't have a signal. A part of her was relieved, knowing she wasn't seconds away from getting yelled at by her younger brother. Besides, it's not like he could stop whatever he was doing to rush out here to troll the ocean, calling out her name.

Chambers tapped her shoulder and pointed at a dark shape that seemed to materialize a mile or two in front of them. "Is that Shady Reef?"

Leah squinted, not sure what to make of it in the dark. At first pass, she expected to see lights emanating from the streets and buildings, but then again, no one was left to keep the lights on. She glanced at the nav unit, which had confirmed the landmass ahead was indeed Shady Reef.

"That's it," she said, tapping the screen.

"Figures," Chambers grumbled. "We're being towed right into the hands of those damn Knights of yours."

Leah raised her eyebrows. "You got a plan?"

"Nope," he said. "This is your shindig. I'm just here for backup."

"I'm assuming locking the doors and hiding until they leave us alone won't work."

Chambers cocked his head to one side. "You know them better than me."

"Right," she said as she tapped her toes. "I think it's a safe bet they'll have a welcome party waitin' for us when we get to shore."

Chambers rubbed his chin. "What I wouldn't give for a decent pair of night vision goggles."

Leah groaned as she covered her face with her hand. "Oh dammit, Logan has a pair he left behind. I should've snagged them before we left."

Chambers leaned forward and jiggled the lever to get the ship to turn. Nothing. "Well, it's too late to go back for it now."

Leah rolled her eyes at him and said, "Ha-ha."

"Just sayin'," he said, and went back to fiddling with the controls.

Leah leaned to her left side, resting her head on her hand as she propped her arm up on the chair's armrest. The island was much closer now, and parts of a dilapidated dock started to come into view. She didn't see any lighthouse nearby, so this could mean it burnt up in the fire from when Maeve and her father were here last time, or, more likely, they were in a different spot.

Chambers leaned forward, his eyes squinted. "You see this?"

Leah followed his gaze but didn't see anything out of the ordinary. She stood up and moved closer to him to get a better angle at what he saw. Silence fell between them until she figured out what Chambers was looking at. It appeared someone was watching them from the end of the dock. But she reasoned that in this poor lighting, it could easily be a bunch of garbage in a burlap sack.

"I guess that could be a person standing there," she said. "But it's hard to tell."

Chambers shook his head. "A person?" he asked. "That's a child wrapped up in a blanket shivering in the cold."

Seconds passed as the jagged shoreline of Shady Reef came into full view. Partially collapsed charred structures from the fire lined the shoreline. It was a grim reminder of how desperate the Blood Knights had been to lure her father and Maeve into their hands.

She turned her attention back to the figure and concluded that Chambers was right about the child. Judging by his round little face and frozen little cheeks poking through the blanket he had wrapped around him, she knew he could be no more than five at best.

"Where are the parents?" she asked.

"Gotta be gone. Knight or no Knight, no parent would let their kid play around a dock like that by themselves. Unless…"

"We're being set up," Leah said, finishing his sentence. "But why? It's not like we can control where we're going."

"Unless someone else is pulling the strings, and at this speed, we're gonna knock him into the harbor when we crash into the dock."

"We're crashing?"

"More like a hard bump, but regardless, that kid is going for a dip if we can't slow this thing down."

Leah opened the starboard door behind Chambers.

He jerked his head around to look at her. "What the hell are you doing?"

"If he goes in, I'll be right behind him."

"Do you know how dangerous that will be? Especially if that dock collapses?"

Leah looked at the child. A wave of adrenaline surged through her body as the reality of her mind went to battle with the emotions of her heart. She wiped her eyes, still confused at what she was seeing as the child waved at them.

"It can't be," she whispered.

"What?" Chambers hollered.

"I don't know how, but that's Lucas," she said, taking the steps down to the lower deck. "Logan's twin brother!"

Her heart raced as she leaned against the deck railing, a genuine smile spreading across her face as she waved back at him. Of all the impossibilities today, it was really him standing there. The world around her seemed more vivid, as if time had slowed down just for her, giving her the chance to savor every moment of this unexpected reunion.

The ship vibrated momentarily, and the sounds of heavy cables clanked below deck. Chambers's voice boomed over the loudspeaker, "The ship's controls are working again."

But Leah didn't respond. Her focus was entirely on Lucas, who still stood at the edge of the dock, his eyes locked on hers as he clutched his blanket tightly around himself.

Leah cupped her hands around her mouth and called out, "Step back, Lucas! You don't want to fall!"

In response, Lucas squatted low, then jumped straight up into the air. He kept bouncing for joy like this several more times as his carefree giggles echoed through the night.

Leah waved her hands frantically, shouting, "No! No! No!"

Lucas leaned forward, wiggling like an excited puppy about to receive a treat as the boat drew closer.

Leah pushed aside the disturbing fact that she could get wedged between the ship and the dock as she leaped over the railing. Her feet clipped the edge and sent her face-forward into the dock. She thrust her hands out and landed with a thud.

"What the hell are you doing?" Chambers yelled over the loudspeaker.

She had one of Logan's zingers lined up to fire back at him but paused when Lucas sprinted past her up the dock. As she bit her lip, she forced herself up and chased after him. She could faintly hear Chambers's voice as he yelled, "Wait for me!"

No time, she thought as she maintained pursuit. Lucas was within arm's reach as he zipped up the gangway, to the pier, and around the corner of a burned-out building. Leah rounded the corner far too fast to stop herself as she crashed into a Spanish teenager dressed in a black suit and tie.

Blinded by fear, she jumped to her feet, ready to take off, not noticing he had a hold of her wrist.

He yanked her back down and laughed. "Well, well, well," he said in a familiar voice. "Who says the gods don't answer prayers anymore."

Her throat tightened as she saw Edgardo, the guy who killed her boyfriend, Mark, after he'd pulled her into a van and sent her to this place. She swung her body around and went to kick him square in the face. Edgardo let her go and rolled out of the way. He hopped to his feet and rubbed the side of his cheek where her foot grazed him.

"When did you get all feisty?" He chuckled.

"Where's Lucas?" she asked as she got to her feet.

"Kid's dead, mi amor."

"No," she glared back at him. "He was just here!"

Edgardo shook his head. "New Orleans must've turned you loco."

Leah spat at him. "Go to hell."

"Lock her up with the other," he said with a snap of a finger.

Leah scooted back, but it was too late. Dozens of Blood Knights dressed in their crimson robes appeared out of nowhere. All she could do now was kick and scream as they dragged her off to some unknown destination.

Chapter 16

United Citadel Field Unit
BRAVO SUBUNIT

CJ sat on the bed in Nieminen's empty room, staring at his wrist computer. His right leg bounced up and down while he wrestled with the urge to message Nieminen for an update. He had left almost an hour ago with nothing but radio silence so far. That was the one thing he liked about working Recon. Usually, you were the first man in and out, which allowed you to kick back and relax since, for the most part, the dangerous stuff was over for you. None of this waiting around to see what will happen next, or, better yet, a last-second change to the whole operation.

They were both hopeful that Nieminen's little black box could tap into the hotel's security system, but the device kept getting booted out. Nieminen postured there were hundreds of thousands of fake nodes on the security system shutting down with each connection he made. One or two shutdowns would probably go unnoticed, but any more would attract attention, letting the security staff know someone was trying to hack in.

CJ got up and checked the peephole again for good measure. It appeared just as empty and dull as it did five minutes ago when he checked it the last time, which he conceded was better than seeing armed men pooling out of the stairwell across from him. At the very least, it gave him something to do rather than sit around and wait. He could always give Logan a call to see how his stalking was going, but past experience told him it would be best to wait for him to check in first. After all, he didn't need a repeat of his call ringing Logan's phone and blowing his cover because he forgot to direct all incoming calls to his earpiece.

Startled, he bumped his nose on the door when his wrist computer buzzed. *Good thing no one was around to see or hear that.* His fingers danced over the screen as he pulled up the message he just received. He grimaced when he saw it wasn't from Nieminen, but Quint. He sat back down on the bed and flipped through all the images Quint had uploaded. It turned out he was able to snag a few pictures of the arriving guest, but he didn't recognize any of them. A few taps later, and he had the photos processed through his face ID analyzer. His head drooped when everything came back as unclear or no ID found. However, he probably shouldn't have been too surprised, since it was only recently that even he became aware of the Mystic Knights.

CJ rolled his head from shoulder to shoulder, accompanied by several large cracks. With a soft groan, he got to his feet and meandered toward the window to peer into the city. Something he had been avoiding with his fixation on the door. Lines of black cars were still pulling up, letting out their guests dressed all in white. At least there was some good news. They most likely wouldn't start their little convention until *all* the guests had arrived.

His ear patch hissed as Nieminen's voice came on the line. "I'm in their security system."

"What the hell took you so long?" asked CJ.

"Well, the easy part was sawing through the metal bars situated between the floors without anyone hearing to get into their secure sector. The rest required more patience and stealth tactics to get a hardline into their main computer system."

"You had to go up and through the ceiling?"

"Affirmative. One guard was stationed near their entrance. I highly doubt I would be able to talk my way past him."

"What about lasers or other silent alarms? You could have tripped."

"Unlikely. This is a hotel, not a bank or government facility."

CJ ran his hand through his hair as he turned away from the window. "All right, I'll take your word for it. What are you able to see?"

"If you were hoping to spy on the convention this way, I'm afraid to report that no cameras show any sort of said activities. However, the guests appear to be heading to the suite on the 70th floor. According to the schematics and brochure, an open-air garden on the roof of the central tower connects to the suite and would have ample room to accommodate a hundred or so guests."

"Righteous suite," said CJ. "Hence why there are no cameras out there because it's considered part of their room."

"I would concur."

"Which means one of us is gonna have to get up there if we want to find out what they're up to."

A short pause followed, which prompted CJ to ask, "You still there?"

"This is peculiar," said Nieminen.

"What?" asked CJ.

"The woman at the front desk has altered her appearance and is dressed as a server."

"Altered it how?"

"She has pulled her hair back and is wearing glasses."

CJ's face went blank. "That's it?"

"You don't find it odd that someone working the front desk would change to be a server?"

CJ shrugged. "Maybe her shift was over, and she wanted some overtime?"

"That is one possibility, but the way she keeps looking around behind her tells me it would be wise to keep an eye on her."

"Fine, whatever," said CJ. "Now, how do we go about crashing their little soiree? Could I get a room within the main tower, overlooking the garden?"

"The probability of them being reserved for the Knights is extraordinarily high."

CJ groaned. "How about you check the hotel database and find a room that isn't."

"I cannot."

"What! Why?" asked CJ. "I thought you were in their system."

"I'm in their system, yes, but I don't have access to their system. I can only observe their camera feeds for now."

"Great, and if I get caught, what's the backup plan?"

"Uncertain, but Quint is at the pool deck on top of the lower tower getting ready to launch a drone."

"Wouldn't they see or hear it?"

"It's possible, but they should be focused on the event. If Quint keeps his distance, he should be able to film it while you record it with your sound amplifier. When this is all over, we can merge the two if that is still an option."

"Wunderbar," said CJ, not too keen on the 'still an option' part. But having either video or sound would be ideal over nothing.

Nieminen continued, "Have you devised an exit strategy?"

CJ paused for a moment. He knew of one way that should work, but it was risky, and had the potential to injure innocent bystanders. If he had more time and help from his teammates, he knew they could find another way, but that wasn't an option.

"I think," CJ hesitated, "I think we need to set some fires."

"Simulated fire smoke or a real fire?" Nieminen asked.

"I'm afraid it's gonna need to be the real deal. In all the confusion, I should be able to blend in with the evacuating crowds."

"Fires and crowds can be—" He paused. "Unpredictable and deadly. Are you sure this is how you want to proceed?"

CJ sighed as he double-checked the contents of his pack. "The unpredictable part is what I'm counting on."

"We'll call that exit strategy one."

"Fine," said CJ. "Now, where am I going?"

"I might have a room for you. I'll need just a minute to confirm."

"Fine," CJ said as he slung his pack over his shoulder.

"There is a couple dressed all in white leaving room 7208."

"That's a long way up," said CJ. "I'm gonna be relying on you to guide me."

"No doubt, now get going. There is an unoccupied service elevator located within the custodial room on this level."

CJ exited the room and eased the door closed so he wouldn't attract any attention. He glanced at his wrist computer and saw it was five minutes till midnight. *Man, we're cutting this one close.*

CJ casually strolled the hall, noting where the cameras were in the ceilings and any emergency exits. It was a safe bet they repeated that pattern across all the floors. So far, he noticed there seemed to be a camera every four rooms, which could work to his advantage.

They would have to have a massive team to monitor all of them, which was highly unlikely since, as Nieminen put it, this is just a hotel. However, facial recognition tech was gaining some traction around this time frame, and once identified, they could easily keep tabs on him. Still, he reasoned it couldn't be anywhere close to the accuracy of that type of technology in his timeline. *Better safe than sorry*, he thought, pulling out his phone to give him something to look at so it wasn't obvious he was trying to evade showing his face.

Nieminen spoke up, "Pick up the pace. It appears there are several teams of questionable hotel staff members doing a floor-by-floor sweep. Yours is up next."

"Thanks for the timely heads-up," CJ whispered.

Halfway down the long hallway, he found an unmarked door with a single card reader granting access. He raised his arm and placed his wrist computer nearby, hoping it could find the proper frequency to unlock the door. This process was always a wild card since it only worked part of the time where he's from, but the odds had to be higher now in this timeline. Or at least he hoped while he waited for the locks to click open.

Thankfully, it took less than thirty seconds for the door to click, which was just enough time for his mind to wonder what he would find behind this door. After all, Nieminen only mentioned that the service elevator was empty.

Not far away, he heard the familiar sound of the elevator doors opening on his floor. *Time to see what's behind door number one.* He gripped the handle, opened the door wide enough to slip in, and gently closed it behind him. He nearly tumbled backward as the dimly lit room automatically adjusted to full brightness. Seeing he was alone, he leaned forward and rested his hands on his knees, taking a moment to catch his breath.

Glancing up, he saw the gray doors to the elevator in the middle of the room. Various cleaning products lined the walls, and somebody had shoved their wayward cart haphazardly in the middle of the room.

"I'm in the cleaning room by the elevator. Am I clear to proceed?" CJ asked. Then he tapped the elevator button, not waiting for a response.

"The elevator is clear, but I should warn you from the camera feed it was obvious that you broke into that room."

"Figured as much. Did anyone else notice?"

"Uncertain. However, they have not changed their pattern in the way they are searching the floors."

"Great," he said through a clenched jaw.

CJ slipped through the elevator doors while they were still opening and smashed the closed-door button, followed by the 72th-floor button. The doors rolled closed just in time for him to see the closet door open through the narrow slit between them. CJ braced himself in the elevator's corner as it rose far faster than expected.

He took a deep breath, trying not to let his anger get the best of him. "Why didn't you tell me someone was right behind me?" he spat out.

"My apologies. I can only watch so many feeds simultaneously, and something else caught my eye."

"Better not be some pretty gal in a short skirt again," he said as the elevator doors slid open.

"Not exactly. Your friend from the front desk is two floors above you and appears to be entering guest's rooms using a master key card. She is definitely doing her own private investigation."

"Potential ally?"

"Can't say for certain, but there are two possibilities. One is she is working for someone who has taken an interest in the Knights. The second would be a personal vendetta. Regardless, your pathway is clear to room 7208."

"On my way," said CJ.

He cracked the doorway ever so slightly to peer up and down the hallway to verify Nieminen was correct. Other than overpriced artwork and elegant gray carpet, it appeared vacant. He did his best to remain calm and collected as he made his way down the hall. His feet felt light as a feather, but truth be told, his stomach was in the middle of a crisis as it pondered which way would be the fastest to evacuate its contents. He reasoned that it was just a side effect of eating that sandwich from the gas station they stopped at while tailing Phillip. But he knew the real reason was that his nerves were on the verge of burnout. It had been so long since he had any sense of normalcy in his life that he wondered if he would even recognize it if it ever came around again.

CJ glanced over his shoulder as he used his wrist computer to unlock the door. He slipped inside the dark room, closed the door, and engaged the deadbolt. After all, he didn't want anyone sneaking up on him. With that in mind, he went to work canvassing the hotel room, which turned out to be several rooms that would put many luxury apartments to shame. All the hotels he'd stayed at consisted of two beds facing a TV with a bathroom tucked to one side. This little suite had floor-to-ceiling windows and a separate bedroom large enough to accommodate a full basketball court, with a sitting room, separate kitchen, and a dining room.

He peered out from the sitting room into the rooftop garden. On the far end, they had erected a plywood set painted in hues of purple and little specks of glitter that appeared to be stars that served as a backdrop to their makeshift stage that was set three feet off the ground. *It'd be a shame if the wind hit that just right,* CJ thought.

Clad in pure white clothing, which CJ figured was way too tight for comfort, were six figures performing some sort of play or opera he didn't recognize. Guests were seated at the many round banquet tables with white tablecloths lit by candles nestled amongst the maze of plant life. Servers walked amongst them, filling their wine glasses as they watched the show.

CJ pulled out his sound amplifier and pointed it at the stage to record everything. The hairs on the back of his neck stood up, and he took a few steps away from the window. Something was off, and it occurred to him that he forgot to do something in his rush to get set up and situated. In an instant, he had dropped to his knee, slung his pack around to the front, and deafly pulled out his thermal camera. With the camera pointed out in front of him, he expected to see a Shadow Knight come flying at him.

Only darkness greeted him and not much else. He glanced back at the stage and saw the opera still going—a good thing too, since it gave him a little time to do a proper search of the suite with the thermal cam. Satisfied that his search came up empty, he took up his perch again near the window, but far enough behind the curtain that the Knights below shouldn't be able to see him.

The six performers stood in a line, spaced evenly with their hands reaching up toward the heavens. The lights flickered out, leaving a thick reddish line projected above them, flying across the backdrop. New spotlights fired up one by one, lighting them in different colors. On the far left, one performer was bathed in deep purple. Beside him, another was shrouded in the darkest gray that was still visible. Then came a bright yellow, followed by a blue, red, and white performer.

The yellow performer clutched his throat and contorted his body as if he was poisoned and fell to the floor, only to have another performer jump out from behind and take up the yellow spotlight. The blue performer went to strike the red one, but Red caught Blue's fist midair as he thrust it toward him. He twisted Blue's arm until he knelt, their colors vacillating between the two. Blue pried Red's hand off his neck.

I bet that red guy is supposed to be a Blood Knight, CJ thought.

The Blood Knight then pointed a finger at Blue, followed by a fire that shot up from the ground in front of Blue—then he was gone. The white performer cowered in fear as the Blood Knight grabbed them by the arm, then paused and glanced behind him as the new yellow figure's light flickered out. The Blood Knight tightened his grip on the white performer's throat until their light extinguished. Kneeling over White, Red grabbed a necklace that wasn't visible on White until now.

Oh no, he thought. *This must be their take on what happened to Jacob Wallace's neighbor when she met up with him in that story Nieminen and Quint told him back in Nebraska. That would mean she was a Knight, but why would he kill her?*

The Blood Knight sang out in an unknown language, which prompted the guests to raise their hands in the air as they chanted a rhythmic phrase back at him. Then he leaped to the center of the stage like a ballerina, where a smoke effect shot up from the floor. He reached into it and gracefully lifted a woman dressed in a long, flowing white gown out of it.

CJ squinted to view her face better, then frowned when he noticed she wore an elaborate white masquerade mask.

"Quint, you catchin' this with the drone?" CJ asked.

"Not sure," he said. "I'm getting a lot of interference. They must have a device that's either jamming or overloading the network."

"Can't you move to a higher frequency?"

"Tried that, and let's just say it made things unstable."

Nieminen spoke up, "Did you lose the drone?"

"Nah, it's coming back down," he paused. "Hey, ah, this security guy I was tailing earlier has entered the pool deck and is walking toward me."

"I would advise you to find an exit," said Nieminen.

"Already making my way towards the stairs," whispered Quint. "I'll find someplace to hunker down until you need me. We can snag the drone later from the rendezvous point."

"Understood," said Nieminen.

"Ah, guys," said CJ as he saw the opera had stopped as the woman addressed the crowd in English. "I think our special guest has arrived."

"Do you recognize her?" Nieminen asked.

"No, she's wearing a stupid mask."

"Understood," said Nieminen. "Continue to record her."

"Copy that," CJ said, not wanting to point out that's what he had been doing the whole time.

The woman on stage was probably very high up, if not the leader of the Mystic Knights. So far, she had mentioned nothing that would denote such, but why would she if she was amongst her sect? She went on about how the cosmos were lining up, along with a bunch of other nonsense that made it easy for CJ to peg her as a loon. In a different time, he could easily see her standing on the sidewalk holding up her THE END IS NIGH sign.

After she finished with her grandstanding, her tone changed. She stood in the center of the stage, hands on her hips, her body rigid. The remaining performers bowed to her as they scampered off backstage. She redirected her gaze not toward anyone specifically, but CJ got the sense that she was glaring at him.

"Above all else, we demand order out of chaos, do we not?" she asked in a lower tone.

Her guests raised their wine glasses and then took a sip. She glanced behind her as two performers carried out one of the servers, dragging her feet behind them. A surge of energy swept through CJ as he recognized who they had captured.

"They got Madison," he spat out.

"Who?" asked Quint.

"The gal that was workin' the front desk," said CJ.

"Strange," said Nieminen. "I somehow failed to witness her abduction."

Quint spoke up, "She probably got snagged from an unmonitored location."

"I'm in an unmonitored location too," said CJ. "Am I still safe?"

"I'm not detecting any dangers at your current location," said Nieminen.

Satisfied it was still only him alone in the hotel room, CJ tossed the thermal camera back into his pack and threw it over his shoulder, itchin' to make a break for it. A wave of relief washed over him as he smiled at the fact it was possible the Knights had been looking for her all this time. However, that didn't explain why there were armed men outside his hotel room. *Gotta stay sharp.*

He kept his sound amplifier pointed at the Mystic Knight who seemed to be in no hurry to wrap it up as she continued berating Madison. Going off her wild movements and the polite applauses from the crowd, she was thriving off of it.

The Mystic Knight turned to face her guest and pointed an accusatory finger at Madison. "If this is the best operative Ordo Veritatis et Iustitiae can turn out, then we are in no danger of failure to achieve our goals."

CJ's ears perked up. "Does Ordo Veritatis et Iustitiae mean anything to you two?"

"It's Latin for 'order of truth and justice,' but I fail to see the connection," said Nieminen.

"Hmm," said CJ. "Sounds like that's the organization Madison works for."

"Never heard of 'em," said Quint.

The Mystic Knight continued, "As we speak right now, I know she is not acting alone."

CJ tried to swallow as his throat tightened.

"We've been tagged," Nieminen blurted out. "Proceed with exit strategy one."

"Copy," said Quint.

CJ watched in horror as the Mystic Knight pointed her finger at him. "The last remnants of the Citadel are here with us now."

CJ turned to run like hell as all the lights in the hotel room sprang to life. He threw his sound amplifier into his pack as he dashed through the front door, not bothering to check if the coast was clear.

"Which way?" CJ asked.

"I've lost my feed," said Nieminen. "Take your best guess."

"Dammit," whispered CJ.

He rounded the corner and saw a young hotel staffer walking his way. The staffer went to pull something out of his jacket, but CJ was already ahead of him. He pointed his wrist computer at him and fired off the taser. The two probes caught him in the cheek and neck. The kid stiffened, fell backward, and smacked his head on the edge of a planter box as he went down.

Quint's voice boomed over the line. "Y'all better hold on to somethin'."

"Wha—" CJ started to say.

The whole floor shook as a loud boom and shattered glass echoed throughout the building. CJ didn't waste any time as he ran through the emergency exit and back inside the stairwell.

"What the hell did you do?" CJ tried to yell over the fire alarms as he took the stairs two at a time.

"Relax," Quint hollered back. "It's just a small fire in the kitchen."

CJ didn't say anything as he ran into a small group of confused hotel guests bumbling into the stairwell. He figured he had to be somewhere around the sixtieth floor as he turned back to see if any

Knights had entered the stairwell. For once, luck was on his side, but he knew it was bound to run out.

He slowed his pace down to let the small group in front of him get ahead. When they were out of sight, he pulled off his shirt and wrist computer, tossed them in his bag and ruffled up his hair, hoping it would help him pass as someone who had just ran out of their room. More guests filled in behind with vicious complaints about taking the stairs since the elevators were non-operational.

It all seemed fairly routine until the smell of smoke wafted into the stairwell. The feeling of dread and panic became palpable as they continued their way down, with a few tripping over their feet. A couple of newlyweds got into a fight as she tried to turn back to collect some valuables. This little scuffle halted their progress for a moment until an older woman talked them out of it. He was actually surprised that the crowd was able to more or less maintain order.

CJ kept his head on a swivel as they reached the thirtieth floor. More hotel guests poured into the stairway, hauling their luggage, which made it difficult for them to continue at a reasonable pace. He glanced over his shoulder and nearly jumped out of his skin when he saw the hotel staffer he tased, hand placed over his forehead and pushing through the crowd with a couple of well-built men dressed in white suits behind him.

His pulse shot up as he fought to remain calm. His heart was screaming for him to run, but he pushed it aside as he focused on putting one foot in front of the other. He slipped past a man holding his small child as he continued down the flight of stairs. His mind raced as he devised new exit strategies, unsure if he was already a fish in a barrel. His ears perked up when he heard someone getting upset with the Knights pushing through the crowd. He reasoned they could only be ten or so steps behind him. Far too close.

"I need another diversion," he whispered.

"What floor you on?" asked Quint.

CJ's eyes darted around until he saw the sign posted near an exit. "Eleven."

"Close enough." Quint chuckled.

"Great," CJ whispered. "You sound just like your brother."

A loud bang sent a shock wave through the stairwell that sent the dust flying into the air like a weak smoke bomb, followed by screams of terror. The cramped quarters turned into a violent mosh pit as they tossed civility out the window in exchange for mass chaos. CJ surged forward, doing his best not to knock anyone over. The noise was deafening inside, but he could hear someone yelling, "There he is!"

CJ gritted his teeth as he slipped past more groups of people. The idea they were close enough now that they could somehow make him out didn't sit well with him.

"What the hell was that?" he whispered. "A concussion pack?"

"Hey, cut me some slack," said Quint. "I'm working with what I got."

"Yeah, well, you got the crowd movin' all right, but the Knights are right behind me."

Nieminen spoke up, "I'll take care of them. You need to focus on getting outside. There's a red car parked on the first floor in the building across the street to your left. It'll be the first one you see."

CJ glanced back and saw that Nieminen was true to his word. The Knights were no longer behind him.

"How did you do that?"

"Now is not the time. Get moving," said Nieminen.

CJ followed the crowd out into the lobby. Several hotel employees stood to the sides, forming an aisle, and waved for them to exit through a side door as firefighters poured in through the main doors.

The cold air hit his face as he exited the hotel. Fire trucks, ambulances, and police cars filled the street. Their flashing lights bathed the area in hues of red and blue with bits of white lights. *These colors seem all too familiar.*

An officer stopped him and asked, "Do you need any medical assistance?"

CJ shook his head. "No, I'm all right."

The officer patted him on the shoulder. "Good, I'll need you to wait over there," he said, pointing to a spot across the street they had set up for evacuees. "A detective should be by shortly to ask you some questions about the explosion."

Great, CJ thought. *They think someone planted a bomb in the building.*

Logan's voice rang through on a private channel. "Are you done screwing around over there?"

"Yeah, it's pretty much a wrap."

"About damn time. Phillip is catching a flight to Egypt. You can join us if you can get here in forty-five minutes."

"Strange. You sure this isn't another wild goose chase or a bird leading us away from their nest?"

Logan groaned. "How about you ask him when you get here, Mr. Recon."

"On my way." He sighed as he took one last glance at the chaos left in his wake before slipping away.

Chapter 17

United Citadel Field Unit
☆Operations Division☆

Leah struggled to get up, but it was no use. She couldn't see where she was with the cloth bag thrown over her head. The musty smell of the burlap pillow under her head, and the restraints holding her down, were a strong clue she was back at that cruddy hospital, where the Knights had held her captive six months ago.

Back then, days and nights blurred together, but she was sure she had been here for at least two days before they transferred her to New Orleans. At least this time, it was quiet—no muffled voices from outside debating what to do with her. She tugged at her arm restraints again. Frustration mixed with anxiety surged in her as they held firm, but that could wait. For now, her top priority was to somehow get that stifling bag off her face. Headbanging seemed to be working, but she couldn't get it past her chain. At this rate, she figured it'd be quicker to chew through the damn thing.

She froze, holding her breath as the sound of footsteps echoed down the hall. A brief thought surfaced. *If I pretend to be out cold, they will leave me alone,* but prior experience told her otherwise. Each click of the heel raised her pulse little by little. The sweat on her forehead merged with the cloth bag, making it harder to breathe.

At this point, it didn't matter what they planned to do with her. Either she suffocated here or die by their hands. She reasoned that with them, she still had a slim chance of getting away. At the very least, she would have a few more minutes to enjoy what little life she had left.

She screamed out, "Help!"

The door slammed open with a loud bang. Leah shook her head, hyperventilating until the sack was ripped off. Two of Edgardo's goons stood in the doorway. The bigger one had his back toward Leah with his arms wrapped around a bloodied Chambers as he dragged him in.

All she dared to do was watch them as they propped Chambers up in the far corner of the room. His face was bruised and puffy from what had to have been a barrage of fists they hurled at him. Thankfully, he was still breathing, but she also found it odd they didn't just kill him. Why bother to keep him around unless he still had some use left?

The other question burning in her brain was, *Why drop him off in here with me?* The best they could do in their current state was talk to each other, which was probably what they wanted. An easy way to extract factual information, since people tend to lie under duress in hopes they say the magical words that buy them some peace, no matter how short-lived that peace is.

She could only think of one way to find out what they were up to. A little trick CJ had taught her is to treat people like they're lower class, and they'll start running their mouths to prove otherwise.

"I don't recall asking for a roommate during my stay here," she snipped.

The short one holding the cloth bag leaned over her. His large, bulging eyes burned with hatred as he glared at her with his hand curled up into a meaty fist.

"You'd best keep your trap shut if you don't want one of these across your mouth." The pungent stench of rotten fish clung to his breath, while bits of saliva danced around his lips as he spoke.

"Oh, I'm sure Edgardo would be thrilled to find out the hired help had busted my lip."

"Lady," he said, "we ain't no hired help. We are true believers in the cause."

"No truer words spoken from a useful idiot. Now, get this lump of meat out of here."

Leah knew she had struck a chord in him when he landed a punch next to her head that formed a nice indentation in her pillow. A little clue that told her he wasn't above intimidating her, but probably wouldn't physically attack her either.

"Keep it up, and this will go back on," he said as he waved the cloth bag over her face.

Leah unconsciously shook her head.

"Yeah," he said. "That's what I thought."

He slammed the door as they left, not bothering to lock it. Another clue they're up to something. Leah let her head drop back down on the pillow with the word *pillow* not being used in the strictest definition. Still, the itchy burlap sack filled with what had to be lawn clippings was a smidge better than nothing.

"Chambers, you awake?" she whispered.

He made some grumbling noises, then settled on "No."

"What happened?"

Chambers raised his head and rested it in the corner behind him. "They came out of the water. Fifty of them or so, carrying their knives in their teeth mere seconds after you took off."

"What?" she whispered. "That can't be. We would have seen them jumping in. No one can hold their breath that long unless they have some scuba gear or something like that."

Chambers winced as he prodded part of his cheek. "Didn't see any scuba gear, but they could've ditched it."

Leah's voice cracked, "Sorry I left you back there."

Chambers sighed. "Don't think it would have made a difference. They were on me faster than a pack of starving wolves."

"Oh."

"There is somethin' else, though, that's off about all of this," he said, getting to his feet.

"Besides them not locking the door?"

Chambers joined her at the side of the bed and went to work to undo all the restraints. "That, and why I'm able to do this."

"Maybe they forgot to tie you up?" she asked, but knew that wasn't the case.

Chambers shook his head. "From all I've heard about these fanatics, it doesn't sound like a mistake they would make."

"You're right," she said as she rubbed her wrist. "They're trying to guide us into doing somethin' for 'em."

"Yep. Like leading a trail of breadcrumbs, 'cept I don't know who's droppin' and who's followin'."

Leah tapped her bottom lip. "I wonder," she paused. "I wonder if we caught them off guard."

"That's not the impression I got."

"No, but it's the one I got. Edgardo wasn't expecting me to run into him. I'm bettin' they were in the middle of somethin' when our boat pulled up."

Chambers flung Leah's last ankle restraint off. It clanged off the metal frame and echoed down the hall. They held their breath as they expected someone to barge in, but only silence greeted them.

"You know," he said. "I think I'm gonna put my money on them not knowing why we are here."

"Seems like a safe bet. I'm sure they're watching us right now. Waiting to see what we're gonna say or do."

Chambers peeked his head out the door. The dilapidated hallway showed no signs of life. He glanced back at Leah. "So what's the plan?"

"Well, we can always wait to see who makes a move first."

"And if their first move is to put a bullet in our heads, I'd rather not wait around to find out."

Leah got to her feet and peered through the cracks in the boarded window. Much of the town had been reduced to ash and rubble, but a few brick buildings remained. She also couldn't see anyone, but that didn't mean there wasn't anyone out there. On the contrary, she knew Knights were hiding out there, eager to report her activities back to Edgardo.

"I guess we play their game until we figure something out."

Chambers leaned in and whispered in her ear, "So where's this research we're lookin' for?"

"Later," she said. *Much later, when I'm certain we're out of earshot of the Knights.*

Leah pushed past him and stood in the hallway. The one light bulb left flickered above what was once a nurse's station. Mold covered the pale green, moist walls. Layers of dust coated the floor, with the Knight's footprints making it clear which direction they took.

Leah took off in the opposite direction down the dark corridor. She reasoned there had to be an emergency exit somewhere around here that would take them down to the ground floor. Each step they took plunged them deeper into darkness. She reached for her phone, forgetting the Knights had stripped them of their possessions.

She wondered if this was what the Knights wanted. Them bumping around in the dark would add some excitement to the Knight's hunt.

Chambers placed his hand on her shoulder. "You know where you're going?"

"Away from them," she said. "You wouldn't have any supplies on you, like a flashlight?"

"Nope," he whispered. "I stashed what I could on the boat. At least this way, I know where they are rather than guessing where they tossed them."

Leah opened a door, letting a trickle of pale light from the room fill the hallway. Not far away, she spotted a faded green sign caked in grime above another door.

"There's our way out," she said, pointing at the EXIT sign.

Down the flight of stairs, they found two exits. One led back inside the hospital, and the other, with a broken window in the door, led outside. Leah held a finger up to her mouth. On the other side of the door, she heard faint voices echoing down another hallway. She pressed her ear up against the door.

"I don't care what he thinks," echoed a deep voice that sounded like the short Knight she'd taunted in her cell. "He's only in charge because there ain't no one else left."

A female voice said, "I'd watch my mouth if I were you. Mathias hand-picked him himself to be his apprentice."

Another man with a velvety voice said, "Those Shadow Knights are sneaky bastards."

A loud boom reverberated down the hall. Leah reasoned someone must've flipped a table over.

"That's the entire point I'm trying to make!" the shorter Knight yelled. "This is *our* stronghold. He has his own in the old country."

Chambers mouthed to Leah the word "Stronghold?"

Leah shrugged her shoulders.

The man with the velvet voice said, "Let's go for a walk. Jürgen and Malia can keep an eye on them."

"No," said the shorter Knight. "I'm in charge of this facility. If they escape, it's my head."

A new voice that was probably Jürgen's said, "I worked that little cop over pretty good. He's not getting up anytime soon."

"Yeah," said the female Leah assumed was Malia. "We could hear the thuds way down here when you dragged him up those stairs."

Chambers rubbed his lower back. "So that's why I'm sore all over," he whispered.

"Go clear your head," said Malia. "Jürgen will go and check on them."

"He's gonna see our footprints," Leah whispered.

Chambers nodded. "Time to move out."

He followed Leah as she slipped through the broken window. The door would have been much easier, but she didn't want to risk setting off an alarm if the door had one. Across from them sat some traditional Japanese buildings that could double as homes or businesses. A wooden deck ran between them, with only minor smoke damage on the white outer walls. The second floor boasted a large swooping roof with blue ceramic tiles and gold trim.

"This way," Leah whispered as she trotted off to the building on the left.

She eased the door open and took a step inside. Broken-up furniture lined the far side of the room, and severe water damage was present. Whatever the ceiling was made up of was long gone, giving way to crossbeams holding up rotten particle boards that made up the upstairs floors. The stench of mildew mixed with decay hung thick in the air. Visible particles, probably toxic, shimmered as they floated by.

Leah pulled her shirt up over her nose. "This building should be condemned."

"I think it is," said Chambers. "They would have to be extra stupid to follow us in here."

"Considering what happened to my father when he was here, they sound more like the burning type."

"Right. We should get moving," he said. "Where's this super-secret research at?"

"Right before I was moved, Rose whispered in my ear that her research lies in the heart of the Acolyte."

"Okay, I'll stop you right here. Why tell you any of this?"

"I can only gather that she was working on something, and if anything happened to her, which sounds like it did, I could finish what she started."

"Seems like a lot to put on some stranger's shoulders."

"Desperate measures call for desperate actions," Leah retorted. "Besides, I don't think there was anyone here she could truly trust."

"All right," said Chambers. "I'll buy this shit for now. So, where's this heart of the Acolyte?"

"I think my father found it with Maeve. In her write-up, she said there was this chamber called the pool of the Acolyte in that factory on the other side of the island."

"Pool sure doesn't sound like heart to me," he scoffed.

"No, but they dragged Logan to another pool in New Orleans to turn him into an Acolyte. Sounds like you could call it the heart of the operation to me."

"Fine," he grimaced. "It's better than nothing. Let's get going."

Leah's heart skipped a beat when they entered the back room, which led out to the alleyway. Someone had left a message in giant letters scrawled out in old blood, *Die Ren Die*, on the wall.

"Ren someone you know?" asked Chambers.

Leah shook her head.

"Hmm," he said. "Must've been a man of the people."

Leah cracked the back door open, checking the angles for any danger. Satisfied she didn't see any, she stepped outside. Charred buildings lined the dirt road, with many of them collapsed in on themselves. On the plus side, she could see several blocks in front of her, but that meant anyone hiding could see her as well.

"We need to keep moving," she said.

Before Chambers could respond, she had swung her leg over a charred beam that used to be the bottom of a window. She took care with each step, making sure not to make any noise or, worse yet, trip and fall. Now was not the time to be limping around the island or leaving a trail of blood for them to follow.

It was slow going, but after an hour, they made it near the edge of what remained of Shady Reef's downtown area. Only suburban scrawl lay before them, and then just a quick hop, skip, and a jump to the factory. Still, it seemed odd that they hadn't seen Knights on their way. When Maeve and her father were out here, it sounded like the place was crawling with Blood Knights. And Chambers had said something like fifty of them came out of the water to nab him. So, where were they?

"Too bad we don't have any weapons," said Chambers.

"Eh, with how things are going, I'm starting to think we may not need any."

"Which means either we are damn good at evading them, or they're sitting back and laughing at us."

Leah smiled. "If Logan was here, he would go with the second option.

"And that's another thing I'm having a hard time believing."

Leah raised an eyebrow. "What part?"

"Logan being from the future."

"Yeah, I get that," she said. "But, as CJ likes to point out, *a* future. Not *the* future."

"Uh-huh, and how would he know it's 'a' and not 'the' future?"

"Probably because his ego told him so, and everyone else is just placating him."

Chambers quietly laughed. "That's the one thing that actually makes sense."

"Now, the confusing part," she smiled. "Apparently, he seems to think you can only go forward in your timeline without causing a paradox. Moving backward would force the universe to correct itself by forming a 'pocket' universe or new dimension to avoid some sort of catastrophe."

Chambers blinked a couple of times, then wiped his forehead. "This is giving me a headache."

"I know the feeling." Leah nodded, then made her way to the first house.

With her back pressed up against the wall, she peered around the corner.

"Anything?" whispered Chambers.

"Nothin'," she said as she went around the corner.

She crouched down low, then duckwalked toward the end of the wall. She glanced back at Chambers. His hands were raised slightly in a don't-shoot gesture. Behind him was the short Knight prodding him with a gun in his back. Leah's brain screamed at her to run and save herself. She even tried to move, but her feet were frozen in place.

"This way." The Knight motioned to the back door with his gun. "There are some things we need to discuss."

Leah didn't question him as she followed Chambers inside the house. If his goal was to kill them, he would have done it already. *No,* she thought. *He needs us for something.*

"If you're inviting us to dinner, there's other ways to ask," Chambers snarked.

The Knight jabbed his gun deeper into Chambers's back. "I just need you two to listen."

Leah nodded.

"If you want to get off this island, I need you to take care of Edgardo."

"Is the hired help gunning for a promotion?" Leah asked.

The Knight redirected the gun at Leah. "It'll do you well to remember I only need one of you for this to work."

Leah rolled her eyes, intending to keep him off balance. "Why? Can't you handle it?"

"Wouldn't be proper."

"You're on the outs with them," said Chambers.

The Knight cocked his head. "I prefer to call it a difference of opinion."

Leah smiled. "I think you're in deep shit because we were able to escape."

"Come now, child, you can't be that stupid," said the Knight. "You're following his plan to the letter. The only real thing about that whole ordeal that wasn't orchestrated was you overhearing me losing my temper."

Leah blushed. "Oh."

"You see, I'm a true believer in the Blood Knight's cause. Edgardo is only after power."

"And what is that cause?" asked Chambers.

"They offer the path to truth and immortality."

"Yeah, and if you don't share their vision of truth, they make you by turning you into an Acolyte," Leah whispered to Chambers.

"And it shouldn't be that way," said the Knight. "The pathway to becoming an Acolyte is reserved for the most faithful and diligent. The unworthy only need to be culled. At least that's how it was until Mathias started to come around, then he went ahead and made Edgardo his apprentice."

Leah countered, "What a noble way of saying the unfaithful should be killed."

"Your mind will come around in due time like the rest of us." He paused. "After what he did to you, I'm surprised you're resistant to the idea."

Leah lowered her eyes. "I don't know what you're talking about."

"Yeah, you do," the Knight snarked. "We all know about Edgardo's wandering fingers and Dr. Lombardi banning him from the hospital."

"Don't you even care why we are here?" Leah asked, changing the subject.

"Irrelevant to the greater good. Edgardo needs to go. You caught him off guard once. You can do it again."

Leah gritted her teeth. "Then you should do it."

"No," he snapped. "I have other things to contend with."

"I'll do it," said Chambers. "If it gets us off this stinkin' rock. Where are the other Knights?"

"Guarding the hospital, factory, and Tengu's gate. There ain't much else left standing."

"I take it Edgardo is at the factory waiting for us," said Leah.

"Of course. There's a good chance you'd end up there eventually since the gate's almost impossible to find."

"What's this gate blocking?" Chambers asked.

The Knight shook his head. "It's not that type of gate. It's a way of quickly traveling, and you need a key to find and unlock it anyway."

Chambers raised an eyebrow. "Huh?"

"Don't worry about it," said the Knight, handing his gun, knife, and their cell phones to Chambers. "I'll be patrolling that area in your boat. After you've taken care of Edgardo, come to the edge of the docks, and I'll hand it over."

Leah crouched behind a rock, taking a break while she caught her breath. They had been jogging for the past forty minutes with a couple of sprints when it felt like someone was behind them. The red-bricked factory loomed above them and sent a chill down her spine. All the windows were dark, with no signs of life other than the smoke stack spewing streams of dark smoke that blended into the night sky.

Chambers kneeled beside her, the Knight's gun at the ready. "You know…I've been thinking," he said between gasps of air. "We should have…just shot him…taken the boat…and cut our losses."

"Can't," said Leah. "It's personal now."

"I get that," Chambers said. "But—"

Leah ignored him as she got from her hiding position and ran toward the back of the factory.

"Oh, dammit!" Chambers whispered as he took off after her.

Leah was moving fast and halfway up the fire escape when Chambers started climbing. Any sense of fear or tiredness was long gone for her. Anger burned inside of her, driving her forward as the memory of being helpless with Edgardo standing over her six months ago resurfaced. She knew he was around back then watching her, but she wasn't sure how she could have forgotten what he did to her. Even with all the meds they were pushing in her to make her drowsy, this memory was too strong to have faded away.

Chambers jumped up on the roof behind her. "What are we doing up here?" he whispered.

Leah looked at him, her jaw clenched. "Maeve's report said they entered the Acolyte's pool through the roof."

"And what makes you think you're going in?"

Leah's eyes narrowed. "You can't stop me."

Chambers sighed. "Listen to yourself. I get it. You want him dead, but you're not thinking clearly."

Leah sniffed. "You don't know—"

"What you're feeling?"

She glared at him. "Yes."

"Kid, I worked Special Victims for ten years, so I know a little about this."

"That's not the same thing," she said.

"No, but that doesn't outright dismiss it either. And I know for damn sure going in there half-cocked without any sort of plan would be suicidal."

Leah groaned. "Yeah, you're right," she conceded. "Rushing in there will just get us killed. So, what's the plan?"

Chambers looked around and gestured toward the skylight. "We can get the layout through there."

They peered through the skylight, seeing the square pool in the center of the room. The room was a black void with no lights other than an eerie glow emanating from the pool. Ripples in the water cast shadows that danced along the low walls.

Chambers moved around the pyramid-shaped skylight as he studied the chamber. He stopped when he saw a figure sitting in a chair next to a door with old blood streaks on the floor.

"Found someone," he whispered.

"Edgardo?"

Chambers squinted. "No. He looks … dead. And not recent either."

Leah circled the skylight to get a better look. "Oh hell, it's him."

"Friend of yours?"

"Hell no. He was in the cell next to me when they transferred me to their police station. Maeve called him the Lazarus man. I think he was one of the early Acolyte experiments."

"Why move him here?"

Leah shrugged. "He's gotta be important somehow."

"Man, I hope he's not the research we're lookin' for."

Leah slapped him on the shoulder. "Of course," she whispered. "The heart of the Acolyte."

"I don't follow."

"Rose must have implanted her research inside of him."

Chambers took a step back. "You've got to be kidding? Why would somebody do that?"

"To protect it. No one's disturbed enough to go diggin' around in there."

Chambers stared at the corpse momentarily, then drew a heavy sigh. "Ugh. You better be right about this," he said. "I'm not exactly thrilled about rooting around in his bug-infested chest cavity."

Leah gave him a thin smile. "Thanks for volunteering."

Chambers narrowed his eyes as he shook his head at her with a crooked grin.

"Okay, here's the plan," he said. "I'll head on down using that roof access panel over there, and you stay up here and shoot at anything that moves that ain't me."

"I can do that," Leah said as Chambers handed her the gun.

"After you've fired, if it comes to that, I want you to run as fast as possible to the docks and flag down that Knight."

"You don't want me to wait for you?"

"No. Once the other Knights hear that gun go off, they'll descend on this place."

"But the research," she protested.

"I'll deal with that. Your job is to secure that ship."

"But I can't leave without you. I don't know how to drive that thing."

"If worse comes to worst, point your gun at that Knight and make him."

Leah knelt by the skylight as she watched Chambers open the hatch and slide down a ladder onto the catwalk that circled the room. Her senses were on high alert as she studied her surroundings. She groaned, frustrated at how anything interesting tended to blend into the darkness.

After all, Edgardo was out there somewhere hiding with the other Knights. That single thought made her jump at the slightest sound. It didn't help that Logan's voice echoed in her mind: "Everyone misses the first time they pull the trigger on a live target." She gripped the gun tighter, scanning the area again. She hadn't come all this way to let some lunatic like Edgardo escape her. No, not this time. He needed to pay for what he'd done. Tonight, he'd take his final breath.

She refocused on Chambers, who had sliced into the Lazarus man. Lucky for him, what little organs were left were all withered and dried up, leaving behind a vast cavity. He pulled out a pocket-sized book sealed in a plastic bag and held it up for her to see.

Out of nowhere, an arm reached out of the darkness and snagged it from him. Chambers dropped to the ground and rolled away from Edgardo, his back hitting the edge of the pool. Leah fired round after round, obliterating the skylight. Large shards of glass rained down into the pool and came awfully close to slicing off parts of Chambers.

She kept firing, never blinking, at the darkness where Edgardo should be standing with the research. He stepped into the light when her gun clicked, looked up at her with a grin, and gave her a wave.

"Thanks, amiga!" he said. "We've been wondering what had become of this."

Chambers leaped forward to tackle Edgardo, who simply sidestepped and disappeared into the shadows. He threw several punches where Edgardo should have been with a final kick for good measure. His knuckles were bleeding as he rubbed his hand. Edgardo had disappeared back into the shadows.

Chambers climbed back up to the roof. "Why are you still here?"

Leah ignored him. "Where is he?"

Chamber shook his head. "I don't know. It's like he just vanished into thin air. Regardless, we need to get out of here."

"Yeah, I know," she said, taking off for the fire escape. "We're no use to them anymore."

Back at the dock, the Blood Knight was leaning over the railing of the Sovereign, waiting for them. He had his arms folded with his hands tucked into his red sleeves. A visible skinny and long bump protruded down his forearm. If he was trying to hide the curved knife he was carrying, he did a poor job at it.

"Did you kill him?" he barked.

Leah pointed the gun at him. "We tried."

The Knight waved her off. "Put that damn thing away. You think I can't count? That gun's been empty for a while."

Leah raised an eyebrow. "Are you sure?"

"Just tell me what happened," he huffed.

"I unloaded everything at him, and Chambers even tried to tackle him, but he just faded away into the shadows."

The Knight lowered his head. "Dammit," he whispered under his breath. "It's really happening."

"What is it?" asked Chambers.

He glared back at them. "None of your concern. But if I were you, I would take this boat and find someplace where the sun never sets."

Chapter 18

United Citadel Field Unit
Beta Team

My stomach rumbled as I sat in Maeve's hospital room, listening to the muffled sounds coming from the hallway, with the soft scent of bleach frying my nasal cavity. I was stuck here waiting for them to wheel her back in from the medical scans she had undergone. The cold, clinical atmosphere did nothing to ease my anxiety. My fingers tapped restlessly on the armrest as I tried to ignore the gnawing unease in my gut.

It had been a while since I last set foot in a public hospital, but they all looked the same to me. The usual speckled vinyl flooring ran underfoot, accented by peach-colored walls with a random framed picture of a mountain providing an alternative to staring at the telly.

It was nearly noon, and the only thing keeping me upright after a sleepless night was the distant prospect of actual food in my stomach on top of the endless cups of coffee. Maeve kept reassuring me until the wee hours of the night that everything was fine, but I knew better. It wasn't the first time I'd had to talk a friend into facing something they didn't want to do. Ignorance is bliss, after all.

Growing tired of sitting, I stood and slipped into a circling pace around the small space, hoping the movement would get the blood flowing and clear my mind. But, as expected, my brain went into high gear with the increased oxygen supply. The goal was to come up with some ideas on how to get Rose out of that institute, which proved to be futile. No matter how hard I tried to think of something different, I kept drifting back to Maeve.

When I was a practicing physician, I never had the pleasure of diagnosing anyone who came close to displaying Maeve's behavior last night. In truth, I could only think of a couple of conditions that could explain her odd behavior and outbursts, but I hesitated to make an official diagnosis. Gastaut-Geschwind syndrome sprang to mind first, but with no history of seizures, it seemed unlikely. Dissociative identity disorder could fit, especially with how she switched from being carefree to spiraling into suicidal rage in the blink of an eye. But for now, the most hopeful explanation seemed to be a psychotic break. At least, with that, we could try to figure out the triggers and remove them from her environment.

Still, none of it sat right with me. I couldn't shake the feeling gnawing at the back of my mind that something vile was happening to Maeve. I clenched and unclenched my fists like I was holding a stress ball as my mind went to battle with itself. It was never easy to grapple with the unsettling reality that my medical expertise might be insufficient to help. I remember having this exact same feeling before my brother died. The overwhelming sense of helplessness made my stomach drop as if I had jumped out of a plane without a parachute. That was something I swore to myself I would never let take control of me again. But now, sitting here in Maeve's room brought it all back. I had to remind myself that that was back then, and my medical skills and knowledge had grown immensely since. At least, that's what I hoped. Being alone in the field with little or no backup from the UC would be my ultimate test—one I intended to pass with flying colors.

I took a deep breath and sat back down, attempting to settle my mind while massaging a kink out of my right leg. A few doors away, I heard soft classical music pouring out, accompanied by cheerful greetings of "How do you do?" and "You're looking well today." It was good to know at least someone was having a good day on this floor.

Their merriment was interrupted by a rather disgruntled Maeve being wheeled down the hallway. An attendant held the door open as the technician maneuvered her bed back into the room. Seeing the poor chap's disheveled appearance and flushed face, it was clear she hadn't been the easiest of patients. Maeve did have a way of leaving an impression, whether people liked it or not.

She sat up in bed, strands of her fiery red hair clinging to her damp face. She fixed a glare on the technician. "And another thing, do you know how loud it is in that tube? I've witnessed demolitions of major resorts that were quieter than that racket. And for what?" She gestured irritably. "You can't even tell me a damn thing about what you saw."

The technician glanced at me, his expression a mixture of irritation and relief. "The doctor will be with you shortly to review the results."

The way he smiled as he left told me he'd be perfectly content if he never saw us again.

"Well, it's lovely to see you're in such high spirits," I remarked dryly.

Maeve blew a few strands of hair out of her face and collapsed back onto the pillow with a thud. "This whole thing is a waste of time," she said, turning her head toward me. "You know it, and I know it. They ain't gonna find a damn thing wrong with me."

"Then we can celebrate the joy of knowing you are physically sound."

Her face lit up as she stared at me with the intensity of a thousand suns. "Physically, huh," she huffed. "But mentally, it's an altogether different story?"

"What? No, I wasn't implying—"

"No, but it's what you're thinking. That I belong in a room next to Rose."

I was about to respond when an idea sparked. I snapped my fingers as a plan took shape. "Actually, that could work," I said with a grin. "It might be the perfect way to get you inside to help Rose escape."

Maeve chuckled. "It will never work."

"And why is that?"

"Well, for starters, they already know who I am and would be all full of questions about why I'm there."

"Perhaps, but I wager we could disguise you sufficiently so they wouldn't recognize you—at least not immediately," I suggested.

"No," said Maeve. "People who go into places like that never come out. And if you put me in there, I'll tell everyone you're a time traveler."

"By all means," I replied with a hint of amusement. "That would keep you in there for sure."

A quick knock at the door broke our little spat as Dr. Foster poked her head in.

"Everything all right in here?" she asked.

Maeve sat up. "That depends on what you have to say."

"All right. So the direct approach it is," she said as she rolled a stool up to the side of Maeve's bed and took a seat.

She took a moment to review Maeve's file, then looked up at her. "I can't find anything wrong with you."

Maeve cocked her head with a smirk. "Really? Um … nothing at all?" she asked as she shook her head. "My father was a serial chain smoker up until I moved out of the house, and you're saying even that didn't affect me?"

Dr. Foster glanced at me. I was starting to get the feeling that Maeve had made such an impression with the staff that word was circulating that it would be best to talk to me over Maeve if they could.

"Let me rephrase that," said Dr. Foster. "I can't find anything medically wrong with you that would explain why you have been experiencing these mood swings your friend described."

In my mind, I knew this may sound like good news, but it was the worst possible outcome. Physical issues tended to be more straightforward to address compared to mental ones. Maeve, shaking her head, told me she felt the same way. Still, I was confident she wasn't an Acolyte, but we were definitely in uncharted territory now.

"So, how would you like to handle this?" I asked, already knowing what she was going to say. This way, Maeve could hear it coming from someone other than me, which, in turn, would allow me to give a second opinion that happened to agree with Dr. Foster's.

"I would recommend a complete psychological evaluation."

Maeve sighed. "How long will that take?"

"As long as necessary. These types of tests are usually dependent on the patient, so there's no real timeline for completion."

"I knew it," Maeve scoffed, folding her arms tightly. "You're gonna keep lookin' until you find something."

Dr. Foster smiled. "That's usually the idea when pinpointing a diagnosis, but it's all up to you on how you would like to proceed."

It was Maeve's turn to smile now because it was pretty clear what she would say next.

"I would like to proceed right on out of here," she said.

Dr. Foster stood up. "That's all right with me, and we'll be here for you if you change your mind."

Maeve's gaze followed the doctor as she left, then focused back on me. An awkward silence fell between us, highlighted by soft footsteps shuffling down the hallway and muted beeps from the medical equipment. Her shoulders drooped as she slumped over. Whatever dark mood she was in had vanished for now. For the first time today, I could see the dark circles under her eyes and how worn out she really was.

I was in a tricky situation with her because, to be quite honest, I wasn't sure what the right course of action would be. The answer was clear if she had been just a regular run-of-the-mill patient I was treating. However, not knowing all the tools the Knights had at their disposal made me cautious in my approach. One thing I did know for sure was that she seemed to do better when working on a case than when she was the center of attention at a medical facility.

"My counterpart that was a friend of yours," Maeve hesitated.

"Yes, what about her?" I asked.

"Do you, um, know if she"—Maeve bobbed her head from side to side, searching for the right words—"if she had, well, these types of spells?"

I patted the side of my leg as I thought about it. "Not that I noticed, but that doesn't mean she wasn't hiding it."

"Well, shit," she muttered as she ran her fingers through her hair.

I lowered my voice. "How long have you had this condition?"

Maeve sighed. "If I thought about it long enough, I might be able to pinpoint a date for you, but it seems like I've always been this way."

"Really?" My alert meter sounded off. Maybe I'd made a wrong assumption all along? I was so sure that this was either medical or the Blood Knights' influence that I failed to consider whether there could be other options.

Maeve chuckled. "Yeah, Kaplan used to say it was my sixth sense or being prophetic, but lately, it feels like it's been kicked up several notches."

"Prophetic, as in how you knew where to find the bloodstone?"

"Yeah, something like that. 'Cept usually I have no recollections of those times, but knowing where to find that bloodstone feels like a foggy memory."

"About how often would you say you're right about this kind of stuff?"

Maeve shrugged. "The way Kap talked, I was always right, but he's probably exaggerating."

I lost my train of thought when my mobile went off in my handbag. In a flash, I was able to fish it out after the second ring and showed it to Maeve so she could see Detective Morgan was calling.

"Hello, this is Eva," I said.

"Detective Morgan here," he said. "Just touching bases with you that the boys found what appears to be the murder weapon used in the murder of Rose's family after a tip from an anonymous caller."

I swore I could hear him winking when he said the word *anonymous*.

"Is that so, Detective?" I asked, trying to keep my voice steady. "What does this mean for Rose?"

"That's another twist in the story. She's being relocated to another facility, but I don't have a clue where she's going."

Maeve's mouth fell open as she leaned in. "How is that possible?" she whispered.

"I'm sorry. I didn't catch that," said Morgan.

"Is it normal not to have a trace on a prisoner's relocation?" I asked.

"I won't say it's not unheard of, but I've never seen it," Morgan admitted.

"I see," I said. "Do you know when she's supposed to move?"

"Very soon."

Maeve's eyes locked on to me as she mouthed the word, "What?"

"And you're sure of this?" I pressed.

"I am," he confirmed. "The other oddity I wanted to tell you is they found some blood from Rose's husband on the handle of the murder weapon with two fingerprints and a partial palm print that matched her son Ted's right hand. So, we're bringing him in for some questioning."

"Wouldn't this new evidence exonerate her?" I asked.

"It has the potential. The whole station is abuzz with this new revelation, but here is the part we can't figure out, and I was hoping you would have some ideas."

"I'm listening."

"All the old evidence from her case has vanished, and I don't mean vanished like we can't find it or lost it. It's gone like it never existed at all in the first place. We can't find anything in our cataloging system indicating we have ever received it, and I've personally done a visual check in the area it should be, and nothing."

I exchanged a worried glance with Maeve. "Yes, I've had this problem as well, when trying to look her up on the internet, and her lawyer also had the same issue. It would appear someone is trying to erase any available information about her."

"Oh, I've gone further than just internet searches. I've checked the court records, and of course, nothing comes up for her. I called up the DA who presented the case, and he has no recollection about any of it. So, what the hell is going on here?"

I thought about what I was going to tell him. Experience has taught me that if he keeps barking, he will have to deal with the Knights sooner or later. Going into their lair was already dangerous enough and going in there unprepared and clueless would be suicidal.

"I'm still trying to figure that out myself," I said. "For someone to go through all the trouble to pretty much erase someone's existence, they must have resources and power greater than I could fathom."

"Great," he said. "What the hell did I get myself involved with now?"

I took a deep breath. I remembered the same mixed emotions I felt when I was on the precipice of learning about the Knights. Once that door was opened, it could never be closed again. And worse yet, you would spend the rest of your life looking over your shoulder, wondering if they were on to you. That lovely soft, warm, and fluffy security blanket is forever torn from your grasp.

"I think it would be best to tread carefully with this one. We have no idea who is pulling the strings, and I intend not to get plucked."

I waited for Morgan to respond, but I was met with dead silence. Not even a faint breathing noise.

"Detective?" I asked.

"Yeah, just a second," he said with a slight tremble in his voice.

I instantly knew something was wrong. A knot formed in the back of my throat that I couldn't swallow. Perhaps someone was with him right now.

"If you need help, say yes," I said.

I watched the seconds tick by as Morgan finally spoke up. "You're not going to believe this."

"Oh, you'd be surprised," I said.

"Ted's gone."

"Missing gone or dead gone?" asked Maeve.

"Missing for now, but they did find his grandfather in the same state as his father."

I felt the blood drain from my face as the realization set in on what had happened. They must have turned Ted into an Acolyte, which would explain why his brother wrote down that secret message about Ted not being Ted anymore. Rose was definitely on the Knights' bad side. So, Ted must have waited for Rose to come home from Shady Reef and drugged her so she wouldn't know what he was up to. Then, all he had to do was take out the rest of his family and frame her for all of it. And now that we have been poking around, he must have killed his grandfather and fled.

"Huh, this is strange," said Morgan.

"What? What is it, now?" I asked.

"They found some black liquid draining out of the old man's nose. They're saying it's responding to heat like how that black ferrofluid stuff responds to magnets."

"Don't touch it!" I shouted.

The door to Maeve's room opened just a bit as a nurse poked her head in. "Everything all right in here?"

Maeve waved her aside. "Yeah, yeah. My friend is just a little worked up right now. Important phone call," she said, holding up an imaginary phone to the side of her head.

"Oh, all right then," the nurse said as she was about to leave, then paused. "If it wouldn't be too much to ask, we need to get the room cleaned and changed over for another patient."

I returned to my call with Morgan while Maeve dealt with the nurse. "I've seen that stuff before, and it can kill you instantly."

"And you saw this stuff where exactly?" Morgan asked.

"A colleague of mine was working on a patient in London when he discovered it. He died immediately on contact, and the research team was never able to identify it."

"Hmm," said Morgan. "If I didn't know any better, I'd say you were yanking my chain, but here we are."

"Indeed," I said. "Look, I need to get going. The nurses here are kicking us out of the hospital."

"Hospital?" he asked. "Is everything all right?"

"Yeah, we're fine. Just do me a favor and burn that black liquid when you get a chance." I said as I walked with Maeve out of the room. "Keeping it around will do you more harm than good."

"Yeah, all right, lady," he said, then hung up the phone.

I opened the door and slid back into the rental, and after all the miles we had put into it, I felt like I owned it. The car jolted as Maeve plopped onto the passenger side and slammed the door.

"So, Ted really did it?" she asked as I pulled out of the parking lot.

"It seems that way, but I'm not too sure now."

Maeve did a double take on me. "Why not? Seems pretty straightforward to me. Why else would he have his fingerprints on the knife?"

"Don't know, but while you were talking to the nurse, Morgan said the kid's grandfather had some black liquid dripping out of his nose that sounds an awful lot like that Acolyte goo they spew when the husk dies."

Maeve raised an eyebrow. "Husk?"

"Oh, that's right," I said. "You weren't there when we talked about it with Detective Kaplan. The husk is what we've been calling the person who has been affected by the Acolyte serum. In every case I've seen, once the Acolyte dies, this black stuff starts to leak out of them."

"What if the person just got a cut or injured some other way?"

"They seem to appear completely normal. Nothing out of the ordinary at all."

"And you're absolutely sure about that?"

"Well, actually that part is somewhat uncertain since the UC's never been able to fully test what would happen if they were to sustain a substantial but non-life threating injurie."

Maeve shook her head. "Damnit. So, they could really be everywhere."

"Perhaps," I nodded. "But it seems unlikely, especially if they're still working out the kinks in the serum."

Maeve gasped. "Didn't CJ mention the UC was infiltrated by at least one of them?"

"Yep. It's a big reason why you'll see me checking Logan's eyes every now and then since it sounds like he was being prepped to be turned into an Acolyte back in New Orleans. That colleague of mine, the one who was killed by that goo, figured out that the whites of your eyes will slightly dim under the proper lighting conditions if you are one."

"I see," said Maeve. "So, if Ted's grandfather was an Acolyte, Ted could have killed him in self-defense."

I nodded. "That is a possibility."

"But that still doesn't explain why his prints were on the knife."

"That is a problem," I said. "You wouldn't perchance have one of your special insights into it?"

Maeve laughed. "That would be helpful, but as I told Kap, those things are more like random déjà vu than anything else."

A few minutes later, I parked at our hotel parking structure, and we took the elevator up to our floor. As we approached my room, I could see something taped to the door.

Maeve studied it for a second, then pulled it off. "It's a flash drive," she said, holding it up.

"Here, I'll take that," I said as I opened the door to the room.

I powered up my laptop and plugged in the drive. Only one file appeared on it. It was a movie file with today's date from two in the morning.

"Aren't you worried about computer viruses?" asked Maeve.

"Nope, not with this baby," I said as I patted the side of the laptop. "It'll isolate everything it finds from that drive from the rest of the system, then purge it when we're done with it."

"Oh," she said.

I clicked on the file, and a small video with no sound opened with Rose's face front and center. She looked like she was strapped down on a gurney and unhappy about it as she looked all around the room and tried to shake her head. A pair of white-gloved hands came into frame and tried to grab hold of her head. Rose tried to bite one of the hands, which led to someone else punching her in the mouth.

In her daze, a pair of blue-gloved hands crammed a mouthguard into her open mouth, and applied a generous amount of tape—the kind that would take the top layer of skin off.

Maeve glanced at me. "Guess they don't want her to spit it out."

I shrugged. "I hope this is the worst of it."

Even as I said it, I knew this was just the warm-up. Rose lay there in a daze for several minutes, and my heart sank when I saw them apply the first set of pads to her forehead.

"They're setting her up for ECT."

Maeve frowned. "I'm guessing the E stands for electric."

"Electroconvulsive therapy," I said. "But they should be putting her under right now."

I had to turn my head when they shocked her. Thankfully for Rose, it was only for a few seconds. I hoped it was long enough to trigger a seizure in her that would block out this memory.

Rose squeezed her eyes shut as she lay there with tears streaking down her face.

"Is it over?" Maeve asked.

"It should be," I muttered. "Unless they're torturing her."

I'd spoken too soon because they were lighting Rose up again. Her back arched as they kept the current going much longer than medically necessary.

My cheeks burned as I watched her go through cycle after cycle until she was left lying there looking dead with her pale skin and huge pupils. Only the faintest of breaths showed any indication of life, then the video ended.

"We have to get her out of there," Maeve snapped.

"You'll get no argument from me," I said. "But maybe that's what the Knights want?"

"How so?"

"Until we can figure out who taped this to our door, I'm not going to wander off into some sort of trap they have laid out for us. The Knights are cunning, and I'll be damned if I'm gonna let them manipulate me into doing something they want."

Chapter 19

United Citadel Field Unit
BRAVO SUBUNIT

Logan glanced at his watch, noting it was just a little past six in the morning. He scanned the gate terminal, looking for any signs of Phillip Wallace, but couldn't find him. Phillip picked up a nice first-class seat on their connecting flight from London to Cairo, while he and CJ were sentenced to another five hours in coach after enduring the first nine. This gave him the advantage of exiting the plane first and vanishing amongst the small crowd forming in the terminal.

Anger burned the sides of his cheeks as this colossal failure on his part sank in. Up until a few minutes ago, he was able to keep his eye on Phillip. He was ready to pounce when the plane landed but didn't count on the other fifty people between him and Phillip. He chalked it up to a side effect of normally flying in a private plane. Still, it had only taken him mere seconds to squeeze down the aisle, upsetting a lot of his fellow passengers in his wake, but by then, he was too late.

Usually, at this time in the morning, most people are running at half speed, which he had hoped would have made Phillip easier to spot. He scanned the people entering and leaving the terminal one more time while he waited for CJ to retrieve their luggage and secure a rental car. While this wasn't the ideal way to follow someone, he knew where Phillip was headed, and that would have to do for now.

He heard a crackle as CJ's voice came in on the line. "Any luck finding him?"

"No," he whispered.

"Well, that's a shame."

"Uh-huh."

"Right." CJ paused. "Well, you'll never guess who I just bumped into."

Logan sighed. "Just tell me."

CJ chuckled. "Your father."

Logan raised his eyebrows. "Which one?"

"The one we know on the Alpha team that trained you on E-12."

"Are you sure? Did you run that test on him?"

"Well, no," CJ conceded. "Didn't feel all that appropriate to grab a man's shirt and lift it up at the airport. Besides, I thought you didn't believe in the test."

"Where are you?" Logan ignored his comment.

"By the exit that leads towards the rental car lot. It's just past the skybridge. You can't miss it."

"Right," Logan said as he slipped through the crowd.

With each step, his irritation grew. Learning he truly belonged to this timeline had only left him with more questions—questions for the man he once believed was his father but turned out to be his counterpart back on E-12. Still, deep down, he knew no answer Alpha Team Kaplan gave would ever satisfy him. His mind subconsciously replayed that memory of his twin brother Lucas with that Shadow Man. Knowing that this was his true home, he couldn't help but think that if the Betas had only been a little faster when they first arrived here, he could have saved Lucas, his real brother. Another scar he would have to bear until the end of time, but that was in the past. He knew he had to keep looking ahead, and with some luck, he could discover the truth after defeating the Knights.

True to his word, CJ was standing off to the side on an exit, chatting with another fellow dressed like a 1930s British Egyptologist minus the pith helmet. The last time he saw this man was almost a year ago for him, but in the future, 2047. After Logan had transferred to the Beta team, Kaplan, Maeve, and the rest of the Alpha team entered the Rift Generator. Something he thought was a fatal mistake for them to make since both Kaplan and Maeve were in their mid to late sixties, and fieldwork like that needed some younger blood.

Logan nodded when CJ spotted him and gave him a little two-finger salute. A half smile crept onto Kaplan's face as he turned his head. He reached out to shake Logan's hand, but Logan didn't reciprocate. His cheeks reddened as he pulled his hand back and tucked it into his pocket.

"You look like a man with a bunch of questions on his mind," said Kaplan.

Logan remained stoic in his response. "Why are you dressed like that?"

"Been playin' the part of a tourist guide—good excuse to rub elbows with the locals and see what shakes loose. But now that you're here, I can finally move on to the next step."

Logan raised an eyebrow. "Which is?"

Kaplan shook his head and stepped outside. "Not here," he said as he held the door open for them, letting the hot air blast them in the face. "Ain't got time to hash out the details now, so you'll get'em on the way."

"That's not how this works," Logan grumbled.

"Look, I know you got your sights on Wallace, who's makin' his way to Memphis or what's left of it. That's where I need your help. I'm goin', whether you're with me or not, so the least you can do is keep me company on the road."

Logan glared at CJ.

"What?" CJ said with a shrug. "I didn't tell him about Phillip."

Kaplan snapped his fingers. "Well now, Logan, it's real nice seein' you all cautious and careful like I taught you, but if we're gonna catch up to Wallace, we best get movin'."

"Fine," Logan shot back. "But CJ's driving."

Logan kept an eye on Kaplan as he followed them into the parking lot. Sunlight had started to cut a path across the sky, lighting up the light brown and beige buildings surrounding the airport. The rear door to a black SUV opened as CJ approached. He tossed Logan's pack into the back, then positioned his pack next to Logan's with much grace and care.

"Run the test," Logan snapped.

"Okay, fine," CJ said, opening his pack and fishing out his thermal camera.

Kaplan tilted his head. "Uh, fellas…what's this test you're goin' on about."

"Just a little test to confirm your identity," said Logan. "Now lift the back of your shirts so CJ can get a snapshot of your back."

CJ leaned over to whisper to Logan. "I thought you thought the test was bogus."

"Yeah, well, I changed my mind," Logan said.

Kaplan shrugged. "Fine, whatever. Let's get this over with."

CJ chuckled as he glanced at Logan. "I believe you said the same thing when you finally relinquished to having the scan."

"Not exactly," said Logan.

CJ went to work scanning Kaplan's back, then stared at his wrist computer while waiting for the results. Various colored lines danced around the image of Kaplan's back, then locked into place as they settled on E-12.

In the meantime, Logan had unzipped his pack, pulled out his holstered pistol, loaded a fresh magazine, and clipped it to his pants. He gave his shirt a solid tug to ensure it was long enough to conceal it.

"He checks out," CJ said, showing Logan the results. "He's from E-12."

Kaplan glanced over his shoulder. "E-12?"

CJ nodded. "It's the designation the Knights have given to the dimensional timeline we're from."

Kaplan lowered his shirt as he turned around. "Satisfied?"

"Never," Logan muttered.

CJ closed the back of the SUV and slid into the driver's side with Kaplan on his right and Logan behind him. Logan kept a keen eye on Kaplan as best he could in the rearview mirror, checking his eyes for any hint of him being an Acolyte. It wasn't long before they left the conveniently titled Airport Road and were barreling down side-streets lined with grassy knolls and palm trees.

Kaplan leaned toward CJ. "What's the deal with Mr. Sunshine?" he asked, pointing his thumb toward Logan.

"How did I end up in your timeline?" Logan spat out.

"Oh, I see," said Kaplan. "So, you found out, huh?"

"Yeah, from a little piece of tech Quint had."

Kaplan turned to face Logan, his face scrunched up. "Who's this Quint fellow?"

"Just your oldest son, Connor Kaplan the fifth."

"Oh," said Kaplan. "So that's the name he would have gone by."

"Would have?" asked CJ.

"Yeah, in my timeline, I guess that's E-12 now, he died a few months before he would have been born, but you already know that, don't you?"

"Oh, right." CJ nodded.

Kaplan sniffed. "It's kinda nice knowing another version of him survived. What's he like?"

"He's a dodgy prick, that one. Now answer my question."

"Look, you know most of the story already. In my timeline, none of my kids made it. Quint, you already know. Leah … well, we never found her. Then there's you and your brother, the twins. Lucas fell at the hands of those Shadow folks, leaving you the lone survivor. That is until a Blood Knight killed you when you were seven."

"What?" Logan gasped.

"Yep, they grabbed you right in the middle of school lunch. But before that, Maeve figured out that you were key to somethin' they were up to, so she and a few others headed out on a rescue mission."

"They wouldn't let you go," said CJ.

Kaplan nodded. "Nope, I was on the horn with the school and police to place you into protection until Maeve could get there," Kaplan paused for a moment. "You know, losing you that way put an awful big wedge between me and Maeve for several years."

CJ cocked his head to one side. "How come?"

"Oh, it was just over stupid stuff like how we could have handled the situation better. Things improved when we learned about the Shadow Knights and the things they could do. It made us realize that with their abilities, we were woefully unprepared to go up against them, but we did well enough considering."

"How bad was it back then?" asked CJ.

Kaplan lowered his head. "Personally, it was the worst for me. The Citadel was just getting started, and we lost several good agents along with Logan."

"And that's when you decided to kidnap me," said Logan.

Kaplan shook his head. "Not quite. We had bigger fish to fry—mainly tryin' to make sense of that Book of Thoth."

"The Book of Thoth?" asked CJ. "As in that mythical book written by an Egyptian god?"

"Well, can't say I know who put pen to paper on it, but it's got the blueprints for buildin' the Rift Generator, sure enough. It's the one item Maeve came back with from another mission. She reckoned it was mighty important givin' how hard it was to obtain."

"Really," said CJ. "I thought the Rift-G was some recent thing the guys in R&D cooked up."

"'Fraid not."

Logan cleared his throat. "When do I come into all of this?"

"Well, took us a good while to piece the whole damn thing together. Just the water requirements alone—that's half the reason we built it at Canary Wharf, with the Thames practically wrappin' around it. Couple years later, we finally figured out what it can do, and with Maeve nudgin' me, I slipped in and grabbed you while you were asleep, then Maeve pulled me out. Figured if the Knights wanted you that bad, they ain't gonna be searching in a place they know you're no longer at."

"Why didn't you go farther back and snag Leah and my brother as well?" asked Logan.

"Well, for starters, I don't exactly know how you end up where you're aiming to go. Truth is, 'til CJ's little test just now, I wasn't even sure I'd made it back to E-12. Near as I can tell, those Shadow folk have a way of pointin' you where they think you oughta go once you shake loose from that delusional paradise you're stuck in that's nothin' more than a creation of your own mind."

CJ glanced at Kaplan. "I thought that tablet we got from that Knight's temple in Belize was supposed to protect us from those Shadow people or grant us safe passage? Something like that."

Kaplan smiled. "Oh, you'll find out that we mixed plenty of falsehoods in with what little truth we've dug up. You, of all people, oughta know that better than the rest of us."

"Hold on, ya old codger!" Logan blurted out. "This ain't addin' up. Why take Leah when I'm three years old but wait until I'm seven when they could have just snagged my ass up whenever they wanted?"

"Now that's somethin' for AD Ben Forsyth to answer. Near as I get it, the Knights are stackin' up dominos to drop all at once. I reckon if one's outta line, the whole thing could backfire." Kaplan sighed. "Man, I'd kill to have his help right now. How come he didn't tag along?"

CJ's shoulders drooped as he hunched forward. His hands pumped the steering wheel as he made a couple of quick glances at Kaplan. It was clear to Logan that he wasn't going to be the one to be the bearer of bad news.

"He didn't make it. One of those bloody Shadow Knights cut him down right before we got yanked outta there by the Rift-G," said Logan.

Kaplan maintained a distant gaze out the front window watching the city fade away into small clusters of farmlands with faint glimpse of the Nile River flowing on the left. His fingers would tap the side of his leg every few minutes, and Logan figured this was how he took the loss of a friend. Hiding his emotions deep inside so no one would be the wiser. Something Logan had grown accustomed to himself. Although, there was the possibility that whatever he had planned had just been derailed.

"You can park over there," Kaplan said as he gestured to an open parking spot next to the Memphis museum in Mit Rahina.

"What do you expect to find here?" Logan asked as CJ parked the SUV.

"If I'm on the money, that Wallace kid can take us straight to the front door of one of the Knights' strongholds, and this timeline's Book of Thoth."

"And how do you know this is where Phillip or their stronghold is?" asked Logan.

"Same as you. Only difference is, I caught him and another Knight talkin' at that hotel in Chicago right before one of your fellow agents took it upon themselves to start tailin' me."

CJ furrowed his brow as he looked at Kaplan. "Were you dressed in a gray suit that night?"

Kaplan nodded. "I was."

"Well," CJ continued, "the agent tailing you was Quint."

Kaplan chuckled as he slapped the side of his leg. "Ah, so that's why he looked so dang familiar. Figured he was just one of those new agents I hadn't crossed paths with yet."

"Right," Logan said as he got out of the car.

He scanned the area to ensure Phillip wasn't mistaken as one of the tourists stumbling into the museum. He could feel the heat from the ground penetrating his shoes while the air felt thick and dusty. Shadows danced along the front of the building. Most of them seemed to be cast from the trees and shrubs, waving in the gentle breeze as expected. The tiny few that remained steadfast sent an unsettling chill down his spine. If anything, this was a good indication that they were on the right path.

"Man, I've always wanted to visit this place," CJ said as he exited the SUV. "They've got some awesome relics here."

Logan moved in behind Kaplan as he got out of the SUV. Unaware of what Logan was up to, CJ continued to make his way toward the museum, babbling on to anyone who would listen.

Logan placed his hand on the grip of his gun and asked, "Where's your wife, Maeve?"

Kaplan took a deep breath as he eyed Logan's hand. "Wish I knew. We got separated in the Shadow Corridor after Ben fired up the Rift Generator. I do know she arrived here sometime in the late 70s. I caught up briefly with her in the early 90s when I showed up."

Logan shook his head. "Uh-uh. That would make you over one hundred years old by now."

"Yeah, that'd be true if I'd stayed put. But I somehow got pulled into a couple other places before gettin' my ass tossed back here two years ago."

"How convenient," Logan snapped.

Kaplan dug his heel into the ground. "My hell, you're so mad at me you can't see I'm the one keepin' you covered. Hell, I got you through those last flights, weapons and all. You honestly think the airlines would just wave you on by with all that gear showing up on an X-ray? That's why I dropped a good chunk of Maeve's stock money on that private jet I gave to Ben for your team to use. I shouldn't have to be watchin' over your shoulder at this stage of the game."

Logan's hand fell from his gun's grip. The ground beneath him seemed to shift as the world around him slowed down with the realization that he may not have been ready for fieldwork. The confidence in his abilities had never wavered like this, and it scared him. How could he have been so clueless that Kaplan, this man who trained him, could remain one step ahead of him without him knowing? Worse yet, was he even qualified to train Leah?

"Aw, hell. I broke you, didn't I?" said Kaplan.

Logan shook his head like he was waking from a dream. "I'm good."

"You'd better be, or we're both done for. Now, where'd CJ get himself to?"

"Oh, I'd say he's probably drooling over some pile of rocks while he commits the placard to memory."

Logan pressed forward as he charted a path to the museum's entrance. His muscles tensed the closer he got to the still shadows at the edge of the building. Out of the corner of his eye, he thought he could see a hint of blue eyes staring at him from the shadows that would vanish when he looked at them. For now, he reasoned it would be best to ignore them since anything else he could think of would likely summon the police.

He found CJ outside in a large courtyard that stretched at least two football field lengths. Many different types of Egyptian statues of all sizes littered the area, with CJ staring up at one that appeared to be a smaller version of the Great Sphinx.

"That ya new best mate now?" Logan asked.

CJ made a double-take as he snapped out of it. "Funny," he said with a dry wit.

"So what's the deal with this thing?" Kaplan asked.

"Oh, nothing really," said CJ. "I've just always wanted to see this one in person. I've seen the one in Giza several times but never had the chance to make it to this one."

"Huh, I always assumed there was just the one."

"Oh no," CJ said with a giant smile. "There has to be hundreds lying about waiting to be dug up."

"Intriguing, sure, but I don't see how this gets us any closer to findin' Wallace," said Kaplan.

CJ made a move with his finger as if he were tracing something on the Sphinx. "You see that sad sap sitting under the tree with his arms wrapped around his legs and his head resting on his knees?"

Logan peered around the Sphinx and eyed the man CJ was talking about. "Ah, damn it, there he is. What the hell's he up to?"

"If I had to take a guess," said CJ, "he's either waitin' for someone or debating if he should clean his sinus out with a shotgun."

"No," said Kaplan. "He's waitin' on someone. The Knight at the hotel said he was due for some reprogrammin'. Just before Alpha team went through the Rift, I dug up intel on a Blood Knight stronghold located somewhere in northern Egypt. Didn't have time to check it out then, but when Wallace's contact mentioned Memphis, I figured that's where he was headin'."

"What makes you think they have this Book of Thoth there?" asked Logan.

"Funny thing, that. When I was out in some other timeline, I ran across a younger version of myself that told me I'd find that book on Prime in one of their strongholds in Egypt. I wasn't sure what Prime was, still not sure, but he said it was where all things seem to collide. No clue what he meant by that, but I got the feelin' he was from this timeline we're in now.

"Well," said CJ. "This current timeline we're in is what the Knights call E-Prime."

"No kiddin'," said Kaplan. "That's some good news there because, truth be told, I wasn't sure where I was at."

"Well, we can't just wait here," said Logan. "Someone is bound to notice us."

"Agree," said CJ. "That's why I'm blending in with the rest of the tourists. I suggest you two do the same."

Logan nodded as he wandered off toward the back of the courtyard. From the looks of it, a bunch of school kids were dropped off doing all sorts of things you're not allowed to, such as touching the ancient exhibits. He could feel his patience running thin as he pretended to marvel at a statue of Ramses II. A couple of boys, around twelve years old, got between him and the statue, standing far too close for comfort, blocking his view of Phillip.

Seeing as CJ and Kaplan had better views on Phillip, he shook his head and meandered off to go inside to watch the courtyard from the second floor. Up a flight of stairs, he found himself leaning over the railing of the concrete exhibit that housed a colossal limestone carving of Ramses II. The chitchat of the dozen or so people viewing the exhibit echoed off the walls, making it impossible for him to eavesdrop on anyone.

CJ's voice crackled over the line. "He's headed in your direction."

Logan looked up and saw Phillip enter up through the stairwell. He locked eyes on Logan and moved in beside him; his hand dangled over the railing. "It's good to see you again, but I really don't have that much time before they find me."

Logan turned to the side and propped one arm up on the railing. "Yeah, I've heard you've got some problems with the Knights."

Phillip sighed as his head slumped. "I'm tired of running from them."

"Looks to me you've been running *with* them," Logan sneered.

Phillip didn't move. He just stood there, watching the people on the ground floor. "Free will isn't easy to come by for some of us."

"And are you acting under your own free will now?"

Phillip shrugged. "Hard to say, but I do know my father wanted … no, that's not the right word," he said as he fished a slip of paper out of his pocket and handed it to Logan. "He demanded that I give this to you."

Logan opened it up, seeing just a string of numbers. "What is it?"

"Your friend eyeing the Sphinx can tell you."

Phillip pushed himself up and off the railing. His eyes were glazed over as he wiped away a tear that had slowly formed. He turned to leave, then paused to look back at Logan.

"There's one more thing," he said.

"What is it?" asked Logan.

"My time is coming to an end."

Logan raised an eyebrow. "They're turning you into an Acolyte?"

Phillip lowered his voice. "They've been trying for a while now. A bunch of us."

"Don't go through with it," said Logan. "We can protect you."

Phillip shook his head. "It's too late for that now. I can see only one clear path to end this nightmare."

Logan pleaded, "Don't join them."

He watched as Phillip turned his back toward him and walked away. When he reached the exit, he paused and looked back at Logan.

Logan nodded, knowing there was nothing he could say or do to convince Phillip to join their side. Then he did something that he hadn't anticipated. He watched in horror as Phillip climbed onto the railing and jumped headfirst into the concrete floor below them.

He turned away, not wanting to see the impact. It was hard enough to see the effect the Knights could have on one person, and this was pure torture. What little time he spent with Phillip told him he was a good person fighting a losing battle. He couldn't help but think that if he hadn't tracked him down, Phillip might have had more time to save himself—another scar he would have to bear.

Chapter 20

United Citadel Field Unit
BRAVO SUBUNIT

The death of Phillip weighed heavily on Logan's mind as the scenario played out over and over. He laced his fingers behind his head as he lay on the hotel bed, staring up at the ceiling fan as it made slow rotations. Out of the corner of his eye, he watched the curtains sway gently in the breeze as his thoughts drifted to the morning's events.

He kicked himself, thinking things could have turned out differently if only he had tried to talk to him once during their flight. He could feel the guilt building up inside him as his stomach churned. However, he had to concede there were multiple forks on that pathway, and dwelling on them wouldn't change the past. Still, there were some lingering questions about Phillip and Quint that he couldn't ignore.

The first from when he was following Phillip to Chicago. He had heard CJ talking to Nieminen in the hotel room, getting a tidbit of information that seemed innocuous at the time, but not so much now. If he remembered correctly, Nieminen relayed that Quint mentioned he saw someone else listening in on Phillip's conversation with a Knight. This morning, Kaplan led him to believe it was him listening in.

Clearly, Quint would have recognized his father, which left Logan with only two possible reasons why Quint didn't identify him. The first being Quint had never met his father, so he didn't know what he looked like. It was possible Quint was taken away in the middle of the night to another dimension like Logan was, except where Quint was too young to remember who or what his parents looked like.

Still, with him hopping around different dimensions like Nieminen suggested, he assumed Quint would have had to run across Kaplan by now. Which leads into the other possible reason is Quint deliberately didn't identify Kaplan to them. As for why, that was currently unknown, but it did echo another inconsistency that involves Quint and Phillip.

Phillip did say his father wanted Logan to have that slip of paper with the numbers on it that CJ was now deciphering. According to the story Nieminen and Quint were telling him back in Nebraska, Phillip's father, Jacob Wallace, was dead. So, either Phillip lied about his father, or Nieminen and Quint were mistaken about his demise. Still, having never crossed paths with Jacob, it raised another question about why he wanted to pass this note to them.

A sharp knock at the door interrupted his thoughts. Logan sprang to his feet and crossed the room to check the peephole. CJ stood in the hallway, one hand tucked under his shirt, clearly gripping his gun.

"What is it?" he whispered as he opened the door.

CJ pushed past him, his gun at low ready, as he swept the room.

"Looking for someone?"

CJ holstered his gun, satisfied they were alone. "Where's Kaplan?"

Logan raised an eyebrow. "Did ya check his room?"

CJ positioned himself inches away from Logan's face. A fire burned in his eyes as he glared at him. "Where were you?" he demanded, jabbing Logan hard in the chest with two fingers.

Logan caught CJ's wrist on the second mid-jab and twisted it, forcing CJ to pull back with a wince.

"What are you talking about?" Logan asked as he pushed CJ away.

CJ wiggled his fingers as he rubbed his wrist. "Kaplan's gone, and my room's been tossed."

Logan poked his head out into the hallway. He could see the door to Kaplan's room was wide open. "Are you sure?" he asked.

CJ narrowed his eyes. "If you don't believe me, check it out yourself."

"Where were you when your room was getting searched?"

"Getting dinner."

"Any idea what they took?"

"Just the notes I was taking on that paper you got from Phillip."

Logan motioned him to take a seat by the window. "All right, mate, hang tight over there, and I'll see what I can dig up. Should only be a minute."

Logan slipped out and crossed the hallway to Kaplan's room. He pressed his back up against the wall and peeked inside. For a moment, he had a fleeting thought at how bad this could look to the authorities if anyone happened to catch him in this position. He stepped inside and closed the door behind him.

The only thing that seemed off to him was the room appeared to have never been occupied at all. Looking at the bed, he noticed the crisp white blankets were still pulled taut with perfect corner seams with a hint of lavender. The highly polished nightstands were free from any dust, let alone any useful fingerprints. He stepped back and noticed the only footprints on the carpet were his. So, either the maids had already been through here, which was doubtful because he would've heard them, Kaplan snuck out or, worse, been taken captive before he even made it to the room.

That last part was plausible since Kaplan had been lingering behind in the lobby as he chatted with the desk clerk after they all got their room keys.

He stepped back into the hallway and left the door slightly ajar in case he needed access later. CJ was waiting for him in the hallway. His arms were folded in a way that suggested he was still holding on to his pistol as his eyes scanned the hallway.

"Well?" asked CJ.

"Not out here," Logan said as he went back inside his room.

The air felt stifling hot as he wiped some moisture off his forehead. There was a definite change in the room, a sense of vulnerability, and he wasn't sure if it was something his brain had manufactured or not. He peered out the window and scanned the area, looking for something like a Knight peering back at him. At least that would have been a clue to explain what was happening. The only thing of interest was the riverboat floating on the Nile behind their hotel. He grumbled as he closed the curtains, pulled the chair away from the window, and sat down.

He leaned forward, resting his forearms on his legs as he clasped his hands. His mission was to secure Phillip, and for better or worse, that mission was over. A new path laid before him, and an unfamiliar one at that. If Kaplan was right, they needed to get their hands on this Book of Thoth. Assuming he could build the Rift Generator, he speculated he could use it to rescue all the fallen members of his family before the Knights killed them and find a place untouched by that cult to live out their days. It could be their own little paradise.

CJ interrupted his thoughts as he closed the door and sat down on the bed. "What now?"

Logan locked his eyes on him. "That slip of paper Phillip gave us. Can you still figure out what it means?"

"Already done," CJ said, showing him the data on his wrist screen.

Logan squinted as he studied what appeared to be a location on a map. "What is this place?"

"Dendera. It's just south of us. They've got this massive temple complex that's a popular tourist destination that the coordinates point to."

Logan raised an eyebrow. "A tourist spot? You sure ya got the right coordinates?"

"I—I think so," CJ paused. "I just used Jacob Wallace's name as a numerical shift in a Vigenère Cipher. I was thinking that when Phillip told you this note was from his father, he might have been talking in code."

"And that worked?"

CJ blushed. "Well, it's the only thing I tried that kicked out anything that made sense."

Logan leaned back in his chair and stretched his legs out in front of him. "Actually, that does make sense."

CJ's jaw dropped. "It does?"

"Yeah. Hiding in plain sight is one of their strong suits. You think whoever tossed your joint could figure out this location from your scribbles?"

CJ nodded. "I had the coordinates scratched out on that slip of paper they took, so yeah."

Logan glanced at his watch. "Looks like it's time to check out of here then."

Their black SUV flew down the road as CJ pressed hard on the gas. They were counting on the idea that whoever had Kaplan was just a little ahead of them, and a surprise rendezvous could go in their favor. The sun had set hours ago as they drove south on their six-hour journey, giving way to a majestic star-filled sky. Very few cars were on the road since most of the locals had already retired to their homes for the night.

Logan pulled out his phone and noted it was pushing 5:00 p.m. back in Kentucky. He knew he was way overdue to give Eva a status report, an observable trait he'd seen in many people who have an aversion to confrontation. Still, as the saying goes, better late than never.

Logan pulled the phone away from his ear as Eva's voice projected out the speaker. "About time you called. I was starting to get worried about you two."

"Change of plans," said Logan. "We're headin' to what might be a Knight's stronghold."

"What? I didn't authorize this. Where's Phillip?"

"Dead."

"How?"

"Self-inflected. Bloke didn't wanna end up an Acolyte."

CJ leaned over. "How's Maeve?"

Eva paused for a moment, then sighed. "Medically, she's fine."

Silence fell between them, prompting Logan to cut through it like a knife. "But…" he said.

"I'm quite worried about her. She's been fine today and even handed over her pistol to me willingly, but who knows when something might trigger her again, and she ceases to be our ally."

"That bad, huh?" said CJ.

"Until I can determine what's going on inside her head, I'm afraid she's a liability."

"What do you need from us?" Logan asked.

"Information, please. What's the stronghold you're going to?"

Logan spent the next ten minutes going over the day's events along with the unexpected run in with Alpha team's Kaplan from their timeline, E-12. Eva remained silent other than a couple of interruptions about the arrival of Kaplan and the whereabouts of the rest of Alpha team, like her friend Maeve.

"Random thought," said CJ. "Kaplan mentioned Maeve arrived here thirty-some-odd years ago, you think she could have stashed some useful information away that we could possibly snag?"

"If she did," said Eva, "I'm certain she would have left us a trail of breadcrumbs to follow. If we had more resources, we could look into it now, but as it stands, we'll have to put that one on the back burner."

"We've got Leah doing nothin'," said Logan.

"True, but I think there's something going on with her."

Logan's ears perked up. "How so?"

"I couldn't reach her until a few hours ago. She claims she was sleeping, but there was something in her voice that suggested otherwise. I tried messaging Chambers for a second opinion, but he hasn't responded yet."

Logan clenched his jaw. "Understood," he said. "I'll look into it."

CJ slowed down and pulled the SUV off onto the side of the road right before a modest but dark empty parking lot. Logan wasn't sure what to make of it all, but it was clear this place was far bigger than the museum they saw this morning. It was more like an excavation of an ancient temple and the surrounding town square. From this distance, he could make out one large ancient square building that seemed to have defied the sands of time that loomed above the others. The caretakers had it bathed in yellow lights that grew darker as they reached for the roof, giving it an ominous appearance. He couldn't make out the finer details, but it looked like someone had carved hieroglyphic figures into the sides of the outer walls, with six pillars holding up the flat roof.

With his hand on the wheel, CJ pointed at the large building. "That's the Temple of Hathor."

Logan curled his lip. "That can't be their stronghold. It's too out in the open and guarded by the locals."

"Oh, I know," said CJ. "We're probably being watched by security right now."

"I'm not authorizing any infiltration unless you have a solid plan in place," said Eva.

CJ chuckled. "Since when have we ever had a solid plan in place?"

Logan shook his head. "Not now."

"Fine," CJ huffed, then turned on his wrist computer and angled it for Logan to see. "Phillip's coordinates tag a rocky mound in the middle of a bunch of brush a few paces west of the outer wall. But I don't see anything noteworthy that would flag it as a hotspot for Knights."

Logan tapped his finger on his leg. "It's gotta be tucked away somewhere."

"Oh, wait. You're right," said CJ. "I'm betting they got one of their security doors hidden out there."

"Only one way to find out," said Logan.

"Fine, you have clearance to proceed outside that historic site's walls," said Eva, "but I expect an update when you find the door and another full report within the hour."

"Acknowledged," said Logan.

He slipped the phone back into his pocket and turned his head to meet CJ's gaze. "You ready for this?"

CJ nodded. "Hell yeah," he said with a smile.

He put the SUV in drive and pulled away. "There's some houses back there on a side street we can park next to, but they are likely owned and lived in by the Knights if this is one of their strongholds."

Logan pointed past the homes to a cluster of tall bushes next to the outer wall. "How about over there? We can keep the car close by for the getaway, and out of sight of those homeowners."

CJ nodded, and parked the SUV behind the bushes. "Hopefully security doesn't spot the car here," he said as he slid out of the SUV.

Logan stepped out of the vehicle and retrieved his pack, then slung it over his shoulder. The air was warm and oddly heavy, yet a cool breeze wafted toward them. Perhaps a sign they were on the right track? Beyond the illuminated temple, everything else was cloaked in darkness. He felt his senses heighten, knowing this was the perfect setting for an ambush by a Shadow Knight.

CJ was already one step ahead of him as he scanned the area with his thermal camera. He looked back at Logan and shook his head, then proceeded forward, following what had to be a centuries-old wall. Logan followed behind him, trying to control his twitchy fingers from unholstering his gun.

CJ stopped abruptly, his heels skidding across the ground like a cartoon character. He checked the map on his wrist computer, then proceeded left, away from the wall. Logan shook his head as he followed him into the dry wooden brush. He picked up his feet higher than usual to reduce the amount of thorns slicing into his ankles. He noticed CJ seemed unfazed by it all, which irked him a little. *A perk of being oblivious to your surroundings,* he thought.

"I'm picking up a heat signature," he whispered.

Logan unholstered his gun. "Knights?"

"No," he said. "I think I've found it."

A few minutes later, CJ stopped again and held his left arm out, scanning the area with his wrist computer. He took a few steps forward, then squatted over a smooth rock about the size of a large garage door flush with the ground.

He looked up at Logan, who hovered above him. "There's something here."

"Can you open it?"

CJ stood up and stepped back off the rock, staring at a squiggly line oscillating on his wrist computer. "I can see the frequency and the wave pattern, but the inverse counter wave isn't working."

"Does it gotta be the inverse counter wave?" asked Logan.

"No, but it's what worked before. At this point, I'm just guessing."

Logan said , "What about your cipher?"

CJ shrugged. "Eh, I guess I can figure out how to work it into the wave pattern, but it'll take a few."

The ground hissed as steam and dust shot into the air from a rectangular groove that formed into the rock. Vertical lines shot across the rectangle as they lowered into the ground, forming steps.

Logan's eyes narrowed. "So, was that s'posed to be a few minutes or a few seconds?"

CJ smiled. "What can I say? I'm damn good at what I do."

"Lead the way, and I'll let Eva know we've found a way inside."

Logan took a picture of CJ descending the stairs and sent it off with a message to Eva, letting her know they had found the entrance and were proceeding inside. He used the light emanating off CJ's computer screen to see where he was going as he descended downward into the long, dusty hallway. The stale air had grown quite chilly and damp the further he went, something he didn't expect to find down here. When the stairs leveled out, they pulled out their flashlights, keeping the beams low to avoid alerting any Knights waiting for them. The chamber they stood in appeared to be solid rock that curved back behind them. A thin layer of dust coated the floor, a good indicator this place hadn't been used for quite some time.

Logan panned his flashlight along the ground and paused when he saw one set of fresh footprints. "Kaplan?" he asked.

"Hard to say," whispered CJ. "I didn't think to check out his footwear today."

This new hallway had thin gold lines curving up and down as they streamed down the corridor, beckoning them to follow. Logan took a few steps in, and felt his heart flutter when he spotted those familiar blue eyes boring into his soul. On the opposite side stood a shadow person, but this one was different than the usual one he had seen wearing a hat. This one appeared to be wearing a hooded cloak, but without any other details, it was impossible to determine.

CJ had his thermal camera out in front, capturing the entity. "This thing is amazing," he whispered.

Logan pulled his gun and aimed it at the shadow. "This thing is dangerous," he whispered back.

The hooded shadow raised a wispy arm and pointed off to the left of him, then faded away. A sound like a metal pipe striking a person's skull echoed through the chamber, followed by a muffled groan.

"Kaplan," Logan muttered under his breath.

Logan picked up his pace as he jogged down the corridor. The gold lines on the wall rose above his head like a gentle ocean wave guiding him. He rounded the corner in the direction the Shadow Man had pointed and saw Kaplan face down in the center of a large square cavern. Six massive columns lined two sides of the chamber, with intricate carvings that seemed to be a mix of runic letters and Egyptian hieroglyphics and a plain stone altar at the front of the room. A red light emanated from the sides of the pillars, as if someone had them backlit, which was impossible given their location and proximity to the walls.

CJ came up behind him, his thermal camera pointed out in front of him. "We're not alone," he whispered.

Logan looked at CJs video display and saw a figure standing over Kaplan. He raised his gun to fire at the Shadow Knight but was struck by another force to his side. He hit the ground hard as his gun flew out of his hand and skidded across the ground with a clink.

CJ turned and fired at the Shadow Knight that had knocked Logan down as it ran past them. His bullets sent a fury of fracture lines as they penetrated the rock wall, missing the Knight.

Logan got to his knees and lunged for his gun. His fingers were a hair away from gripping the handle when it flew away. The Shadow Knight, still in the room with them, had clipped his hand as it kicked his gun away. He yanked his hand back and checked his fingers for broken bones.

CJ spun around, his eyes focused as he scanned the room. The only heat signatures he could find were from Logan and Kaplan. "I don't see them anymore," he whispered.

Kaplan rolled to his side to face Logan. His face was pale, and his eyes glazed over. He tried to speak, but his faint voice gave way to an unintelligible hiss. Drips of blood streaked across his hand and splattered on the ground as he motioned for Logan to come to him.

Logan's heart pounded as he raced toward Kaplan. He knelt down, took his hand, and felt the gash carved into his wrist. His arm felt cold as he pressed down on the wound and turned his head to see CJ dashing toward them with a white bandage in hand. Logan snagged it and pressed it into Kaplan's wrist.

"Make sure this room stays secured," Logan whispered to CJ.

CJ nodded, then went back to scanning the room with his thermal camera.

Logan turned back to Kaplan. "Of course, this'd be the one time Eva's not with us."

Kaplan smiled. "You need the tablet you got from the Knight's temple in Belize."

"Now?" asked Logan. "It's locked away in Vegas."

"Hercules Caves," Kaplan whispered.

CJ came up behind Logan. "We need to get him to a hospital."

"I know, I know," said Logan.

"The altar," Kaplan sputtered out. "Look."

Logan looked up and gasped. For the first time in a long time, he felt the dark sensation of fear rising in the back of his throat. Numerous shadows of people stood along the front wall with their glowing blue eyes, pointing at the altar. CJ aimed his thermal camera at them; his mouth hung ajar. Not a single one of them showed up on his camera. Logan motioned with his head for CJ to check out the altar. CJ nodded and approached the altar inch by inch. When he was close enough to touch it, the shadows faded away.

"What do you see?" asked Logan.

"It's a map smeared in blood," said CJ.

"Of course," he sneered. "Take a picture of it, and let's get out of here. We need to get him to a hospital."

"Already done," said CJ, placing his thermal camera back in his backpack."

He rejoined Logan and placed one of Kaplan's arms around his neck to help Logan pick him up.

Kaplan squirmed a little as his head drooped forward.

"Easy does it," said Logan. "We'll have ya at the hospital and sorted in no time."

Kaplan didn't respond, which worried Logan. He picked up the pace as his fear turned into a fiery determination. He swore to himself that he wouldn't lose another family member at the hands of the Knights.

Chapter 21

United Citadel Field Unit Beta Team

I was awoken by someone banging on my hotel door. *Who in the bloody hell is this?* I thought as I threw some clothes on and stumbled to the door in the dark. Through the peephole, I saw Aaron Sato from the Jasinski Medical Institute. His button-down shirt was half untucked and full of wrinkles. His black hair was matted down like he had just gotten out of the shower, but seeing how hard he was breathing, it had to be from sweat. He had been well-kempt and reserved when I'd talked to him about Rose a few days ago at the institute. Now, he was neither.

I kept the chain on the door as I cracked it open. "Can I help you?"

Aaron glanced up and down the hallway in a panic. "I need your help, please!" he said, clasping his hands together.

"With what?"

"Did you get my video of Rose?"

Well, I guess that was one mystery solved, but it didn't explain why he was at my door at 6:00 a.m.

"I did, and it was rather disturbing," I said. "What's going on?"

Aaron leaned in and whispered, "I think they're after me. Let me in, and I'll tell you everything I know."

I thought about his offer for a second, but better judgment prevailed. Until I was sure of his allegiances, I wouldn't willingly put myself in danger. After all, who says he wasn't one of the ones who was torturing Rose? Or could his changed demeanor indicate he wasn't really the same Aaron at all? Maybe just a husk now.

"You want some coffee?" I asked, keeping my tone casual.

"What? No," he stammered. "Didn't you hear what I just said?"

I met his frantic gaze through the narrow opening. "I did, which is precisely why I'm willing to sit down and talk with you."

Aaron shot a nervous glance over his shoulder. If I didn't know any better, I'd say he was under the influence of an illegal substance. Then again, if Dr. Barnett suspected Aaron had shared that clip of Rose's treatment with us, the consequences would be dreadful. At best, he'd be tangled in expensive legal battles with a team of the institute's top lawyers. At worst, he might find himself on the receiving end of the same treatment plan they had for Rose.

"There's this little café I've found that's open around this time," I said. "Let me grab Maeve, and we'll head on over."

Aaron's head and shoulders both drooped toward the ground. "Okay," he mumbled.

I left the door open a crack as I made my way to the phone and punched in Maeve's room number. On the fourth ring, I heard a click followed by a groggy, "Hello?"

"Hey, Maeve, Aaron from the institute is here at my door. He claims to be the one who dropped off that video of Rose and says he has more information he's willing to share."

"What's the problem then?" she asked.

"He believes the Knights are on to him, so I offered to meet him at the café to hear him out. Get yourself ready, and we'll head over there."

Maeve groaned softly on the other end of the line, but at least I could hear the rustling of sheets as she lumbered. "All right, give me five."

I picked up my gun off the nightstand, quickly checked the magazine, and placed it into my shoulder bag. The last thing I wanted to deal with today was Aaron leading the Knights to us, but if he did, I would be ready for them.

I made sure the door remained cracked open as I left my room to wait in the hall. If something were to happen while I waited for Maeve, I wanted to be able to get back inside quickly. As I stood there, I watched Aaron pace up and down the hallway. I guess, in his mind, if he were still moving, he would be safe. Although I've often found that I do my best thinking when I'm on the move, so there's a slim chance he was collecting and organizing his thoughts.

"Hey, Aaron," I said. "You mind if I run a test on you?"

Aaron shrugged. "What kind of test?"

I pulled my penlight out of my shoulder bag. "Just a quick neurological assessment."

Aaron gave me a crossed look. "I thought you were just a lawyer or paralegal."

"I am," I replied, lying through my teeth. "But I hold a medical degree as well, which is precisely why Ellis sought my opinion on Rose."

"Oh, all right," he relented.

I shined my light all around his eyes until I was satisfied he wasn't an Acolyte. Maeve stepped out of her room not long after. Her eyes were a little puffy, telling me she had just fallen asleep when I called. I only hoped it was because she was debating all night with herself if she should go ahead with the psychiatric help the hospital offered. I knew it was on my mind a lot yesterday. Still, as much as I wanted to help her, I knew I could only show her the way. In the end, it was up to her if she wanted to go down that road.

Aaron gave her a hesitant little wave when he spotted her.

"Hi, Aaron," she said while I closed the door to my room. "You ready for a little pick-me-up?" she asked, then glared at me. "I know I could use some."

Aaron lowered his gaze to the floor. "Let's just get this over with."

Maeve smiled at him. "Oh, cheer up. We'll get you through this."

Aaron smiled tentatively back at Maeve, then shoved his hands in his pockets as he followed her to the elevator.

I wish I had Maeve's optimistic attitude for these types of situations, but experience has taught me otherwise. I couldn't help but feel I was watching a dead man walking.

The elevator ride down was one of those awkward, silent affairs. In my first year of med school, I had a friend who would pretend to be on his mobile when others would join us in these types of cramped compartments. He'd get a kick out of talking about some dubious disease he contracted through questionable actions to see how the other passengers reacted. Meanwhile, I'd be standing there, trying desperately not to burst into laughter. If only he were here now to lighten the mood.

As the elevator doors slid open, we were immediately greeted by the familiar odors of combustion engines mixed with a faint scent of oil. That rainstorm the other day had done a thorough job of cleansing the pavement, leaving behind large puddles of water with unnaturally faint rainbow hues scattered near the elevator. The sun had yet to rise, so the dimly lit parking structure gave way to all kinds of nefarious shadows. I watched them carefully as Aaron got into his car, then I followed Maeve to our car. Lucky for us, no immediate threat emerged as we exited.

It wasn't long before we found ourselves back at Dick's Café, seated in that same familiar booth where we met Detective Morgan. The short line of patrons waiting to get their coffee to go never seemed to die down as they continued to trickle in. I took it as a reassuring sign that the locals would rather step inside here for their higher-quality brew over a questionable one at some quick drive-thru on their way into work.

Maeve slid in next to me with a tray of five cups of the darkest blend I'd ever seen, with the intent to keep two of them for herself.

"So, how's work going?" she asked.

Aaron planted his left elbow on the table and propped his head up with his hand. "Well, I think my career in medicine is over."

"All right," I said. "Let's take this back to the beginning, and you can walk us through everything that's happened."

"Nuh-uh. I want some assurances you can keep me safe."

"Safe from who?" I countered.

Aaron sighed. "I think Dr. Barnett and his nightly visitors know I stole that recording of Rose, and I don't know what to do anymore. They have the power to destroy my life, and if I'm lucky, I'll just get twenty years behind bars."

At first, I couldn't believe he was so naive as to worry solely about potential jail time. This young man needed a reality check about the danger he might be facing, though I wasn't eager to frighten him off just yet. Using him would be a calculated risk, and I don't typically condone putting an innocent civilian in harm's way. Still, he did have access to Rose.

"Answer me this," I said. "Do you think Rose is truly in danger?"

Aaron took his time, but he eventually nodded. "I do."

"Then let them throw a tantrum. From what I've seen, they are harming her, which is illegal."

"Yeah, I know," he said. "But they can frame it however they want and get someone to sign off on it as proper treatment."

I raised an eyebrow. "Perhaps, but that would be risky. 'Bout how long would you say she's been in there?"

Aaron tilted his head. "About a week and a half."

I felt my mouth drop. "Bloody hell. She was a mess when we met with her."

Aaron nodded. "It's from all the abuse they're doing to her."

Maeve said, "I wouldn't worry about them coming after you. Revealing torture and abuse falls under whistleblower laws."

"She's right," I said. "Any judge or jury would have serious concerns about what has happened to her in there. And we have the tape to prove what they are doing isn't proper treatment at all."

Aaron balled his hand up in a fist and lightly pounded it on the table. "You don't get it," he said. "I've done a lot of digging on her background, and there's nothing to find, so nothing to show a judge this woman even exists."

"And," he continued, "it gets worse than that. I can't find any civil or court record abouts her at all. I even did some light searching into our records and found nothing. Hell, even her room isn't assigned to her."

"Yeah," I said. "You're not the first to mention something like that."

I took a sip of hot coffee when a chill of realization hit my spine. Since we left the hotel, something seemed off about this whole situation. I couldn't pin it down at first since he caught me off guard when he showed up at my door, but now, there it was plain as day.

Quickly, I asked, "How did you know where to find me?"

Aaron froze for a moment as his train of thought made a giant U-turn. "Um, well," he said as he tapped the table with his fingers. "You see, um, Rose kinda told me where you were staying. I assumed you must have told her."

Maeve shook her head. "'Fraid not."

I stared at him. "You're lying."

Aaron gulped. "I swear I'm not. You see, she was in this kind of drugged-out daze when I was wheeling her back to her room. When we crossed the threshold, she snapped out of it and told me I needed to find you and the hotel you were staying at right on down to the room number. I swear, she was only lucid for that short little spell."

I wanted to believe what he was saying, and it seemed plausible, having met with Rose. But …

"Why did you believe her?" I asked.

Aaron crossed his arms. "Because this isn't the first time she's done this with me."

Maeve perked her ears up. "What were the other times?"

"Well, she predicted you two were coming to see her when I wheeled her into the visitor's room. She'd also talk about some of the other staff members like she knew them really well, but I know she's never actually met them."

A flash of information hit me about what Maeve had told me at the hospital. She mentioned Detective Kaplan had repeatedly stated she had some kind of sixth sense, an uncanny ability to glean insights into things she had no business of knowing. I glanced at her, wondering if Rose was in the same stage of what was now happening to Maeve.

I focused my attention back on Aaron. "I'll do everything in my power to protect you, but we'll need your help first."

"Yeah, I assumed as much," Aaron mumbled.

"What time are they relocating Rose?" I asked.

Aaron bit the inside of his lip. "How'd you know she's being moved?"

"Oh, I've got my sources," I said.

Aaron scrunched his face. "Then why ask me?"

"Well, I didn't say they were great sources. There are a few gaps you could help fill in."

He sighed. "Well, did you know that because of you two's unexpected visit, she's being moved tonight at around eleven?"

I felt my heart skip a beat. "Tonight?"

Aaron nodded. "Yeah."

I turned toward Maeve. "That doesn't give us much time."

"No," she said. "No, it doesn't."

Aaron raised an eyebrow. "To do what?"

I chose to sidestep his question. "You know who will be moving her?"

"Silver Crest Emergency Services."

"All right, here's the plan," I said, pausing briefly. "That is, assuming you're working today."

Aaron nodded. "I'm supposed to tonight."

"Good," I continued. "I need you to continue acting as you normally would today."

I reached into my handbag, fished out one of the spare communication patches I had on me, and handed it to him.

"Is this a Band-Aid?" he asked as he held it up to examine.

"Not exactly," I said. "It's a comms device that will allow two-way communication between me and you. I'll need you to apply it behind your ear for it to function properly."

Aaron tried to hand it back. "Look, I don't know what you're up to, and I don't care. This isn't the type of help I was lookin' for."

Maeve reached out and placed her hands on top of his. "I know you're scared, but the institute will definitely come after you if you leave now unexpectedly. But if you resign or request a transfer, I bet they wouldn't be the wiser."

"Yeah, you have a point," he conceded. "But that's not exactly a guarantee now, is it?"

"No, but what is nowadays?" She winked.

"Other than death and taxes?"

"Look," I said. "You've already done far more than what I'm about to ask of you."

"Which is?"

"Essentially, just report anything that seems out of the ordinary tonight," I said. "Even the faintest whisper will come through clearly on that comm line."

"All right," he relented. "I'll do it."

"Wonderful, "I said.

Aaron checked his watch. "My shift starts at four today, so I'm gonna go crash for a bit before I head in."

"Sure," I said as he scooting out of the booth. "I'll test the comm line at nine, so make sure you've applied your patch by then. We'll pull you out after your shift is over."

Aaron made a faint nod and left without saying another word.

Maeve downed what was left of her second cup of coffee. "You think he'll go through with it?"

I made a slight shrug. "I'm not entirely sure. At the moment, my biggest worry is he'll mention to Dr. Barnett we were asking rather pointed questions about Rose."

Maeve drove us back to our hotel in her usual fashion of reckless disregard for using signal indicators and flying through what she called yellow lights, which I'm sure a jury of her peers would disagree with. It was something I'd grown accustomed to after spending this much time in the car with her. Back in my hotel room, I had Maeve join me in my room. Things were starting to come to a head now, and it was high time we had a conference call with the entire group.

I called Leah first to give her some time to wake up since it was around 5:00 a.m. back in Vegas. Logan and CJ were already on a plane en route to Morocco, which was another unauthorized trip CJ had chalked up to "time zones." He claimed he didn't want to wake me, though he made it abundantly clear after my tongue-lashing that it wouldn't happen again. With Assistant Director Ben Forsyth and the rest of upper command from the UC gone, the responsibility of keeping everyone in line had fallen squarely on my shoulders, and I intended to maintain order.

I leaned back in my chair while Maeve sat on the bed with my laptop poised to take notes. The last one to check in was Chambers. I still needed to confirm whether Leah truly had been asleep, as she claimed when I couldn't reach her earlier, but I hadn't had the chance yet to ask him.

"All right," I said. "Let's hear Bravo Subunit's update on the Knights' stronghold."

"We ran into a couple of snags," Logan started, "once we made it inside. CJ was able to confirm two Shadow Knights there, along with our injured Kaplan from the Alpha team."

"Any idea what they were up to?" I asked.

"Uncertain, but from the looks of it, they smeared his blood on the altar to reveal the location of the Book of Thoth."

"Book of Thoth?" asked Maeve.

"Yeah," said CJ. "Kaplan said it held the instructions to building the Rift Generator."

"Where's the book?" I asked.

Logan said, "According to the map on the altar drenched in Kaplan's blood, the book's in a cave system in Morocco."

"It's by the Hercules Caves near Tangier," said CJ. "I'm thinking we'll either find the book or another set of coordinates to follow there. Regardless, Kaplan said we'll need that tablet we got from the Blood Knight's temple back in Belize."

I raised an eyebrow. "Where is Kaplan?"

"Took him to a hospital in Qena," Logan said, "then they shifted him to one up in Cairo. Last we saw, he was still in a coma."

"Oh, that's not good," I said sharply. "Sounds like hypovolemic shock. Did you catch the doctor's diagnosis?"

"'Fraid not," said CJ. "We had to leave to catch the plane."

"Yeah," said Logan. "More than likely, the Shadow Knights are already on their way there. If we're fast enough, we just might be able to beat 'em to it."

CJ cut in, "Which is why we need to make a request to deploy Leah. She can meet us in Tangier with that tablet we snagged from that temple in Belize."

I paused to consider it for a moment and nearly decided to send Chambers instead. However, Chambers wasn't under my authority to command. As it stood, he was doing us a favor already. Leah's suggestion made sense, but her absence raised too many questions that I intended to get to the bottom of immediately.

"I'll authorize it if she can tell me where she was the other day when I couldn't reach her."

"What? I already told you I was asleep," she said.

"That's not exactly the entire story," said Chambers.

"Yes, it is," said Leah.

Clearly, the time had come for someone to finally grow up. I couldn't afford to waste precious time like this, and I needed a team I could trust with my life.

"Spill it," I said, snipped.

Chambers started, "Leah tracked down where this Rose lady's research was stashed. I went with her to grab it on some island called Shady Reef."

I couldn't remember the last time I felt this let down by someone. She had been so adamant about never wanting to set foot on Shady Reef again, and yet, she went anyway.

"I thought I made it perfectly clear that you weren't supposed to go there," I said firmly.

"No, you said I couldn't go out there alone, which I didn't. I had Chambers with me the whole time."

I could hear the smugness oozing from the phone, but she was right. The only course of action now was to move past this incident and make a mental note to ensure my instructions are more precise in the future. But for now, I knew I couldn't fully trust her.

"And did you find the research?" I asked.

"We had it briefly," she said.

"All right, what happened?" I asked.

"Well, for starters," she continued, "the island wasn't exactly deserted like we were led to believe."

CJ's voice boomed over the speaker, "What? That's not right. I searched that place high and low."

"Are you sure?" asked Chambers. "We ran across a Knight that mentioned they were keeping an eye on you."

Logan chuckled. "Nice work, Mr. Bond."

"Hold on," I said. "Let's go back to the part about you talking with a Knight."

"No problem," said Chambers. "He told us we were free to go if we took out this kid named Edgardo. Sounded like he had taken over the island, which caused a rift between them."

While Chambers was talking, Maeve got up and stood next to me and said, "Edgardo has the research now."

"Unfortunately, that is correct," said Chambers.

My head snapped to the left, my eyes locking onto Maeve. Perhaps it was just a lucky guess, though that would be the optimistic view. The reality of Maeve, however, suggested otherwise.

"How did you know that?" I asked.

Maeve's voice cracked, "It just came to me."

I raised an eyebrow, my gaze shifting briefly to my handbag next to the phone on the desk. I was certain she hadn't seen me place my gun in there, but that didn't mean she didn't know it was there. If the unseen force simmering in her decided to seize control again, I had to be prepared.

Logan started to speak, unaware of the situation playing out in my mind. "What're the odds that Knight was a plant to push ya into grabbin' Rose's research instead of runnin'?"

"He's not wrong about that," I said firmly. "They set you up, you took the bait, and now they have the research."

"I don't think so," said Chambers. "He had ample opportunity to take us out after Edgardo stole the research. Instead, he handed the ship back over and let us leave."

"Hmm," said CJ. "If there is an insurrection brewing within the Knights, we need to find a way to take advantage of it."

"Agreed," I said.

I paused for a moment, thinking about our next move. Maeve had repositioned herself back on the bed and seemed content for the moment.

She leaned forward and whispered, "You know she's the only one who can bring them that tablet thingy."

"All right," I said. "Leah, you are to escort the tablet to Bravo. And CJ?"

"Yes, dear?"

"You're in charge of getting her a flight and ensuring a smooth trip through security."

"No problemo."

"And Chambers?" I asked.

"Uh-huh," he said.

"I know you've already done so much for us, but if you could ensure that Leah makes her flight, I would greatly appreciate it."

"Sure thing," he said. "I can take care of that."

"Wonderful," I said. "That just leaves the subject of Rose."

"How's it shapin' up?" asked Logan.

"Not well," I said. "But we have a chance to break her out tonight during a patient transfer to a new facility."

"Ooh," said CJ. "This sounds a little dangerous."

I glanced at Maeve. "It has that potential like everything else we've done."

"What do you need from us?" asked Logan.

"I'll need CJ to add me to the transfer team as a State Department health official."

"Hmm," said CJ. "This could be a tough one. I'd like to bring Nieminen in on this one."

"Negative," I said. "This one is for your eyes only."

"All right, I'll see what I can do. Who's doing the transfer?"

"Silver Crest Emergency Services," I said.

"I'm on it," he said.

"So," said Maeve, "Leah delivers the tablet, Bravo secures the Book of Thoth, and tonight we intercept Rose's transfer with Eva posing as a health official. That about sums it up?"

"That's it," I confirmed, "We all have our assignments, and I'll expect an update from everyone in twenty-four hours.

I ended the call, slipping my mobile back into my pocket. A lot was riding on tonight, and it felt as though we were overdue for a bit of success. We could definitely use some more time, a commodity that's always plentiful until you need it. Maeve said her goodbyes as she left to go back to sleep. Something I found fascinating was that she could sleep after drinking that much coffee. I could use a few more winks myself, seeing as I had a long night ahead of me. But with tonight's main event looming overhead, I needed to start planning before things could get underway.

Chapter 22

United Citadel Field Unit Beta Team

It was dark when we left the hotel to break Rose out of her confinement. The city had been reduced to the soft glow of lights casting long shadows broken up by the moonlight with an occasional couple out for an evening stroll. I made one final inspection in the vanity mirror as Maeve merged onto the freeway. Undercover work was more of CJ's forte, but I was slowly getting used to my usual blonde hair dyed a medium brown just a few hours ago. I could feel my face tingling from excitement mixed with apprehension. Thankfully, my makeup covered my flushed cheeks, which could be a giveaway I was up to no good.

The plan was to have Maeve drop me off at Silver Crest while I used my forged credential and a lot of tenacity to get myself onboard the transfer vehicle. Once onboard, I make a peace offering with the crew by offering them my special laced coffee to start their stomachs churning. A few miles down the road, Maeve blocks the road with her car, and I use my gun to force them to stop. From there, it's just a matter of moving Rose and high tailing it out of there.

I checked my watch and saw it was almost 9:00 p.m. We were still a few miles away from the Jasinski Medical Institute, skirting the outer range of our comm patch. I probably should have mentioned to Aaron that there was a slight chance I wouldn't contact him at precisely nine so he wouldn't freak out and run for the hills. I applied the patch and immediately heard his voice in mid-conversation with Dr. Barnett. The not-so-friendly doctor was giving him orders to remain vigilant and to let him know if he recognized anyone who shouldn't be there.

I removed that patch to talk to Maeve so Aaron couldn't hear. "Sounds like he went back to work like he promised."

Maeve gave a half-hearted shrug. "Or someone else has the patch. Hard to say without video."

"Nah, it's him," I said as I reapplied the patch.

"Aaron, it's me," I said. "Is this a good time?"

"Yes," he answered back, but I could pick up the subtle nervousness in his voice.

"Good," I said. "Is it still the plan to move her at eleven?"

"Affirmative."

"Good. Keep me posted if anything changes."

"Sure."

Maeve left the freeway and ventured down a narrow two-lane road lined with your usual assortment of boxed stores and petrol stations on the corners. Most of the businesses on this stretch of road were starting to shut down, giving way to a new influx of cars. Around another corner and down a long stretch of road, I could see

Silver Crest coming up on the right. It was a dingy green building with several garage doors on one side and a tired-looking parking lot out front. Only two cars remained in the lot, and for a moment, I worried they might be shutting down for the night. If so, I'd have to flag them down as they left to pick up Rose.

Maeve pulled up to the side of the road. I nodded to her as I got out with my four-pack of piping hot coffee, two regular and two laced. It wasn't necessary for them to chug it down, but I hoped it'd take the fight out of them when the time came to pull out my gun.

Crossing the lot, I tugged on the glass front door, relieved when it opened with a rush of sterile air. I stepped inside the small waiting room and didn't exactly see the same transformation I'd seen when entering the Jasinski building. The room was slightly larger than a broom closet with that high throughput vinyl flooring that's speckled to hide the dirt and grime. On the plus side, it does look good when waxed and polished. The walls were just as dilapidated, with their dull yellow color far overdue for a fresh new coat.

A man in his late sixties sat behind a thick green glass countertop, looking at a computer. He had a round face and a dark birthmark on the left side of his head that was easy to spot since his hair was long gone. From his ID badge, I could see his name was Terry. His black-rimmed glasses drooped down his nose as he looked up at me.

"Need help with somethin'?" he asked.

I smiled at him as I placed the cupholder on the counter. "Yes, I'm Dr. Turner with the State Health Department. I'm here to evaluate the transfer of" —I paused as I looked at an "official" email from the State Department on my mobile— "one Dr. Rose Lombardi."

Terry squinted as he eyed me up and down. "You sure you got the right information, Doctor? We ain't never had someone from the State come on over for a ride along."

I did my best impression of someone in shock and awe as I raised my eyebrows as high as they would go and slapped the side of my open mouth. "Bloody hell, that can't be right. We're supposed to stop by every two years for an inspection."

Terry squirmed in his chair like a child getting asked to turn in their homework they forgot to do. "Um, well, I'm not sure what to tell you. I've been here for almost ten years, and you're the first to bring this up."

"Dammit, Chris," I said, as my thumbs went into a fury as I typed up a meaningless email to no one. "This is supposed to be his area, yet he's off gallivanting in Africa, 'taking in the sights,' while I'm left to cover his duties. And what do I find? He's been filing fake inspection reports, of all things."

Terry leaned forward and asked, "Is this gonna be bad for us? Should I go get a manager?"

I shook my head. "No, you guys are okay. I'll blame Chris for any minor infraction I find."

Terry shot me a half smile. "I'm sure the CEO would appreciate it."

"Great," I said with a nod. "Do you know who my contact person will be? I was informed your team would provide that information upon my arrival."

Terry held up a finger. "Just a second. I need to make sure you're a part of the transfer team. If not, I'm afraid I can't allow you to board. The last thing we want is a couple of violations that would open ourselves up to lawsuits."

"Excellent job," I said, pretending to tick an imaginary box on my phone. Terry gave me a quick smile before turning his attention back to his computer. Time dragged painfully slow as I stood there, caught in limbo, waiting for confirmation that CJ had done his part. Terry adjusted his glasses, leaning closer to the screen as he read something. I could almost make out the words as he silently mouthed them, but, regrettably, lip-reading was never a skill I managed to master."

"Ah, yes. Here it is," he said, tapping the screen. "Strange it was set up this way though."

His glasses slid back down his nose as he looked up at me. "I guess that's how these requests from the State Health Department come through."

I shrugged, keeping my expression neutral to avoid revealing I had no idea what he was talking about. "Couldn't tell you," I said in a monotone voice. "I've never seen what comes up on your end, only the request being sent from ours."

"Ah, I bet it's a lot nicer lookin' than the old command prompt interface we're stuck with." He chuckled.

"Oh, you'd think so," I replied with a dash of irony. "Yet here we are, still slogging through a similar bloody text-based interface. But, of course, I'm assured that no expense was spared."

"Oh, ma'am, don't get me started." He laughed as he got up. "Wait right here, and I'll let Nurse Farrell know you're here."

It didn't take long before I heard a woman's voice exclaim, "What?" in that loud, incredulous tone people use when they think they've just heard a bunch of malarkey. Leaning over the counter, I tried to catch a glimpse of who Terry was speaking with, but the corridor beyond was empty. The commotion, I assumed, must have been coming from a break room tucked behind one of the closed doors.

I leaned back into the waiting room, not wanting to get caught in a compromising position. I tapped my fingers on the countertop while I waited for Terry to return. So far, the plan seemed to be holding together, but I couldn't shake the worry that Nurse Farrell might throw a spanner into the works. Who did she think she is anyway, going up against a state official? Then again, it was always possible she was a Knight.

"Hey, Aaron," I whispered. "Everything going all right?"

"Affirmative," he said. "But hearing you talking to someone else is throwing off my concentration."

"Yeah, I know," I said. "It does take a bit to get used to."

I heard the soft creak of a door opening, and Terry reappeared at his station. Following closely behind him was a woman in her late forties, her black hair pulled back into a tight, no-nonsense bun. She wore green scrubs and a photo ID badge that confirmed her as Nurse Farrell. She gave me a stern look as she was no doubt deciding on what to do with me.

"Nurse Farrell," I said as I stuck my hand out to shake hers. "I'm Dr. Turner with the State Health Department. I'm here for our scheduled biennial inspection."

Farrell shook my hand, but her facial expression remained neutral. "Yes, I've just been informed you'll be joining us tonight, but I'm not sure why. Every inspector we've had was only interested in the facility, making me think someone has filed a complaint against us."

I offered her my most polite smile. "I can assure you, I have no information about any complaint being filed. As far as I'm aware, these inspections are meant to occur every other year. Unfortunately, it seems the inspector assigned to this area has let that schedule lapse."

Farrell shook her head. "Whatever, just try to stay out of the way. The rig isn't as big on the inside as you would think."

Terry got up and opened the door for me to enter the back. I plucked one of the regular cups of coffee and offered it to him, which he gladly accepted. I moved toward Farrell and offered her one of the laced cups.

"Sure, why not?" she said as she picked it up. "I'm on for another eight hours."

I followed her through the breakroom, which opened into the ambulance bay. Given the state of the rest of the facility, I had expected a similar level of neglect. Instead, I was met with a pristine space. The polished concrete floor sparkled with a reflective sheen, catching the glow of the overhead lights and the clean white brick walls. Green guidelines were meticulously painted on the floor, directing the movements of the four ambulances and two vans. The vehicles themselves were spotless, their white basecoat gleaming, accented by sharp red detailing and lettering that seemed to pop against the polished backdrop.

Farrell took a sip of her drink. "The word you're lookin' for is wow."

"Wow, indeed," I said. "I would have never suspected this was hidden here inside."

Farrell laughed. "Yeah, we get that a lot around here. Most of the revenue gets funneled into this part of the building since it has the biggest impact on our patients. As for everything else, well, you've already seen what little is spent on the rest of the complex."

"Duly noted," I said.

Farrell finally smiled at me. "Come on, and I'll introduce you to the rest of the team."

I nodded and followed her to Bay Four. We circled around to the rear of the ambulance, where a young man in his late twenties was busy stocking supplies from a box resting on the wheeled stretcher in the patient care area behind the driver's seat. His uniform was tidy and professional with black boots, navy blue pants, and a matching button-up shirt with reflective striping. The Silver Crest logo was applied to his shoulder and the front of his hat. His ID badge was clipped neatly to his waistband and jingled as he moved around.

"Yo, Devon," said Farrell. "We've got some company from the State Department."

Devon finished unloading the last of the box's contents, placing them neatly into a drawer before shutting it with a soft click.

"What do they want?" he asked, his tone carefree as he grabbed the empty box. But the moment he turned and saw me standing beside Nurse Farrell, he jumped in startled surprise, the box slipped from his hands, smacked the ground, and rolled out the back.

Farrell snatched it up before it hit the ground. "Oh, just a ride-along inspection."

Devon tilted his head as his gaze flickered between us. "Huh, I didn't know they did that."

Farrell gave me a sideways glance. "Neither did I."

I took out the last tainted cup of coffee and held it out for him. "Sounds like it's gonna be a long night. You want a cup of fresh brew?"

"Sure," he said. "After the pickup, we got a two-hour drive tonight."

Devon took a sip of it and placed it in the cupholder next to the driver's seat."

"Really?" I said, raising an eyebrow. "Two hours? I knew it was going to be a trek, but I wasn't expecting it to take quite that long."

"Actually," he said as he jumped out the back. "It's more like four hours and twenty or so minutes. We still have to drive to the institute to pick up the patient."

"Which means," said Farrell, "we should get a move on it."

Aaron's voice came in over the comm patch. "They are sedating Rose right now."

"Copy that," I said to both of them.

Devon circled around to the front and climbed into the driver's seat. Farrell hopped into the back, turning to offer me a hand as I stepped up. I nodded gratefully and stepped inside. Once the doors clicked shut, she made her way to the front and took a seat. I slid onto the narrow bench beside her, leaning back against the side of the ambulance just as Devon started the engine. The lights in the ambulance dimmed as we began to move with the garage doors lifting to let us out. We turned left, following the road until Devon merged onto the freeway. Other than the soft hum of the engine, we rode together in silence until the Jasinski Medical Institute came into view.

I heard Aaron's voice again. "I don't know if this means much, but Dr. Barnett has been relatively calm and relaxed this evening."

"Interesting," I said.

"What is, hun?" asked Farrell.

"This building's architecture," I said, pointing at the institute.

"Yeah, it's somthin'," she said. "This place gives me the creeps."

Devon raised his voice. "Ditto."

"I take it neither of you are particularly fond of the institute?" I asked.

"Well...," Farrell started to say, before her voice trailed off.

"It's all right," I said to reassure her. "I'm not here to evaluate your feelings about this place. Please, feel free to speak your mind."

"Well, if you want the truth," she said. "I hate this place. The vibes are all wrong, and I swear there are a slew of patients who go in and never come out. If anyone deserves an inspection from the State Health Department, it's them."

"Thanks for the tip," I said with a half-smile.

Farrell gave a quick nod before standing and opening the back doors, letting the cold air rush in. Devon was already there, waiting for her. She rolled the stretcher toward him, and he took hold of it, steadying the wheels as they touched the ground. With ease, he pulled the stretcher the rest of the way out. Farrell followed, hopping down to grab the rear handles. The whole thing felt like a dance they had practiced to perfection.

Farrell turned to look at me over her shoulder. "You comin'?"

I shook my head. "No, this part isn't essential to my inspection."

She nodded and began pushing the stretcher toward the set of double doors. Devon pressed a button on the wall, and the doors slid open automatically. Together, they maneuvered the stretcher through and disappeared from view as the doors closed behind them. Left alone, I sat there, debating whether it would be inappropriate to shut the back doors. The cool air carried a slight nip, and I couldn't shake the feeling of being exposed if the prying eyes of the institute's staff were on the hunt for anyone who didn't belong.

"Hey, Aaron," I said. "What's the latest?"

"We're sittin' pretty," he said. "Dr. Barnett is just about out of here. He's decided to take the rest of the night off."

"Is this unusual for him?"

"It's rare," he said. "But not unheard of."

"How much longer until your shift is over?"

"'Bout another hour and a half."

"Good," I said. "After your shift ends, I want you to head to a public place—somewhere like a bar—and stay there until we can arrange your extraction."

"Extraction?" he said. "Can't I just go home?"

"Do you think you'd feel safer there?" I asked. "You seemed rather on edge this morning."

"Fair point," he yielded. "I'll head on over to the Speedway Depot. It's between the university and Churchill."

"Copy that," I said.

The doors slid open again, revealing Devon pushing Rose on the stretcher while Farrell walked alongside, guiding it toward me. In one fluid motion, Farrell jumped into the rig and pulled the stretcher the rest of the way in. Once she had secured Rose, we were off before I could utter a single word.

"So, how we doin'?" asked Farrell.

"Well," I said with a faint smile. "You haven't slammed a door on the patient yet, so I'd say you're doing just fine."

Farrell chuckled. "Glad to see the State sets such a high bar."

I leaned forward to get a better look at Rose. Her hair was disheveled and matted with what appeared to be mineral oil, giving it a greasy sheen. As I expected, her eyes were partially open, which allowed me to see that glazed, unfocused void I had noticed from my previous visit.

However, her skin was most concerning. It had this pale, damp appearance with an unsettling, almost gelatinous texture. If not for the faint rise and fall of her chest and the steady beep of the heart monitor, it would have been difficult to believe she was still alive.

"What do they have her on?" I asked. "Ketamine?"

Farrell shook her head. "Nope. Just Haloperidol, Lorazepam, and Diphenhydramine," she said. "Our primary concern for now is to monitor her breathing. She'll be like this the entire time she's in our care."

Farrell pressed a hand to her stomach as it emitted a low, gurgling noise. She winced for a moment before she was able to compose herself. "Ooh," she said. "I think I might be coming down with something."

I glanced around the rig, scanning the stocked medications. "Do you need something," I asked. "Perhaps anti-nausea medication?"

Farrell patted her stomach. "It's starting to settle," she said. "I think I'll be all right."

Rose opened her eyes and turned her head to face us. "The shadows lie in a valley of no more, and I will soon join them."

My heart skipped a beat. Rose's words echoed something eerily similar to what Maeve said back in the barn. Back when she'd been teetering on the edge of a murder-suicide.

"Damn, girl," said Farrell. "They got you on something good."

I did my best to keep a neutral tone as I asked, "What do you mean by joining them soon?"

Rose licked her lips. "The convergence is imminent."

"What does that mean?" I asked.

Farrell waved me aside. "She's too drugged up to know what she's talking about."

Rose locked her eyes with mine. "He is coming."

"Who?" I asked.

"Kaplan," she whispered.

I raised an eyebrow. "Whose Kaplan?" I said, knowing my question sounded to the crew like "Who *is* Kaplan." Of course, I knew who Kaplan was, only I assumed she was talking about the Kaplan from the Alpha team who was in a coma back in Cairo.

"Detective in New Orleans," she whispered. "Find Selim."

I had to concur with Nurse Farrell. Rose was far too gone to make any rational sense since Detective Kaplan died six months ago in New Orleans. She must've overheard the Knights mention he'd gone there looking for Leah.

The glass window beside Devon shattered with a loud bang, sending shards flying as the ambulance lurched violently. Devon gripped the wheel, struggling to regain control as the vehicle swerved dangerously. A second shot rang out, piercing the cabin and striking Rose in the leg. Before I could react, Farrell yanked me down to the floor, shielding us both from the chaos.

She looked up at Devon and shouted, "Are you hit?"

"No!" he yelled, then reached for the radio. "Shots fired, shots fired. We are under attack. I repeat, we are under attack."

Damn it, I thought. This wasn't part of the plan. The Knights must be making their move to eliminate Rose before we could intervene.

Suddenly, it all clicked. Dr. Barnett's calmness earlier in the evening now made perfect sense. He must have known this was coming and was glad to have it over. Hell, if Aaron was right, Barnett was going to take off early tonight. I'd bet good money he was out there now, taking potshots at us alongside his fellow Knights.

I checked the map on my mobile and saw we were approaching the spot where Maeve should be hiding. I hoped she was still all right and would back away when she saw we were being shot at.

"They're on the roofs!" Devon shouted.

Another bullet tore through the upper corner of the rig; its downward trajectory struck Rose in the chest. She tried to call out, but I could only hear her gurgle. Farrell got to her knees to check on Rose, and another shot rang out, hitting the nurse on the left side of her upper chest. She let out a pained moan as her hand instinctively moved to press against the wound, her blood seeping through her fingers.

"We need to get to a hospital," I yelled.

"On it," Devon shouted.

I snagged some gloves above me and snapped them on. "Here, let me help," I said to Farrell.

With a quick tug, I ripped the top part of her scrubs and could see air being sucked into the bullet hole. I placed my hand back over the wound and applied as much pressure as possible. Then I leaned her forward to check for an exit wound but didn't find one.

"You have a chest seal?" I yelled.

"Second drawer from the top behind me," Devon yelled back.

Taking Farrell's hand, I guided it over the wound. "Keep applying pressure," I instructed.

She managed a weak nod as I scrambled to the drawer, yanked it open, and tore open one of the metallic pouches. Crouching back beside her, I pressed the chest seal firmly onto the wound, ensuring it was secure, then laid her down.

The piercing sound of sirens grew louder as the cops came up behind us. Their lights flashed and lit up the inside of the rig.

Devon picked up the radio and said, "We have injured on board. En route to Norton."

My gaze shifted to Rose. Blood had pooled around her and soaked into the gurney. My chest tightened with a mix of frustration and sorrow. I knew there was nothing more I could do for her, but she didn't deserve to go out like this. I looked back down at Farrell. None of them did.

A wave of relief washed over me when I heard Maeve's voice crackling over the line. "I'm almost to Norton," she said. "As soon as you can get away, meet me in the parking lot."

Devon pulled up to the hospital and jumped out of the ambulance. The doors flung open, and I was greeted by a team of doctors and nurses ready for action. I jumped out and explained to them where Farrell had been shot, how I applied the chest seal and any other information I could think of. The attending doctor nodded, then turned to follow the team as they wheeled Rose and Farrell into the emergency room.

Devon was pacing back and forth with his hands on his head. Clearly, his nerves were shot. He looked like he was barely holding it together, and it was clear he needed someone to talk to. I was caught in a moral dilemma. The cops were coming up behind us, and I needed to get away before they started to quiz me and unravel the pretense that I was Dr. Turner. But I couldn't in good conscience leave Devon in the state he was in.

I approached him and put an arm around his shoulder. "Hey, there. How are you holding up?"

Devon met my gaze. I could see a tear forming that he wiped away. "I could have died," he mumbled.

One of the cops came up behind me. "Were you on that ambulance?"

I glanced down at the blood staining my clothes. The question was obvious, especially with Devon standing there in his uniform. It had to be one of those obligatory queries they are forced to ask, like, "Have you tried rebooting your computer?"

"Yes, we were," I replied, my tone steady. "But he's not doing so well right now, so I'm going to take him inside. Would you mind keeping an eye on the ambulance until we return? The last thing we need is some druggie making off with all the meds in the back."

"Sure thing, ma'am," he said.

I guided Devon inside and settled him into a seat in the waiting room. A quick glance around revealed only one other man sitting quietly nearby. It struck me as a bit odd that this hospital in a major city was eerily empty. Then again, I'd experienced my fair share of slow nights working in the A&E back home. It seems like there are only two settings in the ER. Painfully slow or painfully busy.

"Thanks, Dr. Lewis," said Devon.

I felt a jolt of lightning shoot down my spine. "How do you know my name?" I asked.

"I'm a member of Ordo Veritatis et Iustitiae, and you should probably sneak on out of here before the cops start poking around."

"But how?" I started to say.

Devon held up his finger. "I'll contact you later and bring you up to speed," he said. "Now, get going while I entertain the police, and dispose of your special coffee."

"Ooh," I said. "How much did you drink?"

Devon smiled. "I'm fine. Just a drop on the tongue."

"Oh, that's a relief."

Devon flashed me a crooked smile. "There's an exit down that hallway you can take." He pointed, then looked me in the eyes. "And thanks."

I nodded in acknowledgment and rose from my seat. Following his directions, I navigated my way to the parking lot, where Maeve was already waiting for me. She had that anxious look about her as she tapped the steering wheel, scanning the area. Her eyes lit up when she saw me making my way toward her.

"What the hell happened back there?" she asked as I slid in next to her.

"I'll tell you later," I said. "Right now, we need to focus on extracting Aaron. I just hope he's all right."

"Should be," she said. "The only thing I picked up on the scanner was a gang shooting that involved the stretch of road you were traveling down."

I laughed. "So, that's what they're calling the Knights now."

Maeve shrugged. "Eh, it seems to fit."

Chapter 23

United Citadel Field Unit
BRAVO SUBUNIT

Logan spotted CJ leaning over a white parapet that overlooked the Atlantic Ocean. The parapet marked the far edge of a sprawling cobblestone plaza. Two white buildings with columns hugged the northeastern corner. Several shops on the ground floor welcomed the many visitors there to browse the trinkets and overpriced regional clothing they had to offer. A set of stairs framed the sides of the buildings, allowing guests access to the upper areas where the restaurants were located that offered first-class panoramic views afforded by the open-air seating.

He joined CJ with Leah in tow. "'Bout time you showed up," said CJ, his eyes still focused on the ocean waves.

Leah gave CJ a little wave as she leaned against the parapet on his other side. "I'm here too."

CJ blinked as he staired back at her. "Oh," he said, then turned to talk to Logan. "I wasn't aware of that part of the plan."

Logan lowered his gaze to watch the people down below enter the Hercules Caves. "Flight's not for another sixteen hours, and I'm not leavin' her behind to sit around at the airport while the Knights are on the move."

"Yeah, I get it," he said as he pushed himself upright, dusting his hands off. "But have fun explaining that one to Eva."

Logan followed suit. "No worries. I'm not scared of her like you, mate."

CJ raised his voice. "What?"

Before Logan could retort, Leah cut in. "Hey, CJ, why do they call these the Hercules Caves?"

"Huh?" said CJ as he turned to face Leah.

"Why do they call it Hercules Caves?"

"Oh," he said, his eyes lighting up. "There are several myths floating around about good old Herc and his quests with this place. Basically, he was on his way out here to gather some apples, um, gold ones, I think. Along the way, he smashed through a mountain, forming the Strait of Gibraltar. What's left of the mountain now straddles the Strait and are known as the Pillars of Hercules."

"And the caves?" asked Leah.

"I'm getting' there." He chuckled. "Once he made it here, he either lived or hung out in those caves below as he figured out a way to get these apples. In the end, I think he was able to trick the Titan god Atlas into fetching them for him."

"So what's in the caves now?"

"Well, it's kind of a hodgepodge of concrete pathways, murals, and some natural caverns. I believe at one point, it used to be a quarry, so much of the cavern is larger than it naturally should be.

They've also got some Greek marble statues down there and some one-of-a-kind backdrops to take pictures with along with other odds and ends."

"And we're supposed to find this book down there using this little rod?" she said, holding up the tablet.

"Not exactly," said CJ. "We're lookin' for a different cave system that's a little south of here."

Logan snapped his finger. "Then let's get to it."

"Sure," said CJ. "Follow me."

Logan followed CJ and Leah down the stairs to the left, their footsteps echoing faintly on the stone. The steps led to a rocky beach where the ocean waves crashed against a natural black rocky barrier. Several different groups of tourists milled about, some lounging on the rocks to soak in the view. Others were drawn to the sounds of a lively drumbeat that blended seamlessly with the soft strumming of a guitar. Their kids resorted to playing games of tag filled with lots of laughter while a few of the younger ones searched for small shiny pebbles to show their parents.

"Which way?" asked Logan.

CJ pointed to an area south of them. "Past the fishermen and over that rocky ledge."

Leah's eyes widened. "Well, screw that. I'd rather take my chances with a Knight than fling myself over a cliff."

CJ shook his head as he stared at her in amazement. "Who said anything about flinging? All we're gonna do is rappel just a few feet, and even if you do slip and fall, it's like fourteen feet to the nice sandy beach below. You'll do fine."

Logan smirked on the inside as he shot her a stink eye. *If she thinks she's ready for fieldwork,* he thought, *this'll be a solid test to prove her wrong. Nothing like a good hit to the ego to bring someone back to reality.*

"Move out," said Logan.

CJ walked ahead of them and surveyed the area. Logan knew it would be tricky to pull this off without raising suspicion. Any tourists wandering too close could easily notice CJ setting up ropes, and the last thing they needed was a crowd gathering. Assuming somebody wasn't already exploring that section. With how busy the Hercules Caves were, he wouldn't be surprised to find someone going rogue and off the beaten path. Or worse, a Shadow Knight could be lying in wait, ready to ambush.

His chest tightened at the idea of the Shadow Knights in pursuit, but it made sense. If Kaplan was aware of the Book of Thoth, it stands to reason that the Knights were as well. There was no doubt in his mind that they had already explored these caves and realized something was missing: the tablet Leah now carried. Capturing Kaplan and using his blood to reveal the hidden map on the altar had just been part of their plan. A simple trail of breadcrumbs to lead them here with everything the Knights needed.

Still, there was a slim chance that only Kaplan's blood could reveal the map, but why? That possibility only complicated things, especially when the simpler, more troubling explanation made far more sense—the Knights were orchestrating their every move. And that was what truly worried him.

He glanced over at Leah, who had taken a hair tie out of her pocket. She smiled at him as she pulled her hair back and tied it into a pony. It was hard to say if she knew he was testing her or was genuinely unfazed. Perhaps the return to Shady Reef was the forge she needed to turn her into a proper, unshaken field operative ready to tackle anything. Then again, maybe this was her way of masking her fears so she could move forward.

They joined CJ at the edge of the rock ledge. Behind them, where the rest of the tourists were mingling, the giant black boulders had somewhat of a steep slope that merged with the Atlantic. This part was nothing more than a sheer drop-off. He could make out a lovely sandy beach not too far from them that would make a better entry. Unfortunately, it didn't extend far enough, forcing them to contend with the waves crashing them against the rocks. One little slip-up and it would be lights out.

CJ had his climbing rig set up and ready to go. He eased himself over the ledge and kicked himself off the rocks as he rappelled down until he was a foot or two above the water. He looked back up to Logan and gave him a thumbs up.

"It's a bit of a squeeze," he said on the comm line, "but this is it."

Leah poked Logan in the arm. "Didn't he say we were only rappelling a few feet with a soft sandy beach below us?"

Logan smiled as he grasped her hand to help her over the ledge. "He also said Shady Reef was abandoned."

"Good point," she said, then lowered herself to where CJ was.

Logan took a good look at his surroundings. Taking care to ensure nothing seemed out of place, and no one was watching them. As far as he could tell, everything seemed as it should be, the only difference being a new song playing in the distance.

He turned and looked back down when he heard Leah say, "I'm in."

Logan nodded and picked up the rope. He fastened it to his harness, giving it a nice little tug to test it wouldn't come loose on him. Taking care to go unnoticed, he eased himself over the edge and slid down to the opening Leah and CJ had entered. Leah was trying to talk to him, but the waves crashing below were far too deafening to make anything out. He grabbed the edge of the opening to pull himself in, but his hand slipped from the cool mist spraying him down. On his second attempt, CJ caught his arm and pulled him through the opening.

The small cavern was dark and slick as it stretched into a black void. At its tallest point, it was pushing five and a half feet, making everyone uncomfortable. CJ shined his flashlight, illuminating the long corridor that looked more like the inside of a pipe than a cave.

Logan wiped a finger along the smooth wall, finding it cold and slick like slime. "You sure this is the right place?"

CJ nodded. "As sure as I am about everything else," he said as he fixed a motion camera to the side of the wall to warn them if someone was coming their way.

Leah flashed Logan a worried look. A smile formed on his face as he made the settle-down gesture with his hand.

"And what are the chances we slip and slide down into a bottomless pit?" Logan teased.

"Uncertain, but probably high." CJ chuckled. "This way."

Logan took a couple of steps, keeping Leah in the middle of them. For now, he was getting decent traction on the ground, which was good news. He looked ahead and saw CJ had his thermal cam out in front. It showed nothing exciting, which was some more good news.

"You think anyone used these caves for somthin'?" asked Leah.

"It's possible," said CJ. "Back in the good old days, when man was just starting to get up and running, they used to make their homes in caves.

"You see," CJ continued. "Back then, everything wanted to kill you, so your best bet of survival was finding a secure place to sleep. Kinda like the way you get the best sleep when it's raining outside since most animals bunker down in a storm, leaving you free from worrying about becoming some creature's midnight snack."

CJ stopped when he saw the end of a tunnel with a small pool in front of it. "So, you see, if you can find a cave that doesn't completely flood when the tide comes in and seals up the entrance, you've got yourself the best shelter in the world."

CJ ran his foot along the surface of the water. Then, he knelt and shone his flashlight under the surface of the water. Its beam penetrated the clear liquid, illuminating an underwater cave they couldn't see before.

He looked up at Logan. "Care for a quick dip?"

Logan shook his head. "Too valuable for that, mate. Anyway, this is more up Recon's alley."

CJ grinned at him. "It's all right to admit you're afraid."

Logan went to kick him into the pool, but CJ jumped in, before Logan made contact with him. His head bobbed just above the surface as he took a big breath. Then, he dove into the underwater cave.

Leah stood by and watched the light from CJ's flashlight dim as he swam away. "Isn't this dangerous?" she asked as she dug out her flashlight and turned it on.

"Most people would say so. CJ's what you would call an adrenaline junky. He thrives off these types of stunts."

"Huh," she said. "So, how long before we send a rescue party?"

CJ's voice came in over the line. "You two need to get over here. There's a massive chamber in here."

"How long of an underwater swim is it?" asked Leah.

"Just a quick one. It's kinda like a P-trap, and there's only one way to go, so it's impossible to get lost."

Logan held his hand out, offering up the pool to her. "After you."

Leah groaned.

He waited for her to jump in, then dived right after her. The salt water felt cool but not uncomfortable on his skin. He followed Leah through the underwater opening, swimming under a jagged rock that would slice through you if you weren't paying attention. CJ's definition of quick must have only applied to Olympic athletes, because a mighty urge to breathe crept up on him all too quickly.

Leah kicked it into high gear as she rocketed herself forward with him catching up to her. They popped their heads above the surface a few seconds later, forcing themselves to breathe over a coughing fit. CJ had squatted next to the pool, shining his light at them.

He tilted his head to one side, squinted, and asked, "You two okay?"

Logan ignored him as he hauled himself out of the water. The cavern they now stood in was massive, its sheer size making it hard to believe the locals were unaware of its existence. The walls and ceiling bore a mix of natural and man-made features, the latter suggested by the smoothness in areas where you might otherwise expect jagged stalactites. Down the center of the cavern stretched a polished, ten-foot-wide pathway flanked by rocky pillars, where stalactites and stalagmites had fused into magnificent columns. These columns were spaced evenly every five feet, creating a sense of deliberate design as they led toward a grand throne at the far end of the chamber.

The stone throne itself sat on a raised platform and was deceptively simple in design. Its rocky surface was shaped smooth to resemble elegant, dimpled cushions. Its armrests curved downward, merging seamlessly into the floor like natural stalagmites. Yet the throne was dwarfed by the awe-inspiring structure behind it. A massive cathedral of intricate rockwork reached out of the throne like crashing waves and curved upward over the throne, arching above like a giant teacup merged with the ceiling.

Leah shone her flashlight around the cavern, picking up bits of sparkles embedded in the rock. "I think we found the real Hercules Cave."

"If that's the case," said CJ, "we may have more than the Knights to contend with when the local government figures out we're down here."

Logan took a stroll toward the throne, lighting up everything he could with his flashlight along the way. "I'm not seeing another way out of here."

CJ caught up to him. "Hmm. I wonder if there's another hidden wall like the one we found back in that Blood Knight's temple in Belize?"

"I dunno," said Logan. "We needed two of their tokens to uncover those," he paused. "And, well, this place feels... off. Like it's got nothin' to do with the Knights."

CJ scanned the area with his thermal cam. "I'm not picking up anything out of the ordinary. Even the Knight's sealed doors give off a little heat."

Leah came up behind them. "I have an idea."

They both looked at her.

"You do?" asked CJ.

"Yeah," she said. "It seems pretty obvious to me."

Leah stepped onto the small platform and sat on the throne. As she glanced down, she saw her right jeans pocket had started to glow red. Reaching in, she pulled out the three-inch-long cylindrical tablet she'd brought with her that the Beta team found in the Blood Knights' temple in Belize. The strange red markings etched into it glowed as they danced around it.

"Wait, wait!" shouted Logan, but he was too late.

She held the tablet up high over her head, the glowing red symbols intensifying into a bright light that lit up the cavern as the growing symbols projected like lasers against the walls as they moved around. New white symbols appeared on the walls, drawing the bright red ones to them and locking them into place. A low rumble echoed throughout the cavern when the last red symbol found its twin on one of the columns.

"What the bloody hell is that?" Logan shouted.

CJ covered his ears as the noise intensified. "That's your sister jumping the gun!"

The water from the pool rose, defying gravity as it flowed up and out onto the walls and ceiling. The vibrations from the rumblings played with the water, causing intricate patterns to ripple across the surface as it converged toward the throne.

"This looks bad," CJ shouted.

"Over here," Leah yelled, motioning for them to join her.

Logan leapt onto the platform and took hold of the armrest. It felt warm, with a soft vibration that somehow felt reassuring to him, almost like he was meant to do this. Once CJ joined them, the throne and its small platform descended with a loud hiss into the ground like an elevator. The walls of the shaft glowed with a soft, bluish light, revealing the hexagonal shaft that shimmered like it had been carved from the largest gemstone in the world. He looked up and saw the hole through which they'd descended sealed up like the iris of a camera as it twisted closed.

"You still think this is Knight technology?" Logan asked CJ.

CJ's body was tense as he held a death grip on the other armrest. "No, I think you're right. This is something different."

"Yeah," said Leah. "But the Knights have to have been here before. I mean," she hesitated, "didn't you find this tablet in one of their temples?"

"True," said CJ, "but I don't think they had access to it. We're the ones that brought it here from our timeline."

The platform ended abruptly, knocking Logan and CJ to the ground. In front of them was an open doorway framed with a block archway. Each block was a different color, alternating between different hues of orange and blue. On the left side of the opening was a life-sized gold hieroglyph of a man with the head of a bird sitting down on a square block, holding a scroll in one hand and an ankh in the other. Opposite of him was a gold-inlaid woman with a feather poking out of the top of her head. She stood tall, holding a staff in one hand and another ankh in the other.

CJ got to his feet and stared at the pair of hieroglyphs, his hands hovering over their surface, not wanting to disturb them. He blinked slowly as he stepped back and captured their image on his wrist computer.

Logan stood up and dusted off his pant legs. "What'd you make of 'em?"

"Well, the one on the right is Thoth," he said. "You can tell by the ibis on his head."

"Ibis?" asked Logan.

"It's a type of bird," said Leah as she stepped off the platform.

"All right," said Logan. "Who's the Sheila then?"

"That would be his wife, Ma'at," said CJ. "You can tell by the ostrich feather she wears around her head. She's supposed to represent truth, justice, and harmony."

Logan raised an eyebrow. "What was that group called that your friend from that Chicago hotel worked at?"

CJ blushed. "I wouldn't call her a friend, but the group was called Ordo Veritatis et Iustitiae."

"And that means what exactly?" asked Leah.

"It's Latin for the Order of Truth," CJ paused for a moment, "and Justice."

"Huh," said Logan. "Reckon there could be a link between the two?"

CJ shrugged. "Don't really know, but it's possible."

"Hold on," said Leah. "You're saying there's another group out there like the Citadel?"

"Looks that way," said CJ.

Logan slid by him and entered the new cavern. Lining the walls were fire basins stacked on ornate pillars that lit up one by one in pairs opposite of each other as he walked by. The rectangular room itself was carved out of limestone and polished to a high gloss. Marbled Sphinx, like the one CJ was admiring back at the Memphis museum, sat on three-foot-tall pedestals. There were twelve in total, six on each side of the room facing each other. Between them rested an ancient red rug that ran the length of the room, ending at another golden-arched doorway.

Leah poked her head through the archway. "Creepy."

CJ grimaced as he leaned away from her. "Creepy? I think it's fascinating. We're probably the first people to step foot in here after thousands and thousands of years."

Logan knelt and picked up some pink flower petals scattered across the rug. He held them up for CJ to see. "These seem pretty fresh to me."

In a flash, CJ scanned the room with his thermal cam. Other than the fire basins, the only other hot spot emanated from the next room in front of them.

"Curious," said CJ.

"Ugh," Logan said as he wiped his hand down his face. "Don't use that word again. You sound too much like Nieminen when you do."

"Whatever," he said. "Someone must have been here. Just get your gun ready. There's definitely something glowing in the other room."

Logan pulled out his pistol and aimed it at the next chamber. He took each step with care, as if testing the ground for weak spots as he made his way toward the next room. Both CJ and Leah followed suit, keeping their pistols at low ready.

Logan pressed his back against the wall next to the opening with CJ and Leah lined up on the other side. He leaned over to get a quick look inside. "You've gotta be kiddin' me!" he said.

"What?" whispered CJ. "What is it?"

Logan holstered his gun and gestured toward the other room with his head. "Go check it out."

CJ nodded and holstered his gun. With his thermal cam pointed out in front, he pivoted and rolled around the corner into the next room. "Oh, wow," he said.

Leah came up behind him. "Wha— Ohh. How is this possible?"

Logan came up behind her. "It isn't. That throne elevator ride wasn't that long. The tip of this place should be pokin' through the ground."

CJ took several more steps inside, snapping as many pictures as possible from his wrist computer. The new room was shaped like a pyramid as large as the smallest one in Giza. The walls were lined in pure gold, with thousands of hieroglyphs etched into them. Treasures of all kinds across many cultures were strewed about, the most impressive being a massive bronze statue of Athena that was almost as high as the pyramid itself. A pillar of white light shone through the center, highlighting a circular dais in the middle of the room.

"This has to be another temple of Thoth," said CJ.

Logan raised an eyebrow. "There's more than one of these?"

"Not anymore," he said. "The other one I'm thinking of was in Hermopolis, but it was destroyed ages ago, and I'm pretty sure it didn't look like this."

Leah pointed at the dais. "Something's going on."

The pillar of light pulsed as it grew in size and intensity. Logan grabbed Leah by the wrist to pull her back, but it was too late. The bright light expanded past them, its brightness indescribable. He tried to cover his eyes to shield them from the searing pain, but it was pointless. He crumpled to his knees, but even with his head down and hands over his eyes, he could still see through his eyelids and make out each individual bone in his hands.

Darkness swept over him for what felt like an hour while he waited for his vision to come back. He got up and looked around, finding himself no longer in Thoth's temple. CJ and Leah were ahead of him, leaning over the railing of a balcony.

"How in the hell…," he said when he saw what CJ was staring at.

"I don't know how," said CJ. "But we're in a floating city above the great eye of the Sahara."

Chapter 24

United Citadel Field Unit
Beta Team

I sat on the edge of my bed in a quaint downtown Brooklyn hotel. Every channel I flipped to had wall-to-wall news coverage on the sudden appearance of an ancient-looking city floating over the Richat Structure in the Sahara. From what I could gather, the Richat Structure, often referred to as the Eye of the Sahara, is a series of concentric rings spanning a diameter of twenty-five miles. From space, it's said to resemble a massive eye staring back from Earth. At least that's what the scientist they were interviewing said.

The Richat Structure had existed for eons, but the headline was about this sudden appearance of a floating city. There was nothing absolute about the city's appearance, or why it was even there in the first place, but I had three good guesses on why it had suddenly appeared.

This intense feeling in the pit of my stomach told me the Bravo Subunit team was involved. My attempts to contact CJ had failed so far, only heightened my uneasiness about the situation. Still, there was a possibility that he was out of communications range. Then again, that didn't explain why my satellite call wasn't answered.

I flipped the telly off as Maeve came out of the bathroom. "Well," she said. "What's the latest?"

"Not much," I said. "But it's a good thing we got here when we did. It appears they've begun grounding all flights for the time being."

I felt the familiar buzz from my mobile, and I snagged it out of my pocket, hoping to see it was a message from CJ. If I had been smiling at that moment, it wouldn't have lasted all too long.

"What is it?" asked Maeve.

"Something's wrong," I said as I flipped the telly back on.

The news had redirected its coverage from the floating city to an airliner that exploded twenty minutes after taking off in Los Angeles. Knots formed in my stomach as I prayed it wasn't the flight Aaron was taking back to Tokyo. Regrettably, I already knew the answer before they flashed the flight number on the screen. He was so hellbent on taking a break from everything and spending quality time with his Japanese grandparents. I had pleaded with him to stay in Vegas, where Chambers could check in on him, but he refused.

"No way." Maeve gasped. "Why would the Knights bother with him? He played a very minor role, if any, in our attempt to extract Rose."

"He's a soft target. Clearly, they wanted to send a message," I said.

Maeve rubbed her forehead. "Or he was a part of the plan all along, and when the Knights got wind that he was defecting, they found an opportunity to remove him. Either way, we'll never know."

I lowered my head, my voice barely above a whisper. "This feels like one of those endless nightmares you just can't wake up from."

Maeve pounded her fists together like a bully making a threat on the playground. "I'm so ready to take them all out."

"In due time," I said. "First, we need to talk with this Selim person."

"Right, are you sure you can trust this Devon fellow?" True to his word, Devon had called earlier and asked us to meet him at the Brooklyn Museum, where Selim worked.

"No," I replied, shaking my head. "But I think he's genuine. After all, he cleaned up the aftermath of Rose's ambush. I can't help but shudder at the thought of what might have happened if the police had discovered I wasn't actually with the State Department."

Maeve smiled. "Oh, I'd say at least twenty years of incarceration, if they let you serve your charges congruently."

I smiled, raising an eyebrow. "I'm fairly certain you'd be right beside me with your aiding and abetting charges."

The hotel room phone rang, and I picked up the receiver. It was the front desk clerk, letting me know a cab had finally arrived to take us to the Brooklyn Museum. A welcome development, as I had no desire to walk that distance today.

"Come on, Maeve," I said. "Let's go."

As we stepped outside the hotel, I couldn't help but be struck by the surreal emptiness of the city. This massive island, home to millions of souls, was a ghost town. Everyone's lives had been put on hold until the current events ran their course. Then there was this strange, icky feeling I couldn't shake that swelled up inside of me. It was like someone was spying on me from afar, and I could do nothing about it.

The cab driver hopped outside to open the rear door for us. He was around his mid-fifties with a gray beard trimmed neatly to his round face, and he tipped his hat to us as we got inside his cab. In the blink of an eye, he was back in the driver's seat, pulling away from the hotel. His eyes flashed in the rearview mirror as he studied us.

"Can you believe what's going on out in the Sahara?" he spat out, full of excitement. "I'd never seen nothin' like it!"

"It's somethin'," I said.

"Oh, you have no idea," he said, shaking his head. "Took me forever to get across the bridge with all those lunatics standing around clogging it up."

"Huh," said Maeve. "Why are they doing that?"

"Who knows," he said. "Just a bunch of doomsayers mucking up the works."

I leaned forward so he could hear me better. "What's the rest of the city like?"

"Eh, pretty much like this," he said, with a shrug. "But I'll tell ya, you won't find an empty pew in any of the churches."

Maeve tapped me on the shoulder and whispered, "That's probably not a bad idea."

I nodded. "You hear anything new about that floating city?" I asked the driver.

He cocked his head to the side. "Heard they tried sending some choppers its way, but it kept drifting off, like some kinda mirage."

"Did they, by chance, see anybody up there?" I asked.

"Not that I've heard," he said. "News guy said the place looks abandoned, which, y'know, makes sense if you ask me."

"Oh," said Maeve. "Why's that?"

"What?" he chuckled. "You two don't know?"

"Know what?" asked Maeve.

"That city? That's what's left of Atlantis. The poor souls living there died off thousands of years ago when it first disappeared. But now? It's back."

Maeve turned to look at me, blinking her eyes. "Well, I'd say that's a new one for me."

I shot Maeve a faint smile. "With everything else that's gone on, who knows if it's true or not."

"Well, looky here," he said. "Made it in record time."

I handed the driver the fare and thanked him for the ride. He gave us a cheerful wave and a broad smile before pulling away, off to search for his next passenger—if there even was one. I imagined only a handful of cabbies had bothered to work today, but chances were good we'd be his only fare for the rest of the day.

Turning toward the museum, I spotted Devon sitting on a curved bench that stretched almost the entire length of the glass entrance. His back was to us as he intently watched a video on his phone, seemingly oblivious to our arrival. The entrance itself struck me as an afterthought, a modern addition grafted onto the building long after its original construction. The main structure resembled a smaller capitol building, with prominent Greek pillars supporting a stately pediment topped off with an impressive dome rotunda.

Devon jumped up when he heard our feet shuffling along the pavement. "Oh, good. You're here."

"Yeah," said Maeve. "Good thing we got here when we did. Traffic was a nightmare."

Devon furrowed his brow. "Huh?"

"She's just jokin' with you," I said.

"Oh," he blushed.

"So, where's Selim?" I asked.

Devon pulled a key out of his jeans pocket. "Right this way," he said. "Oh, and by the way, Nurse Farrell is out of surgery and is doing excellent, thanks to you."

"That's wonderful news," I said.

Devon nodded and smiled, then turned to enter the museum. He slid the key into the lock and adjusted it several times before opening it. We passed through the threshold, and Devon locked the door behind us.

"Not expecting a lot of patrons today?" Maeve teased.

"Not really, but that's not the reason. No one else showed up to work today," he said. "If you would follow me. Dr. Hamza is right over here.

Devon cut across the plaza, curving around a set of benches under the rotunda. We wove through several dazzling exhibit halls, doing our best to keep up with Devon as he zipped past the displays. Eventually, after Maeve and I were out of breath, we entered the Egyptian section of the museum.

Standing in front of a display was a man I assumed to be the Curator of Egyptian Art, Dr. Selim Hamza. He was on the shorter side of the equation, maybe five and a half feet, with his shoes on. He wore a dark suit and tie that contrasted with his white hair and beard. My best guess was to place him in his mid-seventies, but he could be older.

He nodded at Maeve when she came up beside him. "A friend of yours?" she asked, nodding at the statue before him.

"If only," he said. "This is the goddess Isis nursing her son, Horus. She's one of the most powerful figures in the Egyptian divine order."

"That's got to come in handy," I said, reaching out to shake his hand.

Selim reciprocated. "Dr. Lewis, I presume?"

"In the flesh," I said. "I'm with the UC, and this here is my cohort, Maeve."

Selim shook her hand. "Pleasure to meet you," he said, then returned to me. "Sorry to hear about Rose and the ambush."

I shook my head. "We've got to put a stop to them," I said, echoing Maeve's sentiments.

"You'll get no argument from me," said Selim.

"So, what's your connection to the Knights?" I asked.

"Come," he said. "Let's walk and talk."

Following Selim to the next display, he said, "I belong to an organization far older than the United Citadel, born out of an ancient Egyptian religious order known as the Priests of Thoth."

Both Maeve and I exchanged a look.

"And by the looks on your faces," he continued, "you've heard the name Thoth before."

"Indeed, we have," I said. "And fairly recently."

Selim nodded. "As I had expected. Thoth was an interesting character to learn about. His followers believed he was the one who taught Isis her most powerful magic."

"So, Thoth is more powerful than Isis?" I asked.

"He definitely had the potential. However, Thoth was more of a scholar and diplomat. In fact, his book is said to contain some of the greatest knowledge in the known universe."

"Funny," said Maeve. "You speak as if he's a real person."

Selim tilted his head to one side. "Well, up until the arrival of the floating city, I did have my doubts. But now …"

"Likewise," I said.

Maeve's jaw dropped. "Really?"

I tilted my head and nodded. "Yeah. I'm starting to think there's more going on here than just the Knights." I snapped my fingers and said, "You remember back at the institute when Rose mentioned they had Zeus there? The same one you saw die when the Knights shot him in the back of the head on Shady Reef?"

"Well, yeah." She paused. "But we never actually saw him there at the institute. Rose was the only one who brought him up."

I nodded, certain there had to be a connection. In my timeline, CJ had a run-in at the Blood Knights' temple in Belize, where he witnessed a gruesome ritual involving a man named Prometheus. Another person with a mythological name that should only exist in mythology. From what CJ described, Prometheus should had died during the ritual but didn't.

I considered telling Selim all of this, but held back. The UC has a reputation for keeping secrets, and I wasn't ready to break that tradition just yet.

"True," I said, then refocused back on Selim. "But would it be possible to have another man like Thoth out there?"

Selim nodded. "I don't see why not."

Maeve threw her hands up in the air. "I can't believe you're seriously considering this. We're diving off the deep end into the world of fantasy."

"Which reminds me," I said, tapping my chin. "What do you know about the convergence?"

Selim's face turned pale. "How did you know about that?"

"Rose mentioned it before she died, and this one over here," I said, pointing my thumb at Maeve, "has also mentioned it."

Selim covered his mouth with his hand and pulled it down, tugging on his beard in the process. "Hmm, this is something," he said as he wandered to the next display.

"What is it?" I asked.

"The convergence is a tale only passed down from the Priest of Thoth's bloodline. Even still, there's not many of them left that know the tale."

"But I take it you do?" I asked.

Selim nodded his head yes. "I know parts of it. The priest believed the great convergence was to be heralded by a magnificent red comet that would streak across the summer sky." He paused as he moved to the next exhibit. He seemed lost in thought for a moment as he studied a statue of a woman's upper torso with the face of a lioness. "Although, from what my father told me, it wasn't a comet in the original tale."

"Oh," I said. "What was it?"

"Well, that's the problem. You see, that little detail has been lost to the sands of time. I asked my grandfather once about it before he passed, and all he could speculate was it was something else."

"Noted," I said. "You mentioned the comet was a herald. Do you know what it was a herald for?"

Selim waved his finger at me. "Good catch," he said. "The term *convergence* is a good word to describe this event, but I believe *alignment* would be better."

Selim held his arms out wide, making a rotational gesture. "The whole vastness of the universe, the parts you can see and can't see along with other parts that fold into different dimensions, are all rotating into an alignment."

"Then what?" asked Maeve.

Selim lowered his arms. "Yeah." He sighed. "That part is unclear, but my grandfather had some ideas. First, we'll have what some Christians call the Three Days of Darkness."

My knees nearly buckled as I thought about what I saw in London before going through the Rift Generator. I was in Ben's office listening to his briefing while we waited for the Rift Gen to come online. Before we left, I saw a great blackness overtaking the city. It was strange, because I don't think a comet was in the sky to mark the occasion. Perhaps it was on the other side of the world at that time. We were so busy that it's entirely possible we were unaware of its arrival.

Selim continued, "Next to follow would be what the Norse called the Twilight of the Gods, but the truth is probably contained in the Book of Thoth. That is, if your counterparts can find it."

"My, my, good doctor," I said. "You seem to have spies everywhere."

"Not everywhere." He winked at me. "But I'm working on it. But this tidbit came from another member of your organization, Mr. Conor Kaplan, who told me about his plan to head on out to Egypt and search for the book weeks ago."

"And he did," I said, then lowered my head. "And now he's in a coma."

"Dear god," he gasped. "What happened?"

"Shadow Knights got to him," said Maeve.

Selim nodded. "Oh, well then, I'd say he's lucky to be alive at all."

My gaze flickered between Maeve and Selim. "Dr. Hamza, while we were investigating Rose's home…" I hesitated. "Let's see, how do I put this?"

Maeve rolled her eyes while she shook her head. "What Eva is trying to say is that I wasn't exactly acting like my charming little self then. I believe the words she used to describe my episode to another doctor was I was unstable with a different persona while spouting off phrases that made little to no sense."

"That's part of it," I admitted. "But the final act of her episode was pinpointing exactly where to find a bloodstone that Rose had stolen from the Blood Knights. Would you know how she was able to do that?"

"Hmm, let me think on this," he said, pacing between displays.

While Selim was deep in thought, I pulled out my mobile, hoping to see if a message from CJ had come through yet.

Maeve raised her eyebrows and asked, "Any news?"

I shook my head and tucked the mobile away. It was difficult being cut off like this, and worse yet, I didn't have a way to get there to find out what had happened. CJ has always been good about keeping me in the loop, and now the only thing I could think about was Shadow Knights taking them down.

Devon, who had been glued to his phone the whole time, looked up and said, "I'm gonna go check something out."

Selim looked up from a display and said, "Oh, all right, Devon."

He continued to pace, then stopped in front of a display holding a scrap of papyrus where the figure of Thoth was illustrated. "What do you make of self-proclaimed psychics?" he asked Maeve.

Maeve balked at the notion. "Nothing more than con artists who prey on the desperate."

"Yes," he said, still fixated on the papyrus. "That could be true, but have you ever predicted a series of events exactly as they unfolded?"

Maeve shook her head. "I just get good gut feelings."

Selim turned his head and met her gaze. "Would you say these gut feelings are more or less than fifty percent of the time?"

Maeve sighed. "What does that got to do with it?"

Selim held up a finger. "Ah, because even a coin flip is fifty-fifty on average unless there's an outside force at play. I believe human predictions operate on similar principles."

"Okay," said Maeve. "It's fifty-fifty then."

"Uh-huh," he said. "And what about in the presence of that bloodstone you found?"

Maeve's face hardened as she glared at Selim. "Fifty-fifty," she said, making sure to emphasize each syllable.

I took a few careful steps back, feigning interest in a tiny figurine displayed in a nearby case. Neither of them knew it, but I had the bloodstone tucked away in my handbag. It seems that Selim had come to the same conclusion I had with the idea the stone might have some effect on her, and the last thing we needed to deal with was an unhinged Maeve.

Selim kept his tone calm and natural, asking her, "Have you ever heard of the artist Isaac?"

This seemed to do the trick, turning Maeve's rising temperament back down to a low simmer. "I've seen his work but don't really know who he is."

"Yeah," I said. "We've retrieved one of his paintings from Rose's home."

"Isaac is, or was, an interesting man, to say the least," he said. "I met him once in the mid-sixties, and he was pushing eighty-eight years old by then, but his mind was still as sharp as a tack."

We followed Selim with bated breath as he entered the Mummy Chamber. The black room contained various sarcophagi standing upright on pedestals, neatly displayed behind individual glass cases. Large display signs were mounted next to them, letting you know who exactly the sarcophagus was home to and their life's history.

"You see," he said, observing the first sarcophagus. "He used to run with the Knights up until the mid-forties. They were convinced he had the gift of sight."

"Did he?" I asked.

"According to him, no." He chuckled. "All the subjects of his paintings were inspired by stories one of the Knights would tell him. He confessed he never knew the true meanings behind them, but he felt they were meant to be interpreted by others."

Selim took a deep breath and lowered his gaze. "Although, he did tell me that one day, members from a future organization called the United Citadel would contact me and that I should help—"

We all turned our attention to the sounds of feet running in our direction. I discreetly placed my hand on the grip of my gun under my shirt. Thankfully, it was Devon who appeared in the doorway.

His face was beet red as he bent over with his hands on his knees, trying to catch his breath.

Selim placed his hand on Devon's shoulder. "What is it?"

Devon looked up at us. "They're everywhere."

"Who?" I asked.

"The Blood Knights," he stammered. "They're dressed in their red garb, lining the streets in all the major cities."

"What are they doing?" asked Maeve.

"Just standing there like they're waiting for something."

My eyes met Maeve's. "We need to get out of here while we still can."

"I agree," said Selim. "You can take my car."

"You're not coming with us?" I asked.

Selim shook his head. "No," he said. "My place is here."

Chapter 25

United Citadel Field Unit
BRAVO SUBUNIT

CJ hung over the balcony as he tried to wave down a helicopter flying toward them. None of them could tell if the pilot could see them, but something peculiar happened when it tried to fly toward them. The helicopter seemed to hit an invisible wall, its forward motion halting abruptly. The rotor blades slowed down as they sliced through the air like time itself was slowing down. It tilted on its axis in real time, veering off to attempt another approach, each ending with the same results.

The air was deathly cold and faint, but they were low enough to where it was still breathable. CJ looked past Logan toward Leah. "Aren't you glad you came?" he asked, his breath visible.

Leah laughed as she rubbed her arms for warmth. "Beats lying in bed waiting for a Knight to pay me a visit."

Logan took a step back from the railing. "We need to focus," he said. "First objective is to find that book. Second is to find a way off this thing."

"Just the two?" CJ teased.

"Chris," Logan sneered.

"Sorry," CJ muttered. "I'll focus. I'm just a little shaken up, that's all."

"Pull it together," said Logan as he surveyed their surroundings. "Have you contacted Eva yet?"

"No," CJ replied. "I've got nothin' on me that's showing any type of signal, and that includes satellite."

"Perfect," Logan mumbled.

They were standing at the edge of a circular limestone plaza that could have been a road. In the middle was a singular obelisk with a five-foot base that stretched thirty feet into the sky. Flanking the plaza were two tan massive square buildings ten floors high that tapered in the higher it went. Colorful hieroglyphics in six rows of various heights circled the upper portion of the building, with the lower half comprised of one row of Thoth hieroglyphics. Its gold inlay reflected the sun's light toward the obelisk.

The path between the buildings featured a raised planter running down the center filled with palm trees. Metal poles connected the two buildings with banners hung from them that swayed in the wind. Skyscrapers from various known and unknown cultures sprang up haphazardly around them, making it difficult to tell just how large this sky city was.

Logan walked past the obelisk, flexing his fingers against the cold. He scanned the buildings for a doorway to escape the biting air. Everything was sealed up, which only added to his frustration. He was tempted by the idea of shimming up one of the palm trees to snag a banner to use as a makeshift blanket but figured his grip was too weak from the cold, and they were probably out of arm's reach anyway.

Then he spotted it. Up ahead was a circular domed building he hadn't noticed before. It appeared to be made out of some sort of red clay material severely weathered, with a white line only half a foot thick circling the center of it, highlighting an open door.

"Over there," Logan shouted as he pointed at the door.

Leah was already ahead of them as she sprinted to escape the cold. Logan passed her up as he entered the building, with CJ pulling up the rear. The door behind them sealed up with a woosh, locking them inside.

CJ looked at the door, then back at them. "Well, at least it's warm in here."

Twelve gold doors lined the circular room, set into a seamless alabaster wall. Above them, a massive gold dome capped the structure, its surface dotted with bright pinpricks of light. On the polished black floor, six evenly spaced four-foot-tall pillars formed an inner ring, each crowned with a silver dome that projected the scattered lights onto the ceiling. At the room's center, a ten-foot-tall obelisk stood proud with a single, intensely bright, beam of light shooting upward from its peak.

CJ moved toward one of the silver domes, his fingers brushing against its surface. "What is this?" he muttered, inspecting the structure. Tiny laser-like lenses dotted its silver exterior, arranged in what appeared to be a random pattern. A narrow ridge ran between the pedestal and the silver dome, just wide enough for his fingers to fit.

Logan knelt beside him, shining his flashlight into the ridge. The beam revealed a narrow column with the dome's edge curling inward to form a smooth lip.

"Looks like we're meant to grab it," said Logan.

Leah meandered about the room, looking up at the golden dome-shaped ceiling. She would cover one eye with her hand and then the other as she connected the dots with her fingers in the air.

CJ tapped Logan on the arm with the back of his fingers, then pointed at Leah. "What's your sister doing?"

Logan watched her trace an invisible line in the air, then looked up at the dome. "Looks like she's sortin' out a puzzle."

Leah looked at them and held a finger to her lips with an audible "Shhhhh!" echoing all around them.

"Touchy," whispered CJ, which prompted another shush from Leah.

She walked around the central obelisk, dragging her fingers on it. Satisfied with the spot she found, she dropped to her knees and rolled to her back, staring up at the great dome.

Logan knelt beside her. "What are you on to?"

"What do you see when you look up at a nighttime sky?" she asked.

CJ cut in before Logan could speak. "Well, I usually see a thick haze of pollution, but I believe stars are the answer you're lookin' for."

Logan looked up and said, "Of course."

CJ looked up. "This has to be the fanciest planetarium I've ever been to."

"CJ," said Leah. "What's a prominent constellation the ancient Egyptians would worship?"

"Hold on, let me check," he said as he searched the data stored on his wrist computer. "Okay, looks like it wasn't so much constellations they were interested in, but individual stars. Something about a pharaoh's journey, and…" He paused. "Oh, here's an easy one. Orion to them was Osiris."

"And it looks the same now as it did back then?" she asked.

"Of course," said CJ. "The stars haven't drifted that much."

"That's all I need. See if you can rotate that dome over there," she said, pointing at the silver dome on his left.

"Guess we know who the smart one is in the family," CJ boasted.

"Along with which one packs a bigger punch," Logan retorted, accompanied by a snicker from Leah.

CJ waved them aside and slipped his hand into the crevice, gripping the dome's edge.

"All right," she said. "Start rotating it counterclockwise, and I'll tell you when to stop."

"Why not clockwise?" asked CJ.

"Because it's not what I asked for," she said, this time getting a snicker from Logan.

"Hey." CJ smirked. "If you two are gonna team up on me, I'll just go home."

"You know the way?" Logan sneered.

"I'm waiting," said Leah.

CJ rotated the dome, and the lights on the greater dorm spun into place.

"Stop!" shouted Leah, then pointed to another mini-dome. "Now rotate this one."

CJ repeated his actions, only stopping when Leah told him so. A loud noise echoed throughout, vibrating the floor. From the sound it made, it had to be something massive underneath them that groaned in protest as it rotated.

CJ looked back at Leah, his gaze widened. "Oh, this better not be some type of cap twisting open so I can fall out the bottom."

Logan got up to his feet. "Well, we can't just sit around here all day."

"Is there another star or constellation that's related to Osiris?" Leah interjected.

CJ consulted his wrist computer. "There's Sirius, who represents Osiris's wife, Isis. It's part of Canis Major."

"Ooh, I don't know what that one looks like," she said.

CJ joined them and knelt to show her the image on his wrist computer. Leah studied it for a moment. Her eyes darted back and forth between his computer and the gold dome. She pointed at a silver dome on the other side of the room and said, "Rotate that one."

CJ nodded and got to his feet. Once again, he spun a sliver dome, this time creating a loud bang like a cannon going off at a sports game. Leah jumped up and grabbed Logan's arm, while CJ ducked down and wrapped his arms around the pedestal, his eyes closed tight.

Leah elbowed Logan in the side. "I thought you said he was an adrenaline junkie?"

CJ opened one eye and looked around the room. Sensing no other danger, he let go of the pedestal and hoisted himself back to his feet. "Falling to my death isn't the type of thrill I'm lookin' for."

Logan raised an eyebrow. "But crashing into a mountain is?"

CJ groaned. "For the one-hundredth time, we both survived unscathed."

Another rumble echoed through the room. Faster than light, CJ was back to hugging the pedestal. To his right, one of the doors opened with a woosh.

CJ got back to his feet, his heart racing. "Well, all right. 'Bout time something good happens."

Leah shook her head. "I think it's a trick."

CJ looked around the room, then sighed as his head dropped. "Yeah, I think you're right," he said, leaning up against the silver dome. "There's twelve doors in here, and it's doubtful the first one we opened is the right one."

"Yep," said Leah. "Twelve doors and six silver domes."

CJ snapped his finger. "Of course. "Three is a cosmic power number."

"Eh?" said Logan.

"Hmm," said CJ. "I'll start with something simple like birth, life, and death. Groups of three. There's lots of other things that come in three, like the Holy Trinity, or if you want to take the Egyptian path, they tended to group their gods into three complementary forces like Osiris, Isis, and Horus. Hell, even in basic math, it's the first odd prime number you run into unless you count like a crazy person."

"Uh-huh," said Logan. "Don't see how that helps us since there's twelve doors and only six of these dome thingies."

"True," said CJ. "But those are just multiples of threes. If I had to make a wager, I'd say there's nine constellations to figure out, and we've only solved one and a quarter so far."

"Why nine?" asked Leah.

"It's just a guess," said CJ. "I figured since we already know there's twelve doors and six mini-domes, that just leaves nine."

"What about three?" asked Logan.

A cryptic smile crossed CJ's lips. "That would be us."

They spent several hours rotating the silver domes, trying to work out the constellation patterns the room expected. Rotating one silver dome would often destroy parts of another constellation, sending them back to the beginning with various doors opening and closing.

Logan placed his hand on the floor, feeling its cold, smooth texture. "Feels like the vibrations are fading away."

"That's a good thing, right?" asked CJ as he continued to rotate another silver dome.

"Stop!" said Leah. "Big Dipper should be the last one."

The central obelisk emitted a soft hiss. The brilliant beam of light atop its peak shifted across the vast golden ceiling, resembling the sun tracing its path across the sky. Slowly, the light descended toward the horizon of the great gold dome ceiling, finally coming to rest at the center of one of the twelve doors. The door shimmered briefly before sliding smoothly into the ground with a quiet whoosh.

"Think we found our exit," Leah said as she got to her feet.

Through the doorway, they found themselves in a marbled arched corridor. Thin gold inlays ran through the middle of the walls and terminated at the arched doorway at the end. If there was a door, it was already open to the next room. The room consisted of a vast darkness, like staring out into space. Somewhere inside the vast room, a light inside flickered on, revealing a stone lectern with a thick book on top. From their point of view, it seemed to float with a gentle swaying motion.

CJ pointed at it. "There it is!"

Logan led the way down the twenty-foot hallway. His senses were on high alert, unsure if this was a trick. As he got closer to the book, an unexpected wave of serenity swelled in him. It crept slowly in as his head felt like it was underwater. Being so close to the book, he fought to push forward, placing one foot in front of the other. His eyes felt heavy, and couldn't tell if he was awake anymore. As he crossed the threshold into the black void, he reached out for the book only for his fingers to graze the top of the cover.

A surge of energy shot through his body, freeing his mind from its former confines. The book morphed into a stack of papyrus scrolls, then a wood-bound book. He picked it up, and it morphed into a black leather-bound book with a gold inlaid image of Thoth on the cover.

A hand reached out of the shadows and tried to steal the book from Logan. He yanked it back and pulled out his gun in one swift motion. Clutching the book against his chest, he panned the black room, looking for the thief. On his second pass, he saw the lectern was gone, replaced by two armed men holding CJ and Leah in front of them, their pistols shoved into the base of their heads.

Logan recognized the one holding Leah. He had seen him before during the New Orleans mission to rescue Maeve and Leah. He was still wearing his black robe with red accents and a pendent of the runic letter Feoh, ᚠ which signaled him as the leader of the Blood Knights.

His friend, on the other hand, was unknown to him. He wore a similar robe, except his was black with purple accents. Logan surmised the pendant he wore was also a runic letter that looked like the letter "W" on a pole, ᛏ but was clueless about its name or meaning.

Logan kept his gun trained on the Blood Knight. "Malcolm Ward," he thundered. "How did you get here?"

Malcolm licked his lips. "Why, through the ever-so-generous assistance of Mr. Kopache, of course!" he rattled off. "Though I must confess, the sheer ordeal of sitting here, waiting while you fumble about with that pitifully simple little room, was almost more than I could bear."

"Why not just take the book and run like the cowards you are?" asked Logan.

Malcolm tightened his grip on Leah. A little whimper escaped her lips before she regained her composure. "Oh, I did try, and tried, and tried!" he said, nearly tripping over his words. "And I must say, I'm positively offended that you'd imagine me loitering in this dreary little black room waiting for you and your pathetic band of friends to join our little get-together. I do have better things to do with my time, you know."

Kopache's eyes narrowed. "Enough of this tiresome charade. Surrender the book now, and perhaps we'll permit you the luxury of walking out of here alive."

"Fine," said Logan. "Let them go, and I'll give you the book."

"No," Leah snapped.

Malcolm's lips curled into a sinister smile. "Oh, I'll give you the girl. But as for the one who shot me? Oh no, we've still got some... catching up to do."

"Deal," said Logan.

"What!" Leah exclaimed.

"It'll be all right," CJ mumbled, seemingly rubbing his hands together as he covertly unfastened his wrist computer.

Malcolm pushed Leah to the floor, his gun now trained on Logan. "Now, be a good little girl," he purred, "and fetch me my book."

Leah stood up and rubbed the back of her head where Malcolm's gun had been pressed. She took the book from Logan and handed it to Malcolm, stepping to the side.

"Ohhh," Malcolm breathed, clutching the book. "I feel so... alive."

"I can fix that," Logan said, firing several rounds at Malcolm.

Leah dropped to the ground as Malcolm clutched his chest with the book and returned fire. His bullets ripped through the air, striking Logan in the stomach. CJ threw his wrist computer to Leah as Kopache spun around, grabbed Malcolm by the wrist, and dragged both Malcolm and CJ away through the black wall in the blink of an eye.

Logan was on the ground, a pool of blood growing under him. Leah ripped his shirt open and pressed down on the wound.

"Get the Medi-Flex," Logan whispered.

Leah zipped open his pack, pulling out the metallic Medi-Flex pouch. She ripped it open and placed it over his wound, smoothing out the wrinkles in the silicon-like patch. She took the two-pronged remote from the patch, touched it to the surface of the patch, and pressed the button. A gel-like substance flowed through the wound, stopping all the internal bleeding along the way.

Leah bit her lip. "You gonna be all right?"

Logan winced in pain as he sat up. "I will once Eva checks me out, but this should hold me for a bit."

The building shook, sending particles of dust in the air. Leah put on CJ's wrist computer, then helped Logan to his feet. He doubled over in pain, but at least he could walk for now. Leah helped him down the hallway, and the curved ceiling dissipated like white smoke, forming a new cloud.

"I think this place is fading away without the book here," she said.

Logan looked up, seeing the once impressive skyscrapers turn into clouds. "I think you're right."

They reentered the round planetarium room and found that all twelve doors had been opened. The six mini-domes had vanished, leaving only the obelisk in the center with the great light. Its light shone brightly on the ground in front of them, recreating the same pillar of light that brought them here. Flanking the bright light were two statues of Thoth and Ma'at, positioned exactly like their golden hieroglyphic counterparts that greeted them at the bottom of that "throne elevator."

"This has to be it," said Logan.

Leah nodded and wrapped his arm behind her neck to help him the rest of the way. They made it a few feet away from the pillar of light when they noticed that the statues weren't statues but real people. Thoth stood up as the bright light intensified, blinding them as before.

It felt like several minutes passed before Logan could open his eyes. He was lying down with an IV stuck in his arm. He turned and saw Leah sitting on a stool, playing on her phone in a hospital room.

"What happened?" he whispered.

Leah jumped up and came to his bedside. "You passed out after we got on the plane. Don't you remember?"

Logan shut his eyes again. "Where are we?"

"Back in Las Vegas," she said.

"Where's Eva?" he whispered.

"I haven't seen her since she heard the news about CJ, but Maeve's been stopping by to check in on you."

Logan closed his eyes, and a single tear formed in the corner. Thoughts of what the Knights might be doing to CJ kept looping through his mind, each one pressing down like a boulder on his chest. This wasn't like him, and he knew it. He'd long since mastered the art of burying his emotions—yet here he was, crumbling under the weight of it all. Maybe it was the painkillers loosening his guard? At least, that's what he told himself.

"Do me a favor," he whispered.

"Sure," said Leah. "Anything."

"Tell Eva I won't stop until I bring CJ home."

She smiled. "Me too."

Logan took a deep breath. "To the end."

Epilogue

United Citadel
Assault Division Mission Report

Date: 09/20/2019

Team Leader: Dr. Evangeline Lewis / Defense Division / Beta

Report filed by: Logan Kaplan / Assault Division / Beta

Objective:

    1: Rescue former Blood Knight Scientist Rose Lombardi (Failed)

    2: Rescue Phillip Wallace (Failed)

    3: Recover Book of Thoth (Failed)

Operation: Dr. Lewis split the team in half for these objectives. The Beta team, composed of Dr. Lewis and Maeve Donovan, was to follow up on Iris's sister, Rose, who had been convicted and sentenced for the murder of her family. It was believed she could offer vital information about the operations of the Blood Knights.

       The second team, Bravo Subunit, would track down Jacob Wallace's son, Phillip Wallace, who was abducted from his pool by the

Knights in 1980 when he was eleven years old. While tracking down Phillip Wallace, Connor Kaplan from the Alpha team arrived, creating Objective 3.

Outcome: During Beta's team meeting with Rose, she eluded to having some secret research stashed away along with other information that she would give up if they were able to free her. After hearing this information, Leah snuck off to Shady Reef with Officer Chambers. They were able to locate Rose's research, but had it stolen by Edgardo, who appears to be the new leader on the island.

I believe her research has to do with the creation of the Blood Knight's Acolytes. Reacquiring that research will be a top priority.

Unaware of Leah's actions, Eva and Maeve continued with the plan to rescue Rose, where she was killed, possibly by the Knights. In the aftermath, Eva discovered another group similar to the UC, with deep ties to Egyptian priests. This is a relationship we will be exploring in the future.

Bravo Subunit, en route to recover Phillip, also discovered the same organization, Ordo Veritatis et Iustitiae, which is Latin for the Order of Truth and Justice, has been infiltrating the Knights organization.

Upon arrival in Egypt, we reconnected with Connor Kaplan of the Alpha team from our timeline. After his abduction and rescue, we followed the trail to locate the Book of Thoth. After discovering the book in a floating city above the Richat Structure in Africa, Malcolm Ward, leader of the Blood Knights, and Mathias Kopache, leader of the Shadow Knights, appeared and took the book along with CJ as their prisoner. Their whereabouts are currently unknown, but we are hopeful Dr. Selim Hamza of Ordo Veritatis et Iustitiae has some ideas.

There's also another lead involving Hanny, the young girl injured during the Beta team's escape from the Blood Knights' mansion in New Orleans. She spent considerable time in the company of the Knights and may know where CJ was taken. However, shortly after beginning her recovery at a local hospital, she disappeared, leaving behind a note that simply stated she was going home.

I attempted to retrace our path to the mansion to track her down, but whatever mechanism the Knights used for transporting individuals there is no longer active. Either she knows of another way to get back from here, or there's another home she's referring to.

As a side note, with the passing of Rose, and Ted no longer in the picture, Iris was able to inherit the family mansion, which she put up on the market immediately. As of the writing of this report, no one has made an offer to purchase it.

Postscript

The Sea of Never-Ending Voyages

Detective Kaplan leaned over the railing of the old man-of-war frigate, staring into the black water. He was mesmerized by the bursts of bioluminescence that flickered as the waves rippled against the hull. Time seemed to be irrelevant here since he wasn't sure if ten minutes or ten years had gone by. The last thing he remembered was getting shot in the chest while trying to rescue Logan from that eerie mansion in New Orleans.

He pushed himself off the railing and patted his chest. His shirt was intact, along with the rest of him, but something felt off. Perhaps his mind was playing tricks on him, but he could have sworn he didn't feel a heartbeat.

The ancient man, Väinämöinen, steering the ship, had a flowing white beard and wore simple white clothing with a bright red cloak draped over his shoulders. His voice boomed as he called out to Kaplan. "Are you feeling all right?"

Kaplan looked up at him. "I'm not sure."

Väinämöinen licked his finger and held it up in the breeze. "There's a change in the air, one that's unexpected."

Kaplan took a step up the stairs to join him. "Does that mean this ship will start moving?"

Väinämöinen shook his head. "Nothing changes in the Sea of Never-Ending Voyages. That's why it's never-ending, but something is changing in you."

Kaplan cocked his head to one side. "How so?"

"They are correcting a mistake, one they shouldn't have let happen."

"Who? The Knights?"

Väinämöinen grimaced as he shook his head. "This is very bad. I fear we may lose this battle."

"Is there something we can do from here?"

Väinämöinen stomped his foot. "No!"

A sensation of lightheadedness struck Kaplan like a freight train. He raised his hands, watching sparks of light swirled around him like electrons orbiting an atom. Väinämöinen reached out to grab him, but his hand passed through Kaplan's arm like a ghost.

"No!" Väinämöinen shouted again.

Kaplan's legs trembled as he locked eyes with him. "What's happening to me?"

Väinämöinen moved as if in slow motion, his voice stretching through the air. "Find Pallas, the ship's scientist."

The world blurred, colors and light smearing together. Kaplan collapsed backward onto the deck. His head rolled to the side, his vision swimming. A figure in a brown robe stood over him. His unfocused eyes could barely make them out, but they seemed like a monk of some kind.

Pain flared through his cheek as the figure slapped him, bringing his vision into focus. He sat up on a wooden table, pressing a hand to his face.

He was no longer on the ship, but in a cave. Its walls flickering with candlelight. The figure who had slapped him was a woman. Her wild, curly black hair, streaked with gray, had a life of its own. Her right eye twitched as she studied him.

Kaplan glanced past her, noticing shadows dancing along the walls. Another woman, also in brown robes, rushed toward them through an opening.

"Sister Abreo," she whispered, "Moya is coming."

Abreo nodded, then refocused on Kaplan. "Don't tell her anything," she whispered. "I don't know how, but they already know too much."

Kaplan raised an eyebrow. "Are you a Knight?"

Abreo shook her head. "We are the Sisters of Aceso."

Laughter echoed through the cavern as a blonde woman entered, wearing a flowing white dress speckled with blood near the hem.

"I don't know how anyone could mistake this sad little thing for a Knight," she mused.

Abreo immediately knelt before her. "Of course, Mystic Knight."

Moya's gaze snapped to Kaplan. "Can he walk?"

Abreo nodded. "He should be able to."

Moya smiled. "Good, because he's coming with me."

About the Author

Originally from the Las Vegas valley, Shane Miller earned his bachelor's degree in Biology from the University of Nevada – Reno. He currently resides in Salt Lake City, where he can often be found being dragged around the neighborhood by his Huskies and Malamute.

E-Mail: preludeofdarkness@gmail.com

www.ingramcontent.com/pod-product-compliance
Lightning Source LLC
Chambersburg PA
CBHW020527310726
48979CB00014B/2239/J